TEMPESTS OF TRUTH

A MAGE'S APPRENTICE SERIES

Winds of Courage

Storms of Allegiance

Tempests of Truth

And set in the same world:

A MAGE'S INFLUENCE SERIES

Seeds of Glory and Ruin

Vines of Promise and Deceit

Thorns of Hope and Betrayal

Forests of Grandeur and Malice

TEMPESTS OF TRUTH

A MAGE'S APPRENTICE BOOK 3

MELANIE CELLIER

LUMINANT PUBLICATIONS

For Marina
an excellent writing companion
and an encouraging friend

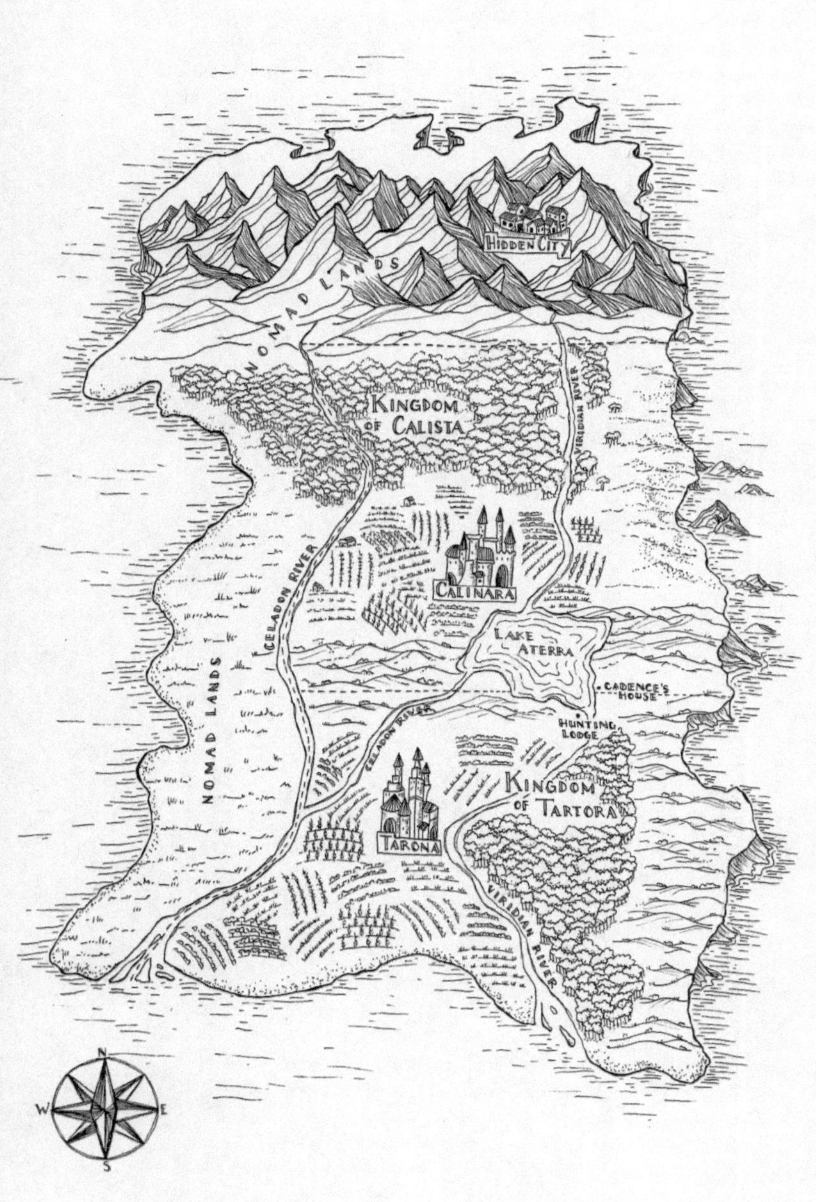

Hidden City
NOMAD LANDS
Kingdom of Calista
VIRIDIAN RIVER
Calinara
CELADON RIVER
NOMAD LANDS
Lake Aterra
Cadence's House
Hunting Lodge
Kingdom of Tartora
Tarona
CELADON RIVER
VIRIDIAN RIVER
N
W
E
S

CALINARA
LAKE ATERRA
ELDRIDA
CELADON RIVER
SPOON RIVER
VIRIDIAN RIVER
CALTOR
TARONA
KINGDOM OF TARTORA
OSTARIA
TARIN

CHAPTER

ONE

I stood on the back porch of the mansion, taking a moment to admire the view of the mountain rising behind the town. The wisps of fog were already starting to burn off in the early morning light. Here on the island, it was hard to believe winter had already started. The season bore few similarities with the winters back home in Tarin.

It was hard not to enjoy the natural beauty and unfamiliar surroundings of the manor house, but I couldn't shake a sense of lingering guilt for taking the time to notice such things when I still hadn't resolved matters on the island—or even in the manor itself.

The servants should have been at the front of my mind, but I couldn't help my rogue thoughts drifting to Nik. He had moved into the manor house in the wake of the disaster, but I still barely saw him.

I wished I could take back everything about that day. If only I had found a way to show Nik I was still alive. If only I hadn't seen him in that room full of bodies and leaped to the worst possible conclusion without even asking a single question. If Nik had truly responded with uncontrolled violence, I could have been proud of myself for having the courage to push him away. But how could I have believed him capable of something so terrible, even for a moment? Why hadn't it occurred to me that his sword might be drawn because he had been desperately fighting for his own survival against the true attacker? Or that he might be crouched over Augustine desperately checking for signs of life?

Nik had been understanding of my mistake, of course—too understanding. His excuses for me only heightened my sense of guilt. And that guilt stabbed at me again every time the scene in the party room sprang back into my mind. I knew what had really happened now, so why was it so hard to shake that one horrible image of Nik?

My guilt was making me avoid Nik, but I was eaten up by the question of why he was avoiding me. I couldn't blame him after my lack of trust, but contradictorily, I also couldn't help being hurt. Our relationship had become a giant mess, and it was all my fault.

"Delphine!" The call came from inside the house, drawing me from both the beautiful scene and my dark thoughts. I sighed. My true responsibilities were waiting.

Ida stepped onto the porch, her expression lightening when she caught sight of me.

"I'm sorry," I said, forestalling her query. "I still haven't worked out what to do about the servants."

The Constantines had rotated new help in and out of the mansion on a regular basis since they couldn't risk anyone getting too close to them and seeing the truth behind their veil of mesmerizations. But the latest group had only started work recently and had all been contracted for at least two months. We no longer needed the services of so many, but they had been promised two months of work, and I couldn't take that away from them. And I certainly couldn't end their contracts early when I hadn't worked out how to pay their wage yet. I was relying on the extra time remaining in their service to find the necessary coin.

The Constantines might have manipulated and exploited the townsfolk—using their skill at mesmerization to lord over them—but they had always paid their bills in a prompt manner. Few things could cut through empty charm as quickly as unpaid gold. So I knew they must have had a stash of coin in the house somewhere, but I didn't have the least idea where. Exhaustive searching had failed to uncover it, and I found myself frequently wishing for Costas. I couldn't blame him for fleeing the murder of his entire family, but I could really have used one person who knew how the administration of the island functioned.

"It isn't the servants." Ida shook her head, and a sense of foreboding settled over me. "My hosts are ill."

"Oh!" I brightened. "They need a healer? Did you bring them with you?" I couldn't help feeling a sense of excitement at being presented with a straightforward opportunity to use my healing power—a welcome alternative to managing the complicated vacuum left by the deaths of the entire Constantine family.

"They're not here." Ida's expression remained grave, and a rising tide of concern began to fill me.

I had suggested Ida relocate to the manor multiple times, but she had been steadfast in refusing, saying she felt more comfortable with the family who had billeted her on our arrival. If they were all too sick to travel, she must be greatly worried.

But perhaps they had remained at home for a different reason.

"Are they afraid of the manor?" I dropped my voice to a whisper. "After what happened here?" I barely managed to stop myself glancing toward the full-length windows that led to the scene of the massacre.

"No, it's not that. They're too sick to walk this far."

"It's that bad?" I winced, my hopes dashed. "You should have come to me sooner! Or did it come on very suddenly?" My mind whirled, running through various possible maladies that might fit with a sudden onset of illness.

"As to that." She cleared her throat, looking uncomfortable. "They didn't want me to come at first. And it seemed mild enough that I thought…" She frowned. "Clearly I should have insisted on coming sooner."

"How long have they been sick?" I asked, alarmed. "And how many are ill?"

"All of them." Ida grimaced. "Their youngest only started showing symptoms last night. I think they would have let me come sooner if he'd been sick from the beginning since they all dote on him so much."

"All of them?" I stared at her. It had to be something highly contagious. "Let's not waste any time!"

As we hurried through the house, I considered searching out Nik and suggesting he accompany us but decided against it. He wasn't a healer, so this was something I needed to handle.

I knew that wasn't my only reason for not searching him out, but I let my mental excuse stand. I didn't have time to consider the complicated dynamics of our relationship when people needed my help.

As we crossed the gardens that ringed the manor, a flash of movement pulled my eyes skyward. A small, feathered body was diving toward me. I stopped just long enough for Phoenix to land on my padded shoulder.

"Good hunting?" I murmured, and he preened, clearly satisfied with his morning's effort.

A quiet yip made me search the surrounding gardens, my

eyes finding a small orange body. Ember was trotting toward me after her own hunting excursion. I stooped and ran a hand down her back. She also looked satisfied, her eyes already growing heavy. She shook it off, though, gazing up at me with what looked suspiciously like a questioning air.

"Go inside and sleep," I said softly. "Phoenix will keep me company."

She hesitated, her eyes moving to the merlin falcon on my shoulder. For a silent moment, the two animals stared at each other. Ember was the first to relax, pressing her body against my leg for a moment and then heading off toward the house. I smiled as I watched her go, despite my underlying worry about Ida's host family. Ember and Phoenix took better care of me than I would have believed possible for a fox and a bird of prey, and their companionship always lifted my spirits.

As we left the garden and entered the town, Phoenix in tow, I quizzed Ida on the illness.

"Is it something your host family recognize?" I asked. "Have they had it before?"

"They downplayed it at first, but now they're saying it's unfamiliar." Ida frowned. "It's not something I recognize either."

I nodded, but I wasn't entirely surprised. In order to maintain their mesmerizations, the Constantines had performed constant healings on the islanders. Not only had their doors always been open to them, but they had even instituted monthly checkups. Most illnesses encountered by the islanders would have been quickly nipped in the bud by the Constantines. There were probably many diseases whose later stages were unfamiliar to the townsfolk.

I had already canceled the schedule of monthly checkups, of course. There was no way I could keep up with them on my own, and just the thought of them was distasteful given they had been an instrument of control and repression. Through those checkups, the Constantines had regularly renewed the mesmerizations on the islanders, beginning their insidious manipulation almost from birth.

I had received no patients in the nearly two weeks since canceling the checkups, but I hadn't been especially surprised given they must all have been in good health at the point of the Constantines' death. But Ida's summons was making me question that assumption. How many others had hesitated to take their illness to the unknown new healer living in the empty house of their old rulers?

I glanced warily up and down the nearly empty streets. It had been over a week since I'd walked into town to the market, but something had changed. The atmosphere then had been somber, a haze of hesitancy and confusion hanging over the populace. The Constantines were gone, but their mesmerizations remained, and the same passivity we had first noticed in the islanders had only been exacerbated by the loss of their leaders. But while the people had all hung back from me then, this time was different. The people weren't dismayed or bemused—they were absent.

The few who did pass within view walked quickly, not appearing to even notice me as they busied themselves with their errands.

Unconsciously my pace increased.

"Go over the symptoms again," I commanded Ida, wanting to focus my thoughts before I started inventing catastrophes in my mind.

"They've been complaining of headaches, and most of them are coughing," she said. "I checked for fever from the start, of course, and they seemed warm but not excessively so. Their condition didn't seem too severe, or I would have come for you before now, like I said. But then this morning..." She grimaced.

I was about to ask for more details when she stopped

outside a door. The house looked almost identical to the ones on either side, but Ida didn't hesitate as she let herself in, beckoning for me to follow.

I hesitated, jerking my shoulder upward. Phoenix recognized the signal and launched himself into the air. Bringing a falcon into someone's home was already questionable etiquette without considering that the family inside were ill. He would be better off waiting outside.

Phoenix flapped across the rooftops, looking entirely unbothered, so I stepped inside. As soon as I was all the way through the door, I flinched at the heat.

"First things first," I said, focusing on Ida. "Get all the windows open and some fresh air in here."

"Nonsense!" an old lady exclaimed, only to go off into a paroxysm of coughs. "It's winter!"

I barely refrained from retorting that there was nothing wintry about the temperature outside. Instead I dropped to one knee beside her chair.

"You need fresh air to aid your recovery. Please trust me, Grandmother. I'm a healer."

"A healer?" She squinted at me in suspicion. "You're that newcomer, then? From up at the manor?" She shuddered at mention of the Constantines' home. "Are you sure you're a healer?"

She regarded my face for a silent moment before her expression cleared. "I suppose you were going to marry young Ignatius. Or maybe young Barnabas." She nodded decisively as if she'd cleared up her own confusion.

I didn't bother to correct her. I already knew the tragic truth about healers on the island. Strong healers didn't make it past childhood unless they were earmarked as future spouses for the next generation of Constantines. If telling herself that story helped her to make sense of my presence, then I was willing to leave the misunderstanding in peace.

"May I examine you?" I held out a hand, my fingers hovering just above her wrist.

She nodded, her hesitation and suspicion apparently gone now that she had fitted me into her world.

I placed my hand gently against her skin and sent my power into her.

Within seconds, my mouth had turned down. My training at the hospital in Caltor had exposed me to a range of the most common illnesses, including some cases at later stages of disease. Those who lived more remotely, especially farmers like my own family, would often wait until an illness was severe before making the trek into a hospital for healing.

But whatever was ravaging this woman's body, it didn't feel familiar. I focused my attention, tracking down each area of her body that felt wrong.

For starters, there was nothing mild about her temperature. Even without my power, I could feel the heat radiating off her skin. And from inside her system, I could easily tell why her body was fighting so ferociously. There was inflammation in far too many places, and her lungs were struggling, her breath making an audible rattle.

We'd arrived only minutes ago, but she was already wilting visibly, clearly exhausted from the conversation. I sent a small burst of energy into her, but I didn't dare risk using too much power when I hadn't seen the state of the rest of the family yet.

"You need to be in bed," I said gently, fighting hard against the urge to pour my power into her and heal all her unfamiliar symptoms.

Ida cleared her throat significantly, and I finally examined the rest of the home. A large open room contained a dining table as well as cooking facilities. Two doors opened off the far wall, both propped wide to allow a view of the room beyond. One bedroom held a large bed that was already occupied by a man and woman. The other held two single beds.

One seemed untouched, while the other was rumpled but currently empty.

I took a second look at the main room and noticed two pallets had been shoved against one of the walls, limiting the floor space. A young boy lay on one of the pallets, murmuring fitfully and staring at me.

"They insisted I take one of the bedrooms," Ida said. "So Grandmother and the boy have been sleeping out here."

I held out a hand, beckoning her to come closer. As soon as she was within reach, I latched onto her wrist. It only took a moment to ascertain she was healthy. I withdrew with a sigh of relief.

"It hasn't infected you yet. Until we know what's going on here, you're moving into the manor with me. And that way these two can move back into proper beds."

Ida nodded, making no protest this time given the circumstances. Launching into action, she helped the elderly lady into the untouched bed. While she did so, I knelt beside the child, chatting mindlessly in my softest voice as I sent my power into him.

By the time I withdrew, my frown had deepened. I helped him to his feet, leading him to the remaining bed. He wasn't in as bad shape as his great-grandmother, since his organs were mostly free of inflammation. But his temperature was raised and, even more concerningly, his heartbeat was slow.

"Does it hurt anywhere?" I asked him.

"My head." He moaned and then gave a cough. "And my tummy."

I frowned, my reply stalled by the sounds of someone thrashing and muttering incoherently in the next room. I handed the boy off to Ida with a quick look, hurrying into the other bedroom.

It was the man who was disturbed, so I went to him first, holding his arm firmly in both my hands. It didn't take long to recognize the same signs I had seen in the grandmother. In his case, the inflammation wasn't as bad—probably because of his younger age—but his fever was raging, as evidenced by the delirium. I sent enough power into him to cool him down and calm him, blocking his pain while I was in there.

He settled down at once, letting out a weary sigh. Cracking open his eyes, he frowned up at me.

"Who are you?" His voice was rough, but Ida appeared at my side with a cup of water which he accepted.

"I'm the healer," I said, and he accepted this statement without question.

"Do you think you could get up now?" I asked him, curious to hear his reaction.

He had propped himself up slightly to drink, and at this question, he attempted to pull himself all the way upright. He didn't make it before grunting and flopping back onto the pillow.

"Sorry," he muttered, a shadow crossing his face. "I don't know what's wrong with me. I haven't felt this tired since the fev—"

"Hush!" his wife snapped from beside him. Her voice was weak, but he still obeyed her command. Apparently she was less accepting of the new healer than he was and didn't like him giving me unnecessary information.

But he'd already said enough for me to guess what he was talking about. I exchanged a glance with Ida, my heart sinking all the way down to my feet, terror rising to take its place. I didn't know about her, but I'd already heard about the infamous fever from three winters before.

Usually the Constantines had intervened in health concerns early, but on that occasion, an entirely new illness had emerged from the jungle to sweep through the town before they realized what was happening. The islanders and their ancestors had carved a home here on this island, but much of it was still uninhabited and densely covered in a jungle-like forest. Environments like that could harbor new illnesses—ones previously unknown to healers—and those were always the most dangerous kind.

In the case of the fever, it had progressed quickly, and given its lack of familiarity, it had taken some time for the Constantines to work their way through the entire town, stamping it from existence. Some of the islanders must have been forced to wait for their healings, and clearly this family had been among their number.

A shiver trickled down my spine, traveling from my scalp all the way to my feet. Three winters ago there had been six powerful healers on the island, and it had still taken them time to handle a new, mystery illness. If the town had been hit by another new illness...

I drew a deep breath, reminding myself to focus on what was in front of me and not assume the worst. Circling the bed, I examined the mother, noting that while she appeared to be at a similar state of progression as her husband, she lacked his earlier delirium. In its place, she bore a nasty looking rash across her torso. I eased her pain as well, soothing the inflamed skin, but once again I didn't dare use enough power to heal her completely, regardless of the cause of infection.

When I let her go, I hesitated, wondering about the best way to proceed. A vision of empty streets intruded on my thoughts, but I pushed it away, trying to focus on practical steps.

The sound of the main door opening made me hurry out of the bedroom. Had others in the town heard I was here and come searching for me?

But as soon as I got a glimpse of the new arrival, I stopped.

The room had seemed large before, but suddenly it felt so constricted I could barely breathe. How could one man take up so much space?

Nik looked the same as he always had—his shoulders just as broad, and his dark hair still contrasting with the burning blue of his eyes—but his expression carried something less familiar. I still recognized it easily, however, and it did as much to shrink the room as his impressive height.

If his eyes had held even a hint of censure for leaving him behind, I could have met them with defiance. But I had no defenses against the sadness he was clearly trying to hide. I had left the mansion without even informing him of my departure, and he couldn't hide his reaction to my omission. Nik might be avoiding conversations with me, but given his choice, he would shadow me every time I left the mansion, taking the role of bodyguard. But he didn't just want to be by my side. He also wanted me to want him there.

And I did. Mostly.

The dynamic between us had become so complicated that sometimes I didn't know what I wanted. The unspoken weight of all that had happened hung in the air making it hard to breathe. I wanted to look at him and see nothing but Nik, but I couldn't stop myself from reliving that horrible moment in the party room—followed, as always, by the spear of guilt for my mistake.

The horror of that moment, and the resultant tangle of our relationship, filled my thoughts even now when something far more serious should have been at the forefront of my mind. Which was yet another reason why I'd been avoiding him while I tried to sort out the confusing administration of the island. It was already hard enough to keep my thoughts straight.

"One of the servants said Ida left a message for me—that I was needed down here?"

His deep voice sparked a visceral response that I immediately tried to tamp down.

He took a step toward me, concern flaring in his eyes. "Is something wrong?"

I let his words remind me of what was most important in the moment.

"I'm afraid there is." I pitched my voice low, trying not to disturb the patients in the two bedrooms. "This whole family is ill with an infectious condition I haven't seen before. And unfortunately it's already progressed significantly. I'm afraid…"

"The empty streets," he said quickly, obviously having noticed the same thing I had.

Hearing him reach the same horrifying conclusion should have made me even more afraid, but instead his words had the opposite effect. They steadied me, relief trickling in to counter the panic. I wasn't alone in this. Nik was here too.

"We need to find out what we're dealing with," I said. "I'll check the houses on either side, but can you and Ida spread further through the town? We don't have time to check every house, but I need to know the rough extent of this."

Given how sick this family already was, I suspected this area would be the epicenter of the spread, but I needed to know for sure.

"Of course." Nik looked at Ida who had entered the main room behind me. "You head toward the harbor, and I'll go back toward the manor?"

She agreed, the two of them murmuring several more clarifications about the routes they would each take. I had already tuned them out, though, hurrying toward the door to start my examination of the neighbors.

In the doorway, I paused to make a final comment.

"We'll meet back here as soon as possible." If things were less dire than I feared and this family was the worst hit, then I would be able to use my power to heal the three adults in this family at least.

Nik and Ida both nodded agreement, and I strode out into the street.

My optimism didn't last two houses. By the time I'd made it

down one side of the street and back up the other, I felt as if I was carrying a pack filled with heavy rocks.

I had expected some of the families to show animosity toward an unfamiliar healer turning up unannounced on their doorstep, but no one had rejected me. And it was tragically easy to see why.

Every single household had someone in at least the first stage of the illness—like the young boy from Ida's host family—and some had members even worse off than the host grandmother.

From my questions, I had managed to track the rough course of the symptoms. In the first week, most patients had symptoms similar to the first boy I examined. After progressing to the second week, the symptoms increased in line with those I had seen in the boy's parents. Only a small handful of people had made it as far as the beginning of the third week, and most of them were even more sick than the first grandmother.

Those whose weakened bodies had succumbed to pneumonia or who had inflammation of the heart or brain were in a severe enough condition that I couldn't just walk away. I had tried to keep my healing to the minimal amount necessary to ensure the patient's survival, but there had been enough of them that even doing that much had drained me to a frightening degree. I didn't dare do anything to ease the suffering of those who were earlier in the illness, lest I end up collapsing like I had in Eldrida.

I tried to cling to some vestige of hope as I waited outside Ida's home. Those who reported being sick the longest had first come down with symptoms just before the Constantines' untimely demise. They must have only just missed having the Constantines heal them in the early stages.

I had thought this street might be the epicenter of the disease, but perhaps it was the opposite. If these families had been the last to get sick, the rest of the town might have already been healed before their illness could progress. If that was the case, and these were my only patients, then I could carefully stagger my healings, relying on power rather than knowledge or finesse to push through, and starting with those who were the most sick.

But the prospect still felt overwhelming, optimistic as it might be. Even Phoenix's appearance did nothing to lift my mood.

Nik returned before Ida, appearing at the end of the street and quickly covering the distance with his long stride. But even before he reached me, my desperate hope had died. One look at his face was enough to read the terrible truth.

When he stopped in front of me, he hesitated, apparently not wanting to put what he had seen into words.

"It's bad, isn't it?" I said softly.

He nodded slowly.

"Every house on this street has at least one person sick, and in some cases it's everyone," I continued.

Nik reached for me, as if he wanted to take my hands, or perhaps pull me close, but he stopped himself, letting his arms fall back to his sides.

"Every house I checked as well," he said reluctantly. "I did a fair sampling between here and the manor as well as a few streets on the western side of town."

I swallowed. It was even worse than I'd feared.

"So it's already made it through the whole town." My voice quavered with the unspoken words behind the spoken ones. This wasn't the sort of sickness you just recovered from on your own—not everyone, at least.

Nik's eyes never left my face, his own expression twisting as anguish filled his eyes. The sight of it leached all the strength from my legs, nearly making my knees buckle.

I knew him well enough to know that anguish wasn't for the islanders who were strangers to him. It was for me. And seeing his fear brought the stark reality of the coming future into horrifying clarity. The whole town was infected with a mystery illness, and there was only one healer of any strength on the entire island. Me.

People were going to die—possibly lots of people—and my only two options were to watch it happen, or else kill myself trying to stop it.

TWO

I swayed in place, and this time Nik didn't stop himself from reaching for me, steadying my elbow and murmuring meaningless words of comfort. His voice was calm despite the raging fear in his eyes.

"This isn't your fault, Delphine," he said once I'd regained my balance.

He wasn't entirely right, though. I had taken responsibility for these people's health, but I had been too inexperienced for the task. I should never have canceled all the checkups so recklessly. I had assumed people would come to me if they needed a healer, but I had failed to consider the state of their feelings.

Their leaders—the ones they had been forced to revere since birth—had all died. And most of them hadn't seen me in person to judge if I was telling the truth when I claimed I wasn't responsible. None of them had attempted to attack me—not even verbally—and I had taken that as more significant than it actually was. Their passive response to me was only in line with their general passivity—a result of the subjugation forced on them. They could regard me with suspicion and hostility without actively launching an attack. And even to those who didn't regard me negatively I was still a stranger.

And into this worst possible moment, before we had the chance to get to know each other, disaster had struck. If the first to fall ill had come to me at once, I might have been able to head off the epidemic. But it was far too late for that now.

My assumption about them taking the initiative had been wrong, and now some of them would pay for my mistake with their lives. I should have checked on the town each day instead of allowing myself to be distracted at the manor. I had focused on the haphazard records left by the Constantines, as well as the management of the manor itself, instead of being focused where I should have been—the people of the town.

"If you push yourself too far, it won't help anyone," Nik said, the alarm in his voice easy to hear. "Without you, they'll be in an even worse position." His expression turned dark. "If anyone is at fault, it's me. If I had acted more quickly and saved some of the Constantines, you wouldn't be the only healer now."

"No." Strength returned to my voice. His useless self-recriminations highlighted the foolishness of my own negative thoughts. "The blame lies with the Constantines. And even that is beside the point. The important thing is how we're going to handle the situation in front of us."

But despite the confidence of my words, I had no idea how to follow them up. How could we possibly handle a disaster of this magnitude?

"Delphine! Delphine!" A high, childish voice made us both turn toward the end of the street.

Two short figures ran toward us, their eyes wide and expressions animated.

"Lumi? Fergus?" I frowned at the brother and sister. "What are you doing here?"

The two were the only non-mesmerized people I had met in the town. Their minds were unfettered because of their mother's avoidance of the Constantines, but that very caution should have placed them far from here. They had been the ones to tell me about the last fever. On that occasion their mother had fled with them into the jungle at the first sign of spreading illness, thus avoiding infection and the need for healing from the Constantines.

A fresh wave of guilt seized me. Had she failed to flee this time because the Constantines were gone?

"We were looking for you," Lumi said. "Mother is sick, and we remembered you're a healer too."

I winced, but Fergus jumped in.

"But never mind that!"

Lumi gave him a reproving look, but he just shrugged.

"She isn't *that* sick. Not like the Tergins down the street."

I winced again, but neither child noticed.

"We heard you were here, so we came to find you," Lumi continued, and once again, Fergus rushed to take over the story.

"We walked past the harbor on our way here, and you'll never guess what we saw!"

"The harbor?" I asked, sounding slightly dazed. My mind was too full of the epidemic to have room for any other topics.

"It was a ship!" Fergus proclaimed triumphantly. "But none of ours went out this morning."

I looked to Lumi, expecting her to refute Fergus's preposterous declaration.

"More like a boat than a ship," she said, "but he's right that it can't be one of ours. With so many people sick, none of the fishing vessels set out this morning."

She said it in a matter-of-fact way, as if she didn't understand the importance of any part of what she'd just said. But each of her words landed like lead in my stomach. The townsfolk were not only all ill, but they had also stopped gathering food due to their condition. We were in dire straits already, and now a fresh disaster was sailing into our shores.

My eyes met Nik's, wondering if he was thinking the same

thing as me. From the angry flash in his eyes, he was. Grey had somehow gotten word of what had happened to the Constantines and had returned. And he couldn't have arrived at a worse time. With an epidemic underway, we had no time to deal with Grey as well.

"Show us," Nik said in the sort of commanding tones that were always obeyed.

The children nodded eagerly, happy to be caught up in the excitement. Clearly they hadn't yet grasped what was happening in their town.

Despite their exuberance, I managed to grab hold of both their hands, quickly examining their bodies. I heaved a sigh of relief when I found them both clear of the illness.

As we half ran through the streets, the brother and sister bickered over whether the arriving vessel was large enough to be considered a ship, and both Nik and I remained silent.

One glance at his grim expression was enough to tell me that he had no intention of allowing Grey to step foot back on the island unopposed. The Constantines were to blame for their own downfall, but Grey was one of them, and he certainly carried his share of the fault. He had done everything possible to upset the balance among his relatives, and he had succeeded beyond his wildest hopes.

I put on an extra spurt of speed as I spotted the end of the street and the glitter of the sea beyond. Everything would be easier if we could arrive before Grey and his people disembarked and disappeared into the town or forest.

From the sound of the siblings' argument, Grey hadn't returned in his full ship with all his followers in tow, so it was possible Nik might have the strength to hold them at bay and send them back the way they had come. Grey himself had no special strength without physical contact.

As soon as we burst onto the waterfront, my eyes scanned the water beyond the long pier. Sure enough, a wooden boat was closing the final small gap, ready to dock. I sprinted down the length of the pier, taking in the details before me.

The boat was a reasonably substantial, sturdy-looking fishing vessel, but it was a long way from a full-size ship. It didn't even have a proper cabin. But I forgot all about the boat itself once I saw the passengers. Coming to an abrupt stop, I burst into tears.

It wasn't Grey at all. Quite the opposite.

Floating in front of me were the people I wanted to see more than anyone else in the kingdom.

Nik halted beside me, his face reflecting the same shock.

"Is that really...?" he asked, not managing to voice the full question.

"I think so," I said, sobbing in relief.

He glanced at me, worry replacing the pleased surprise. I waved a hand reassuringly.

"I'm just happy," I managed to choke out, and he relaxed.

"Delphine!" Luna's delighted cry cut across the remaining distance.

The sound of her voice spurred me into action, and I hurried forward. By the time I reached the end of the dock, she had stepped ashore. As soon as I reached her, she pulled me into an enveloping hug.

"Am I glad to see you!" she said fervently. "Actually, I'm happy just to see land. I could kneel and kiss the dock."

I blinked, loosening my return hug and extricating myself from her grip. I couldn't imagine a passenger of Amara's having any cause to complain about the smoothness of the journey.

I looked past her shoulder, grinning like a fool at Hayes, Clay, and two men I didn't recognize who were wearing the uniform of royal guards and who looked almost as relieved as Luna. When my searching gaze fell on Costas, I gasped aloud, finally understanding how it was possible for the rest of them to be here.

I had assumed the new arrival had to be Grey since he was the only one who knew the route, but I had forgotten that one other Constantine was still alive. Gratitude welled up inside my chest. Costas might have fled after seeing the massacre of his family, but he hadn't abandoned us after all.

As he stepped onto the dock, my eyes jumped to the one person remaining on the boat. Amara. I had never been so pleased to see someone in my life.

She looked as poised as ever, but as she stepped toward me, I noticed the subtle signs of strain and exhaustion on her face. I frowned as I hurried the remaining distance toward her.

"Thank goodness you really are all right," she said in her calm way, as if she hadn't entirely believed Costas's report. "And you even have that bird with you still."

She eyed Phoenix with judgmental eyes, as if the falcon should have stopped me from haring off across the ocean without her.

"Of course I'm all right," I said. "But the town—"

My words cut off as a creaking sounded from the boat behind her. I leaned sideways to get a better view just as the entire vessel collapsed into planks of wood and flotsam that floated on the surface of the harbor.

My mouth fell open and my eyes widened as I turned to Amara, noting again the signs of exhaustion on her face.

"How long have you been holding that together with power alone?" I asked.

"Since we got caught in the storm two nights ago," Luna said in hushed tones.

"Two nights ago!?" I stared at Amara. "I know you did wonders in Eldrida, but even you couldn't expend that much power for days and nights without break."

She smiled back at me. "Which is why it's a very good thing I had help."

"Help?" I looked over my shoulder at the rest of the group, my eyes landing on Costas. "Oh! Of course!"

Costas smiled wanly. Now that I was properly focusing on him, I could see even more obvious exhaustion on his face than Amara's.

"It was actually nice to feel needed and appreciated for once." As soon as he said the words, he winced, looking reflexively uphill toward the manor, as if the reminder of his family and past was painful.

"You came back," I said quietly. "Thank you, Costas."

He met my eyes. "I'm sorry for running like that. I was in shock and not thinking clearly. I was most of the way to the mainland before I realized I had stranded you on the island."

"You never thought I was to blame?" I asked, surprised. It had been one of my biggest regrets that I hadn't been able to explain what happened that night to Costas. Out of everyone he most deserved to know about his family's end.

"I knew you weren't involved." He shot a dark look at Nik. "It was clear you were just as shocked and horrified as me. In fact, it looked like you'd been attacked as well. I've been berating myself for days for not taking you with me when I fled."

Nik stirred, as if he wanted to protest. He would certainly not have allowed Costas to haul me off and shove me on a boat. I sent him a warning look. Until the whole story was explained, the best thing he could do was stay silent. From the way his eyes slid from mine, his tense muscles slumping, he understood the shaky ground beneath his feet.

Amara put a hand on my arm, examining me from head to toe. "There weren't any injuries you couldn't heal? You're healthy now?"

"I'm fine. But it was a close thing. Ignatius ordered armed guards to attack me. Since their swords extended their reach so much, I couldn't get close enough to make contact and use my power. I had to let them wound me enough that they thought they'd succeeded in wearing me down."

Amara's face paled, but it was Costas who spoke.

"Ignatius attacked you?" He sounded shocked. "Not Grey? It took me so long to find Nik that I was afraid Grey might have killed you before we got back."

"To be fair, he did attack me first," I conceded. "But Ignatius did far more damage."

A slow light of understanding grew on Costas's face, and he turned to give Nik another look.

"So that's why Nik…" He didn't seem able to finish the sentence.

I shook my head quickly. "No! Of course he didn't! Nik isn't the one who massacred your family." Perversely, I felt incensed at the idea they had all been misjudging Nik, despite having made the same error myself.

"He wasn't?" He raised both eyebrows, sounding skeptical.

Amara lowered her hand from my arm, but her face didn't immediately relax. She looked across at Hayes. He nodded slowly to confirm he had sensed the truth of my words with his ability. Only then did relief fill her features.

"I was hoping there was a different explanation," she said. "I felt sure there must be."

"As did I." Hayes narrowed his eyes. "But I'd like to hear the truth from Nik himself."

I flushed at his oblique reference to the possibility that I had been taken in by Nik.

"I did not commit the massacre that happened that day," Nik said in a level voice.

Costas looked at Hayes, his brows lowered, waiting for his confirmation. When Hayes gave it, followed by a confirming nod from both Clay and Luna, he let out a long breath.

"They were all adamant that we return to find you both and

seek out the true story." Costas made eye contact with Nik for the first time. "You have loyal friends."

"I think it's loyalty to my father more than me," Nik said caustically.

"Your father?" Costas frowned, clearly confused, and for the first time it occurred to me that he might not know Nik's full identity. That particular piece of information had been lost in the many revelations.

I glanced at Amara and read confirmation on her face. With a sick feeling, I realized she hadn't been quite as confident in Nik as she claimed. She had remained silent about his status, afraid of a powerful foreign mage finding out his family had been murdered by the son of Tartora's king.

But how could I blame her? I had been the first to accuse Nik, and I still couldn't shake the guilt of that or the echoes of the moment that still lingered in my mind. I should never have made such a terrible assumption, and I couldn't blame Amara for doing the same in the face of Costas's testimony.

"My hands aren't completely clean," Nik said in a low voice, bringing all eyes snapping to his face.

"But you were acting to defend yourself and others," I said quickly.

Surely he didn't feel guilty for defending himself against murderers who wanted to make him their final victim? Was that why he'd been acting so strangely ever since?

"You didn't attack anyone for revenge," I added.

"What does that mean?" Costas asked, taking a step toward me, his eyes intent on my face.

I hesitated, unsure how to tell him the full truth. I glanced beseechingly at Amara. "I'm not sure if this is the best place for this conversation. And I have some important things to tell you about what's happening on the island right now as well. Perhaps we should—"

"No!" Costas cut me off, not aggressive but firm. "I don't care how painful it is to hear, I want to know the truth without delay."

THREE

I exchanged another look with Nik. Given what was happening in town—an ever-present pressure in the back of my mind—it would be best to get this whole conversation out of the way as quickly as possible. But that didn't make the words any easier to say.

Nik remained silent, indicating for me to continue with a nod. I sighed. I might not want to be the spokesperson, but I could understand why he thought it would be more sensitive for the story to come from me.

"Ignatius followed Grey and me out into the garden," I said.

"Ignatius?" Amara interrupted, looking to Costas.

"My younger brother," he said heavily. "And the heir apparent to the Constantines. Well…" He shifted uncomfortably. "He was heir apparent before Grey's appearance, at least. Although even then, not without opposition."

I sighed. "I can only assume that was the problem."

Costas looked at me, his forehead creasing. "What are you saying?"

"Sorry, let me start at the beginning. Ignatius overheard Grey and me talking and learned I'm a healer. Grey could tell his deceptions were all exposed, so he decided to sacrifice me to give himself time to escape." My face tightened at the memory, but I pushed myself to continue.

"As I already said, I had to pretend to be dead in order for them to leave, and I still appeared dead when Nik reached the garden and found me."

Amara's eyes widened, and I caught her uneasy expression as she looked toward Nik. I hurried on, all too aware of what she must be thinking.

"Nik hurried back to the party after Ignatius and his guards, but unfortunately he was just a little too late."

"Wait," Costas said, interrupting me again. "Who are these guards you keep talking about? My family never had any guards. They didn't need them," he added, his tone dark.

I paused, struck by his comment. It was true that I'd never seen any other guards before the party or since. In all the chaos, I hadn't given it much thought.

Nik spoke up, looking from me to Costas. "Grey chose the party as his time to make a move, but it appears he wasn't the only one of the Constantine cousins to think that way."

"What did my brother do?" Costas's face was pale, his look of exhaustion deepening.

Nik finally took up the tale, relating the part I hadn't witnessed.

"By the time I returned to the manor house, Grey had already fled, along with most of his followers. When I made it inside, only the Constantines were left. It seems your brother was sick of debating who would be the next heir, and he didn't want to wait to take his turn after his grandmother and father either."

"*Ignatius* killed them all?" Costas asked in barely more than a whisper.

Nik hesitated and then nodded his head. "His guards did, at his command. I tried to stop them, but I only arrived right at the end, and Ignatius ordered his men after me immediately.

My power and training gave me the advantage—even over three of them—but the guards were able to keep me occupied long enough for Ignatius to finish the task himself before he also attacked me."

I thought of Barnabas, who had nearly made it to the door, and shivered. I still couldn't fathom how Ignatius could have done such a thing to his own family. The Constantines might have been the manipulators, but in the end, they had been just as twisted by their behavior as their victims.

"So, to be clear," Hayes said, his gaze trained on Nik. "One of the Constantines murdered the others due to some sort of internal family conflict. You were only responsible for killing the aggressor and his two guards after they attacked you as well?"

"That is correct." Nik held his gaze, his expression confident. But I could read something else lurking behind his apparent calm. Something about that night still tormented him, and whatever it was had been standing between us ever since.

"I'm sorry for your loss," Amara said formally to Costas. "But I am glad Tartora had no hand in it. I hope you won't hold what happened against our kingdom."

Costas nodded slowly. "I wish I could disbelieve Nikolas's account, but Ignatius was always so hungry for power. It always seemed foolish and unnecessary to me—what difference did it really make which of us ruled the family? But I could never convince him of that."

I nodded slowly. Even in my short time on the island, I had overheard an ugly argument between Ignatius and his father. There had clearly been no love lost between Ignatius and his relatives.

"As a healer I can assure you that Nikolas speaks the truth," Clay said, his voice gentle. "But I understand if you might prefer one of your own to confirm that. There may not be healers of strength left on the island, but even the weakest healing ability can truth tell."

Costas shook his head. "That won't be necessary. At first I was driven by shock, but I've had plenty of time to reflect since those first initial moments. As much as I regret every aspect of the situation, my family are guilty of terrible crimes. They lived a life of violence and deception, and I cannot be surprised they met the same sort of end."

"Yes, Ignatius made his choice," I said. "And he paid the ultimate price for it. He didn't know anything about Nik's presence on the island and had no idea what sort of opponent he might face. But I believe the ultimate blame lies with Grey. If he hadn't been deliberately stirring the situation up in preparation for his own coup, then Ignatius might never have made such a move. And Grey is still out there."

I looked to Amara. "What's been happening back in Tartora?"

She sighed. "We haven't seen any sign of Grey. When neither you nor Nik made any contact—" she paused to throw a disapproving look at both of us "—our whole party made our way to the crevasse to arrest Grey. You can imagine our surprise to find it completely abandoned. We were still debating what to do when Costas turned up."

"The route to the crevasse is the simplest," he said, "and since I was on my own, that was important. And I think a subconscious part of me was fleeing toward Aunt Chloe as well. Grey had said she was dead, but I still hoped..." He fell silent.

"Grey himself must have taken a different route," Amara said. "He never arrived at the crevasse. You can imagine our surprise when Costas showed up instead—and our even greater astonishment when he told us everything. I'm not sure if I was more shocked to hear about his family, the island, or your whereabouts."

I blinked, trying to imagine how that conversation had gone.

"You told them everything?" Nik asked Costas, and he nodded.

"There didn't seem any point in holding back. My family and our old life here are destroyed. The Constantine healers betrayed the townsfolk in the worst of ways, but they did look after them physically. Without them, the islanders are vulnerable. They need help, and I'm hoping Tartora will be willing to provide it, despite everything that's happened. Because none of it was my people's fault."

I nodded vigorously. "Yes, the people need help."

We had made it through the most important exchanges of information—the ones that couldn't be delayed—and I couldn't wait any longer to fill them in on the dire situation currently unfolding on the island.

But Amara spoke before I could continue. "You've been looking after them, haven't you." She didn't voice it as a question.

Tears sprang to my eyes. "Nik and I had no way to leave the island. But even if we did, we couldn't have just abandoned the islanders. These people have been affected by what was done to them—they can't think as proactively as you or I. And all their strong healers have been murdered. I'm only one person, but I thought I was at least better than nothing."

The words taunted me. I'd given myself a job and failed at it within two weeks.

"Delphine." Amara's voice was gentle as she wiped the single tear running down my cheek. "I know you would never abandon a whole town in need like that."

I gulped, trying to hold back any further tears. "I wanted you to have a reason to be proud of me this time. But—"

"Don't worry," she cut in. "I was the one to send you to Grey, and I even had the crown's permission to do it. And you couldn't have foreseen ending up trapped on this island. No one would consider you to have abandoned your apprenticeship—especially given we were separated for only a short time."

"My...apprenticeship?" I tried to follow what she was saying. Did she think I was crying out of fear of being branded a reneger? Was that why she had hurried after me at the first opportunity?

Becoming a complete outcast from society in all its forms would certainly be something to cry over, but the thought hadn't even occurred to me. My mind had been too full of everything happening on the island. And while the best of help had just arrived, even more was still needed.

I glanced dubiously into the harbor where the shredded remains of their boat still floated.

"I guess it will be a while before you've recovered enough strength to go back," I said.

"We will absolutely not be going back!" Luna shuddered dramatically. "You weren't out there in that storm, just one tiny boat among all those rocks. Even with the power of both Amara and Costas, I thought we weren't going to make it. No one is getting back to the mainland any time soon."

"What do you mean?" My eyes flew from her to Amara. "Why can't we get back?"

"That was the first of the winter storms," Costas said grimly. "We had two very strong elements mages for only one small boat, and we still barely made it through. It was a dangerous undertaking and not one worth attempting except under dire necessity. And besides, what about the islanders? You were the one who said you couldn't abandon them. I might have run once, but I don't intend to do so again." He crossed his arms over his chest, looking stubborn.

"Actually, we already discussed it on the way over and reached an agreement," Amara said to me. "Costas said none of the fishing boats are big enough to transport everyone, so the plants mages are going to need to work together and build us something bigger. With their power to aid the process, they should be able to have something serviceable by the time the season turns and the storms abate. We don't need something fancy like Grey's ship, since we don't care about creating an impression. Just something sturdy and seaworthy."

Nik looked warily at the flotsam floating nearby. I could easily read the concern behind his expression. Had that boat once been sturdy as well?

But my thoughts were focused elsewhere.

"You're saying we can't get back until the end of winter?" My dismay was evident, and everyone turned their eyes on me, their gazes reflecting varying degrees of worry. "So that means we're not getting any more help from the mainland before then, either. Not for the whole winter."

"Why?" Amara asked sharply. "Do we need more help?"

Tears sprang back into my eyes as the enormity of the situation hit me all over again.

"There's an epidemic on the island," I said. "I'm a terrible healer because I only just discovered it, and it's already spread through the whole town." My voice rose, assuming a hysterical edge. "And I can't even recognize what disease it is!" I swayed on my feet, the effect of all my power expenditure hitting me hard now that the initial shock and excitement had worn off.

Nik started toward me, but Amara was already at my side. She steadied me with an arm around my shoulders, her concerned gaze flicking to Hayes. "An epidemic?"

I tried to pull myself together to give them a proper report on the situation. "I've only examined the patients on one street so far, but I found multiple people in a dire situation. I had to heal them on the spot or they might not have lasted until I got the chance to return."

"It's that bad?" Hayes asked, clearly alarmed.

"I don't have much experience yet, so maybe you'll recognize it?" I quickly outlined the symptoms for him along with my limited understanding of the disease's progression.

Hayes and Clay exchanged a long look, both of their brows furrowed.

I leaned into Amara, guiltily relieved to no longer be the most senior healer present. I didn't have to be in charge anymore, and I'd never been happier to lack authority.

"It sounds like typhoid," Luna said hesitantly.

I tried to remember what I'd read about typhoid and failed. I'd certainly never encountered it in an actual person.

Hayes grimaced. "I'll have to examine a patient before I can say for sure. But it sounds like it has some similarities at least."

"Our mother is sick," Lumi piped up suddenly, making me start. I'd entirely forgotten the two children were still lurking nearby. "We could take you to her."

Hayes glanced at me, and I nodded. "Their mother kept them away from the Constantines. They're not like the rest of the town."

A shadow crossed Hayes's face, but he merely nodded and turned to the children with a smile.

"If you could do that, I would appreciate it." He glanced at Clay and Luna, and they both nodded, moving toward him.

I reluctantly pulled away from Amara, already missing her support. "I can take you to Ida's host family as well. They're the first ones I examined, and they have someone in every stage of the illness."

"No," Amara said firmly, making me frown. "Absolutely not."

"What do you mean?" I tried to work out what she was talking about. "No one else can—"

"I can take them there," Nik said. "I know this town as well as you, and I was at the house earlier. I'm also not exhausted from over-extending my power."

His eyes met Amara's, and for once they appeared to be in perfect agreement.

"I didn't overextend myself," I argued. "I'm still awake, aren't I?"

"Not for long from the look of you," Amara said. "You need to get some sleep before I'm allowing you to use another speck of your power. Otherwise we'll have you comatose for days again."

I grimaced, embarrassed at the reminder.

"I was careful this time," I said meekly, and her face softened.

"I'm sure you were. But you're also a single healer suddenly faced with an epidemic. I have no doubt you pushed yourself as far as you dared."

I bit my lip, unable to deny the truth of her words.

"Where have you been living?" she asked. "Is there room for us as well?"

"More than enough room." I glanced at Costas. "That is, if Costas doesn't mind."

"You're up at the manor?" He sounded a little surprised.

I shrugged. "It seemed the most practical place to stay while I was trying to sort everything out. But if it bothers you, I can—"

"No, no, it's a large house and the only place where we won't put anyone else out. It makes sense for us to stay there, especially if there's an epidemic underway."

I smiled, relieved I didn't have to come up with another living arrangement when I could hardly think straight.

"Delphine isn't the only one who's exhausted." Hayes gave Amara a stern look. "You and Costas need to get to bed as soon as possible as well. I'll find out what's happening in the town, and we can talk up at the manor once I get back. But only after you've had some rest! You've been holding on for days. You can safely hand over to me now."

She smiled, a softness in her eyes I'd never seen before.

"Thank you," she said softly. "This is your area of expertise anyway. But I'll try not to sleep too long."

"Take as long as you need." He hesitated, as if he wanted to say something further, but after a shake of his head he took off after Lumi, with Clay and Luna at his heels.

The two guards hesitated, looking from Amara to the retreating mages.

"Go with them," Amara said. "They may have need of assistance, whereas we'll all be sleeping. Nik, you too."

Nik also hesitated, although his eyes were on me. I gestured for him to go, sending him off with a reminder to try to find Ida while he was in town. We'd had to hurry off before her return, and she had to be worried.

Nik agreed and finally left to follow the others, sending one lingering look over his shoulder.

"There are several conversations still to be had," Amara said dryly, watching him go. "But they'll have to wait until we've all had some sleep."

"Yes, please," Costas said fervently.

More guilt picked at me as Costas led us through the streets toward the manor. The town was too quiet, and now that I knew the reason, the empty streets haunted me.

"I assume you came in the boat Costas took?" I asked, desperate for something to fill the unnatural silence.

Amara blinked, clearly distracted by other thoughts.

"Yes," she said at last. "We brought as many as could be crammed into it."

"And the rest of your group?" I asked. "You sent them back to the king?"

She nodded. "I wrote down everything Costas told us and instructed the guards to deliver it straight to the capital and directly into the king's hands. They had to return to Eldrida on foot, but they will have taken horses from there. They may even be in the capital by now."

"So Tartora has warning about Grey, at least," I murmured.

Amara nodded. "If King Marius and the Triumvirate believe it. I'll admit it's a hard tale to swallow."

I remembered my own astonishment on first learning that healers could mesmerize—and I had been offered firsthand demonstrations.

"I hope King Marius takes the warning seriously," I said fervently.

"He's a cautious king. He won't dismiss a message from Hayes lightly," she said. "But either way, there's nothing we can do about it until the weather changes. We only encountered one storm, and that was bad enough. I wouldn't want to try again any time soon."

FOUR

I woke up groggy. For a moment, my thoughts were muddled and confused, and then I shot out of bed as my memory fully returned. Scrambling into the first clothes I could find, I peered at the light coming in the windows. I had meant to sleep for just a few hours, but it didn't look like late afternoon. Apparently I'd slept through the rest of the day and the night as well. From Ember's warm presence curled in the sheets, I guessed morning must be well underway.

I hurried off in search of the others, but thanks to the size of the Constantine manor, it took me some time to track anyone down. Eventually I found Amara in the room we used for breakfast.

She smiled at me over a steaming cup of tea and gestured for me to take one of the empty seats around the table.

"Isn't it too hot for tea?" I asked, slipping into one of the places across from her and reaching for a slice of toasted bread. "I've barely drunk the stuff since I got to the island—and this is winter!"

"It's never too hot for tea." She assessed my face as she spoke, checking my condition.

I glanced uncomfortably out the window. "How long was I asleep?" I tensed as I waited for her answer.

"Just since yesterday," she replied, and I breathed a sigh of relief.

"You weren't in a comatose state from overusing your power," she added, "but you must have been pushing yourself a lot to need that much sleep. Now that I'm here, there'll be no more of that."

I shifted in my seat, considering her words. On one level, they were just what I'd been longing to hear. I couldn't wait to hand over responsibility for the island and its inhabitants. But I suspected it wasn't going to be that easy. Emergencies didn't care if you were an apprentice or a proficient.

"What's going on in the town?" I asked, sidestepping the issue of my exhaustion.

A cloud settled on Amara's face. "Hayes and Clay worked most of yesterday and then took shifts through the night. Luna, at least, was sent back here to sleep the night through, but she's already eaten and gone back into town this morning."

I straightened, stuffing the rest of the toast into my mouth. "I should be off too," I said around the mouthful.

"Absolutely not," Amara replied without any change in her steady tone.

"Amara!" I stared at her. "There are only three of them, and the whole town is sick. Four healers is better than one, but it's still not enough for an epidemic of this size and strength."

"I know you're powerful, Delphine, but you're still largely untrained," Amara said. "Even Luna is more experienced than you are, and Hayes and Clay are both masters. They can heal more people with less power than you can."

"Still," I said, clinging stubbornly to my point. "If they worked through the night, they must be getting tired. I'm sure they could use fresh assistance."

"*Fresh* is not a word I would use to describe you, even with all that sleep."

When I glared at her, she just raised an eyebrow, and I slumped back in my seat with a sigh. It had only been a matter of weeks, but apparently I'd already forgotten what it meant to be an apprentice with a master. It wasn't all positives.

Looking at my dejection, Amara relented, putting down her teacup and leaning forward.

"Costas and I were also tired enough to sleep most of the day and night, but I did manage a conversation with Hayes yesterday evening."

"What did he say? Did he recognize the illness?"

She shook her head, and my anxiety surged. So we really were dealing with something new.

"Apparently new illnesses sometimes appear out of the jungle," I said. "There was a fever a few years ago, but back then the Constantines…"

She nodded, allowing me to trail off uncomfortably. I still didn't know how to think or talk about the deceased Constantines who had lived terrible lives and met a terrible end.

"There is good news," Amara said. "It might be a new strain, but Luna was right that it bears many similarities to typhoid. So they aren't dealing with something entirely unfamiliar. By the end of yesterday, Hayes and Clay had finished their assessments and agreed on the best approach to treatment as well as a plan for general epidemic management."

"Already?" Tears welled behind my eyes.

Thank goodness two masters had arrived. I was used to relying on my strength to make up for my lack of knowledge and experience, but that could only get me so far. This had been a disaster far beyond anything my strength could compensate for.

"You'll be better off hearing the details from them. I admit I didn't absorb the finer points of it all. But the important thing is that the three of them have already recruited all those in the town with a healing affinity—however weak—and together they've made it to every household and completed a triage."

"That's incredible!" I hesitated. "How many are in immediate danger?"

She grimaced. "I don't know exact numbers, but since the situation is already so advanced, it's more than is ideal. And unfortunately a few have already died."

I paled. The townsfolk had started dying on my watch, and I hadn't even realized.

"The first deaths have only just happened," Amara said quickly, correctly reading my emotions. "It seems the real danger doesn't start until the third week of illness."

"That's something to be grateful for, at least," I muttered.

"At this point, we'll take any advantage, however small," she said. "Hayes and Clay spent the night doing limited healings on the most severely ill patients. Unfortunately, given how far the epidemic has already progressed, they can't do anything to get ahead of it—not yet at least. It will take everything they have just to help those in the most danger."

"Exactly!" I gave her a piercing look. "And that's why I should be out there helping!"

She ignored my words. "Thankfully, since the illness develops over weeks rather than just days, Hayes thinks that better management will eventually be possible. If the four of you can work through the worst cases quickly enough, you should eventually reach the point where you can start treating less advanced patients before they reach the danger period. That's going to take a while, and it will be much longer again until we can truly get on top of the epidemic, but time is the one thing we have."

My ears pricked up at her mention of the four of us. "You are going to let me go and help, then?"

"Tomorrow. As I said, this is a marathon, not a sprint."

"Not for those in immediate danger it isn't," I fired back. "How can you expect me to sit around at the manor doing nothing all day while people in the town might be dying?"

She surveyed me in silence for several moments.

"That does seem a bit much to ask," said a friendly voice from the doorway.

I looked up to see Costas leaning against the doorframe, his eyes on Amara. How long had he been standing there?

"Shall we bring her with us?" he asked.

"That's an excellent suggestion." Amara stood, her manner turning brisk. "Some fresh air and exercise will no doubt be of value." She looked at me. "How quickly can you be ready to go?"

"Immediately." I jumped to my feet. "Where are we going?"

"Did you get as far as typhoid in those medical texts of yours?" Amara asked.

I shook my head. "I might have skimmed past it, but I don't remember if I did. I've been focusing mainly on the anatomy books and those illnesses I encountered in the Caltoran hospital. But I haven't even been able to do that for a while since my books are all back on the mainland."

"While typhoid is infectious, it's largely spread through contaminated food and water. Hayes and Clay are in agreement that this new illness is likely the same."

"How can they tell?" I asked, fascinated.

"I can't give you all the details," she warned. "You'd have to ask one of them to get the technical reply. But I gather it's a combination of factors. The nature of the illness and its close relation to typhoid is a clue. But also the way it has spread so evenly across the town. That suggests a communal source rather than a gradual spread from an initial infected patient. If it was spreading person to person, the most advanced cases would be grouped together in clumps of close associates."

"That makes sense." I frowned, considering her words. "So you're going to search for the source of the infection?" I looked back and forth between them. "You must suspect it's in a water source if the two of you are going?"

"We're not making any assumptions," Amara said. "I'll be leading the investigation since I've helped in epidemic situations before, but we're keeping open minds."

"Which is why I'm coming along," Nik said from behind Costas.

Costas came all the way into the room to make way for Nik who took his place in the doorway, his eyes on me.

"I'll help in case the issue is coming from stored food, the soil, or a wild plant," he said.

"And if you come along, Delphine, you can keep an eye out for an animal host as well." Costas sounded pleased.

I guessed he felt similarly to me. If we couldn't be in the town healing people, it was a relief to at least have something constructive to do. And he didn't even have the assurance I did that I would soon resume work among the infected. It had to be difficult not to have a healing affinity in situations like an epidemic.

Amara led the four of us out of the manor and to the edge of the garden. I was acutely aware of Nik's presence, but neither of us addressed the other directly. Just like in town the morning before, we needed to put aside the tension between us to focus on the epidemic.

"Ida!" I cried, distracted from thoughts of Nik by the arrival of the older woman.

She nodded at me, her face grave. But when she caught sight of Phoenix and Ember approaching, her expression lightened. Her fondness for the animals had only grown with each passing week.

She bent over to place a gentle hand on Ember's back. "Shouldn't you be sleeping, beautiful?"

Ember allowed the pat for a moment before slipping away to join me. It was unusual for her to be out of bed during the day, and I could only assume she'd sensed something unusual was going on.

"I'm sorry we rushed off without you yesterday," I said to Ida. "We got word of a boat arriving and feared it might be Grey."

She nodded. "Nik found me and explained everything. We are fortunate your friends arrived in such good timing."

I nodded fervently.

"I spent the day and some of the night helping Masters Hayes and Clay, and they are both highly skilled." Her expression of distaste didn't match her words, so I threw her a questioning look. She shook herself slightly.

"Sorry," she murmured. "Seeing them at work reminds me of Grey—the only other healing master I know. It's a relief to know they aren't all like him."

Her sour expression made it clear she had shaken off the last of Grey's hold and no longer held him in any reverence. It was a far cry from her attitude back in the crevasse when she had excused his lack of care for his people. I was sorry for all the terrible things that had happened to break the hold of her mesmerizations, but I couldn't be anything but happy that she was free of his lies.

"Are you coming with us?" I asked.

"Master Amara thinks I may be of help. Whenever I can, I've been exploring the mountain and the wilderness areas surrounding the town. This is a very beautiful place, and I enjoy the solitude and peace away from the bustle of the town. So I offered to act as guide since the locals are either sick or have sick family and friends to care for."

"We're heading into the jungle?" I looked from her to Amara.

"It's not a true jungle," Ida said. "Although it's more like one than anything in Tartora." She led the way into the dense trees that bordered the manor gardens to the north.

We all trailed behind her, coolness enveloping us as we stepped beneath the canopy. "But shouldn't we be checking for contamination in the town first?" I stepped over a jagged branch that had obviously fallen a long time ago since it was half covered in moss.

"I did some initial investigations late yesterday, once we knew what we were dealing with," Nik said, the familiar sound of his voice humming through my bones.

I could feel his presence at my back and didn't dare turn to look at him. I longed to feel the comfort of his arms around me more than I was willing to admit.

"I couldn't find anything amiss in any of the major food stores, or any obvious sources of poor sanitation that might be corrupting the environment."

"For all my family's faults," Costas said, "—and they were many—they were still a family of healers. From the beginning, we've had a comprehensive sanitation system, and they always kept a close eye on the town's food and water sources."

"But Grey disrupted everything here," I said slowly, considering his words. "Even from before our arrival, but especially after. They must have lost focus on the normal day-to-day issues."

"The timing seems to line up," Amara agreed. "I would guess the source of contamination first appeared shortly before their deaths."

We were all silent for a moment as we considered the timing and everything that had happened on the island before and since that moment.

"Where are you leading us?" Amara asked Ida as we turned sharply west, following a trail that was so faint it barely counted as a track but which gave us a fairly straight passage through the trees.

"There's an area just ahead that is well used by locals," she said. "A number of families regularly forage among the trees there for the goods they sell at market."

"What sort of goods?" I asked, frowning at the tall trunks and dense foliage around us. While the bright blooms were a pleasant sight, I couldn't see anything that looked edible.

She glanced back over her shoulder. "All sorts of things. Mushrooms, for one. Plus various roots that grow at the base of the trees. And some of the leaves have health benefits as well."

"Do they use it for medicine?" I frowned. "Didn't the Constantines freely heal all ailments?"

"They eat them," Costas explained. "Or make tea with them. My family encouraged the locals to take care of their health even outside their appointments."

"Could something like that really be the source of such a virulent sickness?" I looked doubtfully toward Amara.

She shrugged. "If there's a contamination source where they grow and they aren't properly washed and cooked, perhaps? We don't want to rule anything out."

I didn't need Ida's announcement to know when we'd arrived. The dense tree trunks thinned, allowing much more sunlight through to the forest floor. In response, a profusion of bushes and other ground plants covered the area. In several spots I could even see freshly turned earth where some small plant had recently been pulled out by the roots.

"Let's spread out," Amara commanded. "Nik, you examine the plants and the earth. Delphine, please let me know if you sense anything wrong with any of the animals in the area."

I stopped walking and reached out with my power, assessing the area around us. As expected, our immediate area was mostly devoid of creatures—our arrival having scared them away—but a few still lingered in burrows and nests, and further out the forest teemed with life.

There was only so much I could sense from a distance, but even so it was fascinating. My attention caught on a long snake hidden among the leaves of a tree a short distance from our location. I had never encountered anything like it—I had little experience with reptiles in general—and the unfamiliar feel of the cold-blooded creature fascinated me.

After a moment, I shook my head and forcefully pulled my focus away. I wasn't here to learn about the local wildlife.

I spread my power out, skimming lightly over a myriad of creatures. While I couldn't tell any details of their condition, I could feel the steady beating of the life inside them. I was confident that if any of them were in significant pain, I would sense it, as I had once done with Ember.

Nothing caught my attention, though. If any of the animals were ill, they were hiding it well.

I tried to push my power out, calling to the animals around me. If any of them could be coaxed close enough, I could make contact and get a more exact picture of their health.

The attempt brought back memories of trying to call to the trapped eagle. Tears sprang to my eyes as I remembered how that incident had ended. And now there was more death around me.

I pushed harder, attempting to throw my power across the surrounding forest. It was a desperate, unfocused effort, but my ears caught a rustle in the surrounding ground coverage. I turned hopefully toward it, only to see familiar orange, white, and black fur as Ember appeared from between two bushes and rushed to my side.

I dropped to one knee and scooped her up. "Of course you came, old friend. You always do."

A small chip alerted me a moment before Phoenix flew in low beneath the branches, executing a tight maneuver to land on my shoulder.

"And you, too, fine sir." I ran a finger along his feathers. "You never let me down either." I sighed. "But it's your wild brethren I was hoping to meet. And I don't think the presence of the two of you is going to help in that attempt."

Phoenix cocked his head and regarded me with one beady eye. He didn't look in the least repentant, and I couldn't help smiling.

Amara strode toward me. "Have you noticed anything strange? Anything at all?"

"The animal populations look quiet as far as I can tell. I can try to get close enough to touch a few of them to confirm, but that might be hard to achieve with so much disruption to their normal environment." I glanced doubtfully around the disturbed section of forest.

"No, let's leave it there for now," she said, only half paying attention. "It was always an unlikely option that it might come from animals. They aren't carriers for traditional typhoid."

I nodded, relieved I didn't have to attempt to capture a selection of wild animals.

"Did you find anything?" I asked, hopeful despite her serious expression.

A startled cry made us both spin eastward, staring into the trees.

"Was that Costas?" I asked, and Amara nodded.

She took off without a word, heading in the direction of his voice, and I hurried behind. Had Costas been the one to find something?

CHAPTER

FIVE

Phoenix took off from my shoulder, racing ahead of us, just beneath the canopy.

The forest had gone quiet again, but somehow that only made me more anxious. Was Costas in trouble and unable to call out?

We wound through the trees toward him, my straining ears picking up nothing except the sound of running water. Then came the glint of sunlight on water, followed by the sight of a small huddle of people standing on the bank of a small river.

Costas was there, looking unharmed, and Ida and Nik stood beside him. I slowed to a walk, huffing out a relieved breath as they turned to look at us.

"Sorry." Costas sounded embarrassed. "A wild boar took me by surprise. I didn't mean to bring everyone running."

"So you didn't find anything?" Amara sounded disappointed. "Did you check the river?"

He nodded. "Nothing to report, I'm afraid. The water felt the same as in the river beside town."

"That makes sense," Ida said, "since it's the same river."

"It's not actually," Costas corrected, making her frown.

"I suppose it's not exactly the same one," she acknowledged

after a moment. "The main river bends westward, and it's only a branch that breaks off and goes south toward the town."

Costas shook his head. "I think you're getting confused, which is understandable. The town's river starts further south from here. It isn't a big one, and it starts from an underground source, so to all appearances it just springs out of nowhere not far above the town. It would be natural to think it comes from a larger river up north."

"I..." Ida paused, frowning, before giving a shrug. "Of course you would know the island better than me."

I looked between them, surprised Ida would be wrong on something of that nature. She was the sort of steady person who could be relied on to have accurate information and considered opinions. And while it was true that Costas had lived his whole life on the island, it was Ida who was serving as our guide because he had lived his life almost entirely separate from the regular islanders.

But then this was a matter of geography, not of where the islanders preferred to forage for herbs. As an elements mage, in particular, surely Costas would be familiar with the nearby rivers.

"Hmmm...I'm starting to regret not going with you to check the town's river," Amara said. "I won't be able to make a comparison with this one."

She knelt swiftly and plunged a hand into the flowing water. Her brow creased as she stared downriver. When she stood, it was slowly, the water flowing off her hand until it was completely dry.

She turned to Costas. "You really didn't feel anything at all unusual about this water?"

His brows shot up. "Did you?"

She hesitated. "Maybe?"

"Are you stronger than Costas?" Nik asked. "If you sense something he doesn't, could that be why?"

"I think we have a similar level of ability, actually," she said. "But there is one crucial difference." She turned to me. "Could you check the water, Delphine?"

"Me?" I stared at her. "I can, of course, but I don't know if I'll be able to sense anything."

"You think it's your cross-influence that's the difference, then?" Nik asked Amara in an intrigued tone.

"Cross-influence?" Costas asked. "What do you mean?"

"I have an elements seed," Amara said, "but I was activated by a healer."

"By a healer?" Costas stared at her in astonishment. "But that makes no sense. Don't you come from the Tartoran capital? Surely there was an elements mage available to do the activation for you?"

"There was, of course," she said, "but I preferred the healing master I chose—both for personality and affinity."

Costas's brow wrinkled, as if he couldn't understand what she was saying, and I remembered what Grey had told me about the island.

"They don't allow cross-influencing here," I said. "I suppose they had to do everything possible to preserve and strengthen their power, given their community is small and isolated."

"No cross-influencing at all?" Amara asked. "That's a loss."

"But what would be the benefit?" Costas asked. "We were taught it just weakens your ability."

"In the sense of brute force, it can," Amara agreed. "But there are many advantages to be received in exchange. I may not have proper healing power, but my power will always be tangled with traces of my influencer's power. It expands my ability in ways that are impossible for a straight elements mage. And in this case, it's given me an important capacity to sense life—however incomplete my sense might be compared to a true healer like Delphine."

"You think there's something alive in the river—something that shouldn't be there?" I asked.

"Possibly?" She sighed. "I can't be sure. I'm not familiar with what the disease feels like since I can't connect with a human body. I'm hoping you might be able to recognize it, though, since you're healing cross elements. I'm not sure a straight healer could sense life at such a minuscule level when it's suspended in water instead of inside a living creature. But I'm hoping my elements influence will give you that ability."

Kneeling, I leaned toward the water. As I neared it, I wobbled, nearly losing my balance and falling in. Someone caught me by the arm, steadying me, and I didn't have to look back to know it was Nik.

I could feel his warm presence beside me, but I forced myself to focus on the task at hand, merely murmuring a quick thank you.

As soon as my hand was immersed in the river's current, other thoughts fell away. I couldn't sense the water, exactly, but when I pushed out my power, searching for life, it slid eagerly and quickly through the water, latching on to the various river dwelling creatures with ease. I focused harder, looking for a different sort of life.

"Oh!" My exclamation made the rest of them crowd in close, peering over my shoulder as if my discovery might be visible.

"Did you sense something?" Amara asked.

"It's faint, but it's definitely there." I couldn't help sounding excited. "And it felt similar to the disease in the bodies of the townsfolk. I'd be surprised if such faint traces could make someone ill, but maybe it gets stronger downstream?"

"The two of you can put your hand in a river and sense traces of disease?" Ida looked at the two of us with hints of awe in her expression.

I was growing used to people looking at Amara like that, but I felt uncomfortable being viewed the same way.

"I'm sure any healing cross elements or elements cross healing mage could do it," I said.

"The important thing is that we find and eliminate the continuing source of infection," Amara said. "This river seems like it could be the answer, but we need to find out how the infection got from this river to the other one."

"Why don't we follow it south?" Ida suggested. "We can track its route as well as anything it comes into contact with."

Amara glanced at Costas before nodding. "That sounds sensible."

We quickly formed ourselves into a single file line with Amara at our head. She led us along the edge of the river for several minutes before holding up a hand to signal a stop. I put Ember down and peered around Costas and Ida, trying to see what Amara was doing.

Kneeling again, she once more put her hand into the flow of the river. This time she took even longer to rise, her eyes narrowing. When she said nothing, Costas copied her movements, also making contact with the water.

Almost as soon as he did so, his eyebrows shot up.

"You can feel the branch?" Amara asked.

"Of course. But where did it come from? That definitely didn't used to be there. I swum this river many times as a boy."

The melancholy tone of the final sentence brought to mind the image of an ostracized boy with an elements seed, seeking comfort in the water since he was unwanted within his healer family.

"Is it possible this new branch joins with the town's river?" Amara asked. "It seems to be heading in the right direction."

"Entirely possible." Costas looked up at Ida. "I apologize. It seems you were right. I shouldn't have dismissed what you were saying so readily. Something has changed since I was last in this part of the island."

"If this branch has connected the two rivers only recently,

that seems like further evidence this is the source of infection," Ida said. "And it might explain why I'm still healthy as well. I didn't like to say anything to my hosts, but when we first arrived, I found the taste of the town's water unpleasant. I fell into the habit of boiling a pot for myself and letting it cool since I found it produced a more familiar taste."

"It must be the water source causing the problem," I said. "Everything fits. It even explains why no one at the manor is sick since we use a well on the grounds rather than traipsing across town to the river."

Amara stood, shaking water from her hand. "We'll follow the branch when it appears and confirm that it joins the town's river. But I now feel confident about what we'll find."

We resumed walking, but this time chatter passed up and down our line.

"How could a new branch suddenly form out of nowhere?" I asked.

"It happens more often than you might think," Amara said.

"Is it also normal for a new branch to carry a new disease with it?" Nik sounded skeptical.

"No. That bit isn't normal at all." Amara glanced back at us. "A new branch explains how the infected water is reaching the townsfolk en masse, but it doesn't tell us any more about the actual source of infection. How did it get into the water in the first place?"

"Between us all, I'm sure we'll find the source," Ida said with conviction.

I glanced back at Nik, but his face was carefully blank, giving no indication of what he thought of our chances. But when his eyes caught on mine, I glimpsed a fire raging beneath his calm exterior.

I whipped my eyes back to the front again. I was fairly certain that particular blaze had nothing to do with the epidemic or the town, and it was something I couldn't deal with right now.

But now that I'd glimpsed it, I could feel the warmth of his gaze on my back, making it hard to concentrate. When Ida stopped in front of me, I walked straight into her back, nearly sending us both tumbling into the river. We would have gone over if not for the cushion of air that pushed back against our momentum, righting us both. I threw a thankful look at Amara who was watching me with amused forbearance.

Ember was less impressed. Having only just managed to avoid my stumbling feet, she took off for the front of the line, apparently having decided Amara would be a safer walking companion.

I couldn't fault her since the near accident had clearly been caused by my distraction. I murmured a second apology to Ida, but she waved it off.

Once I was paying attention, I could clearly see why we'd stopped. The river bent sharply away to our right, while a small stream broke off and continued south, in the rough direction of the town.

After only the briefest of comments, we resumed our progress, but now following the stream instead of the main river. As we walked, I resolved to focus on the issue at hand, but the more I tried to force my mind away from Nik, the more aware I was of the heat from his body and the soft rise and fall of his breath. I stumbled slightly, and a strong hand steadied my elbow from behind. The touch was withdrawn again as soon as I regained my balance, but the tingle of contact remained, distracting me even further.

The flap of wings made me look up to see Phoenix zipping toward me. He was flying above the stream, as if it were a road for birds, its purpose being to clear a path free of trees. I shook my head at my own whimsy, but the thought of a path stuck in my head.

The ground beneath my feet was becoming easier to walk, as if someone had already started wearing out a track along the route. It would be natural for the townsfolk to do the same as Phoenix—following the course of the stream as they made their way to the best foraging ground. But this stream was new and the townsfolk had been falling progressively ill for the last couple of weeks. Was it possible they had already worn down the ground this much, even this far from the town?

A rustling in the undergrowth nearest the stream made me turn in time to see Ember come shooting out from between two bushes. She was moving fast enough that she might have slid into the stream if I hadn't scooped her up. I wasn't sure if she was afraid, but something had set her trembling. Whatever she had encountered in the forest had certainly caught her attention.

Making a fast decision, I changed direction, stepping away from the stream in the direction she had come. Nik immediately stopped as well.

"What is it?" He sounded concerned.

I didn't turn to look at him, just holding up a hand to ask him to wait. Closing my eyes, I sent my power out into the surrounding forest. Dimly in the background I heard Nik calling to the others ahead of us to stop, but I ignored his words as well as their replies, focusing on my search.

This time I ignored the feathered, furred, and reptilian populations I encountered, skimming over them as I looked for something else. Someone had made a path beside this stream, but what if it wasn't the townsfolk? What if someone else was here in the forest?

It was a large island, and the town only covered a small part of it.

I stiffened as my power brushed against the familiar feel of people. Nik's hand braced my elbow as he murmured a question I wasn't paying enough attention to catch. For once, his presence wasn't enough to distract me as I reached toward my new discovery.

"What have you found?" Amara's question—delivered in the voice of a master to an apprentice—broke me out of my focus.

I blinked, shaking my head as I turned to look at her. The others had abandoned their single line to cluster around me, all of their faces intent.

"There are people." I pointed straight into the trees. "Through there."

"We're still a way north of the town." Costas frowned in the direction I'd pointed. "But not everyone forages in the same place. They must be out gathering supplies. Perhaps they're hoping they can find something that will help with this disease."

"It's possible." I hesitated. "But would they bring sick people along on a foraging expedition?"

"Are they ill?" Amara asked, her voice turning sharp.

"It's hard to say for sure from this distance." I hesitated again. "I don't think they all are. But there's one—a child—who doesn't feel right even from this distance. I'm afraid she must be very sick for me to sense it from so far away."

"A child?" Amara's frown deepened. She exchanged a look first with Costas and then Ida. "Is it possible someone came out here in desperation and didn't want to leave their sick child behind? Regardless, it sounds unusual enough to warrant further examination." She turned to me. "Do you think you can take us to them? Are they moving?"

I checked again before answering. "They seem to be stationary, and I can certainly take us in their direction. But I can't tell what obstacles might be between us and them."

"I'll take care of any obstacles," Nik said in a matter-of-fact way, and I didn't doubt his ability to deal with anything the forest might throw at us.

I glanced up and down the river, considering the path that wasn't quite a path. My instinct told me these weren't towns-folk who'd come into the forest to forage. And if I was right about that, perhaps...

I stepped away from the river, pushing through the bushes in the same spot Ember had emerged from. At first I could see nothing but more trees and varied undergrowth. Nik strode through behind me, and I turned in time to see him stop abruptly.

Following the direction of his gaze, I sucked in a breath.

"I'm not imagining it, right?" I asked. "That's a path?"

"A path?" Amara reached us, following my pointing finger to see for herself. "Did you know this was here, Delphine?"

"Not for sure, but I wondered." I gave Ember a light squeeze. "Ember found something in this direction, and it occurred to me that whoever made that path," I gestured back toward the stream, "might have made more."

"Impressive." Amara smiled at me, and I couldn't help grinning back despite the seriousness of the situation. If I couldn't be in town healing people, at least I could be useful out here.

"If there's a path, we need to see where it leads." Costas took off, the rest of us hurrying to fall in behind him.

The narrow width of the path through the undergrowth kept us in single file again, but the conversation continued regardless.

"The path just ends abruptly back there instead of connecting with the path by the stream," he said, and for a moment I thought he was discounting my theory. But when I caught the look he threw Amara, I realized he had something else on his mind.

"You think they're hiding themselves, then?" Nik asked. "Would they have reason to do that?"

"I think you know the answer to that," Costas said in a tired voice, and Nik fell quiet.

"Are they hiding from us?" I asked, horrified.

The idea hadn't even occurred to me, but now it seemed to fit all too well, given the newness of the paths. Had our arrival driven some of the islanders from their homes?

I glanced back at Nik, and he frowned at the expression on my face. I expected him to say something comforting—however meaningless given our lack of information—but instead he turned a speculative look northward.

"Hold on a moment," he said, and we all stopped, everyone turning in his direction.

Plunging into the trees, he disappeared from view, only to call for us to follow him moments later. I had to wind my way around several dense bushes, but as soon as I was out of sight of the path, the undergrowth abruptly cut off, giving way to an unnatural clearing.

The trees had been cleared, as well as the undergrowth, replaced with neat rows of what looked like vegetables, and even a whole section of some sort of grain. I gaped at it, everyone else taking in the sight in equal silence.

"I thought I could sense something out of the ordinary through here," Nik said at last. Looking at me, he continued. "Whatever is going on here, I don't think it has anything to do with us."

I nodded, relieved, although my curiosity was now burning out of control.

"Look!" Ida pointed at a spot to our right. "That looks like a more established path."

"That makes sense," Amara said. "The stream is quite new, so the paths to and along it are also new. But this clearing has obviously been here a long time."

She led the way toward the second path, and we all followed. This track was much more obvious and had enough room for two people to walk side by side. From the look of the packed dirt beneath us, I suspected some sort of cart made regular use of it, as well as people on foot.

"How close are we?" Amara asked me.

"Very," I said quietly. "There are five adults and the sick child. I suspect two of the adults might be older, but they're not elderly enough for it to be obvious in their bodies from this distance."

"Sounds like a family," Nik murmured as he drifted closer to me. Despite his words, his hand strayed to his sword hilt.

Amara nodded. "Regardless of who they are, I feel confident we can handle the situation."

It was a reasonable assumption given the nature of our group. With two powerful elements mages, not to mention a strong plants mage, there were few people who would pose a risk to us.

"Relax," I whispered to Nik. "The last thing we need is more of that." I nodded toward his sword but regretted it immediately when his face paled.

He drew away from me, and I immediately felt the distance. I didn't need his protection, but I had appreciated his presence anyway. I bit my lip. How long would it be until the sight of Nik with a sword didn't bring back unwanted images of that awful night? I hated the lingering effects of what had been a misunderstanding on my part.

And as usual since then, I couldn't find the right words to bridge the gap that had sprung up between us. Nik had done nothing wrong—the horrible assumptions had all been mine, and it should be my responsibility to fix matters. If only I knew how.

"I'm sorry," I murmured, and he gave me a tight smile.

I wanted to say more, but it was hardly the time for a proper conversation.

"They're just ahead," I whispered, unsure if we were trying to hide our approach.

Amara nodded to show she'd heard but didn't stop walking. Ahead of her, the trees thinned and then disappeared completely, revealing another clearing. This second one was smaller, but it looked well established.

My mouth fell open as I took in a log cabin with another, smaller garden spreading in all directions around it. Whatever I had been expecting, it hadn't been this.

"How long have they been here?" I asked. "This isn't a camp but a long-term house."

"It certainly is. And the only polite thing to do at this point is knock." Amara walked up the neat path that led to the front door and rapped loudly on the wood.

A glad cry sounded from inside, and the door was wrenched open. A man appeared, but as soon as he took in Amara's appearance, his face fell, his expression changing from glad welcome to horror within seconds.

CHAPTER
SIX

"Please don't be alarmed," Amara said quickly. "We don't mean you any harm."

"Don't touch me!" the man said roughly, pulling out a knife and holding it up defiantly, although the hand that held it trembled.

I swayed forward, wanting to run to support Amara, but caution held me in place. I didn't want to cause the man to panic and attack.

"Don't worry," she said. "I'm not a healer." An unnatural wind swept past us and through the cabin door, clearly demonstrating her affinity.

The man relaxed slightly although he didn't lower his knife. Peering over her shoulder, he narrowed his eyes at where the rest of us were grouped together in frozen stillness.

"I did, however, bring a healer with me," Amara continued, making the man start violently. "And my healer tells me that someone inside this house is in need of medical assistance."

She met his gaze, her eyes steady, and I wasn't surprised to see him flinch. I had been the recipient of that gaze often enough myself to know its effect.

I finally let myself step forward to join her. Nik grabbed at my arm, his eyes on the knife blade, but I shook him off and he let me go.

"I'm Delphine," I said in as calming a tone as I could manage. "And I'm a healing apprentice." I nodded toward Amara. "She's my master."

His eyes widened. "You're cross-influenced? My grandma told me about that, but I've never met anyone who was."

I nodded. "Then you must know I don't come from the island. I'm not like the Constantines. All I want to do is assist the sick child."

He hesitated, glancing over his shoulder, and I could guess what was making him waver. From this proximity, I was certain the child inside was extremely ill. This family must have been avoiding healers for years, but now they had desperate need of one.

"Do you have any strength?" he asked roughly.

"My apprentice will be a master one day," Amara said with complete certainty.

The man's eyes widened as he gave me a second look. I shifted uncomfortably.

"I don't know about that," I said. "But I think I know what that girl in there has, and I'm certain I can help her."

I had encountered enough cases to know what the slow heartbeat and rattling breaths meant.

"You're sure?" he asked, and I could hear the indecision in his voice.

"Yes." I tried to look as trustworthy as possible. "But the sooner I help her, the better. I can't be sure without a proper examination, but she sounds like she's already well advanced in the illness."

"She's not the only one who's sick," Amara told him gently. "This disease has spread through the whole town. My apprentice may be young, but she knows what she's doing."

"Fine," the man said, "but she comes in alone. And she doesn't touch anyone except the patient."

I nodded eagerly, my concern for the girl growing as I heard her give a racking cough and sensed her heartbeat dip even further in response.

"Absolutely not," Nik said in a harsh voice.

He stepped forward to my side, and the man's eyes narrowed, his gaze taking in Nik's stance and the weapon on his hip.

"How about a compromise?" Amara said. "I will accompany my apprentice inside, and the rest of our group will remain out here."

The man's eyes flicked to the remaining two, but he was too distracted by Nik to give them more than a passing glance. If that distraction was the reason for him failing to recognize the one Constantine among us, then Nik's protective instincts had achieved some good at least.

"Very well," he said after a moment. "Just the two of you."

He stood back slightly, gesturing for us to pass him and enter the house. Amara went first, with me following close behind. The man shrunk back from me as I slipped past, clearly afraid of any contact, no matter how minor.

I winced but was soon distracted by the inside of the house. The first thing I saw was a second man stepping forward to provide backup to the one already in the doorway. He was a generation older than the first, and from the resemblance, I guessed them to be father and son.

This man also gave me a wide berth, clearing my view of the house beyond. A large, open room contained a wooden table with six chairs, a stove, a number of storage cabinets, and several more padded chairs. Unlike the smaller home of Ida's host family, the cabin had a number of doors opening off the central room. Judging from the different timbers used to make the various internal doors, I guessed the house had been expanded over time.

Two women—one older and one younger—sat at the wooden table, their postures stiff and their expressions torn between hope and fear. There was no sign of the child.

"Please take me to the patient." I'd barely finished the words when another round of weak coughs made me look toward one of the doors. "She's in there?"

The older woman stood and wrung her hands. "Please save our Nina." The look on her face almost brought tears to my eyes, and I nodded, determined.

Amara reached the door first, opening it for me and ushering me inside. The room beyond held two beds, one against each wall, a dresser, and a small table bearing a pitcher of water. Scattered across the floor and bed were a number of toys, each one clearly carved and polished with care.

But the small girl lying in one of the beds was too far gone to pay any attention to toys. Her eyes opened at the sound of the door, but from the glassy, unfocused look to them, she was barely conscious.

A woman lay beside her, her arms wrapped around the girl and a look of anguish on her face. The girl's mother.

"Please," she whispered, her eyes on my face. "Please."

Unlike the others, her face bore no hint of fear at our presence, and I guessed it was because a far worse fear already had her in its grip, leaving no room for anything else. She knew how close her daughter was to death, and she would clearly risk far more than our presence to save her.

I didn't waste any time on words, hurrying to the bed and kneeling beside it. Gripping Nina's thin arm with both of my hands, I pushed my power into her.

It only took seconds to confirm that our assumption had been right. This girl had the same thing that plagued the townsfolk, and her condition had already progressed beyond anyone else I'd encountered.

I didn't need my power to feel her burning up—my hands were enough to tell she was dangerously hot. I cooled her first, easing her pain while I did so. Just those two things were enough to get a response. She stirred, her eyes brightening as she regarded me with curiosity. But she didn't try to sit up, her condition still clearly extremely weak.

I sent my power to her brain next and her heart after that. With both essential organs in such a state of inflammation, she wouldn't have lasted long without intervention.

As I poured my power into her, letting my natural instincts guide the process, I wished I'd had a chance to talk to Hayes before we left. Not having learned the techniques he'd devised for treating the disease, I was going to have to expend a lot of power to save her. And as I poured it into her, I wondered how many other children in the town were approaching this level of illness.

Hayes and Clay had triaged the population, but sometimes conditions like this could progress unpredictably, and I preferred to keep as much of my power in reserve for other patients as possible. I didn't hold back from the healing, though. Considering the extent of her illness and the family's isolation, it seemed important to complete the healing while I had the chance.

By the time I had finished, the mother was shaking with sobs. When I let Nina's arm drop with a tired sigh, I reached for the mother's wrist, concerned. She waved me away, however, recovering herself enough to speak.

"I'm just so...grateful," the final word came out on another sob, but she pushed herself into a sitting position, helping her daughter to ease herself up as well.

"She'll still need recovery time." I stood. "Given the length of her illness, her energy reserves will be low, and her nutrient levels will be depleted."

The mother nodded, but she couldn't keep a beaming smile off her face.

"We'll take excellent care of her."

"Mama, I'm hungry!" Nina announced, her high voice strong, despite her recent ordeal.

Her mother swept her into her arms and squeezed her tightly. Meeting her eyes over Nina's head, I saw fresh tears spilling out.

"We tried so hard to coax her to eat and drink," she said. "But it was a struggle to get her to take anything. And we couldn't keep her temperature down. At first we were taking her to the water every few hours to immerse her, but even with the new stream so much closer than the river used to be, she got too weak for the journey."

Amara, who had been standing back near the door, straightened, her eyes focusing on the woman.

"You were bathing her in the stream?"

"Yes." The woman faltered before the intensity of Amara's expression, looking from her to me. "Was that wrong? We just wanted to cool her."

I rubbed the back of my neck and looked at Amara.

"Bathing a patient with a high temperature in cool water is often a good idea," I said carefully.

The mother remained tense, clearly understanding there was something more behind my broad statement.

"I'm hungry!" Nina repeated, escaping her mother's arms and sliding out of the bed.

Seeing her standing, I guessed her to be about five. Dropping to one knee, I offered her my hand and she shook it gravely.

As soon as she'd finished, she looked over her shoulder at her mother, her eyes bright.

"Did I do it right?"

"You did an excellent job," her mother assured her, then looked at me, vaguely embarrassed. "She hasn't met anyone outside the family, other than her ladyship, of course, but we've tried to teach her proper manners in case…"

She trailed off at the confused expressions on both Amara and my faces.

"Why don't we join the others," Amara said, "so we can talk properly, and you can get this young lady some food?"

Nina jumped in excitement and raced for the door. Her mother watched her go with the dazed expression of someone who'd just had a violent and unexpected shift in emotion.

Amara put a gentle hand on her arm. "Don't worry, she really is better. My apprentice might be young, but she's strong."

The woman flinched, pulling away, and Amara quickly removed her hand.

"Don't worry," she said. "I have an elements seed myself."

"You're cross-influenced?" the woman asked me, showing the same amazement as the man at the door.

"Yes, that's right," Amara said. "We're not from the island."

"Not from the island," the woman repeated slowly, as if she couldn't quite wrap her mind around the concept.

"I'm sorry to hurry you," I said. "But we need to talk to you about an urgent situation."

The woman still looked bemused, but she allowed us to lead the way out to the main room. Nina was already seated at the table, being plied with food by the two delighted-looking women there. Even the men at the door had relaxed since Nina's appearance. My healing had done far more than our words in convincing them of our intentions.

"Could the rest of our party come inside now?" Amara asked, looking from the matriarch of the group to the patriarch.

"It sounds like there's a lot you don't know about the current situation on the island, and our time is limited."

Glances flew between all five of the adults, but after a moment the older woman nodded, and the two men slowly moved over to the table to join the rest of us. I hurried to the empty doorway and leaned outside.

Nik appeared in front of me before I could even wave them over. From the tension in his muscles, he had been poised and waiting to spring into action.

"You can relax," I told him. "I healed the girl, and everyone seems willing to listening to us now. She was close to death, so we arrived just in time."

"But who are they?" Costas asked, half to himself.

"I have no idea," I said. "But did you really not have any idea there were people living in the forest?"

He shook his head. "I've never heard of anyone living outside the town."

"It's a very sensible set up if you ask me," Ida said. "It must have been very peaceful out here without the Constantines breathing over them." She calmly entered the house and nodded a greeting to the group gathered inside.

There weren't enough chairs for everyone, but we gathered around the table anyway, some remaining standing. I would have liked to stand myself since my body was buzzing with nervous energy, but Nina's mother insisted I take her seat.

In the face of her earnest protestations, I couldn't refuse. But as soon as I was settled, their attention turned to the rest of my companions, and a reaction spread through them. Several of them leaned forward, the others exchanging whispers as they examined Costas.

He cleared his throat awkwardly. "Do you know me?"

"You look just like her!" The matriarch exclaimed. "Who are you?"

"Do you know where her ladyship is?" the mother asked in a

rush, not giving him a chance to answer the grandmother's question. "Has anything happened to her?"

"That's your second mention of this ladyship," Amara said. "I didn't realize the island had any royalty or nobility. Is she the descendant of someone of rank in Calista from before the kingdom's fall?"

"Ah…" The mother looked at the older couple. "I'm not sure. That's just what we've always called her."

"She wasn't born into a noble family," the older woman said heavily. "But she married one of *them*."

A hush fell over the table. No one needed to ask who *they* were.

A strangled sound made me look at Costas. He had gone from slightly pale to an uncomfortable red, his hands tightly gripping the back of Ida's chair.

Ida turned to give him a confused look before surveying the others around the table. "Are you talking about Lady Isolde? My host family mentioned her once, but I thought she died?"

"Lady Isolde?" I looked from Ida to Costas, but his attention was on the matriarch.

"She did die," he said in a rough whisper. "When Ignatius was still a baby."

"No," the matriarch said simply. "She didn't."

Costas leaned forward, his eyes glued to her. "You're telling me my mother is still alive?"

This time the woman hesitated. "All I can tell you is that she was alive when we last saw her over a month ago. We expected her to be back before now, though, and we even went out looking when…" She trailed off, clearly uncomfortable at the level of emotion on Costas's face.

"I don't understand," he said, and this time he sounded dangerous. "Someone explain it to me right now."

Amara and Nik exchanged a look, Nik's posture shifting slightly in response. He had already positioned himself a step back from the table where he could see everyone and move easily, and he was clearly ready to take action if Costas was about to have a violent breakdown.

"My host family are convinced she's dead," Ida said, cutting through the tension in her matter-of-fact way.

I'd wondered about Costas's mother myself but hadn't dared ask since I was staying up at the manor instead of in the town. Part of me hadn't wanted to ask either, afraid the Constantines might have murdered their son's wife as they had their daughter's husband.

"Did the family not approve of her?" I asked tentatively.

"They were the ones to choose her since she's a powerful healer," the older man said, a note of either bitterness or disgust coloring his words. "But their lies can only take them so far. You can't make someone do what's not in them to do."

Nik shifted in place, and I shot him a look. He refused to meet my eyes, making me frown, but once again, we were in no position for a conversation about us.

"Hush, Pa," the second younger woman said, glancing at us fearfully. Her eyes lingered on Costas the longest.

"Did she live here with you?" Costas asked. "Until she disappeared a month ago, at least."

"Oh goodness, no," the matriarch said. "But she visited regularly. All the forest dwellers gladly house her when she comes past, and she could never bring herself to show favoritism by settling with anyone. Now there's a truly noble lady, whatever her blood."

"Ma!" the younger woman hissed, even more urgently.

"There are more of you?" Amara asked before holding up a hand. "Wait, no, don't answer that yet. I think I should start by letting you know what's been happening on the island. It sounds like this Lady Isolde was your link to news beyond this clearing, and much has happened in the last month."

"New arrivals to the island is news indeed," the younger man said, his gaze roaming over each of us.

"Perhaps more important, however, is that the Constantines turned on each other and are all dead," Amara said, keeping the news as concise as possible. "With the exception of Costas who has an elements rather than healing ability."

"Dead?! They're all dead?" The ringing voice from the doorway cut through the astonished exclamations of the rest of the group.

Everyone turned to see a middle-aged woman outlined in the doorframe. She had a wan, exhausted air, overlaid with an expression of deep shock. While we stared at her, the woman's eyes rolled up into her head and she collapsed.

Everyone at the table leaped to their feet, but Nik reached her first. He arrived just in time to cushion her head from the fall, and by the time I shouldered through the milling people, he had her lying flat on the ground.

I dropped down beside her and grasped one wrist. Someone behind me murmured a protest and someone else shushed them. I kept my eyes on the unconscious woman.

I could find no sign of injury or illness in her body, beyond a few minor scratches and a blister on both heels. I looked up at the others.

"Is she dead?" Nina asked, staring at us with wide eyes.

I shook my head. "Happily not. As far as I can tell, she collapsed from a combination of shock and exhaustion, nothing more."

I pushed some energy into her, and the woman stirred. As soon as her eyes fluttered open, she tried to push herself upright. I steadied her, holding her gently down.

"You've pushed yourself too hard," I told her sternly, adopting the healer tone I had learned in the Caltoran hospital. "I've given you some energy, but you need proper rest before you attempt anything strenuous."

The woman stared at me, her eyes even wider than they had been when I first saw her in the doorway.

"You're a healer?" she whispered.

Before I realized what was happening, her arm shot out, her fingers closing around my wrist like steel.

I tried to yank myself free as her power speared into me, but her hold was too strong. Throwing up my wall, I pushed her back out, but not before I felt the shape of her power inside me.

Nik, who had drawn back while I worked, appeared at my side. Grabbing the woman, he pulled her roughly away, using enough force to break her hold.

"Wait!" I cried, before he could do anything more drastic. "Wait! She wasn't trying to mesmerize me or hurt me."

"Of course she wasn't!" the matriarch exclaimed, clearly offended at the suggestion. "Lady Isolde would never do that."

"Lady...Isolde," Costas repeated in a numb voice. He alone hadn't left his original position by the table, although his eyes were glued on the woman. "You're my mother?"

SEVEN

Isolde's eyes flew to Costas, and she gasped. The two were frozen for a moment, staring at each other while the rest of us watched them in an equally motionless state.

Slowly two tears slipped over her eyelids and tracked down her cheeks. "My son," she whispered. "My little Costie."

"How can you be my mother?" he said stiffly, clearly not recovered from the shock. "You can't be my mother. That's impossible!"

She struggled to her feet and started toward him, but he flinched back and she stopped.

"After a few months had passed, I couldn't remember what your face looked like anymore," he whispered. "I was too young. When I met you during my adventures in the forest, I thought you were someone from the town out foraging. I used...I used to imagine you were my mother. I would pretend I was a normal boy, and we were a family."

More silent tears ran down her face.

"I'm sorry," she said in a broken voice. "I wanted to tell you the truth every day, but I didn't dare. Too many lives were at stake. Possibly even yours after they murdered your uncle."

He shook his head violently. "No. No, it doesn't make any sense. It can't be."

"You know each other?" I looked back and forth between them, utterly confused.

"Sit down, your ladyship," the patriarch said, pulling out a chair and gently helping Isolde to sit. She allowed him to guide her, hardly seeming aware of her body's movements.

Once she was seated, however, she looked back at me. "You're a healer—a master level healer. And you brought my son to me. How is any of this possible?"

"That's exactly what we'd like to know," Amara said, resuming control of the conversation. "But first I must ask you not to touch or test my apprentice without her permission again." Her voice was ice, and the woman's eyes widened, a look of guilt coming over her face.

"I'm sorry! I didn't think. It's been so long since I've been around anyone who—" She cut herself off and shook her head. "I apologize. Please allow me to introduce myself. I'm Isolde—not Lady Isolde, just Isolde. I don't hold any rank—and officially I'm married to Augustine Constantine, although I haven't seen him in many, many years."

Amara's stiff stance softened. "I'm afraid I have to inform you that you are now a widow. Your husband was murdered."

"By your son," Costas said baldly. "Your son murdered his father, his grandmother, and everyone else he could get his hands on."

Isolde gasped again, her hand flying to her mouth. "Ignatius? Ignatius did that? But why...how...?"

I expected even more tears to flow, but strangely the news dried the last of them. Her brow furrowed, and I could almost see her turning the information over in her head, trying to make sense of it.

"He was such a chubby, beautiful baby," she said at last in a soft voice. "But he was a healer, so they shaped him into one of them. I knew from the beginning they would do that."

"So you just left?" Costas snapped. "You just abandoned him—and me?"

"No, of course not!" She sighed and ran a hand down her face. "Leaving you both was the last thing I wanted to do."

"Then why did you do it?" he asked in a quieter voice.

Amara cleared her throat. "This is clearly a very personal matter for the two of you, and I wish we had the luxury to respect that and offer you some privacy. But given the situation we all find ourselves in, I think it would be best if everyone was brought up to date on exactly what has been happening on this island."

Isolde nodded slowly. "I, too, would like answers about the current situation."

When she inclined her head toward the seats, the house's residents launched into movement, returning to the places they had occupied before. The rest of us followed, although Isolde was now in my seat. I lingered at the back, standing close to Nik, and this time no one took any notice of me.

"Let's progress in chronological order," Amara said, looking at Isolde. "You said you didn't want to leave your young children, so what happened to compel you to do so?"

"The Constantines have ruled this island from the beginning," she said. "But over the years they've become complacent and over-confident, too used to a docile population. I was one of those compliant townsfolk, once upon a time, and I was even flattered to be chosen as the future bride of Augustine. I knew that was my future from a young age, and I was delighted with it." She shook her head, as if unable to believe her youthful naïveté.

"But once I was actually married, everything began to unravel. Being in such constant contact with the Constantines gradually stripped away the mesmerizations that had been with me from childhood. At first I was confused and frightened —and even more so once Augustine explained mesmerization to me."

"So they taught you to do it too, after you were married?" Amara asked.

Isolde shook her head. "I'm not a true Constantine, so they didn't go that far. But they spoke openly in front of me, and when I asked questions, my husband answered them." Her face twisted in disgust. "I don't think it even occurred to him that I might be horrified by the information."

"So that turned you against Father and Grandmother and the others?" Costas asked. His eyes hadn't left her face the entire time she talked, as if he was weighing and measuring each word.

"Of course!" She shuddered. "Although in truth, I had already reached the point of being afraid and unhappy before that. I had worked out something was wrong, but I didn't understand what until the revelation about mesmerization. I thought I had just idealized them out of youthful ignorance or something."

"So you decided to leave?" The crease between Amara's eyes told me she was unconvinced by her own suggestion.

"No." Isolde's eyes were on Costas. "I would never have left my children just because I felt uncomfortable. And while I deplored the state of affairs on the island, there didn't seem anything I could do about it. But then they went too far."

"Of course they did," Costas muttered.

"There was a boy in the town who possessed a strong healing seed—one of those situations where a child is born with a much stronger seed than his parents."

I shifted on my feet, all too familiar with that situation. Nik glanced down at me, and I nodded slightly, managing to muster a strained smile.

"At first the Constantines did nothing," Isolde continued.

80

"In retrospect, I think they were waiting to see if either Costas or Ignatius turned out to be a girl. If I had borne a daughter, the boy would have been marked as a future Constantine son-in-law. But my children were both boys, and Grandmother knew I didn't want any more."

"So they had to get rid of the child," Costas said bitterly. "They couldn't have any strong healers outside the family."

Everyone at the table stirred at his words, their faces twisting into various expressions of displeasure and grief. No one disputed his words, however.

"I see you've already worked out how the family ran things," Isolde said to her son. "I'm afraid I was slower to realize than I should have been. But the boy grew sick a number of years before reaching the age of activation, and I was the one sent to treat him."

My eyes widened, and Nik and I exchanged a look. The hubris of the Constantines really had grown beyond reason if they had sent an outsider to do a task like that.

"My instructions were to claim I had arrived too late and that he was beyond saving," Isolde confirmed. "But in reality, I was to use my power to end his life. Augustine mesmerized me himself just before I left, but he overestimated the effect of his lies. There is no truth under the sun that would convince me to use my power to kill a child. And any claim that the boy was a threat melted to nothing when I saw him weak and ill in his bed."

"Augustine forgot that he never had control of your mind," I murmured. "He could convince you of his lies—at least briefly —but he couldn't force you to do something so contrary to your nature. And especially not in the face of evidence to the contrary."

It made sense. There was a reason Grey had made so much use of his charm, despite his ability. He had tailored his mesmerizations around each person—to me he had spoken of a bloodless coup to save the kingdom, and to Ida he had promised a life of peace and safety.

Isolde turned to look at me, her brows drawing together. "I don't think I caught your name?"

"I'm Delphine," I said. "And I have more experience of mesmerizations than anyone should have."

Her brows rose almost to her hairline. "You know how to mesmerize? They taught you even though you're not a Constantine?"

I nodded and she sank back with a sigh. "I had hoped..."

"That the end of the line of Constantine healers meant an end to mesmerization?" I asked, and she nodded. "Unfortunately, not all the Constantines with a healing affinity are dead."

Her eyes widened. "But you said—"

"When I said all the healer Constantines are deceased," Amara interjected, "I meant all the Constantines who resided on this island."

Isolde gasped. "Chloe?" she asked, instantly understanding.

"My aunt died many years ago," Costas said, "but her son survives."

"Grey is alive and trained to mesmerize? But he was just a baby when his mother fled from her parents..." Isolde stared from Costas to Amara and finally to me. "Is he the one who trained you?"

I nodded. "And unfortunately, after instigating chaos on the island, he was able to escape to the mainland."

"The story has gotten out of order," Amara interrupted. "We now know why you fled, Isolde, but not how."

She shook her head, as if trying to put her thoughts back into order. "Yes, sorry. Obviously I couldn't kill the child. But I also knew he would never be safe in the town."

"So you smuggled him out to the forest," Costas breathed, looking around the house with fresh eyes.

"Lady Isolde was our rescuer then, and has been many times since," the matriarch said firmly. "My son would have been murdered without her intervention—and us none the wiser." Fury still blazed in her eyes at the memory of the long-ago crime.

"So you're a strong healer?" Amara looked at the younger of the two men in confusion.

I could understand her emotion. If he was a strong healer himself, why had they been in such desperate need of my services?

The man shook his head. "They're talking of my older brother. He died in an accident two years ago." Grief clouded his eyes.

"A strong healer died in an accident?" Ida asked, clearly confused at the idea.

"We were cutting wood and—" His voice choked slightly. "Death was immediate. There was no time for healing."

I swallowed. Healers had a better chance than most, but we weren't impervious to danger.

Nik tensed at my side, his eyes on my face, and I knew he was thinking the same thing, remembering all the times I'd been in danger. Careful not to look in his direction, I kept my focus on the people around the table.

"But he lived many extra years beyond childhood and even survived long enough to give us a beautiful granddaughter," the matriarch said in a muffled voice. Her eyes came up to meet mine. "We cannot thank you enough for saving Nina."

"Delphine had to heal Nina?" Isolde looked at me again. "She was sick with this new illness?"

"You know about it?" I asked.

"Of course." She ran a hand over her face, the exhaustion from earlier still showing on her features. "I discovered it several days ago and have been constantly on the go since.

Because of where I started, yours happened to be the last house on my circuit."

"You pushed yourself too hard." Costas's voice softened for the first time since his mother's arrival. "You're fortunate Delphine was here to help you. Otherwise you might not have survived trying to heal Nina."

"These are my people," she said fiercely. "I couldn't leave any of them to die."

"So these people aren't the only ones you've smuggled out of the town?" Amara asked. "They were just the first?"

Isolde nodded. "I helped them pack up and flee as soon as it was dark. And then I returned to the manor and told them the matter was taken care of. So great was their confidence, they didn't even check on the family or notice they were gone. I thought I might have gotten away with it, but two weeks later, I tested a young boy and discovered he had a strong healing seed. I thought it would be easier to get him and his family out of town before they ever came to the Constantines' attention."

She sighed. "And that's when I discovered the difficulty of making solo trips into town and the forest without arousing suspicion. It took weeks before I got the chance to approach the child's family and get them out. I took them to a different location from my first evacuees—it's easier for individual families to escape notice than a whole second village—but on my way back, I checked in here."

"And she found me sick," the matriarch said. "We were unused to living in such a wild place, and I had been infected with something unfamiliar. By the time her ladyship arrived, I was stretched out on the bed too ill to move."

"I healed her, of course," Isolde said. "But I also realized that I couldn't bring these people out here and abandon them. They had no experience of living in a wilderness like this, and they had no strong healers of their own—at least not until their children grew old enough to be activated. And when that time did

84

come, those children would need someone to activate and train them."

"And so you faked your own death," Costas said, his jaw tight.

"I made sure to go over the waterfall when half of them were there to see," Isolde said. "I needed to be sure they wouldn't come looking for me."

"Why didn't you take us with you?" Costas demanded.

Isolde shuddered slightly. "There was enough danger in what I did for an adult healer. I couldn't possibly have taken a small child or toddler over that waterfall with me. And besides, they didn't care about losing me—I'd fulfilled my purpose and delivered the next generation of Constantines—but their own blood would have been a different matter. For all I knew, they might have torn the forest apart just to find your bodies."

"Not me," Costas said bitterly. "They never wanted me."

Isolde sighed. "They were fools until the end if they couldn't see your value. But remember, back then you hadn't been tested yet, and they were still assuming you had a healing seed."

"And after?" he asked. "All those hours I spent in the forest alone. I'm not sure they would have even noticed if I never returned."

"I wanted to tell you so many times," she said. "But by then Chloe had married, lost her husband, and fled. I had seen just how far they were willing to go, and I was being more careful than ever to hide the existence of the forest families. I couldn't be sure they would ignore your disappearance, so I couldn't risk it. All I could do was watch over you when you were away from the manor," she said softly.

"I used to call you Forest Lady, and I thought you were so kind," Costas said quietly. "You were nothing like Grandmother or Aunt Kendry or Father. Whenever I came out, I would look for you, and I was always disappointed if you didn't appear with a kind word or special treat to share."

Fresh tears slipped down Isolde's cheeks. "It was all I could do for you, but it was far from enough. I'm painfully aware of that."

"So over the years you've been smuggling out families in danger and setting up a network of homes in the forest," Amara said slowly.

"Not a network," the patriarch said with a frown. "We've never met any of the others."

Amara looked doubtfully at the two younger women in the circle.

"Except for our daughters-in-law, of course," the matriarch said quickly.

"I kept everyone separate in case the Constantines ever stumbled on one of the families," Isolde explained. "Given their abilities, they would easily have extracted any secrets. This way none of them could betray the locations, identities, or even the total number of the others. And it also prevented the families from banding together. There are enough of them now that it would be dangerous for them to do anything as a whole group."

"So you travel between the houses, providing training for their young ones," Amara said.

"And also healing as necessary. Not all the families had to flee because they had a child in danger. Mesmerization can be broken, as I experienced myself, and it occasionally happens among the townsfolk—especially those who've served a term at the manor. I'll help anyone who wants to get away from the town and the Constantines."

"I understand that as a healer, you could easily test the town's young children before they even reach the age of official testing," Amara said. "Especially since it isn't something that needs physical contact. But how do you know about the discontented townsfolk?"

"Not all discontented people have actually fled the town," I said slowly, putting something together. Looking up, I met Isolde's eyes. "I'm guessing you know Lumi and Fergus's mother?"

She smiled. "I do. She is one of the few who chose to stay, and she acts as a go-between when she discovers anyone who wants to disappear."

"That's why she fled up the mountain during the fever," I muttered. "She wasn't just escaping infection but was fleeing to a healer who wouldn't mesmerize her or her children while healing them."

Isolde caught my words, her brows lifting. "You really do know her if you know about that."

"Actually I've never met her, only the children. They're so clearly different from everyone else in the town that they attract attention."

A shadow of fear crossed Isolde's face before she froze, her expression slowly changing. She had lived half a lifetime in fear, and it would take time to absorb that the source of that fear was gone forever.

"I'm one of those who realized something strange and terrible was going on after being a maid for several months at the manor," the second younger woman said in a timid voice. "Isolde found me and offered me the chance to escape."

She smiled first at Isolde and then at the younger man who was standing behind her chair. He squeezed her shoulders in response, smiling back at her, and I realized the two must be married.

"It was my parents who realized something was wrong," Nina's mother said. "They were concerned enough to keep me away from further healing checkups, but they were too scared to leave their comfortable life in the town for an unknown future in the forest. But once I finished my apprenticeship, I couldn't bear to stay in the town, surrounded by mesmerized people and watched over by the Constantines. Since I knew

Isolde had offered my parents a different life, I set off by myself to try to find her."

She shook her head, as if recognizing her youthful foolishness.

"It was a blessed day for our family when our son found you wandering in the forest," the matriarch said with a warm look for both her daughter-in-law and her granddaughter.

Nina, who was seated in her mother's lap, still eating, looked up and beamed at her grandmother. Her mother wrapped her arms around her daughter and pressed a kiss against her hair.

"It was a fortunate day for me, too," she said softly. "I think I was already in love before I even reached the house."

The whole table went quiet, a communal shadow falling across their faces as they remembered their missing son, brother, husband, and father.

"How did the Constantines never notice?" Amara asked. "Didn't the other townsfolk ever say something about their missing neighbors?"

"Of course not," Costas said in a dark voice. "How could my family get rid of anyone they found inconvenient unless the islanders were mesmerized to accept disappearances or *accidents* among their neighbors without question? My family's behavior was so ingrained, that if any of them noticed a missing person for themselves, they probably assumed someone else in the family had dealt with them quietly and never bothered to even ask."

Nik made a quiet growling noise deep in his throat, his eyes on Costas and his expression thunderous. These were the people attacked during the party, and yet his instinct had still been to try to save them.

Was it any wonder he was upset that I had thought him a mass murderer—however briefly? Isolde had said not even mesmerization could turn her into such a person, and yet I had believed it of Nik without mesmerization even being involved.

"It's a relief to know that not all the missing children were murdered," Costas said. "But someone's going to need to visit the foresters to explain the current situation. From what you've described, I'm guessing there's still some quiet trade going on between the foresters and the town, so they need to know the entire town is about to disappear."

"They're what?" Isolde asked blankly.

The forester eyes were all firmly fixed on Costas, showing varying levels of shock.

"Actually, about that," Amara said slowly. "Perhaps it isn't necessary after all..." Her eyes were on Isolde's face as she spoke. "This discovery changes the situation significantly."

CHAPTER

EIGHT

"What is the situation, exactly?" Isolde asked.

In succinct words, Amara summarized Grey's return to his mother's home and the dramatic events that had unfolded as a result.

"Grey has returned to the mainland, which means we need to get back to Tartora as soon as possible," she concluded. "But we couldn't abandon the population without any healers—especially not when they are now leaderless and ill equipped to take command themselves. So we thought we would need to take everyone back to Tartora with us. But now it turns out their forest is full of young, powerful healers—ones led by a strong, experienced healer. So tell me, Lady Isolde—are you willing to leave the forest and take your rightful place in the manor house again?"

Isolde's face slowly paled as she stared at Amara. "You want me to lead the entire island?"

"Why not?" Amara's level tone issued a clear challenge. "I can't think of anyone with a greater right. You might not have been born a Constantine, but you bear their name which will help the islanders to accept you. You have the power and experience, and you've amply demonstrated the necessary compassion. If you lead the way, will the other foresters follow?"

Isolde looked down into her lap, staring at her tightly clasped hands as she considered Amara's challenge. When she looked back up, her eyes went to Costas.

"The manor isn't empty," she said quietly. "One of the true Constantines remains. Whatever my reasons for doing so, I abandoned my young son, and I will not take his home or position unless he willingly opens the doors for me."

Costas gazed back at her, and I couldn't read his face. I held my breath until he spoke.

"I don't know if our relationship can be healed or not. I think only time will tell that. But I won't disadvantage the whole island for the sake of my pain. I'm not ready to lead on my own, and I can't keep the people safe without healers. I was planning to leave the manor as soon as the seas clear, so I can't bar its door now. If you will come, I will support your efforts to protect and lead the town as well as I'm able."

Tears welled in Isolde's eyes. "Thank you," she whispered. "You turned out far better than I could have hoped."

Costas's cheeks flushed despite his earlier words about their relationship.

Whatever hurt our parents inflicted on us, part of us still yearned for their approval. An image of my own father appeared in my mind. Would he be proud of the person I was becoming? For the first time since discovering his betrayal, I wanted to find out.

Amara gave a satisfied smile, but almost immediately, her brow creased again.

"That takes care of the longer-term future of the islanders, and I thank you for lifting the responsibility from our shoulders. However, we are still in the middle of an immediate crisis."

Isolde leaned forward. "The new illness? It's hit the town?"

"Unfortunately, yes," I said, still feeling guilty. "And it had spread through the entire town before we discovered it."

"The entire town?" she whispered, and from the horror on her face it was clear she knew what that meant. "What are you doing here, then, Delphine? They must have need of us…" She leaped to her feet, only to sway at the sudden movement.

"My apprentice is here under my orders," Amara said sternly. "And she's here for the same reason you need to be—healers have limits, and you'll help no one by pushing yourself past exhaustion."

Isolde collapsed back into the chair, reluctantly nodding her head.

"The town has not been abandoned," Amara continued. "Thankfully I was accompanied by three powerful healers who have already completed an initial triage and are working among the populace as we speak. Our role is to discover the source of the infection, and I believe we have done so."

Her eyes slipped momentarily sideways to rest on Nina.

The girl's mother pulled her closer, looking worried. "Are you suggesting my daughter infected the entire island? She's never even been into the town!"

"No, but she has bathed regularly in the stream," Amara said gently. "You may not be aware that this stream merges further down with the river that runs past the town and which is used by the townsfolk as their main source of water."

"They've been drinking downriver of this stream?" As a healer, Isolde didn't need any further explanations to be horrified.

"The people in the town have no idea anyone is living in the forest," Costas said. "It won't have occurred to them that someone might be contaminating the water upstream."

"And we didn't realize the stream ran past the town," the matriarch murmured. "We never thought we were doing any harm…"

"When I get back to that dolt," Isolde hissed through her teeth, her expression furious.

"Who do you mean?" Amara asked, instantly alert.

Isolde relaxed. "Oh, he didn't mean any harm." She sighed. "The most recent addition to the forester population is a young couple. They both have strong elements seeds, and the husband kept going on about how much easier it would be to source water for their crops if there was a closer stream. A few weeks ago, he decided to divert a small portion of the river. Between the two of them, they had the strength to do it, and he was convinced there was no harm done."

"And this is why elements mages are taught to be so careful about interfering." Amara gave her own sigh. "And this is why all three affinities are so important. Elements mages won't think of this sort of consequence unless they have healers to remind them."

"Is that where the stream came from?" the patriarch exclaimed. "We were pleased to discover it, but we couldn't imagine where it had sprung from."

"I'm amazed only Nina is sick," Isolde said. "Are you sure none of the rest of you have any symptoms?"

The rest of the family hurried to assure her of their health, but I agreed with Isolde. It was strange.

"I think you should all come back to the town with us," I said. "That way Master Hayes can examine you. He has far more experience and training than I do."

To my surprise, Isolde readily agreed. "I would like to meet this master for myself. While I was born with a powerful seed, the training I received was limited. I couldn't compare with a Tartoran master mage."

"How soon can you be ready to make the journey to the manor?" Amara asked, gazing around the table.

Several murmured conversations broke out, and it was soon decided that everyone would leave for the manor in an hour, with the exception of the childless couple. They would stay to prepare the house for a period of inoccupancy before taking Isolde's carefully written out directions and setting out to contact the other forester families.

"No one will force them to move into town," Costas said, "but they should at least come to see the situation for themselves. And if any of them are activated healers, we could really use the help right now. Naturally they won't want to leave their families behind unprotected in the case of a reinfection, so they are all welcome at the manor."

After that, the conversation gave way to a flurry of activity and movement as everyone prepared for departure. Nik took one look at the chaos and suggested we wait in the garden. We didn't have the chance for private conversation, though, since Amara and Ida accompanied us.

"Are we really free to go back to Tartora without taking the whole island with us?" I asked once the four of us were alone. It seemed too good to be true.

"I won't be entirely easy until I've seen how Isolde and Costas manage," Amara said. "But I feel optimistic. This really is excellent news for both the epidemic and the island as a whole."

"Of course we can't leave until the epidemic is over," I said. "But does this mean we don't have to wait the entire winter? We won't need a ship large enough for the entire population anymore."

Amara shook her head. "I wish we could go back earlier. I feel uneasy about what might be happening in Tartora in our absence. But I don't think it's possible. We don't need to take a lot of people now, but we've also lost Costas. I don't think we would have made it here without his assistance, and that was after encountering a single storm. One elements mage isn't enough to make that journey in winter—especially not when I'm unfamiliar with the route. It's just too far."

I slumped, disappointed. But I couldn't remain downcast for long. My situation had improved beyond all expectation. I was no longer separated from my master. I was able to hand over responsibility for management of the epidemic to more experienced healers. And now we had even found extra healers to assist. There was no reason for me to get discouraged about being temporarily stuck on the island. Tartora might not have experience with Grey, but they had warning and a whole host of powerful mages. It was foolish to think they were in desperate need of me, or even Amara. They would survive one winter without us, and we would clearly be busy enough here, even with Isolde and her healers.

It took more than an hour for everyone to be ready in the end, and I was more than eager to get moving again by then. I knew my impatience wasn't achieving anything—after completing a major healing on Nina during my rest day, Amara wouldn't let me anywhere near the town until the next morning—but I couldn't help my desire for action of some kind. Even if I couldn't help, I wanted to know what was happening with the epidemic.

Ida had departed ahead of the rest of us, heading for the town instead of the manor, so it wasn't a surprise when we arrived at the manor's door only steps ahead of Hayes.

"Ida told me," he said immediately. "You've found more healers?"

The combination of exhaustion and hope in his eyes made my heart sink.

"Deaths?" I asked, and he quickly shook his head.

"None since our arrival, but I'll be honest, we're hanging on by a thread."

I looked to Amara. "Couldn't I—?"

She shook her head, only to hesitate and glance at Hayes. "What do you think?" she asked him, inclining her head toward me. "I had intended to send her to you this afternoon, but we encountered a gravely ill child, and Delphine healed her completely."

I bit my lip. Now that the family was joining us at the manor, I was second-guessing that decision. I could have just done enough to keep her out of danger.

Hayes held out a hand, his eyes assessing me as I laid my wrist over his fingers. I felt his power press into me, skimming through me with a light touch before withdrawing again.

"Considering the circumstances, I think you could allow her to spend a few hours in town, at least," he said. "Luna will be here shortly because I've insisted she come back for food and some sleep. Delphine can take her place, just for a while."

"You haven't been eating or drinking in the town?" Amara clarified, and when he shook his head, she looked relieved. "That was wise."

We stepped inside the manor as Amara completed proper introductions between Hayes and Isolde.

"I understand you're to take charge of the island," he said. "I can explain what we've done so far, and you can—"

"No, no," she said rapidly. "I may have strength, but I lack your training and experience. Please continue managing the epidemic—I'll be watching closely and learning as much as I can."

He inclined his body in a slight bow, accepting the authority she was handing him.

"You should feel free to test me," she added. "That way you'll know how to put me to best use. And all my students as well, once they start arriving."

"You need to rest before being put to use," I said in my best impression of Hayes's own healer tone.

Hayes threw me a surprised look, and I smiled. "Said in my official capacity as her healer. She collapsed from a combination of shock and exhaustion not long ago and is only upright and functioning now because of my efforts."

Isolde made a rueful face, not trying to deny it.

I glanced around, noting that the others had moved away to discuss accommodation with the manor's servants. I stepped a little closer to Hayes, lowering my voice anyway.

"You must be tired, but do you think you could examine the adults we brought out of the forest with us?"

Hayes frowned. "Do they have the illness too? None of them look severely ill, and if they're still in the early stages, I'm afraid they'll have to—"

"Actually, it's their apparent health that's confusing me." I glanced at Isolde who nodded encouragingly. We had spoken about it during the walk to the manor, and she had been as confused as me. "The girl's condition was advanced —she must have been one of the first cases—and yet none of the others are sick. There's another couple who didn't come with us, so that's five adults total. I know that those who are more vulnerable usually succumb to the exposure first, but from what we've seen in the town, at least two or three of the others should be showing some symptoms by now."

Hayes looked at the older couple who were standing nearby talking with Amara. "They have weaker healing abilities, don't they? Is it possible they healed themselves while the symptoms were still very minor?"

Isolde twisted her mouth to one side as she considered the possibility. "If it was so easily done by someone of their strength, one third of the town would be well right now. Is that the case? Do you have no healer patients?"

Hayes shook his head. "Unfortunately, we have many."

"According to their account, they haven't had to heal themselves of anything lately," I said. "So you can see why I'm confused. They both let me check them during the walk, but I can't see anything amiss. Even so, I was hoping you would check for yourself."

Hayes nodded slowly. "It can't do any harm. If they're not sick, it won't cost me much in the way of energy."

He strode toward the elderly couple, with Isolde and me following close behind. As he examined the woman in silence, a crease appeared between his eyes. When the expression slowly changed to one of surprise, I couldn't resist holding out a hand to the woman with a questioning look.

When she nodded permission, I made contact as well, sending my power to combine with Hayes's as I had so often done before. His power was in her abdomen, examining each of her organs, although they appeared healthy to my power.

I closed my eyes, concentrating harder. It was true her insides were healthy, but still—there was something there.

My eyes sprang open, and I stared at Hayes in shock.

"Is that…?"

He opened his eyes slowly, his expression thoughtful. "Yes, I believe it is."

"Am I sick?" the woman asked. "Can you heal me?"

"You're not sick," I said. "But also, you are. Sort of."

"What?" She looked to Isolde, who shrugged, clearly just as confused.

"I never would have noticed it," I said to Hayes, once again impressed by his skill.

"That's because you didn't know to look. It isn't something our power picks up instinctively like a wound or damaged organ. But I've seen it once before with a different illness."

"What is it?" Isolde asked.

"The disease is there inside her," I said. "It's just not making her sick."

"We call it being a carrier," Hayes said. "Some diseases are more prone to the issue than others. I hadn't even considered it for this epidemic, given how many in town are sick, so it's a good thing you discovered it early. If we heal only the sick and leave the carriers, then we'll just see constant reinfections.

We'll need to heal everyone—symptomatic or not—before this will be over."

"There can't be many carriers in town, though," I said. "Almost everyone is sick."

"Hmmm...And you're saying five adults in this one family are all carriers?" Hayes let the woman go and stared at the far wall while he thought. "Is it something special about them, then? Something passed on by blood?"

"They're not all related, though," I said. "There were three married couples."

Hayes ran a hand along his jaw. "I'll have to examine the others to be sure they're carriers too, but if they are, then it must be environmental. Something they've consumed or been exposed to has protected them from symptoms."

"If we could find out what it is..." I said excitedly.

He nodded. "If it was something that could be replicated, it might be a big help in getting this epidemic under control. We'll still want to eradicate the disease from the population completely, but it would be helpful to be able to do it more slowly, without worrying about more and more people reaching a dangerous level of illness."

"I suppose you'd be looking for something Nina wasn't exposed to," the matriarch said consideringly. "I'll have a think and talk to my family and daughter-in-law. Between us, we should be able to come up with a list of possibilities."

"Thank you," Hayes said.

"I can lead the investigation," Nik said suddenly from behind me. "There's a good chance it's something they ate, so it makes sense to have a plants mage in charge. I'll probably need assistance from a healer at some point, though."

"I'll manage assigning you one," Amara said. "Costas and I are about to head out to cleanse the river, but once that's finished, my ability won't be of use to anyone, so I can take on a management role. You'll be the one making the overall decisions, of course, Hayes, but with the shortage of healers, you won't have the energy for purely administrative matters."

"Thank you, Amara," he said, with a speaking look.

She smiled back, a note of tenderness in her eyes that made me look rapidly between them.

"I know you healers well enough to know you'll need someone to remind you about taking regular rests," she said. "I'll oversee that and make sure no one is working themselves dangerously hard—and while you're each having a turn resting your ability, you can help out with searching the forest."

"We're very fortunate your boat turned up when it did," Isolde said. "The island would have been in trouble without you."

"We're not out of trouble yet," Hayes said grimly. "But I'm starting to think we have a chance."

CHAPTER

NINE

The following days passed in a blur, day and night blending together as I slept when instructed and woke when told. Every waking moment was full of healing as I trailed either Hayes or Clay, learning how to better heal this particular strain and then immediately implementing everything I learned.

Two full weeks had passed before I once again had the chance to stand on the back porch of the manor and admire the dawn light over the mountain. And, just like the last time, Ida's voice calling my name interrupted me. I waited, letting her come to me as I enjoyed a final moment of peace.

As soon as she appeared, she handed me a piece of paper, and I scanned it quickly before giving another sigh. The list was still so long.

"I'll leave immediately," I told her, but she stopped me with a hand on my arm, her face concerned.

"Have you eaten?" she asked. "We don't want a repeat of last week."

I flushed at the reminder. The first few days had been chaotic as we scrambled to first identify and then harvest and distribute the plant which had protected Nina's family—the one she had hated and refused to eat. When I had collapsed halfway through my rounds, everyone had panicked, thinking I had driven myself past my limits. Most people had been relieved when they learned I had simply forgotten to eat for almost twenty-four hours—too caught up in my work to take the time for basic self-care. But Amara and Ida had both had stern words for me.

"I had a quick breakfast before I came outside," I assured Ida. "I'm not going to faint again."

She examined my face closely. "You're sure you're not pushing yourself too hard?"

I mustered a smile, wondering when I would be free of the bone-deep weariness that clung to me these days.

"I'm fine, I promise. I know we can't afford to have any of the healers out of action for multiple days. There are too few of us as it is."

Ida nodded fervently. "Thank goodness Master Hayes and Master Clay arrived when they did. As well as Isolde and her students. We wouldn't have made it this far without them."

I pondered her words as I hurried out of the mansion and into the town beyond. My resolution to stay and care for the people of the island seemed distant and foolish now. I could never have held back the current disaster on my own. As it was, we had passed the initial crisis but were still far from eradicating the disease completely, as evidenced by the list in my pocket of the next patients in line for healing.

"Delphine!" Hurrying footsteps from behind made me turn. When I caught sight of the man hurrying to catch up with me, I slowed to wait for him.

"What are you doing up?" I asked Costas. "Weren't you on night duty with Hayes?"

He shook his head. "Nik and I swapped, so he's just heading for bed, and I'll be accompanying you."

He spoke of the prince as casually as I did. Those of us

residing at the manor had long since ceased to worry about formalities or honorifics. Island life was far from the realities of Tartoran position and rank, and all our efforts were focused on keeping the islanders alive and healthy.

"Sorry I didn't wait for you," I said. "I was already running late, and I thought Nik might be waiting in town already."

"No matter," Costas said with an easy smile. "Ida informed me you'd already left."

I was grateful he let the topic drop, making no comment about the awkwardness between Nik and me. The tension between us must have been obvious to everyone at the manor, but thankfully everyone was either too busy or too considerate to comment on it.

I cast a sideways glance at Costas, unable to put the matter out of my own head so easily. Why had he and Nik swapped shifts? Had it been Nik's request? Was he avoiding me again? I felt like I barely saw him these days, but my long hours in the town, paired with the never-ending exhaustion, provided an easy explanation for our lack of connection. I just wished I could believe that was all it was.

I couldn't stew on it for long, though. Once I arrived at the first house on my list, all my attention had to be on the patients inside. We had moved past the early days when we were pulling dangerously ill patients back from the brink of death. Those healings had required power and instinct, but not the finesse required for full eradication. Now that we were working on full healings, focused attention was needed.

At least I wasn't responsible for finding and healing the carriers. Those healings required even more skill and finesse, so I was happy to leave that work to the masters.

We progressed slowly, moving from house to house down our list. Costas charmed the inhabitants while I worked, too absorbed to be aware of my surroundings. Amara had decreed early on that we should work in pairs with a non-healer accompanying each healer. She said it was important that someone actually talked to the families while the healer was lost in their work, and after the first few visits, I appreciated her wisdom. Costas did all the explaining and socializing, and I was able to focus on the healing—something that became even more valuable as the session wore on, and I became more and more tired.

By mid-afternoon when I finally finished the final patient on the list, I was too weary to do more than muster a weak smile for the woman who had just been healed. She murmured a quiet thank you but wouldn't meet my eyes. I wasn't surprised at her manner—thanks to the mesmerizations, many in the town still viewed me with suspicion. Given my exhaustion, I was almost relieved, rising quickly to head back to the manor.

But when I looked around the house's spacious main room, there was no sign of Costas. The woman saw me peering around and muttered something about him leaving already.

He'd never left me alone mid-healing before, so I hurried from the house, concerned. Had something happened back at the manor?

I paused as soon as I got outside, looking up and down the street in case he had just stepped outside briefly for some fresh air. But the only person I saw was a boy skulking against the wall of the house with the sort of scowl some youths seemed to perpetually wear in those awkward years leading up to their activation and apprenticeship.

I turned in the direction of the manor and made it two strides before something solid hit the back of my head. Pain shot through me as I was flung forward. I hit the ground hard enough to rob me of breath, fresh pain spreading through my middle.

Rolling onto my side, I doubled over, wheezing as I tried to regain my breath. What had happened?

A shrill, chattering call made me look toward the sky. Before

I could find Phoenix, however, I saw a solid wooden staff whipping toward my head. Acting on instinct, I pushed my power through my body, letting it heal me without guidance as I rolled away from the descending weapon.

It never made contact. A hand appeared, catching the staff and ripping it from the grip of the youth. A second later a feathered arrow shot down from the sky, pulling up just before colliding with Nik and the boy.

Phoenix chattered again, somehow managing to sound approving this time as he swooped down to land on my stomach.

The boy fell back several steps before regaining his courage and standing his ground, rage twisting his face.

"You killed them!" he shouted, pointing at me. "Just admit it! It was you, wasn't it?"

I scrambled to my feet, sending Phoenix soaring skyward. A sick feeling rushed through me as I saw the look of naked fury on Nik's face as he advanced on the boy, his fist going white where he gripped the staff he had torn from the youth's hand.

"Wait, Nik!" I cried as he reached the boy, only to instantly regret my words.

I had reacted on instinct, the sight of him a reminder of that terrifying moment at the party, the one I couldn't shake from my mind. As always, the sudden memory had momentarily brought back the shock and fear I had felt then, but there had been no need for me to speak. Just as then, he wasn't going to attack indiscriminately.

Thankfully Nik didn't even seem to hear me. Reaching out with his free hand, he grabbed the boy's collar, lifting him slightly so that he was off balance. Throwing the staff down, he dragged the boy in my direction.

As Nik came, he turned his head and finally absorbed my reaction. The heightened color on his face immediately drained away, and I wished I could take back every moment of my reaction rather than see his anger replaced with pain.

Why did I keep hurting Nik? It was my own fault that I still saw echoes of that awful moment at the party when I saw him bending over Augustine's body. I now knew he had been checking Augustine for signs of life—something he had rushed to do without even dropping his sword—and I should have known it then, too. No wonder Nik was avoiding me when I kept letting my terrible mistake stand between us.

Recovering himself in an instant and hiding his emotion, Nik's face returned to a stony expression as he dragged the boy the rest of the way to face me.

"Look her in the face." He gave the boy a slight shake. "This is the woman who just healed your mother, and yet you struck her over the back of the head?"

"She claims she healed my mother," the boy said in a sullen voice. "But how do I know that's true? She's a murderer."

"Delphine is a healer," Nik said in an ice-cold tone. "She has never—and will never—murder someone. I was there. I saw it happen. Your precious Constantines turned on each other."

"You're lying!" the boy cried, his face twisting and showing a glimpse of something far more heartbreaking than his attack.

Beneath his aggression lay barely masked terror and confusion. It wasn't transient fear of Nik's larger frame and stronger muscles, but something far deeper. Already in the most confusing and tempestuous time of life, his emotions had been tangled further—first by the Constantines' mesmerizations and then by their abrupt and violent deaths.

All my anger disappeared, replaced with compassion and a bone-deep exhaustion. We could heal every person in the entire town and eliminate the epidemic, but how could they begin to heal from what the Constantines had done to them?

The boy exploded into sudden movement, trying to get to me, but Nik's grip only tightened further, holding him in place.

He shouted further accusations, getting more and more worked up in the face of Nik's unyielding stance and blank face.

"You must know someone with a healing affinity," Nik said when the boy paused for breath.

The youth hesitated, giving Nik the space to keep talking.

"Of course you do. Have you asked them about this epidemic?"

The boy's eyes slid sideways, away from our faces, giving us our answer.

"Precisely," I said. "Believe me, we're not doing all this for fun. Any healer in this town, however weak, could tell you that the people who were sick have now been healed."

"Your own eyes could tell you that," Nik said with impatience. "And those same friends will be able to confirm I'm telling the truth about what happened to the Constantines. Shall we go find one right now?"

He took a step as if he meant to drag the boy off to find the closest person with a healing affinity.

The youth shivered, and for a moment I thought it was from fear or embarrassment. But when he shivered again, it racked his whole body in a way that made me hesitate.

"Wait," I said, putting a hand on Nik's arm. He stilled instantly. "Let me check something."

I put a hand to the boy's head, not even using my ability as I confirmed my sudden suspicion.

"He has a fever. No wonder he's acting so irrationally."

I sent my power into him, confirming that he had the illness, likely in the second week.

"How did you conceal this?" I muttered, mostly to myself. "Have you been hiding from the healers every time they came past?"

He shrank into himself at my words, looking guilty and scared.

"It's a good thing I discovered it now, or you could have

ended up in a dangerous situation," I scolded him as I drove the illness out of his body. "Everyone who's ill needs to be monitored for disease progression—surely you know that by now."

As I healed him, my earlier discouragement and desperation rose up inside me. My power could easily drive the disease from his body, but what I really wanted was to drive out the lingering effect of the mesmerizations.

The Constantines might be gone, but the lingering echo of pain in my head told me people were still being hurt by them. How much longer did it have to go on? Would these people ever be free?

A protective instinct rose inside me, fueled by my anger. I stopped trying to hold it in, letting it fan into flame inside me as I did a final sweep of his body to check for any missed pockets of illness.

As my power tried to roll through him, something sprang up inside him, barring my way. A wordless exclamation fell from my lips as my power was abruptly expelled from his body.

I dropped back a step, as if I had been physically shoved, although the boy was still slumped limply in Nik's grip. Nik immediately let go of the youth, stepping to my side and examining my eyes.

"What's wrong?" he asked in a low voice. "What happened?"

"I...I'm not sure. I think...I think...Quick!" I shrieked as the boy attempted an escape. "Stop him."

Nik moved instantly, not losing any time to questions. He had the boy back in a firm grip before he'd made it more than half a dozen steps.

"Let me go!" the boy cried, some of the fire back in his voice.

"I'm sorry," I said breathlessly. "I just need to talk to you for a moment. I need to—" I held out my hand, hovering just over his skin. "May I?"

The boy opened his mouth, presumably to reject my request, only to pause, the words unspoken. A look of confusion came over his face, as if his own thoughts didn't make sense to him.

A heady, implausible possibility overtook me. Was it possible? Surely it couldn't be...

"Why did you attack me?" I asked, my tone coming out too eager. He gave me a wary look, and I tried to calm my manner. "What made you target me?" I asked.

Nik's hold loosened, but the boy didn't move, his earlier fury having completely disappeared. Reaching up, he scratched the back of his head.

"I'm not sure," he said at last. "Some people were saying you might have killed the Constantines yourself, and I was so..." He frowned as if the end of the sentence didn't even make sense to him.

"You were so angry?" I finished for him. "Because I might have killed them?"

"Yeah," he said weakly. "I suppose so."

"You were close to them, then?" I asked, ignoring the odd looks Nik was giving me.

"Well, not close to them exactly," the boy said hesitantly. "I didn't know them personally or anything."

"But you were enraged about their deaths because they were such good people," I suggested.

"Well." He rubbed the back of his head again. "I don't know about that. They did heal us, I guess."

"And now you're left without healers," I said.

He frowned, giving me a sideways look. "Not exactly. All of you people seem to be healers—aren't you?"

"We are!" I said with such excitement that he and Nik exchanged a confused look, united suddenly by bemusement over my odd behavior.

"But the important thing is that the Constantines were wonderful people and excellent leaders worthy of loyalty to the end," I said earnestly.

"I...suppose?" It was a question not a statement.

"Yes! Yes, yes yes!!" I jumped into the air, unable to contain my excitement.

My unexpected movement brought Phoenix winging back in my direction, one of his shiny eyes focused on me. I settled enough to allow him to land on my shoulder, stroking his soft feathers with one gentle finger.

"Thanks for warning me earlier, fine sir."

"Ah...Delphine?" Nik asked tentatively, placing a gentle hand on my arm. "Are you all right?"

"Absolutely wonderful!" I turned bright eyes on him. "We have to get back to the manor! No, wait! I have to check—"

Once again I held my hand out toward the boy, silently asking for permission to make contact. This time he willingly put his wrist into my fingers, although his expression was still bemused.

I cautiously pushed my power into him, but it encountered no barrier. I might have raised his wall, but it hadn't stayed in place once I lost contact with him. I activated it again, but this time when my power was shoved out of him, I maintained my contact with his wrist.

Trying a third time, I encountered a solid barrier, preventing my power from accessing him.

"Interesting!" I dropped his wrist and then repeated the entire experiment with the same results. "Very interesting!"

"What is interesting?" Nik asked, still in the same careful voice.

I burst into laughter. "Oh, Nik, you should see your face right now."

He smiled back, responding to my happiness, but looking

adorably confused in the process. It felt good to laugh with him again, even if he didn't know the reason.

"Can I go now?" the youth asked, starting to edge away.

"Yes, yes, feel free." I wiped tears from my eyes as the boy took off at a run.

He didn't make it more than three steps, however, before he tripped over the discarded staff and went sprawling. Nik reached him in a single stride, reaching down to haul him back to his feet.

I stared at Nik, transfixed, as he thumped the boy's shoulder, shaking free some of the dust that clung to him. The boy had been flat on the ground, and for a moment Nik had been bent over him—the tableau a stark reminder of the memory that plagued me.

But this time when the emotions of that moment rushed back, they were overlaid with something different. This boy had attacked me, as the Constantines had done, and yet even so, Nik had helped him. When he reached down, it had been in the role of protector, and for the first time, I could feel that truth wound through my old memory. My mind had repeated the truth a hundred times, but now my emotions had finally caught up.

I remained in place, frozen, as the boy muttered something in an embarrassed undertone and rushed away. He disappeared into the house, closing the door firmly behind him.

I had no idea what emotions were showing on my face in the wake of my realization, but some of them must have been visible. When Nik turned to me, his brows drew down, his earlier look of confusion deepening.

"The boy must think all the healing has driven me over the edge," I said with a weak chuckle, worried it might be Nik who thought so, not the boy.

"It hasn't?" Nik asked, but his look of amused long-suffering told me he still had faith in me.

"Not in the least!" My earlier elation came rushing back as I remembered my discovery. "Did you hear that boy's responses?"

"He sounded about as confused as me." Nik gave a reluctant chuckle.

"Exactly! He didn't know what to think about the Constantines." I gripped both of Nik's arms and looked up into his face. "Do you know what that means?"

Slow understanding broke across Nik's face. "The mesmerizations broke? How is that possible? Are they gradually fading away now that the ones who created them are dead? We haven't seen signs of that in anyone else who was under their thrall."

"No, we haven't, because mesmerizations will last forever without evidence to break them. Not having the Constantines around anymore actually made them harder to destroy since there was no way to show they weren't who they claimed to be."

"So what just happened, then?"

I ran back over the sequence of events in my mind. "I was just checking my healing when something changed inside him. I think...I think I somehow activated his wall, and when it pushed my power out of him, it pushed out the mesmerizations as well—just like my wall does for me."

"You made a wall in him?" Nik asked. "I thought you couldn't do that. Didn't you and Grey spend hours and hours trying?"

"Actually," I said, "I was never trying to activate someone else's wall for them. I was trying to teach them how to make their own. I don't think I've ever tried to do it for someone else before. It never occurred to me it was even possible."

"So what you're saying," Nik said slowly, finally realizing the full import of my discovery, "is that you can not only protect yourself from being mesmerized or attacked with healing power, you can also protect someone else?"

"As long as I have physical contact with them." A grin spread across my face. "And I can purge mesmerizations that already exist in others like I do in myself."

"Delphine," Nik whispered. "That changes everything."

CHAPTER

TEN

I thought it might be hard to replicate, but to my joy it turned out to be much simpler than I expected. Like with my own wall, once I was familiar with the feeling, it was easy to reach for it again.

What wasn't so easy—what turned out, in fact, to be impossible—was teaching anyone else how to do it. I tried with Hayes, then Luna, then Clay, and even with Isolde. But just like with Grey and his followers, no one else could repeat my accomplishment.

When we finally gave up, the disappointment in the air was palpable. I knew Hayes and Clay, at least, were thinking about more than the islanders. My wall was useful against more than just mesmerizations since it could also protect against an attack from a healer. And calling up a wall for someone else was even more valuable than being able to create one for yourself, since it allowed those with other affinities to also be protected.

"I don't even understand how it's possible to do," I said to the other three healers in the wake of the failed lessons.

We were all gathered on the back porch, enjoying the mild weather as we worked. Even Ember had ventured out of my room for her sleep and was curled up at my feet, although Phoenix was nowhere in sight.

Due to our continued efforts to eradicate the epidemic, it was a rare event for all four of us to be together. But when my attempts to teach them individually had failed, Hayes had insisted on one final session all together, just in case that somehow brought a breakthrough.

"I always thought my wall was made from my healing power," I said. "How could someone from a different affinity create one?"

"We must have been wrong about its source," Clay said thoughtfully. "It must come from the body itself—it's just your power that controls bringing it up and down."

"If you think about it, it does make some sense." Hayes sounded fascinated despite our failure. "We know the body develops a resistance to healing power over time—both due to age and due to excessive healing. So we know everyone has the innate ability to resist our power. This must just be another aspect of that natural ability."

"Do you think non-healers could learn to activate their own wall?" Luna asked.

Hayes narrowed his eyes. "That's less clear. My instinct is no. Non-healers can't control their resistance to healing, unfortunately, so I don't see why they would be able to control this. Delphine uses her power to raise and lower the wall, but a non-healer can't connect with their body that way."

"Except a healer can't control their own natural resistance either, can they?" I asked.

Hayes and Clay exchanged a look, making my stomach sink, although I couldn't explain why.

"It's a bit more complicated than that," Hayes said. "Healers can't prevent the natural resistance of old age. If we could, we would never die except through the occasional accident. But when it comes to the resistance created by repeated healings, healers do have a heightened ability to push past it—particularly when healing themselves.

"That's good," I said, unsure why he and Clay looked so concerned.

"But there are still limits to that," Clay said gently.

I nodded. It made sense. No one had ever claimed healers were impervious to everything except old age.

"We're worried about you, Delphine," Hayes said when I clearly still wasn't getting it.

"Me?" I stared at him. "What do you mean?"

Hayes grimaced. "You've had an unusually dramatic apprenticeship."

"You certainly have!" Luna's expression caught up to the worry on the faces of the men. "I've nearly completed mine, and I've barely had to heal myself the whole time. I think at most I've intervened in the early stages of a few infections I picked up at the hospital. But you've had so many run-ins with Grey!" She shuddered.

"I'm particularly concerned about the attack from the Constantine son," Hayes said. "You did what you had to do to survive—and it was an ingenious solution, I must add—but it was far beyond a normal healing, even in the case of extreme injury. And it came after a number of other significant healings..."

"Have you noticed any difference since?" Clay asked. "Do you need more power when you heal yourself from small things?"

My hand moved of its own accord to rub at the back of my head where the youth from town had struck me.

"I don't think so?" I said hesitantly. "Not that I've noticed—although I haven't been paying attention."

"That's good." Clay sounded pleased. "Your natural

strength should give you a high ability to push past the resistance. But you can't get complacent. You're young—very young —and you still have your whole life ahead of you. If things continue as they have been, you could soon find that even your strength isn't enough."

I gulped. "You mean it might get to the point where I can't even heal myself?"

"It's possible," Hayes said before rushing to add, "We don't mean to alarm you! But you need to be warned. I've already spoken to Amara about the matter, and she agreed that it made sense for us to talk to you about the issue."

"Oh." I swallowed. "Thank you for warning me. I'll try to be more careful."

I looked up, and my eyes caught on Nik, frozen in the doorway. From the horrified look on his face, he'd caught the latter part of our conversation.

I looked back at the others. "We're going to go back to the mainland and deal with Grey once and for all." I was speaking more for Nik's benefit than theirs. "And that will be an end to all the violence."

Luna agreed enthusiastically, but I wasn't sure if that was because she'd also seen Nik hovering in the doorway.

He cleared his throat, his expression closing off. "Amara asked me to fetch you all for the meal. She wants to take the chance to eat together to discuss where we're up to with the epidemic and the next steps for management."

Hayes nodded. "That's a good idea. We've come a long way, but we haven't reached the end of the business yet. And now that Delphine has discovered she can purge others, we'll need to make a plan for that as well."

"A plan?" I asked, still a little dazed from the unexpected turn of the conversation.

Clay nodded enthusiastically. "We'd hoped to be able to

help with the task, but I'm afraid you'll have to do it on your own."

"I'm going to need to purge everyone before we leave," I said slowly, the answer obvious. If I had the ability to free people's minds, I couldn't walk away and leave anyone still trapped by lies.

"It will help that we've just surveyed everyone in the town," Hayes said. "It just means we'll have to start again and cover every single person all over again."

"And you'll be doing it alone." Luna linked her arm with mine, giving it a sympathetic squeeze.

"It's a good thing we have all winter," I said, trying to speak with a cheerful note.

It was an overwhelming task, but only days ago it was something we thought impossible. Despite the disappointment of my failed training attempts, it was still good news overall.

Luna glanced at Nik who hadn't made any move to return inside. Slipping her arm out of mine, she took hold of both Hayes and Clay's elbows and propelled them into the house with her.

"Come on!" she said cheerfully. "We can't keep Amara waiting."

Hayes had time to throw a single raised eyebrow in my direction, making me flush, before the three of them had disappeared into the manor.

Nik still stood motionless, his eyes on me.

"Every healing you have to do is putting you at greater long-term risk. And I let that youth hit you." I knew his anger and recrimination was directed inward, but it hurt me just the same.

"That wasn't your fault!" I said heatedly. "You weren't even supposed to be there at all."

It turned out the boy had planned the attack, getting one of his friends to lure Costas away at the crucial moment. I should have been totally alone, and yet Nik had been there to protect me as usual.

What I didn't know was why he'd been there. And why had he swapped shifts if he was worried enough about me to come into town to check on me during his rest time?

"No," Nik said softly. "I was supposed to be there. I should have been there from the beginning. And if I had been, that boy would never have touched you."

"You've been avoiding me." It wasn't a question, and he didn't deny it. "You're still affected by what happened...that day."

He swallowed visibly but didn't speak.

"Are you angry with me?" I asked hesitantly. "For creating the problem in the first place and then blaming you before I even gave you a chance to explain? I know it was terrible of me to assume the worst like that, and I don't expect you to just forgive me. I've been trying to give you space, but I've been sorry every day since."

"What?" He strode over and took my hands, moving as if he couldn't hold himself back. "Of course I'm not angry with you! How could you think I would blame you for that? You didn't ask to be attacked, and you must have been in a state of shock afterward. I know what that scene must have looked like."

A spark zipped through me from the place our skin touched, but I couldn't quite meet his eyes. "Then why? Why have you been avoiding me?"

He swallowed, letting my hands drop. But he didn't step away.

"I'd seen you injured before, but not like that." He looked away, the muscle in the side of his jaw jumping. "You can't imagine..." He shuddered, his voice dropping low. "I can't look at you without seeing you lying there, covered in blood. So still. Too still. Even now I can taste the panic and rage and fear of that moment."

"I'm sorry," I whispered, although the words were inadequate for the moment. I knew just what he meant because I had also struggled to escape the traumatic images of that night. A silent tear slipped down my cheek.

He reached up and brushed it away with his thumb, his hand cupping my face.

"But that wouldn't be enough to keep me away from you," he whispered in a rough voice. "Not on its own. If it was just that…"

"Then what?" I asked, my words hardly more than a breath. "What else have I done?"

"Nothing!" His response came quickly. "You've done nothing. It's what I've done."

He fell silent, and I knew we were both seeing the scene from that night.

"You didn't do that," I said in a stronger voice. "Ignatius and his guards did that. All you ever did was defend yourself and try to defend others. It isn't your fault you didn't succeed in saving them. It was over for the Constantines before you even arrived in the room."

"But it could have been me," he said in a low voice. "I walked into a scene of chaos and violence and reacted as anyone would. But what if I'd walked into something else? What if I'd walked into that room and everyone was talking and eating and laughing? I keep reliving that night and remembering the rage I felt as I walked across the garden. You were dead—lost forever, I thought—and I was pursuing Ignatius. I can't deny that."

"That doesn't mean you would have murdered him in cold blood!" I exclaimed. "Let alone murdered his entire family!"

"But how can I be sure of that?" he asked in a tortured voice. "I may not have murdered anyone that night, but that doesn't mean I'm not capable of doing it. The most powerful mages in

Tartora are convinced I'm a terrible person. What if they're right?"

"Stop!" I took his face between both my hands, forcing him to look me in the eyes. "The Triumvirate didn't think you were suited for the throne—that's hardly the same as being a mass murderer. Do any of us truly know the depths of what's in our hearts? We can't judge ourselves by what we might have done if circumstances were different. We have to look at what we did do."

I tried to think how to make him understand and stop blaming himself. "Would you give yourself credit for something good you might have done if only you were in a different situation?" I asked. "If not, then you equally can't judge yourself for something bad you might have done if the surrounding circumstances were changed. It's our actions that matter. I've had plenty of time to think about it since then, and I trust you, Nik. No matter how angry you were, I don't believe you would have started killing people indiscriminately. And the very fact you feel this guilt now—despite doing nothing except defend yourself—proves you're not going to do it in the future. It was wrong of me to make such a terrible assumption, even for a moment."

He was shaking beneath my hands, but gradually the shivers ceased, his body going still.

"Do you really believe in me so much?" he whispered.

I held his gaze steady. "I do. I love you, Nikolas of Tartora. It doesn't matter what the Triumvirate think. You are a good man."

He gave a reluctant laugh. "They might be surprised to hear you say that."

"That's their loss, then. You may not be suited to be king, but you could be an excellent prince, if they'd let you."

His arms wound around my waist, pulling me close. "If

that's true, it's because of you, Delphine. You showed me a different way to think about myself."

My hands slid up to his neck, my fingers curling in the hair at the back of his head. He closed his eyes and sighed with contentment.

"I wish we could always be like this," he murmured against my hair. "Just you and me alone here."

I pulled back slightly so I could see his face. "On this island? Do you like it so much here?"

His face clouded. "It's not the island specifically. I just like being away from everything—with you."

I bit my lip. "Don't you want to go home?" I hesitated. "You know we have to, right? We have to go and find out what's happened with Grey. I can block his mesmerizations, and even purge them, and for now I'm the only one who can do it. We can't just abandon Tartora."

He sighed again, but this time it sounded heavy and sad. "I know. And I would never seriously suggest we stay. I want this moment to last forever, but I know it can't."

He pulled further away from me, and the movement hurt with a pain that was in my heart, not my body. I could sense the movement was symbolic. Despite clearing the air between us, despite reaffirming our feelings, Nik was still pulling away from me.

"Sorry," Luna said ruefully from the doorway, making us spring the rest of the way apart. "I gave you as long as I could, but Amara really does want everyone there for this meeting."

"No, no. Of course!" I flushed, hurrying forward to join her while carefully not looking at Nik.

He seemed less flustered, giving a low chuckle as I rushed past him. But he refrained from saying anything, picking up Ember for me and falling into place behind Luna and me as we hurried for the dining hall.

I thought I'd have to endure three more sets of knowing

eyes when I reached the table, but Hayes, Clay, and Amara barely looked our way. They had fallen silent at our approach, but there was no denying the charged atmosphere in the room. I just couldn't tell if the tension lay between the three of them or was due to the interruption.

I faltered as I slid into my chair, glancing questioningly at Luna. She was looking between the three of them, an interested gleam in her eyes. I could almost see her leaping to her own conclusions.

I looked at the older three again, trying to see them from Luna's perspective. Amara did look less calm than usual—possibly even flushed—and Clay was determinedly looking out a nearby window. Only Hayes remained calm, although his gaze kept going to Amara's face, as if drawn there irresistibly.

"Do you think people can change?" Luna chirped into the awkward silence around the table.

Nik started noticeably, but Luna was too absorbed in the situation with the others to even look his way. Apparently, she wasn't talking about us or our conversation.

"That's a broad question." Amara took a bite of her meal, speaking with her usual calm, although I knew her well enough to recognize an underlying agitation.

"I guess I don't mean the people themselves," Luna clarified. "Do you think people can change what they want out of life?"

"That's a question I'd dearly love to know the answer to." Hayes was still looking at Amara, but she was staring fixedly into her plate.

"Why do you ask?" Clay raised an eyebrow. "Are you thinking of abandoning your plan to return to Calista once you graduate, Luna?" He seemed aware—and mildly disapproving—of whatever she truly meant, although I had no idea what it could be.

"No, of course not! I could never do that." She hesitated, as if realizing what she'd just said. "But that's not to say I might not change my mind one day—in the distant future, I mean. Maybe one day I'll return to Tartora. Life moves through seasons, however long or short they may be."

When no one immediately answered, Hayes gave her a repressive look. "I think that's enough life wisdom for a midday meal. I believe we need to make some plans for how we're going to get through every person on the island—twice—before the end of winter."

Luna subsided at the mild reprimand, but I could see from the twinkle in her eyes that she wasn't truly put off. Whatever was lurking in her mind was still bubbling just as strongly as before.

When the day finally ended, we headed for bed at the same time for once. We had been sharing a room ever since the manor filled with returning foresters, but we were usually on different schedules.

"What was that about?" I asked as I slipped into bed, turning on my side to face her.

"Huh?" She finished brushing her hair and dove into her bed in her usual exuberant fashion.

"At lunch. All that talk of life seasons and people changing. You weren't listening in on Nik and my conversation, were you?"

She giggled. "If you try to tell me he's fallen out of love with you because his devotion was just a phase, I'm not going to believe you."

I flushed. "No, of course not. I just wondered...What were you talking about?"

"Amara and Hayes, of course!"

I pulled my pillow into a more comfortable position. "What do you think they were all talking about before we came in?"

She sighed dramatically. "I wish I knew!" She sat up abruptly. "Do you think Hayes told Clay to back off? I know

Clay's interested in Amara, but Hayes isn't doing anything about it!" She groaned and flopped back onto her pillow.

"What do you think he should do about it?" I asked.

"Declare his passionate love, of course," she said promptly. I laughed and she gave me a hurt look. "Don't try to say he doesn't love her because I know he does."

"Oh, he confided in you, did he?" I asked still chuckling.

"He doesn't need to," she said airily. "I can see it."

"Do you really find it so thrilling?" I regarded her curiously from across the room. She seemed so invested in the romance story she'd crafted in her mind.

"Can you blame me? Hayes has stayed loyal to her through all these years, and now circumstances have brought them together again." Her excitement fell away as she added, "I just really want it to work out this time."

I examined her face with a bemused smile. "You sound like you're worried about him."

"I am!" She gave me an earnest look. "Master Hayes has been nothing but kind and considerate since the moment he activated me. And not just me. He literally saved my people. I couldn't tell you how many of my friends and family would be dead right now if it wasn't for him. And when we arrived at the Guild, everything was so new and overwhelming, but he helped me to adjust—and my family as well. He looked after all of us."

"I understand," I said softly. "Amara has been the same for me, even if my family isn't involved."

The start of Luna's apprenticeship had been even more dramatic than mine, but I felt the same gratitude toward my activator as she clearly did to hers. I had only adjusted to the dramatic changes in my life because of Amara's care and understanding.

"It sounds like Hayes is on his way to becoming the Master of Healing, though," I said. "Why would you be worried about him?"

She gave an exaggerated sigh. "My two year apprenticeship finishes this winter, so I'll be officially graduating as soon as we get back to the Guild. And then I'll be returning to Calista. I'm excited to go back to my homeland and join in rebuilding it, but I don't feel like I can leave with an easy heart."

I tried to hide a smile at my nineteen-year-old friend's world-weary air as she considered the burden of caring for her more powerful and more experienced activator.

"Was he having such a hard time before he took you on as his apprentice, then?" I asked.

"Before he activated me, he was Master Colton's second, and seconds don't take apprentices," she explained. "So he'd been alone for a long time."

"You don't think he'll take on another apprentice after you graduate? Maybe even more than one?"

She pursed her lips. "He probably will. Affinity heads are expected to have a whole group of apprentices since they're so strong themselves. But that doesn't mean they're close relationships—especially since it's their seconds who do the heavy lifting of training and corralling the students. Besides, Hayes doesn't need more people who regard him with grateful admiration. He needs an equal who loves him. Someone who can help him take on the difficult role of guiding an affinity and helping to run the kingdom."

"And you think Amara is the right one for that role?"

She nodded, looking somehow both sad and hopeful. "After he gave his heart to her, no other woman has been able to measure up. It has to be her."

"They've known each other for so long, though," I said softly. "If either of them wanted to change the decisions they made back then, they've had plenty of opportunity. Maybe the barriers between them really are too large to ever be overcome."

"No!" Luna sat up straight. "I refuse to believe that! There's always hope for a better future."

I lay on my pillow, staring at the ceiling for a long time after we finished talking. Nik didn't want to go back to normal life, and I should have realized why immediately. He was both a royal prince and a reneger, forcefully outcast from society. What was there for him to go back to?

But at the same time, it was also true that we couldn't stay here. So where did that leave us?

With nothing but hope that our situation might change.

CHAPTER
ELEVEN

The weeks passed all too quickly. Knowing an uncertain future loomed in front of us, I tried to spend as much time with Nik as I could, but several things stood in our way.

Completely healing everyone in the town, even the carriers, was a massive undertaking since it sometimes involved circling back to the same people two or even more times due to our rationed resources and the chance of reinfection.

Isolde had also asked for our help with an education program designed to prevent such a widespread calamity from happening again. The healers in the town might not have significant strength, but they could be trained to look for and recognize sources of contamination.

And, on top of all that, I was solely responsible for visiting every person in the town and purging them of the Constantines' mesmerizations. Nik insisted I couldn't be alone even for a moment. If he wasn't free to accompany me, then Costas, Amara, or Ida were always at my side. And his fears were far from groundless.

The boy who had attacked me in the street wasn't the only one who blamed me for what had happened, and while everyone had been willing to accept healing, no matter who brought it, they were less willing to accept a checkup from the person they suspected and resented. I had thought the job would become routine, and the physical effort of activating their walls certainly became so. But the social problem of my task only grew as more and more of the town were freed from their mesmerizations. Removing the lies left an increasing number of people unsettled and dissatisfied, and their change in attitude provoked those who were still enthralled.

"The problem," Amara said one evening, "is how young they were when the mesmerizations started." It was a rare occasion where we were all eating the evening meal together, and the conversation had turned to the islanders' state of mind. "The effect of such early tampering went further than the specific lies implanted in their minds and impacted their whole patterns of thinking. The problem is a complex one, and it will take a long time for them to relearn and retrain their minds."

She looked across the table at Isolde. "I'm sorry we're leaving you to deal with the ramifications. But we have to head home as soon as winter ends, and Delphine can't stop freeing people just to make your job easier."

"And I would never ask her to," she said forcefully.

"Given the perpetrators are already dead," Amara said, "we'll leave it to you to decide when and how much to tell the general populace about mesmerizations. I know you won't be able to hide the truth forever—there are too many foresters who already know what was happening for that—but it might be strategic to wait until everyone is freed before explaining everything. There's no telling how those who are still under the mesmerization effect might react to what they would see as lies."

Isolde sighed. "That is a question that has been weighing heavily on my mind. But I appreciate your forbearance. The issue will need to be handled delicately."

"The people may end up turning against everything related to the Constantines," Hayes warned.

Isolde nodded. "If that is the case, I'll accept it. I didn't take on leadership because I thought it would be easy. And if the people end up deciding they want someone else to lead them, I'll gladly step aside. I would prefer to be a straight healer than deal with administration anyway." She glanced sideways at Costas. "But whatever happens, I have hope the people will recognize that the two remaining Constantines were never part of the plot against them."

I guessed from her expression that her hope went beyond that. I suspected she would happily hand over leadership to her son the moment he was ready to accept it.

"I'm relieved to hear you say that," Amara said. "But I still feel sorry. If we weren't so concerned about the state of affairs in Tartora, then I'd offer for us to stay and back you up for longer."

"You've already done so much," Isolde said. "We couldn't ask more of you."

"I hope you'll still feel the same way when it comes to nego-tiating an alliance and trade treaty with Tartora," Hayes said with a twinkle in his eyes. "Or, if you prefer, I suspect King Marius would be willing to accept you all as subjects of the Tartoran crown—with the benefits and responsibilities that conveys."

Isolde raised her eyebrows. "That is definitely not a decision I could make on my own."

"Nor am I delegated to make any official offers," Hayes said. "But consider it food for thought."

"I certainly will." She glanced again at Costas who looked thoughtful.

Clay cleared his throat, gaining everyone's attention. "Actu-ally," he said, "while we're on the topic, I've been considering the matter of our departure, and I'm unconvinced we all need to return."

Amara's brows lowered. "You want to stay?"

"I think I should—if the islanders would like me to, that is. I'm satisfied the epidemic will be eradicated by the end of the season, but the island's healers are mostly young, and none of them have undergone proper training. Isolde has done the best she can for them, but even she did not receive proper training in her youth. While the islanders are not currently bound by Tartora's strict laws around apprenticeships, I believe an apprenticeship of sorts would be of value to the stronger healers."

"You'd stay for two whole years?" Isolde asked, sounding shocked. "That's a very generous offer, and we'd be delighted to have you, of course. And not just for your healing strength and skill. We would appreciate your input on our unique administration challenges."

"I'm not an expert administrator by any means," Clay said, "but I'd be happy to help in any way I can. I just can't feel right about abandoning you all with the current state of the island."

He looked over at Amara. "I can't help you with the sea journey back, and given my lack of success in learning from Delphine, I can't help with Grey either. For now, at least, I think the island is where I am most needed and wanted."

Something unspoken passed between them before she bowed her head in acknowledgment.

Clay smiled in response, his face lighting up with his usual good cheer. "I'm sure my junior partner in the clinic back home will be happy to be rid of me for a while longer. He's been ready to take a more senior role for some time now."

Both Isolde and Costas gained a new animation after that, although the rest of us were subdued in exchange. If Clay was willing to stay, he could be of great assistance to the islanders, but it felt wrong to leave him behind.

"Do you think Clay will be all right here for so long?" I asked Amara and Hayes later that evening. "Should we be trying to convince him to come back with us?"

Hayes grinned at me. "Is Luna's condition catching? Don't tell me you think you need to start looking after master mages as well now?"

I flushed. "No, of course not. It's silly of me, I suppose. I just feel bad. I was the one who led us all here in the first place..."

"Don't worry." Amara gave me a sympathetic smile. "Clay is more than capable of looking after himself, and he can make a big difference here."

"Do you think the island will want to become part of Tartora?" I asked. "I suppose Clay's presence might help sway them toward us."

"I couldn't say." Amara glanced laughingly at Hayes. "But I can tell Hayes would rather they became part of Tartora than Calista."

"We have done a lot for them," Hayes protested. "So there's no harm in planting the seed."

"None at all," she said, still with a chuckle in her voice, but I could see a sliver of hurt in his eyes.

If Luna was right, this was the problem that had stood between them from the beginning. Hayes wasn't a naturally ambitious person, but he had chosen to invest in the politics of his Guild and kingdom. Whereas Amara had been so scarred by her mother's power-hungry nature that she'd rejected politics completely.

Amara and Hayes might love each other, but their lives were incompatible. The discomfort of that thought weighed on me. They weren't the only couple whose love didn't match the practicality of their futures.

After finally purging the last islander of mesmerization, I walked home to the manor in pouring rain. Ida was my companion for the day, and she had enough elements power to keep the rain off the two of us, but the atmosphere was unavoidably gloomy.

My mood lifted, however, when I spotted Amara and Ember waiting for us just inside the door. Even Phoenix had come inside, unimpressed with the unrelenting wet outside, and Ember happily trotted over to join us.

As I bent to pick up the fox, Amara spoke. "I've been monitoring the situation for weeks, and I'm confident this is the last storm of the season."

I blinked, trying to work out her point. I had been focused on the rain, the completion of my task, and the difficulties facing Isolde in the town, so it took me a moment to realize the significance of her words.

"You're leaving?" Ida asked, catching on more quickly than me.

Amara nodded. "I've already talked to Hayes and Nik, and we'll be sailing the day after tomorrow. That should give us enough time to pack and say our goodbyes."

"So soon." I didn't know what to feel.

At the beginning, the winter had stretched before us, impossibly long. But the magnitude of our task had easily eaten the weeks. Now I couldn't believe it was already time to go home.

After a moment my thoughts caught up with me. "Wait, Ida. You said *you're* leaving. Aren't you coming?"

She shook her head. "Isolde has offered me a place here, and I already told her I would stay. I came here because I wanted to live in safety and peace. The island didn't turn out to be the haven I expected, but I still think I have as much chance of finding that peace here as anywhere. Whatever their reasons, the islanders welcomed me with open arms, and now they could use my help in return."

I swallowed, sadness clogging my throat. I had become used

to Ida's solid, dependable presence, but I should have foreseen this possibility. I would miss her, but I was glad for Costas and Isolde's sake. Ida had stepped up to help me from the beginning, even before the others sailed in, and she had become as much an expert on the island's administration as Costas himself.

"I hope you can build the life you want here." I wrapped her in a tight hug. "But if you can't, you'll always be welcome with us in Tartora."

Ida smiled. "And I won't forget what you've done for me. If you ever want to come back, I'll make sure there's a place for you."

I smiled a wobbly smile. Ida had broken most of her mesmerizations herself, but she had still been ridiculously grateful to me for purging her mind completely.

"I'll miss these two." Ida stooped to run a hand down Ember's back. "I'd try to lure them into staying except I know it would do no good."

My smile steadied as I squeezed Ember tight. "Don't worry. I'll take good care of them."

Ember pressed into me, as if she understood what I was saying, and Phoenix made a small chip note that made us all smile. He didn't usually like coming into the manor, but he liked the rain even less.

The following hours passed too quickly. A final walk through the town and a farewell dinner with Isolde, Costas, and Ida had to suffice for my goodbyes, and the rest of the time was consumed by sorting and packing my various belongings. I had come with very little, but somehow I had acquired more things during my stay than I could account for. It took time to decide what to take back with me, but at least I wasn't alone in having this problem, since Luna was even worse. Between the two of us, we filled five large bags.

"You must be especially excited to get back," I told her as we lugged our bags to the manor entrance on the designated morning. "You'll finally be graduating and returning home."

She had refused to tell me which winter day had marked her two years as an apprentice, saying we would celebrate together at her official graduation in the capital. She wouldn't even accept my apologies for getting her caught up in the entire mess with Grey. If she'd been back home, she wouldn't have had to wait to graduate.

"I'm excited and sad at the same time," she told me. "I can't wait to see my parents and all the progress in Calinara. All last year they were writing to me about the restoration work in the city, and I want to see it for myself. But then I think about leaving you and Hayes..." She stopped abruptly, dropped all her bags, and flung her arms around my neck, sobbing into my shoulder.

I froze in place, unable to put down my bags due to her tight hold and equally unable to keep moving forward.

"I'll miss you too," I told her, "although we're not saying goodbye yet."

She pulled away, mopping at her eyes. "It feels like a good-bye, don't you think?"

"It is a goodbye," I agreed, starting forward again. "But not between us two. And even once you do graduate, we'll see each other again. If you don't come back to Tartora, I'll go find you in Calista. I'll be free to travel once I'm a graduate too."

"Will you really?" Luna brightened instantly. "I'll show you everything! Promise!"

We reached the front door to find the others already waiting for us. Amara and Hayes were both watching us with amusement, but Nik turned away as soon as he saw me look in his direction. He didn't turn fast enough to hide his expression, though. One among us had no positive feelings about what was waiting for him back on the mainland.

He said nothing, however, and we quickly moved through

the town toward the harbor. I threw a final glance over my shoulder as we left the manor and its beautiful gardens behind. Would I ever be back to the island? If they allied with Tartora, it was possible, although I couldn't imagine what the isolated community might look like in the future.

The islanders had gifted us a boat in gratitude for our extended service, and Costas had given Amara detailed instructions on the route back to the crevasse. She had traveled the path once before, but Costas had led the way on that occasion.

There were only five of us going back since both the Tartoran guards had elected to stay with Clay. They claimed to be staying to guard him, as if he was an official Tartoran delegate to the island community, but in reality we all knew they had more personal reasons for their decision. They had been chosen in the first place because they didn't have families waiting for them at home, and both of them had become attached to forester girls during the winter months.

For a while everyone was busy in the bustle of loading onto the boat and setting sail. But as the island dwindled to nothing behind us, I sat beside Amara on the small deck.

"Can you really do this on your own?" I asked.

She laughed. "Don't you think it's a little late to be asking that question?"

I grinned. "I suppose it is." I turned my face into the ocean breeze. "It's hard to believe we're really going home."

"Don't worry," she said after several minutes of comfortable silence. "With the winter storms behind us, I won't have any trouble navigating a boat this size." She gave a rueful smile. "I just might be very, very tired by the time we arrive."

True to her word, Amara barely slept for days as she negotiated us through the tricky passage. By the time land finally came into sight again, I was immensely relieved. My master was strict on my not pushing myself near exhaustion, but she was apparently willing to take herself right up to the line.

I wasn't the only one glad to see land. We were all sick of the confined space, with the tiny cabin providing the only relief from the elements. Even Luna had run out of topics of conversation, and Nik had barely spoken five words in at least a day.

As soon as we were positioned in a straight line for shore, Amara turned to Nik and gave a weary smile. "I trust you can bring us the rest of the way in?"

He nodded. "You can leave her in my hands."

I knew he was talking about the boat, but Amara still shot me an amused look before lying down right where she was on the deck and going to sleep. Nik frowned down at her, and even though he didn't say anything, I could see the concern in his eyes. As much as he might have fought it at first, Amara had worked her way into his inner circle.

Phoenix launched himself from my shoulder and winged straight for the distant land. Ember immediately padded to the boat's prow and stood watching him go.

"Don't tell me you miss him!" I took my place at her side, grinning down at her. "Don't worry. I won't tell him."

I laughed to myself, too delighted at finally finishing the interminable journey to care who might be listening to my nonsense.

The remaining distance flew past, the land growing closer and closer. At first we had been too far out for me to identify the crevasse, but soon I could clearly see the thin line of green standing out from the surrounding desert.

And by the time Nik brought us gliding gracefully into the dock—using his power on the wood of the boat and the wood of the dock itself to achieve it—I could see all the details of the slim crevasse that pierced the desert cliff. It felt like years since I had sailed away, and yet at the same time only days. Everything looked just the same, all the tents still in place although they were no longer inhabited. The tall walls of the crevasse must have protected them from the winter storms.

Ember was the first to alight, with me close behind her. I took up a position on the dock, receiving the stream of bags that Luna tossed in my direction. Hayes unloaded the rest of the luggage in a more dignified manner while Nik secured the boat to the dock with firm knots.

No one woke Amara, although I saw Hayes throwing her concerned looks. When we were finally ready to leave the boat behind, he scooped her into his arms and carried her off the deck, still sleeping peacefully.

Luna, her eyes enormous, tugged on my arm, inclining her head toward Hayes's retreating back with an excited look. I watched them go myself, wondering what, if anything, Hayes's action meant.

If Amara did decide to change her mind about Hayes, I would be happy for her. But what would it mean for the rest of my apprenticeship?

"Are you all right?" Nik calmly took the many bags from my hands, swinging them over his shoulders like they weighed nothing.

"I'm fine." I smiled up at him. "And I'm also capable of carrying bags."

He just gave me a slow smile, but it didn't quite reach his eyes or dispel the tension in his frame.

Hayes's shout of surprise made us all freeze for a second before launching into action. Racing toward him, my thoughts moved even faster than my legs. Was there someone in the crevasse? We should have considered the possibility that Grey might return to reclaim his old camp.

I had almost reached Grey's house when I saw the source of Hayes's shock. As I had feared, we weren't alone.

Two strangers were waiting for us.

CHAPTER

TWELVE

"Nik!" A short young woman, all motion and energy, threw herself into Nik's arms.

The bags went tumbling down as his hands closed around her. I froze, staring at them both as I tried to work out what was happening.

Nik didn't seem impressed, however, despite enduring the embrace without complaint. And as soon as she lightened her tight hold, he gripped her by both arms and pushed her away from him.

"What are you doing here, Gia?" he asked. "And where have you been for the last year? I didn't find a trace of you in Tartora."

Gia? I stared even closer at the woman. This was Princess Morgiana, Nik's twin sister? She looked different from how I'd expected—shorter and less regal, perhaps. And despite Nik's gruff greeting, she practically sparkled. They were clearly nothing alike in temperament.

"I've been in the nomad lands," she replied, undaunted by his cold expression. "And then Calista. And then the nomad lands again." She threw a glance at a tall young man who was standing slightly back, watching her with amusement. "When did we get back, Renley?"

"Didn't you know about the troubles we've been having here?" Nik asked, cutting off any reply the other man might have made. "We could have done with your help, Gia. Don't you care about your own kingdom at all? Or have you forgotten your people now that you married a Calistan? The people no longer matter to you since you're not taking the throne?"

I expected her to stiffen and take offense at receiving a bevy of accusations instead of a proper greeting, but instead her eyes widened and a smile grew across her face.

"Who is she?" Gia shook free of his hold only so she could grab his arms in what looked like an iron grip. "Is she here?"

Nik's eyes flicked toward me for the briefest second, but Gia caught the involuntary gesture. Twisting around, she peered in our direction, but since I was standing next to Luna, her eyes flicked back and forth between us. She looked back at her twin, her smile growing even larger.

"But this is amazing! You have to introduce me to her immediately!"

"I don't know what you're talking about," Nik said stiffly, all his earlier antagonism completely forgotten.

Gia shook him lightly. "Don't try that on me. I know you too well. All this talk about caring about our people—even without the throne. And you really seem to mean it too! Plus, I heard you've been working with Master Amara and Master Hayes of all people. Actually *collaborating* instead of sulking around the kingdom on your own."

Nik cleared his throat. "I don't know why that makes you think—"

"Ha! Didn't you hear me say I know you too well? The only person you ever listened to even a little was me—and I'm well aware that wasn't because I have any great wisdom. You listened to me because, despite yourself, you couldn't help loving your own twin. That little bit of softness was the only way I ever got through to you. So if you've suddenly started *listening to other people* and *learning things*, then obviously you've found a love that's softened you much more than I ever did. Something has made you open yourself to new ideas, and I want to know who she is. Immediately!"

Nik sighed loudly, but a smile was creeping across his face. I stared at him, fascinated by this new insight. I had always known he had a twin, but she had been a distant concept. A crown princess who had abdicated her throne. The one Nik could never live up to. I had never imagined someone who treated Nik like this.

"Well it isn't me," Luna said with a wicked grin. "Hello, Renley," she greeted the man standing behind the twins.

He smiled and waved back. "I'm glad to see you back in one piece, Luna. You've been keeping Hayes in line, I hope."

"I think that might be someone else's job now." She gave a significant look toward the cabin where Hayes had disappeared, still carrying Amara. Presumably he was finding her a bed so she could continue her much-needed sleep. I just hoped she wouldn't be disturbed by all the commotion outside.

Renley's eyebrows went up slowly, and he threw a considering look at the cabin. I elbowed Luna, glaring at her. She might speculate to me, but it was much too early to be making comments to strangers.

But as they continued to chat, exchanging news, it became apparent they were far from strangers. Luna finally noticed me staring.

"Renley and I grew up together in the Calistan settlement," she explained. "It was a small enough place that everyone knew everyone, but our parents were particular friends."

She turned to Renley. "And this is the dearest of my new friends, Delphine."

I couldn't help smiling at the label, but the expression froze when Gia whipped around to face me. She had been wheedling Nik in a quiet voice while Renley and Luna spoke, but she had clearly been listening for the introduction.

"I'm Gia!" She held out her hand, beaming at me with her whole face. "It's lovely to meet you, Delphine."

I stepped forward to take her hand, relieved to see my arm wasn't shaking. But when I began to bow over it, she snatched it away horrified.

"No, no, no! You can't do that!"

"I'm sorry, Your Highness," I said, startled.

"Please don't do that either," she begged me earnestly. "It's just an honorary title these days, you know. I left court precisely because I couldn't stand all of that. Just call me Gia."

I shot a glance at Nik, who was watching me intensely, something on his face I couldn't read.

"Very well, if you insist," I said, pulling myself together. Gia was probably the most important person in the kingdoms to Nik, and I wanted to salvage as good an impression as was still possible. "I'm Delphine," I added unnecessarily. "Master Amara's apprentice."

"The hero of Eldrida! I've heard of you," she said, making both my hands fly up and wave in protest.

"No, no, those stories are all exaggerated! I didn't—" My words broke off as I caught the mischievous twinkle in her eye.

"Please forgive my mannerless twin," Nik said stiffly. "She's well aware of how public opinion can distort matters."

"Oh, Nik." Gia sighed. "I'm glad you care about people now, but couldn't you also try being a bit more fun?"

He glared at her, and I moved to his side, offering him my silent support. He smiled down at me, his expression softening, and Gia gave a happy sigh.

His face immediately closed off again, but the damage was already done.

"I knew it!" Gia said, her eyes shining. "Delphine, I really am *very* glad to meet you."

"I'm glad to meet you, too," I said, warming to the intense girl in spite of myself. It was hard to resist her irrepressibility or her obvious affection for her brother.

"So you're elements affinity?" she asked, giving her brother a quick sideways look.

"Actually I'm a healer," I said awkwardly.

"Ooh, cross-influenced! Yes, of course, I should have remembered that from the stories in Eldrida. Interesting." She gave her brother another look.

A wave of irritation swept over me. "You don't have to keep looking at him like that. He isn't obsessed with elements anymore."

Gia's eyebrows sprang up to her hairline, and I flushed as I realized what I'd just said. I glanced apologetically up at Nik, but he was looking down at me in amusement.

"Healers can be fierce when roused," he said with a grin.

Gia's eyes widened at his reaction. "I really, really like you, Delphine," she said with a beaming smile. "I can barely recognize my brother."

I frowned, looking at him again. "Really? Maybe it's just that everyone always underestimated him."

Both twins laughed at that, making me squirm.

"Don't worry." Gia winked at me. "I'm sure he'll never entirely lose that dark and brooding thing he has going on. He just can't help himself."

"Gia," Nik said in a warning tone, but Hayes emerged from the cabin at that moment, interrupting the twins' reunion.

"Oh good, you're all still here," he said. "Amara will need to sleep for a while, so we have time to talk. I don't suppose you've been here long enough to prepare any interesting food?" he asked Gia and Renley hopefully.

Renley chuckled. "That we can help you with. Sick of ship fare, are you?"

The two led the way into the main room of the cabin, and everyone was directed to find seats around the table. I sat, running my hand along the wood and remembering the last time I had been here. This was the location of my first mesmerization, although I hadn't known it at the time, and I had expected the presence of Grey to linger. But somehow, with the room crammed full of familiar bodies and bits of conversation floating back and forth, it was hard to picture him at all.

We were a chair short, and Gia looked at her brother.

"Delphine can sit on your lap, can't she?" she asked innocently.

"Gia," Renley said in warning tones, pulling his wife onto his lap instead. "Your poor brother will be wishing you back in the nomad lands soon."

Gia just laughed, putting an arm around his neck and placing a fleeting kiss on his lips. "He's had a lifetime of putting up with me, so he's used to it."

Nik did have a look of long suffering on his face, but I also noticed he was carefully avoiding looking in my direction. I was glad because I could feel the flush on my cheeks. Gia and Renley were so comfortable and natural with each other, and it made my heart ache. Would Nik and I ever get to that point? Our relationship had been all heat and intensity with little room for the sort of relaxed familiarity I saw between his sister and her husband.

"If you've just come from the nomad lands, how did you end up here?" Nik asked Gia.

"We spent a year in Calista and the nomad lands," she said, "first recruiting for Calista, and then doing some negotiation for Father. So we were gone longer than I expected."

"Father trusted you to do negotiations for Tartora?" Nik asked skeptically.

She threw him an impatient look. "You're the one who has issues with Father, Nik. He knows I still want the best for Tartora—I just don't want to be tied down. It's not like it was a major trade treaty. Some things are best handled outside of the official channels."

I raised my eyebrows, but she didn't explain further, and I wasn't going to ask. Nik didn't ask either, his brows contracting as he looked at the table. Beneath its surface, where no one could see, I slipped my hand into his. He glanced at me and smiled slightly. His sister might not know his thinking about his father had changed, but I did.

"Calista isn't the most recent place we've been, though," Renley interjected. "We heard there was trouble in Tartora and hurried back to Tarona. That's when we heard you'd been found —and then lost again."

Gia rolled her eyes, as if she thought it very irresponsible of everyone involved. I had to stifle a smile since she gave the impression of being someone who would lose anything that wasn't attached to her.

Hayes leaned forward. "Do they truly believe we're lost? Didn't they get the information we sent about Grey?"

"Maybe you'd better let me tell the story," Renley said to Gia before turning to Hayes. "The guards you sent arrived promptly in the capital, and King Marius knows where you've been all winter. That's why we've been here waiting for you since the moment the last storm passed."

Hayes sat back slightly, but he didn't look that relieved. "So you worked out we were stuck there for the winter. But does that mean the king also assumed Grey and all the Constantines were stuck with us?"

I drew in a breath as I realized Grey might have been free to infiltrate the court all this time with no one on the watch for him.

"No, thankfully not." Despite Renley's words, his face

remained grave. "His ship foundered close to shore just past the southernmost point of the desert. Some herders saw it and helped the passengers and crew reach land. Most of them scattered immediately, but a couple were injured and ended up being taken to local healers. The name of their leader and their place of origin made it back to some law keepers who knew Anka had been searching for Grey last year."

"You've caught Grey, then?" I asked hopefully.

"No." Renley's response made everyone in the room tense up again.

"I can understand his initial escape if there were only a few herders on hand," Hayes said. "But it's been months since then. How could they not have found him?"

"Finding him would require looking," Gia said flatly.

Luna propped her chin on her hand. "Let me guess, they're all holed up in the capital, afraid to come out in case they run into Grey?"

I frowned as something occurred to me. "Were you officially sent to meet us? Are you even supposed to be here?"

Gia and Renley exchanged a look, Gia chuckling. "Busted! You're quick, Delphine. I can see why Nik likes you."

Nik's hand tightened around mine beneath the table while Hayes sighed, rubbing his brows with his fingers as if he was developing a headache. "So you heard where we were and decided to run off on your own. As if we didn't have enough to deal with already with Grey on the loose."

"It's true that Gia was eager to see Nik," Renley said gravely, meeting Hayes's gaze. "But that wasn't our main reason for coming to find you. I know Gia has earned herself a certain reputation for recklessness, but I'm equally concerned about the situation in Tarona. We wanted to talk to you first—to prepare you for the situation and hear your perspective."

"It's that bad?" Hayes stared at him, clearly appalled. "Don't tell me Grey has wormed his way into court!"

150

Everyone around the table exchanged panicked glances as we imagined Grey mesmerizing the royal family and Triumvirate.

"No, no, it's not that bad," Renley said quickly.

A relieved sigh rippled around the table, and his face tightened in response.

Hayes frowned at his reaction. "What is going on, then?"

"The king and Triumvirate are extremely concerned about the possibility of exactly what you were just picturing," he said.

"Paranoid, you mean." Gia scowled.

"It's a real danger," Renley said, and I could tell from his tone that they'd had this conversation many times. "They're right to take the possibility seriously."

"They're right to be cautious, yes," Gia said. "But there's a difference between that and living in fear. While they're busy protecting themselves, where is Grey? The danger will never end unless we find him."

"The idea of having someone playing with the thoughts in your head is terrifying," Luna said quietly. "Surely we can understand their fear. Are you really saying they've done nothing?"

Gia snorted. "No, they've recalled Anka from Caltor so that the one senior official in the kingdom who knows what Grey looks like is sheltering at the capital with them, keeping *them* safe."

"Anka's at the capital?" Amara asked from the doorway of one of the bedrooms.

Hayes stood up, offering her his seat. "You should still be resting," he murmured as he helped her sit down, but he didn't try to convince her to return to bed.

She accepted the offered seat, her pale face betraying her underlying exhaustion.

"Master Amara," Gia said politely. "I don't think you've met my husband, Renley, yet."

Amara smiled and inclined her head toward both of them. "It's a pleasure to meet you, Renley, and to see you again, Princess Morgiana. I'm sorry I missed your wedding. I was traveling through the eastern hill country at the time, and I didn't receive the general invitation issued to all masters until it was too late to travel back."

"I'm glad you didn't inconvenience yourself," Gia said with an easy smile. "If it had been up to me, I would have gotten rid of all those formalities. There was no reason for you to uproot your plans to attend the wedding of someone you barely know."

Amara's lips twitched, and I could see Gia had a similar effect on her as she did on me. It was hard not to smile around Nik's vibrant twin.

"That is gracious, Your Highness," she said, and Gia immediately shook her head.

"Gia. Please."

Amara shot a glance at Hayes, and he nodded slightly. She looked back at the princess.

"Very well, Gia. I want to be sure I understand the situation correctly. The king and Triumvirate are aware of the danger from Grey and have taken measures to protect themselves. In particular, they have brought in Anka who can ensure he doesn't sneak into court under a false pretense. Is that the sum of it? Are you telling me they've done nothing to actively find Grey?"

"Of course it's not that bad," Renley said quickly. "Anka is working from court to head a kingdom-wide search for him. But he must be lying low because we've had no word of his location. He's certainly not stirring up public trouble like he was before."

Amara's shoulders relaxed slightly. "Some of Anka's people from Caltor know what he looks like, so even if she's not free to travel, she'll have sent them out, I'm sure."

"That depends," Gia said. "Were they mages? The Triumvirate have all but shut down the Guild. They're afraid of what will happen if Grey manages to enthrall enough mages of strength, so the mages are confined to the Guild and palace grounds or the capital at most."

"So Anka is leading a search, but she isn't allowed to make use of mages?" Hayes asked, sounding half bemused and half annoyed. "That's like searching with one hand behind her back."

"Exactly. I see you grasp the problem." Gia sighed. "I love my parents dearly, but they were raised to protect the throne and Triumvirate first and foremost. It's not that they don't care about the people—they just think the kingdom will crumble if the systems of government break."

"They're not entirely wrong," Amara said with a sigh. "There are many things I don't like about how we manage mages and the distribution of power in this kingdom, but I've also seen firsthand the ways they hold everything together. I don't think we even realize all the things that would collapse if the system itself broke down."

I nodded slowly, thinking of the literal collapse of the unsanctioned dam Amara and I had encountered early in our travels, and of the capital healers who kept Tartora's hospitals running. I had seen far less of the kingdom than Amara, but I knew what she meant.

"But the government isn't serving the kingdom if they're too focused on protecting themselves," Gia said. "They need to send out their best people and track this Grey down before he can twist more minds. It's the only right thing to do."

Renley grimaced. "It's awful to think that every day we delay may mean more minds forever tainted by Grey's lies."

"Actually...about that." Nik's hand tightened around mine again. "There's something Hayes and Amara didn't know when they sent that message. Delphine has worked out how to purge mesmerizations. So once we find them, we can free the minds Grey has touched."

Gia shot upright. "Really?" She stared at me. "But that's amazing news! Father can stop being so afraid and start actually doing something."

"It's certainly an unlooked-for boon," Hayes said. "But at this point, Delphine hasn't been able to teach anyone else to do it. So the skill is limited to Delphine herself."

Gia winced. "That's unfortunate." She shot a look at Renley. "Maybe we should hold off telling Father about this new development just yet."

"You want us to defy the king and go hunting for Grey on our own?" Luna asked in a neutral tone.

Hayes's frown deepened, and I caught the worried look he sent in her direction.

Gia waved her hand airily. "Oh, nothing as subversive as that. I'm merely suggesting that you aren't under any explicit orders to report directly to the capital, so it might be worth our while to take a more circuitous route there."

Nik nodded slowly, and Gia grinned.

"I like rebellious Nik," she said. "If I hadn't been so worried about you for the last two years, I would have been cackling and rubbing my hands in glee to see you go rogue."

This time it was my turn to squeeze Nik's hand. Hayes had clearly been right about Nik's family being worried about him.

"I'm not so sure about this." Hayes looked to Amara. "Anka is a trained law enforcement official, and she's very good at what she does." He turned back to Gia. "I don't know why you think we could do any better."

"Actually," I said slowly. "There's someone in Tartora who was tracking and studying Grey before Anka even knew he existed. The same person who found this camp when she couldn't." I looked at Nik. "And he's here with us."

Amara considered my words, looking thoughtful. "Nik

154

certainly knows more about Grey than I do. So tell us, expert—
if we were to entertain this plan, what would you be
advising?"

Nik disentangled his fingers from mine so he could lean
both his elbows on the table, his eyes narrowing.

"Did you talk to Anka?" he asked his sister. "What's her
strategy?"

"They're assuming his goal is the capital—it's the only
thing that makes sense given his ability," Gia said, glibly
handing out what I could only assume had to be state secrets.
"Grey doesn't need to spend time raising an army before
attempting a coup. All he needs is direct access to those at the
top."

"And so they've made a fortress around themselves," Nik
murmured, his eyes narrowing. "But it's been an entire season,
and Grey clearly hasn't managed to infiltrate the court. So what
else have they been doing?"

"He's in hiding, clearly," Renley said. "So the theory is that
he must be either laying low in some remote region, trying to
avoid notice, or else he's lurking somewhere nearby, ready to
make a move. So Anka has split her forces. She only has a few
who have personal experience with him in Caltor, and she's
sent some of them to circle through the more remote towns,
while others have finished scouring Caltor and have now
moved on to Ostaria, working their way out from the capital. Of
course constant rumors about him crop up everywhere, but
none of them have borne fruit yet."

"As far as they know," Gia said. "Because of course there's
the constant fear that the people they sent to investigate may
have encountered Grey and been forcibly turned."

Nik raised an eyebrow. "In that case, it's obvious. We should
start in Eldrida."

"Eldrida?" Hayes asked.

"If I'd been in the capital, I would have recommended they

start there, but instead it seems to be down the bottom of their list of places to focus."

"Why Eldrida?" Amara asked, her expression giving nothing away.

"It's not an obvious staging point for the capital," Hayes added, his eyes also fixed on Nik.

Nik shrugged. "Maybe not, but it's the place Grey knows best. He and his people must have contacts there. They were stationed at this camp for a long time, and Eldrida was their only trading point."

Gia jumped to her feet. "See! I knew there would be something we could do. And this is perfect. No one could criticize us for returning through Eldrida. It's basically on the way."

Hayes and Amara exchanged a look. Finally Hayes spoke.

"Very well, then. We can travel from here to Eldrida and from there to the capital. It would have been our likely route anyway."

Amara stood. "Given there has been no solid news of Grey, I can't see any rush for us to get to the capital. We can afford to spend a few days in Eldrida before moving on. But first, I need a proper sleep."

Everyone stood, moving away from the table, but Gia only moved around to latch onto Nik's arm.

"You will be coming with us all the way to the capital, won't you?" she asked quietly, her eyes fixed on his face.

"Don't worry, Gia. I intend to see this through."

"That's not what I mean, and you know it," she said fiercely. "It's been long enough, Nik. You need to come home."

He opened his mouth to speak, but she rushed on.

"I know what the Triumvirate did to you was awful. And Father treated you badly, too, in his own way. But he didn't know it was going to happen, and it wasn't as if he was offered a choice. He and Mother miss you. She's been so worried, not even knowing where you were."

"And so you wanted to make her feel better by leaving home the second your apprenticeship allowed and wandering the kingdoms yourself, then?" he asked, but it was amusement, not bitterness, lurking behind his words.

Gia had the grace to flush. "I understand why you had to get away. I had to as well, at least for a while. I'm just saying it's been long enough."

"Gia, stop." Nik cut her off gently. "I'm not avoiding Mother and Father, not anymore. I'm seeing what I started through to the end and making sure Grey can't hurt anyone ever again."

"So you'll be going to the capital with us?" she pressed.

He sighed. "I don't know what you're expecting. I've been gone a long time, and everything has changed. There's no place for me there, anymore. Or are you forgetting what I am now?"

She groaned. "Why couldn't you have waited to run off until after you finished your apprenticeship? Would that really have been so hard?" She gripped his arm with both hands. "But couldn't you ask them to take you back? If your master accepts you back, and you complete your apprenticeship, you won't be a reneger anymore."

He rubbed the back of his neck, giving a laugh that held a tinge of his old bitterness. "And you think Master Augusta will accept me back just for the asking? Unlike our parents, the Triumvirate always wanted me gone."

She bit her lip, her eyes worried. "But you could at least try."

He gently removed her hands from his arm. "I'll stay with you all the way to the capital, sister. But I can't promise you what will happen after that."

I stood frozen, hardly breathing since they seemed to have forgotten my presence. But as soon as Nik finished speaking, he flashed me a glance loaded with more emotion than I could name.

I stepped toward him, my mouth forming his name, but he

was already gone, out the front door of the cabin and off into the greenery of the crevasse.

CHAPTER

THIRTEEN

The trip due south to Eldrida was uneventful since it took us largely through desert. Gia took every opportunity to initiate conversation, quickly wheedling my entire life story out of me. She shared freely about herself as well, regaling me with stories from her childhood with Nik.

Nik, on the other hand, was clearly avoiding me. He never did anything pointed enough that I could protest, but neither did we have opportunities to talk unless there were several others present.

"Why does he have to sabotage his own happiness?" Gia asked sadly as we approached Eldrida on the final day. She was gazing at Nik, who was walking ahead of us in conversation with Renley.

I didn't pretend not to know what she was talking about or that the matter hadn't occupied many of my thoughts during our journey.

"I think he thinks he's doing it for me," I said with a sigh. "He knows I won't leave my apprenticeship and Amara—he wouldn't even ask me to—and he thinks that means it will never work between us. Like Amara and Hayes. So he's trying to create distance between us now, to minimize the pain."

Gia groaned. "That would explain why he's always looking at you."

"He is?" I frowned. I hadn't noticed him watching me. I was always the one looking at him.

But Gia nodded assuredly. "Whenever you're distracted and not looking at him, he stares at you like his life depends on memorizing every one of your features. Just seeing his expression makes my heart hurt—and that's despite thinking he's being a fool."

I looked down at my feet, my face burning. Did he really look at me like that?

Gia was right—he was a fool.

"Can't you straighten him out?" Gia asked. "I've tried, but he stonewalls me."

I sighed. "What am I supposed to say? What if he's right?"

"Don't you be like that, too!" Gia cried. "My brother has never cared about anyone the way he cares about you. We have to find a way for you to be together."

I sighed again. "If you have any suggestions, I'm listening."

When she fell silent, I gave her a look, and she winced.

"There's still time," she said quickly. "We'll find a way. Maybe Augusta will take him back."

"And what if she does?" I murmured. "Then he goes back to being a royal prince, and who am I?"

"Definitely none of that!" Gia exclaimed. "Look at Renley! He doesn't have a title or position. He's no different in rank from Luna."

I gave her a skeptical look. It had taken a few days, but I no longer felt awkward arguing back to a princess. "I think you're forgetting that Renley is Calistan, and from what I gather, he's a close ally of their new king and queen. Things are different in Calista—it's basically a new kingdom. Is there anyone of high rank? Since your marriage, you've become part Calistan, too.

And that's given you freedom to distance yourself from being a Tartoran princess. But I'm only a very junior member of the Tartoran Mages' Guild. I don't have any alternative position or home to offer Nik. If he does finally reconcile with his family and take back his rightful place, how can I ask him to give it all up for a second time?"

Gia linked her arm with mine. "I'm sure it will work out. It has to."

I sighed and nodded, not wanting to dispute her words a second time. Especially when I was holding on to the same nebulous hope myself.

My eyes lingered on Nik's back, taking in the breadth of his shoulders and his easy stride, before slipping sideways to where Hayes and Amara walked, their heads bent close in conversation. Nik had been there for me from the start—from before I was even activated—and I desperately wanted him in my future too. But hadn't the same been true for Amara with Hayes? Their case proved that love wasn't always enough. You couldn't build a life together if circumstances forced you apart.

I tried to move forward to walk with Nik, but as usual he outmaneuvered me, and I ended up in the lead next to Amara. She took the opportunity to quiz me on what I had learned during the epidemic—an ongoing process that was being completed in snatches whenever we had the chance.

"It's not the teaching program I'd planned for you," she said. "But there's no denying that these constant crises are pushing you to develop your power far faster than an ordinary apprentice. You may be lagging behind on academic learning—Hayes tells me you still have plenty of memorization to do from both the anatomy and general medical texts—but you're far more capable than the average first year apprentice. Catching up on academic learning can happen easily enough later on."

"Even if I'd had my books with me on the island, I don't

think I would have had the chance to open them," I said. "I feel like I barely drew breath the whole winter. But I promise I'll make more of an effort once we're reunited with our possessions. You left the bulk of them in storage in Eldrida along with Acorn, didn't you?"

Amara nodded. "I'm looking forward to that reunion myself."

"Have you missed the freedom of having your cart, Acorn, and an open road in front of you?" I asked. "I'm afraid taking me on as your apprentice has proven far more disruptive than you expected."

Amara gazed ahead at the walls of Eldrida, which were growing larger before us.

"A year ago I would have been itching to be off again after so long. But I actually haven't even thought about it. Although I will be glad to get to the capital."

"Really? I thought you didn't like Tarona?"

"It feels different now," she said thoughtfully. "So much is happening and changing in Tartora, and the capital is the hub of it all. In the past, I've always felt certain that the place I was most needed was in the smaller cities and towns. But now I feel needed in the capital. I suppose it's all this business with Grey."

She shook herself slightly and smiled at me. "Don't worry. Once everything has been resolved, we'll be back on the road again. I haven't forgotten that I promised you your apprenticeship wouldn't be spent at the Guild."

"About that..." I paused before continuing. "A year ago I thought differently, too. I'm not saying I want to be at the Guild, necessarily, but I now recognize how hollow my old prejudice against it was. If we need to stay there for some reason, I wouldn't consider it a betrayal."

Amara's eyebrows lifted slightly, her eyes distant. "I'll bear that in mind."

The sun was lowering toward the horizon as we approached the city, but the gates didn't close until sunset, so we joined the main western road without concern. But when we reached the gates, we found them closed and barred. Only a single door, cut within the left gate, was propped open. And standing in front of it were four armed guards wearing stern expressions.

Amara and I exchanged a surprised look. On our previous arrival at the city, the gates had been wide open and unmanned. On that occasion, the anomaly had been due to the storm, but this situation seemed almost as unusual.

"Are the gates closed for the day already?" Amara asked carefully, the others remaining silent as they clustered close behind us.

"That depends who's asking," the guard at the front said aggressively. "What's your business in Eldrida?"

"We're travelers seeking rest and shelter before we continue our journey," she said, making no mention of our identities.

I glanced over my shoulder and saw Nik and Gia had melted to the back of our small group, the other three attempting to block them from view. I quickly looked front again, hoping I hadn't attracted any attention.

"And what brings you traveling in these remote parts?" the same guard asked, clearly taking note of our lack of trading goods.

Amara shrugged, doing a good job of appearing unaffected by the strange situation. "It's not remote to our way of thinking. We've come south from eastern Calista."

"Calista?" The man glanced behind him, and one of the other guards nodded.

I realized, belatedly, that Amara had been picking her words carefully, wary of any guards with a healing affinity. And it looked like her caution had been called for.

The guard in front of us stood motionless for a moment,

clearly torn about what to make of us. But two of the men behind him had started whispering, their heads bent together. The speaker was watching us with wide eyes, his words inaudible but rapid. The other started out frowning, but his eyes gradually widened as well, his gaze locking on us.

I shifted uncomfortably. If they intended to deny us entry, would they leave the matter there? Or would they attempt to arrest us? I couldn't imagine why they would do so, but nothing about the situation made sense. Travel around Tartora had never been restricted, and city inns relied on travelers to survive.

The speaker at the back had finished, and his listener responded by stepping forward to murmur something in the ear of the leader. This time he was close enough for me to catch the words *heroes* and *storm*.

Just like before, the leader's whole manner changed on hearing the whispered message. He peered first at Amara and then at me before dropping into an abrupt bow.

"We are honored!" he exclaimed. "Please forgive my earlier questioning. Of course the heroes of Eldrida are welcome in our city any time!"

My mouth fell open, but Amara took it easily in stride, inclining her head and smiling graciously.

"Thank you for your welcome."

"I apologize for not recognizing you at once," the leader said. "But I hope you can understand our caution. You must have heard the rumors and know there are dangerous people loose in Tartora. We can't be too careful in protecting our citizens and our city."

"An admirable goal," Amara said in a steady voice. If I hadn't known better, even I would have believed she found nothing about the situation odd.

The fourth guard had disappeared during the latter part of the conversation, and I realized his purpose when a loud creaking rang out. Slowly the full gate swung open, giving easy access to the city. All four guards jumped to attention, lining up on either side of the gate and bowing deeply as we passed through.

Amara led the way, the seven of us staying close together as we walked. I smiled at the guards as naturally as I could manage, but I wasn't sure how well I succeeded. We continued into the city in unnatural silence until well out of ear shot of the guards.

"It wasn't just me. That was weird, right?" I asked Amara. "I'm not even sure which aspect of it was more unsettling."

Amara nodded grimly, the calmly gracious expression she'd worn at the gate gone completely.

"So that was all about keeping Grey out?" Luna asked, but her voice made it clear she didn't find it a satisfactory explanation.

"So it would appear," Amara said.

"Or so someone wants it to appear," Hayes muttered, making me shoot him a horrified expression.

"Are you saying—?" I started, but Amara cut me off with a hand on my arm.

"Later," she murmured, and I nodded.

For several streets, I followed her with quick, jumpy strides, trying not to see a threat in every shadow. The people we passed appeared normal enough, going about the regular business of a coastal city. For the most part, they ignored us, although more than one took a second look at Amara and me before bursting into speech with their companions.

"I thought they would have forgotten about us by now," I said to Amara, acutely uncomfortable.

"A disaster like that storm isn't soon forgotten," she said. "And we can be grateful for it on this occasion. I honestly don't know if we would have gotten into the city if we hadn't been recognized."

"As long as it was only us who were recognized," I said.

I didn't know what was going on in Eldrida, but I was already uncomfortable about everyone soon knowing Amara and I were here. They didn't need to know both of King Marius's children were here too.

CHAPTER

FOURTEEN

After another turn, I recognized a landmark.

"Aren't we going to the inn?" I asked Amara, sure that had been her intention. She had waxed poetic for several minutes during the morning about the warm bath waiting for us.

"Change of plans," she said shortly.

I didn't question her further, and neither did any of the others. After what had happened at the gate, I even felt relieved. Anyone who got word of our arrival would expect us to be at one of the city's inns. While I didn't know where else we could go instead, anywhere seemed better than there.

We had nearly reached the large central square—our route bringing back unpleasant flashbacks of the storm's destruction and violence—when Amara stopped abruptly in front of a large, closed wooden gate.

"What is this place?" Luna asked over my shoulder, looking at the worn wood with curiosity.

"It's a small, private stables," I said, recognizing it. "When we first arrived in Eldrida, the stable master was sheltering people from the storm. He kept Acorn, Ember, and Phoenix here while we went out to help. Oh!" I exclaimed, suddenly realizing what must have happened. "Has he been looking after Acorn while we've been gone?"

Amara nodded. "When we left for the desert, I organized for Acorn to board here until I came back. Since we were being labeled as heroes, he agreed easily enough, although I think his personal view was that I was pushy and self-righteous." She smiled slightly, obviously not offended.

"Why didn't you just leave her at one of the inns?" Luna asked. "Especially if you thought the stable master didn't like you."

Amara raised an eyebrow. "What difference does it make whether he likes me or not? Liking me isn't the measure of someone's worth. His first instinct during the storm was to open his doors and shelter as many as possible. And he even opened the doors a second time just because he heard hoof beats through the noises of the storm. And when I first came back to check on Acorn in the aftermath of the storm, she had been well groomed and looked fast on her way to becoming fat and happy."

Luna subsided, looking suitably chastened.

"I wish I could be so uncaring about whether or not people like me," she whispered to me, and I nodded agreement.

Amara had to rap on the wood several times, but eventually the large gate creaked open. The grumbles of the elderly man behind it ceased as soon as he got a good look at who was there.

"Oh, it's you," he said sourly, but his heart didn't seem to be in his ill temper. "I suppose you've come for that cantankerous mare of yours?"

Amara led the way inside, the rest of us trailing in behind her.

"Been causing trouble, has she?" she asked.

"See for yourself." He nodded toward a stall halfway down the short aisle. We peered over the closed half-door to see a contented Acorn feeding from a trough.

She hadn't looked up at the sounds of our arrival, but when Amara laughed, her ears pricked, and she turned her head. For a moment she surveyed her mistress before swishing her tail and returning to her feed.

"Who is that calm horse?" Hayes asked. "Do you think he swapped Acorn out with another mare with similar markings and a rounder belly?"

Amara chuckled again. "It's a good thing I have Delphine with me, or I'd never convince her to leave this stable."

I eyed the mare doubtfully. "I'm not sure my presence will be enough."

"I've never liked that animal," Hayes muttered, and Acorn pricked an ear, stopping eating. Turning her long neck, she gave him a look that could only be called a warning.

Luna and I burst into laughter while Hayes glared back at the horse.

"There you go!" I said. "It is Acorn after all."

"You were gone for long enough," the stable master said from behind us.

"Yes, we were held up for much longer than expected," Amara said. "Which is why I left her with you in the first place. I knew you wouldn't get rid of her when my original payment ran out. Of course I'll pay the balance now, with a bonus as well for your understanding."

The stable master's face lightened considerably, and he even nodded respectfully.

"If you'd like to earn a bit extra," Amara added, "I seem to remember you have several rooms on the second level above the stalls."

The elderly man eyed us uncertainty. "They're nothing fancy. You'd be more comfortable at an inn."

"Perhaps," Amara said lightly. "But we'd rather stay with Acorn if it's possible."

Out of the corner of my eye, I saw Hayes and Renley once

again positioning themselves in front of Nik, attempting to block him from sight.

For a moment I wondered if they thought the man was a threat and why they weren't blocking Gia as well, if so. Then I remembered Nik's official status. He was a reneger—the kingdom's most famous reneger—and if the stable master realized his status, he would be legally required to refuse him service or lodging.

The man didn't even glance in their direction, however. Instead he started toward the stairs, gesturing for us to follow him. "Don't go saying I didn't warn you," he grumbled as he began the climb.

Next to the stairs, I noticed a bulky shape with a large length of canvas thrown over it. From the dimensions, I guessed it was Amara's cart. Apparently our remaining belongings had also been stored here in our absence.

Upstairs there were only two rooms available, so we split in half with men in one and women in the other. I wondered if Gia and Renley might protest, but they made no complaint about being temporarily separated.

"I didn't expect Nik to be proven correct so immediately," Gia said as we deposited our bags in the room assigned to us. "But I'm glad we came to Eldrida. Something is going on here that's worth further investigation."

"We have to keep an open mind," Amara warned. "It's still possible this is a reaction to the rumors about Grey and nothing more. It's easy to see things that aren't there when you're already suspicious. I suspect we'll find the capital equally tense."

She sent Gia a questioning look, and the younger woman shrugged.

"It isn't quite like this—or wasn't when we were there—but I can't deny it's been unsettled."

"What's the plan now?" I asked. "Are we going to head out into the city and see what we can discover?"

Luna bounded over and wound her arm through mine. "The two of us should go together," she announced.

"That's a good idea," I said before noticing Nik in the doorway, his expression disapproving. "And you're not invited," I told him. "Who's going to gossip with us if you're hanging around all silent and menacing?"

Luna nodded fervently. "Two female apprentices will get a very different reaction from any of the rest of you."

"I agree," Amara said calmly. "And beyond that, I am officially forbidding Nik and Gia from stepping foot outside these stables until we get a better idea of what's going on in the city."

They both began to protest, but she silenced them with a stern look. "I'm pulling rank on both of you, and don't try to argue you're royalty. Nik, you're a reneger, and Gia, you were the one to ask us not to consider your rank. As a master mage, I am the senior member of this expedition, and I expect both of you to obey this command."

She continued to stare them down until they both nodded reluctant agreement.

"I'm a master mage as well," Hayes said meekly from behind Nik. "Are you also pulling rank on me?"

She gave him a long-suffering look. "If you intend to cause trouble, I'll be forced to remind you that since you resigned your position as Colton's second, I'm back to being your senior due to having taken the mastery exams before you—at least until you're actually appointed the next Head of Healing."

"Yes, ma'am," he said meekly, and the corners of her lips tugged upward.

Nik cleared his throat pointedly, and the mood of the room shifted.

"Are you really going to let the two of them wander around

alone?" he asked Amara, inclining his head toward Luna and me.

"Certainly. We have no immediate reason to think there's a physical threat lurking in the streets of the city, and you saw Delphine and my reception at the city gates. They're more in danger of being revered than attacked."

"And neither of them is helpless either," Gia added heatedly. "If two mage-level healers can't protect themselves, who can?"

Nik was reluctantly forced to concede, and I threw him a smile. I knew his concern stemmed from an excess of care rather than a lack of belief, and I couldn't bring myself to fault him for that. I also couldn't really blame him for thinking I would be safer with Amara than Luna. But Luna was right that we would create a different impression on our own—especially given Amara's hero status in the city. I had been dragged into the reverence due to my connection to her, but she was the much more recognized figure.

"The two of us will also go out." Amara indicated herself and Hayes. "We both have contacts in the city among different circles, and between us all, we can hopefully get a picture of what's going on."

She looked at Renley with a contrite expression. "I'll be leaving you to babysit these two. My apologies."

He laughed. "I think some quiet brother-sister bonding time is an excellent idea and long overdue." Both the twins rolled their eyes, but I also caught Gia shooting him an affectionate look. It was no wonder Renley was so calm and steady when he constantly had to balance out Gia.

Although the day was coming to a close, no one wanted to wait a whole night without doing anything, so we set out immediately. The two master mages disappeared quickly, heading for their individual contacts, while Luna and I strolled the short distance into the central square.

The day's market had almost wrapped up, with many of the

stall holders busy packing away their remaining wares. We wandered around aimlessly, listening to snatches of conversation from both shoppers and sellers.

Unlike at the gates, nothing in the market gave the overt impression anything had changed. The salt tang in the air, slightly different from the one that had permeated the island, took me straight back to my previous stay in the city, and the people we saw were occupied with the usual business of life. But the longer we listened, the deeper the crease between my eyes grew.

"It's not just me, is it?" I asked Luna. "There's a different tone now from before."

Luna nodded slowly, her eyes scanning the closest row of stalls. "It does seem subtly different. More fearful and insular, maybe? And I haven't heard a single complaint about the guards at the gates, although some of these stallholders must have traveled from out of the city for the market."

"Of course, it could just be because of the rumors about Grey, like Amara said." I frowned at a nearby clump of people who were talking animatedly.

"Yes, it's possible," Luna agreed, although she sounded doubtful.

"Do you think we should try approaching someone directly?" I asked as we neared the fountain at the center of the square. Whatever damage the feature had sustained during the storm had been expertly fixed, and several groups of people lingered around its enormous rim.

I eyed one of the groups whose members appeared around our age. One of the girls caught me looking and stared openly back. I was about to look away when her expression changed, her eyes going round.

She tugged at the arm of the boy beside her, saying something I couldn't catch.

"We might want to move on," I murmured nervously to Luna, but before we could do so, the girl called out loudly.

"Delphine? Luna?"

We both turned to stare at her as the entire group surged toward us. My eyes jumped from face to face until one of them triggered a memory, bringing the identities of all of them rushing to my mind.

"Oh!" I said. "From the hospital!"

The first girl laughed delightedly. "Don't worry if you can't remember our names. I don't know if we even got introduced. But of course we couldn't forget you—our own sleeping beauty."

I winced, flushing painfully while Luna laughed.

"Have you graduated yet?" Luna asked the girl. "Weren't you nearly finished with your apprenticeship last time we were here?"

The girl smiled. "Only ten more days!"

I frowned, confused by their familiarity, and Luna grinned in response. Prodding me lightly in the side with her elbow, she explained, "We worked together while you were slumbering, Hero."

I winced again while the others all jumped in, clamoring to know if Amara was with me and what we'd been doing since our departure from the city.

We answered as evasively as we could, Luna turning off many of their inquiries with questions of her own about the hospital and their work there. She couldn't shield me completely, however.

"Did you marry your prince?" one of the girls called from the back of the group, and most of them laughed.

I froze, remembering how they had exaggerated their own stories, making the tale more and more outlandish until they accidentally stumbled on the truth regarding Nik's identity.

Luna jumped into the gap on my behalf. "Not yet," she said

breezily. "She's been too busy single-handedly holding off an epidemic."

I glared at her as the healing apprentices exclaimed among themselves. I didn't need her spreading more false rumors about my exaggerated heroism.

She just grinned back at me, clearly unrepentant. But her expression changed as the first girl began to press us with questions.

"There's been an epidemic? Where? We haven't heard anything about that."

Luna shot me a concerned look, recognizing her mistake.

"It wasn't near here," I said vaguely, and the girl looked relieved.

The boy next to her shook his head disgustedly, though. "An epidemic? If it's not one thing, it's another. The kingdom isn't what it once was."

My ears pricked up at his comments, and I tried to think how to keep him talking. But another boy jumped in immediately making any response from me unnecessary.

"Some days I think we really should just shut the gate completely," he said, and several voices murmured agreement.

When I frowned, the first girl jumped in quickly. "Not against you, of course! You're one of us now! The heroes of Eldrida will always be welcome in the city."

The rest of the group murmured their agreement, and one of the boys generously added, "You, too, Luna. Everyone who helped us in the storm is welcome here. Those are our true friends." The last was muttered with enough feeling to make me blurt out a question.

"What do you mean? Did some people not help?"

"Where was the capital when our city was being destroyed?" one of the girls said with feeling. "Not here, that's for sure."

"How could they have been here for the storm?" I asked, confused. "No one knew it was coming."

"Precisely," the girl said as if my point flowed perfectly from hers. "They claim everything would fall apart without the Mage's Guild, but where was the warning about the storm from the elements mages?"

"But the storm—" I cut myself off when I realized it wasn't my place to spill the truth about the storm to a group of random apprentices.

"As I said, *you* carry no blame," the first girl said earnestly. "We all saw how hard you worked. Our masters have all been holding you up as a cautionary tale ever since."

They chuckled among themselves, as I tried to hide my astonishment. We had been afraid of people wrongfully blaming the Calistans for the sudden killer storm, but I hadn't expected them to blame the Guild for failing to see the unnatural weather coming. The Eldridan mages must have known for themselves that there was nothing normal about that storm.

One of the girls hissed suddenly, pointing at where the sun had slipped below the buildings on the western side of the square.

"We have to get back to the hospital," one of the boys said, "or else we'll hear it from our masters." He sent us a questioning look. "Do you want to come with us?"

I shook my head quickly. "We have to get back to our own masters."

The other apprentices all accepted this without question, hurrying away in the direction of the hospital.

"I think we really should get back," I said to Luna. "I don't know how long the others will be out, but the market is about finished now."

She agreed without protest, and the two of us hurried back toward the stable that had become our temporary accommodation. I didn't know about Luna, but I had plenty of food for thought. And the more I thought, the less I liked the picture I was building.

FIFTEEN

Nik was waiting for our return in Acorn's stall. I caught his murmured voice before I saw him and peered in at him in surprise.

"She really has mellowed," I said with a grin when I saw how calmly the mare had accepted her visitor.

"You just don't know how much work I put in during our travels." Nik came out into the stable aisle, securing the door behind him. "Did you discover anything?"

"Maybe?" I glanced at Luna who shrugged. "It's hard to say."

He raised an eyebrow, but I just shrugged as well. "There was nothing definitive. Let's wait and find out what the others have discovered before I say anything."

He narrowed his eyes. "You have a theory."

I looked away. "Maybe."

It was unsettling how well he understood me. He was right that I had a theory, but I wasn't willing to say it out loud until I'd heard any other information on hand.

It took several more hours for Amara and Hayes to return. We had prepared a meal in the meantime, and as soon as everyone had finished eating, we gathered in one of the bedrooms.

Luna succinctly described what we had observed about the mood in the city, as well as the unsettling conversation with the other healing apprentices. She apologized for mentioning the epidemic, but none of the others seemed concerned.

"What did your contacts have to say?" I asked Amara.

"The elements mages I could find were withdrawn and cagey," she said.

"The ones you could find?" Gia asked with raised eyebrows.

Amara frowned. "Every time I asked for one of them, I was told he was at the law enforcement hall. It was always said as if I should understand the significance of that, although no one was willing to be drawn out on the topic."

Nik leaned forward. "He's been arrested, then?"

Amara shook her head slowly. "I don't think so. It didn't seem like it from their manner, anyway."

"Did they say anything about the storm?" I asked. "Why aren't they correcting the people's mistaken impressions?"

"All of them seemed weary of that topic," she said. "As if they've grown tired of explaining and being ignored."

"But why would the people ignore them?" Luna asked. "It doesn't make any sense."

"It does if there's someone they trust more telling a different story," Hayes said. "It sounds like I got straighter answers from the healers since they aren't directly involved in the matter. According to them, there's been a great deal of unrest since the storm, with many feeling the capital didn't send enough assistance in the aftermath. One or two loud voices started suggesting the city should have had warning from the capital ahead of time and claiming it showed how little Eldrida is valued and prioritized."

"That doesn't make any sense," Gia said hotly. "Even if it had been a normal storm and a warning had been possible, the

180

warning wouldn't have come from the capital. Eldrida's own elements mages provide that sort of information."

"There's always someone who wants to be enraged about something." Hayes sighed. "And too many people died in that storm. The grieving populace would have been looking for someone to blame, and those in power are the easiest targets. Their own head law keeper was probably the first to be criticized—especially since he happens to be an elements mage instead of the more usual healing mage. So he was probably just trying to deflect blame away from himself, regardless of the consequences. That seems like Miro, from what I know of him."

"He never had the right temperament for the position," Amara said. "I told Anka that years ago."

Hayes shrugged. "There weren't exactly a lot of options. They wouldn't have assigned an elements mage—let alone him —if they had someone better suited who was willing to take the role."

"Which at least partially bears out the people's complaints." Amara sighed. "Eldrida is the furthest city of its size away from the capital, and we all know typical Tartorans have a tendency to look down on those who live east of the forest."

I stayed silent, unable to refute it. Even in distant Tarin I had encountered the occasional snide comment about easterners.

"How long has this issue been fomenting?" Nik looked across at Gia. "Why hasn't Father done anything?"

"Ordinarily he would have," Gia said. "But this is exactly the problem with the fortress mentality they've all adopted. With Miro stirring trouble in order to defend himself, they'd need to send out high level officials to address the issue. At any other time, he would probably have been recalled over this. But they're too afraid to let anyone of strength leave the capital."

"I actually overheard Anka having a conversation about it

with some of her people," Renley interjected. "She seems to have reached a similar conclusion that Miro is transferring blame. While she took the situation seriously, it was prioritized below finding Grey, which is understandable. I think she would have come herself if she wasn't being kept chained to the court."

"That sounds like Anka," Amara said. "I wouldn't want to be the one telling her she has to stay sheltering in Tarona. I can imagine how that conversation went—even if it was with the king. There's a reason a mage as powerful as Anka had a position in Caltor, not the capital."

"They made her Royal Mage," Gia said simply. "Forcibly."

"They did what?" Amara stared at her.

Gia shrugged. "It's a position usually held by an elements mage, but there's no law that prevents a healer from taking the role, and Anka has the strength for it. If she'd cared to, she could have challenged Colton to become Master of Healing when the previous one retired. So there were no arguments she could make against the appointment. And as Royal Mage, she's part of the kingdom's government—the official liaison between the crown and the Triumvirate—so there was no question of her going rogue after that."

"Poor Aunt." Amara gave a pained chuckle. "Not only forced to the capital but chained to the heart of government. I wonder if they realize what they're in for by now?"

"But where does that leave us?" Luna asked. "Should we try to do something about the situation in Eldrida, or do we stay focused on trying to find Grey? Did anyone get word of him?"

Amara shook her head immediately, but Hayes hesitated before following suit. I focused in on him.

"Are you sure—*completely sure*—you didn't hear anything that could have been referencing Grey? Any hint at all?"

Everyone looked at me, surprised, except for Nik, who gave a small smile.

"Delphine has a theory," he said.

Amara raised both eyebrows. "Do you, now? Go on then."

"First I want to hear an answer to my question." I kept my attention on Hayes.

"I specifically asked after any new healers who'd come to the city since the start of winter," he said. "I figured other healers would be the most likely to know about a newcomer. But the only one mentioned was a younger female, a recent graduate of the Guild who I've met myself."

"But?" I said, given how he'd hesitated earlier.

"When they were complaining about the elements mages, a couple of them mentioned a newcomer who sided with Miro and promptly received a position in the law keepers' hall. He's elements affinity, though, not healing. And his vocal support of this nonsense was probably just his way of securing a desirable job despite being a newcomer. But since we're on the lookout for anything out of the ordinary and newcomers in particular..." He shrugged. "It did occur to me that the man in question might be one of Grey's followers acting as his agent."

A tight feeling in my chest robbed me of breath. "Anything else?" I asked, my voice barely above a whisper.

Out of the corner of my eye, I could see Nik watching me with concern, but I was too focused on Hayes to respond to him.

"My reception was markedly chillier than last time," he said, "which seemed suspicious in itself given how much assistance I provided during the storm. But then everyone knows my close connections with the Triumvirate."

"I'm sorry, Hayes," Amara said softly, no doubt comparing her own reception as a hero with his.

He smiled at her. "I'm hardly going to crumble due to a few unjust attitudes. But I grew curious enough to try going directly to the law keepers' hall myself."

Gia raised her eyebrows. "That was bold. What did Miro have to say for himself?"

"I don't know, since I wasn't permitted inside."

"What?" Amara straightened. "That can't be right. Law keepers' halls are required to be open and available for all to enter so that anyone can lodge a complaint."

"Officially, yes," Hayes said. "But who's going to reprimand them for not following the rules when Tarona has stopped sending senior visitors from the central law keepers' hall? From the state of things at the gate, Miro feels a similar fear to the king himself. He's created his own little fortress at the Eldridan law keepers' hall."

"That's one possibility," I murmured, hoping Hayes was right.

"Are you going to tell us the other possibility now?" Nik asked.

I took a deep breath. I had been hoping the others would dispel my fears, but instead their information had only strengthened my concern.

"I've been uncomfortable about something ever since we talked in the crevasse," I said. "I thought about it all the way here to Eldrida, and even so, I couldn't quite make sense of our theory about Grey's plans."

"What theory do you mean?" Hayes's tone was respectful, and he was obviously taking my concerns seriously which only put me more on edge.

"Everyone has been talking as if all Grey needs to do is get access to court, and he'll be able to take over the government and throne—like a puppet master in the background."

"Is that not the case?" Gia's eyes were fastened on my face with almost painful intensity. "That's the impression I had. Can't he use his mesmerizations to control someone's mind?"

"Yes and no. It's not that simple." I paused as I tried to work out the best way to describe it. "Mesmerizations aren't about controlling someone's mind. They're about lies and truth. Of course lies can be used as a vehicle to control someone, but there are significant limits—in particular that it won't last if the lie can be disproved. Just look at the island. It took an entire family of mesmerizers to keep one town subjugated, and even then they couldn't manage it completely. Isolde is a perfect example of the sort of limits I mean—and she was someone who'd been shaped by their lies since birth."

"Isolde?" Renley asked.

"Costas's mother," I explained. "Everyone thought she was dead, but it turns out she was in hiding, leading a sort of passive resistance." I briefly explained her story. "They told her a lie and ordered her to do something in line with that lie. But instead of compelling her to act according to their wishes, their order broke the mesmerization completely."

I tried to think of another example. "Take what the Triumvirate did to Nik. Imagine that Grey was there and had mesmerized both the Triumvirate and the king into believing Nik was a danger to Tartora. That lie would be enough to have them skip Nik in the line of succession in favor of Evermund— we know it's possible for them to act that way because they did it. But what if Grey said that since Nik's such a danger, King Marius should have him killed?"

"Father would never do that," Gia said with confidence. "Nik is his son, and he loves him."

I smiled at her, hoping Nik was hearing her words and believing them.

"Exactly," I said. "It doesn't matter what lies he tells the king, Grey couldn't compel him to kill his own son. And Nik's behavior would soon disprove the original lie, thus breaking the entire mesmerization. There are a hundred traps like that, situations where someone won't react to the lie as intended or where something unforeseen breaks the mesmerization."

"Grey could still cause a lot of damage and chaos," Renley said.

I nodded. "He could, of course, but what would be his

motive? That's the part that had me confused all the way across the desert. As a single individual, he would have to work incredibly hard and incredibly carefully just to maintain a position that would always be insecure. And the attempt would be infinitely harder now that the court is on high alert. Everyone must be afraid of doing anything the least out of character in case others think Grey has gotten to them."

"He might just want to destroy Tartora," Gia said. "From what you've said, he destroyed his own family—and nearly their whole community along with them—and ended up with no personal benefit from it."

As little as I wanted to speak up for Grey in any matter, I couldn't accept the likelihood of her suggestion.

"Grey doesn't have any reason to destroy Tartora," I said. "On the island, he had a personal vendetta against the family who killed his father and caused his and his mother's exile. I dislike Grey as much as anyone—I'm the only one here who's experienced the stomach-churning reality of his mesmerizations—but he isn't some well of endless evil. He's motivated by his own advantage, and I just can't see how destroying the kingdom he wants to live in would be advantageous."

"He might plan to topple everything so he can take over and rebuild from the ashes," Nik said.

I shook my head. "Some people might want that," I said, "if their primary motivation is seeking power. But I don't think that's what Grey wants the most."

"You don't think he wants power?" Hayes sounded unconvinced.

"I think he wants adulation," I said, "which is similar, but not quite the same thing. If he seized power in the situation Nik described, he would hardly become a beloved leader—not when the majority of people would be beyond his ability to mesmerize."

"So you think we've all been focused on the wrong thing," Amara said. "You don't think he's planning to make a move on the throne at all. You think he has something else in mind."

I nodded. "Grey told me a lot of lies to start with, but on his final night on the island—when he realized I'd found a way to break his mesmerizations—his mask dropped, and he admitted a number of truths. In particular, he revealed his greatest grievance against his mother, which seemed to be the source of all his bitterness. Grey wanted back the life she had stolen him away from—not a life where he was head of a vast kingdom, but one he described as a life of luxury, living like a prince among the island's rulers."

"So you think Grey wants a life of wealth, respect, and comfort?" Nik said.

"Yes, and for all Grey's moral failings, he's never been a fool. I think he knows he won't easily find that life anywhere near the Mages' Guild or the court. In the time I was with him, I never heard him say anything about the capital. In fact, in his whole time in Tartora, he always carefully avoided it." I looked at Nik with a challenging expression. "Isn't that right? You tracked him the longest."

Nik brows lowered. "You're right. He never went near the capital."

"Isn't that a good thing?" Gia asked. "If Grey never actually wanted the throne, shouldn't we all be relieved? Why do you look so uncomfortable, Delphine?"

I grimaced. "He didn't talk about the capital, but he did mention somewhere else. Here. Grey spent his childhood and youth believing he and his mother should be living a life of comfort in Eldrida instead of scratching out a lonely existence in the crevasse. He believed his mother could have used her ability to mesmerize to make a place for them here."

"And Nik said from the beginning that Grey had contacts

here—that it would be the most likely place for him to come," Amara said slowly.

"And now that we're here," I said, "we've found that the city is changing. They've closed the gates and all unrest is being directed toward the capital. People are complaining that Tarona doesn't care about the easterners and that they do nothing for Eldrida." I looked at Hayes. "You described Miro as turning the law keepers' hall into a fortress against Grey, but it seems to me it could be something else. Miro could be turning it into a palace."

Gia and Nik sprang to their feet simultaneously.

"You're saying Miro is trying to secede from the kingdom with the eastern part of Tartora?" Gia cried.

"I never liked him," Nik said in tones of contempt. "He was the sort to muss your hair and say something condescending just because you were a child."

"I'm not sure that makes him villainous," Luna said, earning herself a united glare from the twins.

"I agree with Luna," I said. "This Miro might be self-important and self-serving, but the timing is a bit too convenient, don't you think?"

"You suspect Grey has already mesmerized Miro and is working from the shadows?" Amara asked.

"That's what I'm afraid of," I said. "Who knows how many lies he's pumped him with? If Grey is happy with a high position and a luxurious life, he might be willing to lurk behind Miro's rule for the rest of his life, knowing his position of influence will always be secure. Grey has always been good at working out what motivates an individual and how that can be used to his advantage. If he's familiar with Eldrida, then he likely already knew Miro's nature. He would have known that Miro had the conceit and ambition to tear Tartora down the middle, if he only believed he could do it safely."

"The rest of the kingdom won't stand for it!" Gia said fiercely.

"Oh, they won't be happy about it," Hayes said. "But how far do you think they'll go to stop it? If Grey can use Miro and the other officials to convince the easterners they're better off on their own, it would mean all-out war to stop it."

Gia instantly deflated. "Father won't want to kill people in large numbers—not the soldiers he'd have to send, or the easterners either. Instead, he'll try to send a few powerful individuals to infiltrate Miro's circle and put an end to it at the top. But all he'll be doing is sending them into Grey's clutches."

"Calista are close allies, but they're also still in the beginning stages of rebuilding," Nik added. "They won't have the resources to aid us in a drawn-out conflict."

I glanced at Luna who was biting her lip and looking away. Nik was right.

"And the nomad tribes are used to doing things a different way," he continued. "They elect their monarchs, so if Miro can convince them he's acting according to the will of the people, they may side with him over us."

"But the people won't actually be better off," I said, remembering the islanders. "It's all lies about the capital not helping them. Grey himself is the one who first created that storm, and he's the one who provoked the Constantines into strengthening it. King Marius might not get everything right, but the very fact he won't attack proves he does care about the people. Grey, on the other hand, only cares about using them for his own gain. If Miro becomes king of the east with Grey behind him, no one in the new kingdom will ever be safe, even inside their own minds."

"We can't let that happen," Gia declared.

"But hold on," Hayes said. "The theory bears weight, but if Grey's here already, preparing a position for himself, shouldn't there be some sign of him? It can't serve his purposes to be too far in the background, not from what you're describing, Delphine."

"Actually," I said, "I think we already have had news of him."

Everyone frowned at me with varying levels of confusion.

"You were the one to hear, Hayes. You said there was a newcomer who immediately took up a position close to Miro."

"But he has an elements affinity," Hayes said. "Do you mean Grey is using one of his followers to stand in on his behalf?"

I shook my head. "Grey is wily, and even without using mesmerizations, he's well practiced at presenting lies in a way that will evade a healer's truth telling ability. In fact, this is one particular lie he's used before. When we first arrived on the island, he successfully convinced the rest of the Constantines that I had an elements affinity since he didn't want to confess I was a healer. What if he's done the same thing here for himself?"

"That's a sickening thought," Luna said in a horrified voice. "He's already here and right under our noses!"

"Coming to Eldrida seems reckless now," Amara murmured. "We didn't even consider that Grey might not only be here but in a position of power already." She looked at me, fear in her eyes. "We practically announced ourselves at the gate, and then we let you wander all over the city. If Grey hasn't already heard of it, he will soon."

"Me?" I stared back at her. "Why me in particular? We were all out and about."

"But you're the one person Grey must fear the most." Nik's eyes burned into me, hard and determined. "You're the one who not only knows all his secrets but is more powerful than him. He can mesmerize, but so can you—and you can block him and purge his lies as well."

"Thank goodness he doesn't know you worked out how to

purge other people of mesmerizations," Amara said. "If he knew that, he'd tear the city apart to find you."

"Thank goodness for your foresight in coming to this stable instead of an inn," Nik said to her. "How many people know you left Acorn here?"

"No one, as far as I know. Unless the stable master told anyone."

"Someone will need to talk to him," Nik said, brisk and focused now that the threat had narrowed in on me. "He doesn't seem the loquacious type, though, so we might be fortunate."

"We need to get you out of the city, immediately." Luna's eyes were wide, her expression panicked. "But not through that gate. The guards might have orders to stop you. Does anyone know another way out?"

"Wait, stop!" I stared around. "Are you all serious? Do you really mean to smuggle me out of the city? What about stopping Grey and freeing Eldrida before he gets his claws the rest of the way into it? We can't just flee now!"

"We don't have to flee," Hayes said. "But you do. It's too dangerous for you here."

"I can't just leave! You all just said it. The only way to stop this turning into a proper war is to send someone to infiltrate Miro's so-called palace, and I'm the only one it's safe to send. I'm the only one who can protect myself against Grey, and the only one who can reverse his power."

"You want to walk straight into Miro and Grey's arms?" Nik asked, incredulous.

"Think about it," I said. "I can purge Grey's mesmerizations, which means all I have to do is get close enough to Miro to touch him and I can end this whole thing. Miro must be inclined to vainglory if he's ripe for Grey to use like this, but he never tried anything treasonous before. Grey must have convinced him of all kinds of things, including that he's not going to suffer repercussions from Tarona. Everything is playing into Grey's hands because with the capital locked down, there's no one coming to Eldrida to shake those lies. So we need to strip them away ourselves."

I looked directly at Nik. "You don't have to tell me you don't like the idea. I already know that. But it's the only plan we have that might actually work."

CHAPTER

SIXTEEN

The fight only ended when Nik stalked out of the room. I'd managed to convince everyone else—even Amara —but he was stubbornly resistant.

I watched him go with equal parts frustration and sadness. It might be easier if I thought he was being unreasonable, but who wanted the person they loved to throw themselves into danger?

"Is it wrong of me to be a little glad?" Gia asked in my ear as everyone got up and began to spread out, beginning the preparations for bed.

"Glad?" I turned to stare at her.

She gave me a cheeky grin. "I'm not saying the changes in Nik aren't great—they are. But it's nice to know he hasn't turned into an entirely different person."

"Gia." Renley gave her an exasperated look, but she just laughed.

"I like this new kind of selfishness, though," she said. "It suits him better than the old kind."

"Don't worry," I said. "He won't actually try to stop me from doing what needs to be done. He never has before."

Gia shook her head. "Just how much danger do you perpetually throw yourself into?"

"Far too much." Amara approached us with a look of long suffering. "I knew there was a reason I never took apprentices! I'll be gray by the time Delphine graduates."

I threw her a guilty look, and she smiled.

"I know, I know, you can't help yourself," she said. "And how can I stand firm against you when your motives are always so reasonable? I'm the one who chose an unusual apprentice and gave her the promise of an unusual apprenticeship. I can hardly quibble now when things have turned out to be so very unusual."

"Very sensible." Gia nodded approvingly. "My parents could have saved themselves a lot of heartache if they'd accepted it the first time I told them I was never going to fit their plans for me." She glanced toward the door. "Things might have turned out differently if they'd invested in Nik from the beginning and shaped him to be the future king."

Amara followed her gaze, letting her eyes linger on the empty doorway. "Actually, while the path may have been painful, I'm inclined to think things turned out just as they should have. I'm not saying Nik couldn't have been shaped into an adequate king, but I don't think he would have been either a great one or a happy one. Whereas now..." She paused for a moment. "Let's just say I have hopes for him."

Gia burst into laughter, causing both Amara and I to give her affronted looks.

"No, no, I perfectly agree." Gia wiped at her eyes, her mirth finally subsiding. "I just wish Nik could have seen your face and expression when you said that."

Amara gave a reluctant smile. "Your brother may be a powerful mage—officially or unofficially—but he is still a young man, and I know how young people view old fogies like me. Don't worry, I wouldn't say it to him directly."

"Old fogey?" Hayes leaned his head into our little circle. "Speak for yourself. There's never been a more youthful or in touch master mage than me. Just ask all of Colton's apprentices from back when I was his second and did most of their training."

Gia instantly went off into peals of laughter, regaling Luna with tales of how the apprentices had really viewed Hayes. Amara just smiled silently, her eyes meeting Hayes's with both humor and something warmer and more personal. I turned hurriedly away, feeling like an intruder in something private.

"Are you worried?" Renley asked me quietly. "The kingdom is in danger of being split in two, a whole people are blindly walking into the worst kind of subjugation, and you've just volunteered to take an enormous risk on your own, and here they all are—laughing."

I grinned back at him. "Isn't it excellent? How awful it would be if everyone was shuffling around in depression. When I think of everything that has been happening since the moment I got activated..." I shook my head. "Just think what a negative year I might have had if this group of people wasn't able to carry everything lightly!"

"That's the spirit." He smiled. "I know it can take some time to adjust to this crowd, though. I remember my own period of adjustment very clearly. But having a serious air isn't always the mark of those who actually take matters the most seriously when the moment of action comes."

His words reminded me of Clay, who would have been right at home in the center of this moment. Since the first time I'd met him, he had always been smiling and laughing, a cheerful presence in any situation. For the first time I wondered how much of that was his natural personality and how much was a purposeful approach to a life that was often unfair and difficult. When I was as experienced and skilled as him, would I still approach each new moment with the same relaxed good cheer? If not, I hoped I could at least match Renley, who lacked Gia's exuberance but was never a dampening presence. He was like the steady foundation that allowed her wildness to shine.

Gia's stories were still going, but I slipped away from the rest of the group. Descending the stairs, I entered the cold darkness of the stable. The quiet sounds of the horses surrounded me, the occasional swish of a tail, the munching of teeth, or the shifting of hooves. None of them stirred at my arrival, though, and I walked easily down the central aisle, peering into each stall as I passed.

The occasional lantern illuminated some more than others, and when I finally spotted Nik, he was inside Acorn's stall, sitting in near darkness. He looked up, meeting my eyes.

Jumping to his feet, he vaulted over the half door and landed in front of me in the light of the closest lantern.

"You've finished pacing up and down, then?" I asked with a small smile.

He ran a hand through his hair and gave me a rueful smile in return. "You know me too well. I thought I was going to lose my mind cooped up in that tiny room with so many people."

I refrained from pointing out that the rooms we had been given were hardly tiny. Instead I slid my fingers into the hair on either side of his head.

"I could see you were about to lose it in there."

He sighed, leaning his head slightly against my right hand.

"Do you know how many times I've wished you weren't the sort of person who considers the greater good before your own safety?" he asked. "And do you know what I always think next?"

"No, what?" I asked, playing along.

He slipped his hands around my waist. "I remember that I love you for the person you are. So how can I wish for you to turn into someone else?"

I ran my hands down the side of his head, cupping his face

196

in my hands. "If you could take my place in this and go in my stead, would you?"

"In a heartbeat," he said instantly.

I smiled. "In that case, now that we've established we're *both* selfless people—in our own ways—shall we move on to more practical matters?"

"Practical matters?" His eyes had dropped to my lips, and he only seemed to be half listening.

"Yes. Namely, how are we going to infiltrate Miro's law keepers' hall?"

"We?" Nik's eyes sprang back to mine, his full attention restored. "When you say we…"

"You will come with me, won't you?" I asked. "I might be willing to risk myself in a situation as dire as this one, but I'd rather not go in there without any backup."

"Delphine!" He pulled me flush against him and pressed his lips to mine.

I leaned into the kiss, ready to let the rest of the world fade away for as many moments as he wanted. But all too soon he was drawing back, his eyes a little wild.

"Do you really mean it? You want me to come with you?"

I nodded, and he squeezed me close again, burying his face in my hair with a shudder.

"I've been down here trying to work out how to not lose my mind while you were off attempting to take on Grey and his minions on your own."

"I know." I smiled tenderly up at him. "I understand why you don't want me to go, and I also appreciate that you know you can't stop me. But most of all, I want us to do things together." I hesitated, afraid to keep going. "That's the future I want, Nik. Doing things together with you for the rest of my life."

I held his gaze, even as the color drained from his face, his arms going rigid around me. For a long moment we stayed locked there, motionless.

"I wish…" He shuddered again. "There's nothing I want more, Delphine. You know that, don't you?" He sounded desperate. "But I won't turn you into an outcast at my side. I can't do that."

I nodded slowly, fighting back tears. Did he really think it impossible he could return from being a reneger?

Swallowing, I forced a brisker tone. "As I said, we really do need to think about practical matters. It's all well and good for me to say I'm willing to go into the law keepers' hall to confront Miro, but how am I going to get inside? From Hayes's experience, we know they're not just letting people walk in."

"Especially not you," Nik said, relaxing slightly at the change in topic. "Of all of us, you're the one whose face Grey and his followers know best. Most of them still haven't actually seen me, and even Grey himself has only seen me briefly on a couple of occasions, both at night."

"So going in the front door isn't an option," I said. "And I'm guessing any back doors are sealed tight."

Nik let me go, pacing a few steps away and staring into the darkness of an empty stall, clearly thinking.

"If it was just me, I'm confident I could get in," he said. "All the law keepers' halls across Tartora are the same, and I've spent time at two of the ones in the capital. If you can climb up to the higher levels, the design of the windows…" He trailed off as he looked back at me.

"Given your height and all those arm muscles, I'm quite sure you could do it," I said. "Me on the other hand…" I held out my arms and did a spin on the spot. "We're going to need a different plan, I'm afraid."

A sudden throat clearing made us both startle. Nik strode forward to shield me with his body, but it was only the stable master who stepped out of the shadows.

"I wondered who was making a ruckus in my stables," he said gruffly, eyeing us disapprovingly.

I flushed, hoping he had only just come out to investigate and hadn't seen our earlier interactions.

"Apologies," Nik said curtly. "We'll return upstairs."

He took my hand, starting to lead me toward the stairs. But the stable master cleared his throat again, making us stop. A chill ran through me. Had he recognized Nik?

"I might be able to help with that problem of yours." He looked at us expectantly while we stared back at him blankly.

"Problem?" I asked tentatively when he stayed silent.

"Getting into Miro's lair," he said matter-of-factly. "Not you." He eyed Nik's height disapprovingly. "But I could get you in." He nodded at me.

Nik frowned, taking a step toward him. I wasn't sure if he intended the effect to be menacing, but I would have backed away if I'd been the other man. The stable master held his ground, however, looking unbothered.

"Couldn't help overhearing that last bit," he said. "The girl said she couldn't climb in, so seems to me, she'd be better off going through one of the doors."

"We understand they're not allowing people to just walk in anymore," I said cautiously.

"Aye, that's the case," he said. "But some people are allowed in."

I waited, eyebrows raised, and he sighed and continued. "My brother-in-law supplies fresh produce to the hall. He takes a hand cart all the way through to the kitchens and storerooms from what he's described.

"Why would you help us?" Nik asked. "Why would your brother-in-law?"

"I may be an old stable master in Eldrida," the man said, "but that doesn't mean I've never been anywhere else. I've visited the capital more than once. Seen the royal family, even, a number of years ago now."

Nik stiffened, and I gasped.

He gave a raspy chuckle. "I always had a way with faces. Your hair's changed, but your face is the same. And that sister of yours hasn't changed a jot. You can't fault a man for being curious about royalty, renegers, and master mages hiding out in his stable."

"You were listening upstairs?" I asked, mentally scrambling to remember everything we'd said.

He shrugged. "Didn't quite understand everything. This whole mesmerizing business is a mite confusing. But I got the gist, and it explains the strangeness that's been going on here lately."

Nik's stiff, threatening posture hadn't changed, but I placed a restraining hand on his arm, my eyes on the man as he continued.

"Not everyone likes what's been going on in the city," he said. "Ain't no good going to come from cutting ourselves off. And as for Miro and his cronies..." He shook his head. "They might not lie directly to the crowds, but I went to hear them speak myself, and there's no hiding the whiff of deception about them."

I raised an eyebrow. "Did you ever consider a career in law enforcement? Master Anka would be glad to have you." It wasn't surprising he had a healing affinity since he worked with animals, but he clearly had the sort of law keeping talent I'd heard Anka talking about.

The stable master chuckled. "That's a business for young heads like you two. Me, I've always preferred horses to people. They're more straightforward. No need to look for lies with them." He looked me straight in the eyes. "My brother-in-law has an elements affinity, and he's told me more than once that the storm came out of nowhere, and there's nothing the capital could have done about it. We both think this city would be better off without Miro. If you're going to put a stop to his nonsense, we'll do what we can to help you. Including turning a blind eye to this one." He nodded toward Nik.

I relaxed completely. "He's telling the truth."

I smiled at the stable master. It was nice working with another healer, even a weak one. He understood that I wanted to hear him state the situation clearly. After seeing Grey at work, I was becoming all too familiar with the ways people shaped words for deceptive purposes.

"If I get in via the produce cart, you're confident you can get yourself in?" I asked Nik.

He nodded, his expression determined.

"In that case," I said. "We should go talk to the others. I think we have a plan."

CHAPTER
SEVENTEEN

The stable master's brother-in-law was next due to deliver supplies to the law keepers' hall the following morning, so we didn't have long to debate the details. But considering how much couldn't be known, I preferred it that way. Waiting around would only make me nervous and give more time for Grey to track us down.

When the stable master returned from an early morning visit with his relative and instructed me to come with him, Amara protested. She wanted to accompany us as far as the cart, at least, and Hayes only just managed to convince her to let me go alone.

I could understand her feelings. Hayes, Luna, and I could all sense the truth of the stable master's words, but she had to go on faith. If she wasn't so well-known in Eldrida, I would have been tempted to let her walk with us as far as the brother-in-law. But with her hero status, it wasn't worth the risk.

Nik would have volunteered in her place, of course, but he was already long gone. He had disappeared into the night the moment we agreed on the plan and was hopefully already inside the hall. I had been spending the hours since his departure trying not to picture him discovered and mesmerized by

Grey. I could now understand firsthand why he hadn't wanted to be left behind with nothing to do but wait and wonder.

There was enough cool bite in the morning air to justify my wearing a cloak as we walked through the city, and it took all my self-control not to keep tugging the hood down further over my face. Instead I kept my head down as I wound through the streets in the wake of the stable master.

The morning was advanced enough that many other people were also out on various forms of business, and snatches of their conversation drifted past my ears. Some talked of their children or the day's prices for vegetables, but any time anyone mentioned the capital in a disparaging way, my insides clenched a little tighter. Did they really believe the throne and Guild were to blame for their recent woes, or had they already had the misfortune to run into Grey?

The stable master moved at a surprising pace given his age, and we were soon in an unfamiliar part of the city. When a tall, white marble building loomed before us, I jumped and came to a standstill. Staring up at it, I forgot to keep my face covered.

"What are you doing?" The stable master jerked my arm, pulling me back into movement.

I stumbled behind him, my thoughts churning. "Why are we at the law keepers' hall? Aren't you supposed to be taking me to your brother-in-law?"

Suspicious tension flooded my body, although I couldn't make sense of it. There had been no lie in his words when he had repeatedly stated his intentions and our destination. But I couldn't be mistaken in the building either. The law keepers' halls across Tartora had all been built in the same era to the same plans, and I had come to recognize one easily, even despite the similarity they bore to the public hospitals.

"My brother-in-law lives on the other side of the hall," the stable master said. "We'll be meeting him a few streets further on."

"Oh." The possibility was so obvious that I didn't know why I hadn't thought of it immediately. "Of course."

But now that my nervous tension had exploded, I couldn't easily get it to recede. I was practically trembling as we turned down a side street and passed down the side of the hall.

A plain, unembellished door swung open as we approached. I faltered, but the stable master kept moving steadily. I pushed myself back into movement as well, not wanting to draw attention to us, but my pace had slowed to a crawl.

My face was angled downward, keeping my features from view, but I couldn't resist a quick glance upward as two young men exited the building. They were moving slowly despite the air of excitement that clung to their frame and words.

"I thought you were just coming to keep me company," the first said. "I didn't expect you to sign up yourself!"

"How could I not once I heard the situation?" the second exclaimed. "If the capital won't assign us enough law keepers to ensure the city's safety, we have to step up. It's the only right thing to do."

"Won't your master be upset?" the first asked as I drew level with them. "Mine has already signed on another apprentice. He couldn't afford to keep me on now that I've graduated since he would have to pay me wages and not just room and board. But yours was expecting you to stay and work with him, wasn't he?"

Neither spared me a glance as we passed each other, too absorbed in their conversation, but I caught the shadow of uncertainty cross the second's face. He quickly shrugged it off, however.

"I'm graduated now, just like you, which means I'm free to choose where I work. He has no hold over me. I'm sure when I explain the situation, he'll see that I'm doing this for the good of..." His voice faded as they turned onto the main street.

I looked forward again to find the stable master waiting for me, an impatient look on his face.

"Sorry," I murmured, hurrying to catch up with him.

A sick, churning feeling was growing in my gut. Miro was building a private army of youths, and something—or someone—was swaying them to sign up, despite their previous plans and intentions. I had to stop him before he started sending them off to die.

Nik's parting message echoed in my mind. He had leaned in to press a brief kiss to my lips, despite the presence of the others, and I had been so flustered I had nearly missed his quiet words.

"Protect yourself," he'd whispered, the words fierce. "Don't forget what Hayes told you. Every time you get injured, you're putting your future at risk."

I shivered at the memory, the words more frightening now than they had been then. Because now my mission had a face—two faces—and I couldn't afford to give up, no matter what risks were required.

I was still thinking of the two boys when my guide directed me into a small, fenced yard. A stoic-looking man, some years younger than the stable master, waited for us beside a sturdy hand cart that had been piled high with crates, barrels, and sacks of food.

"About time," he said, and the stable master grunted in reply. "All I have to do is get you in, correct?" he asked me.

I nodded. "Just get me inside the hall. I don't want you getting caught up in this any more than you need to."

The man nodded, looking satisfied with my answer.

I hesitated, clearing my throat. "Could you please—?"

The stable master elbowed the other man, whose frown turned into a look of begrudging understanding.

"I'm not looking for extra trouble, but I've seen the strangeness of things inside that hall for myself. They may all worship that Slate fellow, but I don't want him anywhere near me." He shook himself. "I won't betray you, if that's what you're worried about."

I nodded my thanks for his speaking his assurances out loud, but I couldn't resist questioning him.

"Slate?" I asked.

"That new elements mage Miro is so fond of. From the way everyone talks, you'd think he's keeping things running single-handedly, but I've never seen him lift a finger myself."

Slate. Grey. It had to be. My heart sank at the further confirmation of my theory.

"You'll just need to hop in here," the man said, driving out immediate thoughts of Grey.

"I'm sorry, where?" I asked, sure I must have misunderstood.

"You're a small enough thing, like me brother said. You should fit in," he said, as if climbing into a barrel was a perfectly ordinary thing to do.

"I thought you were just going to throw a blanket over me or something," I said.

"Not if you want to go undiscovered," he said. "I'll be met at the door and escorted to one of the storerooms where I'll receive assistance unloading the cart. You'll just need to sit right and tight until we've all departed. The lid won't be nailed down or anything, so if you give it a firm push, it will pop right off, and you can climb out easy enough. Look, there are even holes that will let the air in."

"An excellent plan." The stable master clapped him on the back, as if proud of his family member's good thinking.

I eyed the barrel dubiously. Although I could think of no solid objection, the idea of being restrained inside the barrel sent a bead of sweat running down my back.

But thought of the young soldier made me straighten. I could do this. I had to do this.

The barrel had already been loaded onto the cart, so I had to clamber up a fair way before I could lower myself into it. Both men offered me steadying hands, however, and the feat proved easier than I'd feared.

It was a harder task to make myself sit down, curling my body to fit the shape of the barrel, but that was due to mental resistance rather than physical difficulty. The brother-in-law had picked a good-sized barrel, and if anything, I would have to worry about flopping around when I was unloaded from the cart.

The lid went on, sending me into near darkness and muffling the sound of the two men exchanging final words. All too soon, however, we lurched into motion, sending me bouncing against one side of the barrel.

I was definitely going to have a problem when I was unloaded. If one of the helpers picked me up, they needed to believe there was grain or pieces of fruit in here, not one large, awkwardly shaped girl.

By the time I was dragged up a ramp and heard greetings being called out, I had finally arranged myself to my satisfaction, my arms and legs braced against the sides of the barrel. I waited, new pricks of sweat breaking out all over me as the cart was pulled through the back corridors of the hall.

When a thump finally sounded and we settled into stillness, my muscles were so tense I thought I was going to burst. I had to continue waiting, however, as the contents toward the back of the cart were unloaded first.

"What about this one, then?" an unfamiliar voice called out just above me.

I held my breath and squeezed my eyes shut, as if that would make a difference.

"That one's apples."

The man beside me grunted in response, the location of the sound suggesting he had squatted down. I strained my limbs against the sides of the barrel, holding myself in position as I was lifted suddenly into the air.

"Oof!" The man exclaimed as I was rocked violently from side to side, barely holding my position. "You really packed them in this time!"

"Only the best for the law keepers' hall," the delivery man responded, making the helper grunt again.

I dropped suddenly downward, barely suppressing a cry of pain as my rear end hit the ground. Tears welled in my eyes as I held another breath, waiting for the sound of footsteps moving away from the barrel.

Finally they came, and I allowed myself to relax, my arms and legs dropping limply. I couldn't relax for long, however. I needed to listen if I wanted to work out when everyone had left the room.

Now that my barrel had been unloaded, it seemed to take forever for them to unload the remaining supplies. But finally I heard the creaking of wheels as the cart was pulled out of the room, followed by a number of clomping feet and dwindling voices.

I remained motionless until I heard the door close, however, and even then, I made myself count to a hundred. When no further sounds reached my ears during that time, I placed both hands against the lid of the barrel.

Pushing upward, I displaced it, carefully keeping hold of the edges rather than letting it fall to the floor with a crash. I wanted to burst out of the barrel at all speed, but I forced myself to move slowly.

As soon as my head was free, I froze and examined the room. It was mostly dark, although some light leaked in from under the door and through the one dusty window in the far wall. But my eyes were already adjusted after the dim inside the barrel, and I quickly ascertained that I was alone.

The moment I reached this conclusion, I clambered the rest

of the way out of the barrel, nearly knocking it over in my haste. I caught myself and it just in time, placing it carefully back upright and setting the lid in place.

Stepping back, I examined it and nodded. From the outside, it looked undisturbed.

I crept toward the door, wondering what I would do if I found it locked. Thoughts of a locked door made me think of Nik. He could easily take care of that problem, but where was he now?

He had to be inside the hall, but where had he chosen to hide? I looked over my shoulder, although I knew it was only wishful thinking that he might appear out of the depths of the room. It was better if I thought of myself as alone, anyway. It would make me that much more careful.

Pressing my ear against the door, I checked for silence before even attempting to turn the door handle. To my relief, it responded easily beneath my hand. Apparently the hall's residents trusted their own and didn't feel it necessary to lock away their supplies.

Easing the door open, I slipped out into the empty corridor beyond. I had spent some time in Caltor's law keepers' hall, so I was familiar with the location of the suite of rooms used by the head of the hall. But that did me little good when I didn't know my starting point. I had never had occasion to visit the kitchen or storerooms of Caltor's hall.

I had two options. I could keep my cloak and skulk around, keeping to back corridors and attempting to avoid running into anyone. Or I could leave my cloak behind and walk confidently through the hall, trying to look like I belonged. With the doors barred to outsiders, anyone already inside would be assumed to be a legitimate presence.

Taking a gamble, I folded my cloak and stashed it back inside the storeroom. Forcing my head high, I headed left, moving toward the main part of the hall. Once I reached the more public areas, I would be able to work out where I was and go from there.

The true test came when I heard footsteps. It was too late to change strategy, though, so I kept my pace steady, hiding my hands in my skirts to conceal their trembling.

The approaching people turned out to be servants. The older woman was too busy berating a timid-looking girl to pay me any heed. The girl glanced up as they passed me, a slight wrinkle appearing between her brows. But she quickly cast her eyes back down, making no comment. Even if she questioned my presence, she didn't look like she was going to say anything.

I breathed a little easier as I rounded a corner and left their sight. My spirits lifted even further when I recognized a staircase ahead of me. Hurrying up it, I finally found myself in a familiar corridor. Best of all, I didn't have far to go to reach Miro's office. They must have positioned his rooms so his food wouldn't get cold while it was being brought from the kitchens.

Hurrying down the corridor, I almost didn't hear the footsteps approaching from a side hallway. There was more than one pair of feet, by the sound of it, although they weren't moving in sync.

"Excuse me!" a strident male voice called. "Who are you?"

I froze, the blood draining from my face. But when I looked around, no one had come into sight. Both sets of footsteps had stopped, however, and I realized the man was addressing an unseen person in the side corridor.

Creeping forward, I peered around the corner to see an astonished-looking girl with a duster in her hand.

"I'm one of the maids," she said with a confused look.

The young man confronting her frowned deeply, clearly trying to look more important and officious than his years suggested.

"I don't recognize you."

The girl rolled her eyes. "I didn't realize new maids were brought to you for inspection before starting work."

The man bristled, clearly not appreciating her tone.

"Unapproved people are not permitted to wander the law keepers' hall," he said pompously. "If you are who you say you are, I'm sure you'll have no problem coming with me to—"

The girl put her hands on her hips and glared at him. "Of course I have a problem with it! We're behind work for the morning as it is. If you have an issue, you can go on your own."

The man swelled with wrath, his eyes bulging, but before he could say anything, another woman appeared from a side room.

"Where are—oh." She gave the man an unimpressed look. "It's you. I should have guessed. Stop harassing the new maid and let her get back to her work, or I'll have to report you again."

The young man drew himself up to his full height, but he couldn't entirely hide his chagrin.

"It is the duty of all law keepers to question the presence of anyone who might not belong in the hall," he said. "I was merely doing my duty."

"Well go do your duty on someone else's time," the woman said tartly. "I've had enough of your nonsense."

The girl with the duster laughed and hurried into the room behind the other woman, leaving the young guard sputtering alone in the corridor. I whisked my head back around the corner, my heart racing.

He was clearly the last person I wanted to run into, even before he'd been embarrassed and enraged by the two women. If he caught sight of me, there would be no one to shield me from his pompous meddling, and I might actually find myself dragged off to whatever authority figure he'd been intending to appeal to.

I glanced around wildly, my eyes landing on the smooth door used for storage closets. Prying up the ring that lay

212

recessed in the wood, I pulled the door open and propelled myself inside, gently closing the door behind me.

It was nearly pitch-black inside, but I ignored the closet's contents, my attention on the door as the sound of the man's footsteps resumed. My breaths kept pace with his steps while my heart raced wildly ahead, pattering away as if I was already in his clutches.

Thank goodness he'd been held up in the other corridor, and I'd had the chance to see who I was dealing with. If I hadn't hidden myself away—

My thoughts cut off as the speed of his steps changed. Surely it was coincidence he was slowing down so near my hiding place. There was no way he could have seen me from around the corner.

"Why am I being asked to fetch supplies?" The indignant mutter reached my ears through the wood of the door. "It's a waste of a soldier and an insult to my dignity. If they knew what they were doing, they wouldn't—"

The door swung open, and the law keeper cut off mid-sentence. Taken by surprise, we both stood frozen, staring at each other.

EIGHTEEN

"What...?" the guard spluttered, his eyes roaming over the closet behind me. "Why are you in here in the dark?" A suspicious look descended over his face, and he lunged for me.

I moved at the same time, making a grab for his wrist. He was obviously inexperienced because he hadn't even considered the possibility I might be a healer. By the time he realized what I was doing, I had already latched onto the exposed skin.

For half a second, I considered the option of mesmerizing him. All I had to do was convince him he'd seen me cleaning the hall previously, and the problem would be solved without harm to anyone.

But before the temptation could properly set in, I rejected it. During the weeks I had spent purging the minds of the islanders one by one, I had made myself a promise. I was never mesmerizing anyone again, no matter what the reason. Reaching into someone's mind by force was a line that should never be crossed, no matter what.

If I decided it was all right to do it now in order to save lives, where did the argument end? Would I one day find myself enthralling my children to keep them away from any possible dangers?

But even without mesmerization, I was still a healer. As soon as I made contact, I pushed my power into his body. With only a small effort, I could easily end his life or even leave him permanently incapacitated. But this guard, no matter how officious, was not my enemy.

Instead of harming him, I used my power to put him to sleep. His eyes drifted closed mid protest, and he slumped forward onto me. I staggered back into a row of shelving, only just managing to catch him under his arms.

Struggling with his weight in the small space, I managed to get him down onto the floor and then onto his back. His legs sprawled out into the corridor, however, where they would draw the attention of anyone walking by. Leaping over him, I propped both of his knees up, but his legs immediately flopped back down.

I stepped back and considered the problem, my eyes landing on the door. Closing it part way, I wedged his feet against the wood so that as I pushed it closed, his feet moved back as well, pushing his knees up into a steeper angle.

I barely managed to get the door latched, stepping back with a sigh of relief. I had no time to waste, though. He might wake at any moment, and he would instantly raise the alarm when he did. I had to find Miro immediately.

Abandoning subtlety, I took off down the corridor at a sprint. When I tried to stop outside a door with an elaborate handle, I was moving so fast that I continued to slide forward. Spinning, I leaped back toward the door and pulled it roughly open.

Gasping for breath, I stumbled inside the room, pulling the door closed behind me. For a blank moment, I thought I'd come to the wrong place. The dark wood desk I had expected to see was nowhere in sight. Instead, an enormous, carved wooden

216

chair with a high back and thick arms stood on the far side of the room. A row of simpler chairs ran down the room to the left and right, creating a space that felt far more like an audience chamber than an office. Even more shocking was the change from the familiar red carpet and curtains I had grown used to in Anka's office. In Eldrida, they had been replaced with a deep purple—a shade whose use was forbidden beyond the royal family and Royal Mage.

I gasped. If we hadn't already guessed Miro's intentions, the room clearly announced them. Its very brazenness took my breath away. How far had his plotting already progressed?

"And who might you be?" The oily voice, amused rather than shocked, made me spin toward the row of tall windows.

A middle-aged man stood in one of the windows, holding a document to the light. A second, younger man stood with him, but I recognized with sweeping relief that it wasn't Grey. The assistant stared at me with his mouth open, displaying all the surprise the older man lacked.

"Are you Miro, the head of this hall?" I asked boldly.

Both men raised their eyebrows at my impudence.

"I am," the older man said, still amused. "Do you have a grievance to bring to the law keepers?"

The younger man bristled. "If so, there are proper avenues! You can't come bursting in here."

I ignored him, my eyes on Miro. "I come with a warning."

"How fascinating." Miro looked me up and down as if I were some sort of unique specimen, briefly interesting but ultimately unimportant.

I edged slowly closer, eyeing the assistant. He looked like an administrator, not a soldier, but I didn't want to discover my mistake too late. It might be safer to put him to sleep before I attempted to make contact with Miro.

"I'll go and fetch someone," the man muttered to Miro who still hadn't looked away from me.

He started toward the door. I waited until he passed closest to me before lunging for him. He exclaimed, trying to evade me, but I was quicker. Thrusting my hand at his face, I made contact with his skin and put him straight to sleep.

He slumped to the ground so quickly that I barely managed to catch him before his head hit the ground. Laying him down, I immediately rushed back toward Miro, spurred on by the distant sounds of shouts and running feet. The guard in the closet must have woken up.

"You're more resourceful than I expected," Miro said.

"What—? No, never mind." I shook my head.

There was no point trying to have a conversation with him before I purged his mind. When I was finished, we could talk properly, without hurry, since he could call off the approaching guards.

I expected him to try to evade me when I reached for him, but he allowed me to take his wrist without protest. Brushing aside the strangeness of it, I pushed my power into him and called up his wall.

As it pushed my power out, I fell back physically as well, panting as I looked at him with wide eyes. He continued to look back at me with the same disquieting smile. I waited a breath and then another, ready for the look of confusion and horror to overtake him. Nothing happened.

"Slate said we didn't need to go looking for you, that you would come to us," he said conversationally. "But I didn't entirely believe him."

"What?" I asked, my thoughts stuttering at his unexpected reaction. "Don't you see? Slate is Grey, and he's been lying to you this whole time. We call it mesmerizing, and it's the reason you've been doing all this."

I gestured around at the transformed room, my breath coming heavily as I tried to make sense of what was happening.

"I'm not sure whether to be flattered at your belief in my

loyalty or offended that you think I'm a mindless follower." His eyes narrowed. "I can certainly see how you might be useful, however. There's always value in an insurance policy. I wonder..." He tapped his chin thoughtfully, breaking off when the door to the room was wrenched open.

The man who walked in was clearly unwelcome, given Miro's startled, unhappy expression. His irritation was quickly swallowed by a welcoming smile, but his true feelings had been visible long enough for Grey to smile knowingly.

"Not quite ready to see me?" he asked mockingly. "However useful she may appear to be, Miro, she's not worth the risk. Take my word on that. Or has she already gotten to you?"

His mocking look made Miro straighten, his face turning cold.

"Of course not. I'm not such an easy target."

"Naturally not. My mistake." Grey bowed slightly, but in a negligent way that robbed the movement of any respect.

I stood motionless, staring across the room at Grey. I had thought my theories so clever, but I had made a terrible, fatal mistake. I had said we didn't know how many lies Grey had forced into Miro for him to choose this path, but it had never occurred to me that the number might be zero.

"You really are an appealing tool, Delphine," Grey said conversationally. "You have more value than all my other followers put together. Such a pity." He strolled closer but carefully stopped outside of touching distance.

I glared at him, my hands balling into fists at my side. "I am not a tool to be used at whim by others!"

"Yes, that is precisely the problem," he agreed, but even as he said it, there was a hungry look in his eyes.

"It rankles, doesn't it?" I poured every ounce of disdain and superiority I could into the words. "We both started out with a special skill, but I was able to learn yours and you could never learn mine. It must gall you to know you aren't the strongest person in this room."

Grey scoffed, but something unpleasant flashed in his eyes. Even so, he didn't step closer.

"Smart, strong, and beautiful," he said softly. "Are there any limits to what we could have achieved together? I think not. But you won't find me an easy target now. No matter how much you goad my pride, I'm too wily to offer you a contest." He flicked his arm, briefly exposing a flash of skin along his wrist while he watched me with a knowing smile.

My lips tightened, flattening into a thin line. I had walked straight into their trap, and now there was no easy way out. Everything had depended on Miro waking up from his enthrallment and turning on Grey in betrayed wrath.

Fear clawed at my throat, making it hard to breathe. But I couldn't give in to it now. If I was going to survive, I had to keep all my wits about me.

"An impasse, then?" I asked calmly, proud of my voice for not shaking.

"Oh, I hardly think that." Grey inclined his head toward the open door and two guards stepped into the room, determined looks on their faces.

Miro might not be mesmerized, but I would have been willing to bet these two were from the fanatical gleam in their eyes.

"You're really all right with this?" I asked Miro, desperation making my voice harsh. "You have no problem with Grey mesmerizing your people, as long as you get to sit on a pretty throne?" I glanced derisively at the elaborate seat.

"And why wouldn't I be?" he asked. "Marius's line is unworthy of the Tartoran throne—the Triumvirate themselves gave that ruling."

The slightest twitch of movement in one of the floor length curtains caught my attention. I kept my gaze on Miro, my heart somehow beating even harder as a terrible possibility occurred to me.

He was still talking, although I was barely listening.

"The Triumvirate's problem is that they're cowards!" he declared, working himself into a rant. "They recognized the problem, but they're too weak to look further afield than a cousin. I will never be given the recognition I deserve in Tartora, so why shouldn't I take something they don't even value and make it great? Who in the rest of the kingdom even values the east?"

222

The two guards nodded, as if they found this slightly unhinged spiel inspiring.

I flinched, the desire to look toward the curtain almost mastering me.

"I don't know how you escaped Ignatius," Grey murmured. "But I should warn you that I'm much more thorough than my cousin."

"Ignatius is dead," I said baldly. "Along with your entire family. The island is free of the lot of you now. Only the Constantines who actually cared are left."

Something flashed in his eyes, some glimmer of distant surprise and grief, but he shrugged it off quickly. "So poor, outcast Costas is on his own, is he?"

"Far from it," I said. "His mother is with him."

"Aunt Isolde?" Grey stared at me, his face blank for a moment before he shrugged and smiled again.

"The island is no longer my concern. I have a larger prize in mind now."

The guards behind him drew their swords, distracting me from Grey's face.

"Don't worry," he continued. "They've been trained how to deal with healers. It really hasn't been a pleasure, Delphine."

With one final mocking smile, he disappeared out the door, leaving a clear path for his guards to reach me. I backed up, putting myself closer to Miro, but he called out in a panicked voice and several more guards ran into the room, rushing to form a protective ring around him. His assistant had also woken and stood to join the guards, shaking his head as if to clear his groggy thoughts.

As Grey's guards advanced toward me, I pulled out the knife at my belt. It wouldn't do much good against their longer blades, but I wanted to go down fighting, at least. The feel of the hilt in my hand recalled the memory of when Nik gave the knife to me. I should have kissed him then. I wished I had. I wished I hadn't let any of our moments together slip away.

The curtains on the side of the room swung dramatically aside, and Nik lunged into the room as if pulled out by my thoughts. I dropped instinctively to the ground, curling into a ball as he leaped straight over me to meet the blades of my attackers with his own.

Miro gave a startled cry, and the guards surrounding him rushed forward to support the two now facing Nik. But Nik fought with a ferocity I'd never seen, his blade moving too fast to follow. Even so, his skill alone wouldn't have been enough against so many opponents. But Nik had more ways to fight than with a sword.

The chairs from the two rows shuddered into movement, their wood creaking as it responded to the pull of Nik's power. They rose into the air before flying across the room in every direction, exploding spectacularly into spears of wood as they collided with walls and people.

The guards shouted, some abandoning their weapons to shield their heads, while others went down, hit by one of the chairs. The two who had come in with Grey kept their focus, however. Ducking and weaving through the chaos, they closed in on Nik as he retreated toward the throne—the only chair not to have moved.

I looked around, wondering how I could help, and my eyes latched onto Miro. His earlier assurance had vanished completely, beads of sweat appearing along his brow. Inching along the wall, he was attempting to reach the door and escape the fighting.

Narrowing my eyes, I crawled across the floor, keeping below the smashed pieces of wood shooting across the room. Grey had already escaped, but I wasn't letting Miro get away as well.

He let out a sigh as he reached the door, pausing briefly to glance back over his shoulder at the chaos he was escaping. The brief pause gave me just long enough to reach him.

Stretching out my arm, my fingers latched around his ankle, burrowing until they found skin. He shrieked and tried to pull his leg free, but the effort only sent him toppling sideways.

I clung on as he fell hard, most of his body outside in the corridor. Dragged forward by my arm, my muscles strained to maintain contact as I sent my power spearing into him.

He stopped fighting instantly, his body relaxing into the ground as sleep took him. I took a deep breath and crawled forward to sit on his chest. The pounding of feet preceded the arrival of another column of running guards.

I grabbed Miro's floppy arm and held it aloft, my fingers curled obviously around his skin.

"I'm a healer!" I shouted in my loudest voice, and they all froze.

The men inside were Grey's people, and they wouldn't stop to protect Miro, but these were ordinary law keepers trained to respect their head of hall.

"Who are you?" called the captain at the front of the line.

"I'm an agent of the crown," I said, thinking on my feet. "And I'm arresting Miro on charges of treason against Tartora."

"And if we don't recognize your authority?" the captain asked in a hard voice.

"Are you a healer?" I asked, taking a gamble based on his rank.

He hesitated before nodding curtly.

"Then you can see the truth of my words. Any of the rest of you who are healers should listen closely too. You've been lied to, manipulated, and tricked by Miro and the man you call Slate."

The law keepers in the corridor shifted, looking at each other warily.

"You can't trust the thoughts in your head or even your own memories," I said.

"What are you saying?" the captain asked, but the tone of his voice had changed, a look of horror creeping into his eyes.

I focused on him. "From the look on your face, you've heard the official warnings from Tarona about the healer Grey."

The captain slowly nodded.

"Slate is Grey," I said. "And Miro knows it."

"Impossible." The man's voice sounded dry. "Slate is an elements mage."

"Tell me," I said. "Did you see evidence of that before you touched him for the first time? If your only memories are from after that time, they may be false ones, created by your mind to support his mesmerized lies."

"Captain," said one of the men tentatively. "What's she talking about? Everything she's saying has the ring of truth, but it doesn't make any sense. What's this about mesmerizing?"

As I had suspected, only those of sufficient rank had been included in the official warning from the capital. The king must be worried about creating mass panic if the story of Grey's powers spread freely across the kingdom.

"I can see you believe your own words," the captain said. "But that doesn't make them true."

A jagged spear of wood that had once been the leg of a chair flew through the open door behind me. Several of the law keepers dodged, only just avoiding it before it hit the wall of the corridor with enough force to damage the stone.

The men craned to see over each other's shoulders, all attempting to peer at the heated battle happening inside the room. I desperately wanted to look back myself, but I knew I couldn't afford the distraction. If Grey's guards were still locked in battle with Nik, they must have strong abilities of their own, and my best chance of helping him lay with the men in front of me.

A loud crash sounded behind me, and the knuckles on the hand holding Miro's arm went white as I fought to keep my focus.

"If you'll let me make contact with you, I'll prove it," I told the captain, desperate enough to take the risk of revealing my secret. "I have the ability to purge Grey's lies."

The captain hesitated, his eyes flashing from the unconscious Miro, to the battle behind me, to the men watching him with wide eyes.

"I swear I will do nothing but purge your mind of the lies," I said, knowing he would see the truth in my words. "I swear I will not harm you or use my power for any other purpose." Extending the risk even further, I added, "If you'll let me do this, I'll hand Miro over into your charge. If I'm proved right, I trust you'll arrest him yourself. If I'm wrong, he'll be free."

When he still hesitated, I put my whole heart into my eyes. "Have you ever been to the capital, captain?"

He blinked at the unexpected question and nodded. "Five years ago."

"Did you see the royal family?"

He nodded again.

"Then look into that room and tell me who's fighting Miro and Slate's men right now."

For a silent moment, the captain stared into the room, and I allowed myself a quick glance as well. Nik had leaped on top of the throne chair, using the higher ground it afforded as he held off multiple attackers, a haze of increasingly small wood shards whirling around him.

The captain swallowed, looking back at me with wide eyes.

"Very well," he said hoarsely.

A couple of the men behind him called out protests, but he ignored them, holding my eyes as he moved forward and held out his arm.

Using my free hand, I lightly brushed my fingers against his.

Reaching into him, I called up his natural wall. His eyes widened as it sprang to life, driving my power out before it and Grey's lies along with it.

He fell back a step, breaking the remaining physical contact between us. One of his men stepped forward to steady him, glaring at me suspiciously.

"Captain! Are you all right?"

"Yes, I'm..." He cleared his throat. "I'm fine. It's...I don't..." He looked at me, and I looked back sympathetically.

"I've experienced it myself," I whispered. "I was once fooled by Grey as well."

He shook his head, a wild look in his eyes that felt all too familiar. He couldn't be putting more blame on himself for falling prey to Grey than I had when I first realized the truth.

"It's true," he said in a loud voice. "We've been deceived."

"Please." I stood, letting go of Miro. "Help the prince."

A murmur passed down the line of law keepers when I mentioned Nik's rank. The captain nodded grimly, gesturing for the men behind him to come forward and calling out orders as he did so.

"Wait!" I said. "Let me help them too."

I didn't stop for more debate. Reaching for the first bit of exposed skin I could see, I called up the wall of the person it belonged to. He gasped, jumping away from me, but I was already done. Reaching for the next person, I did it again and again. Several of them grabbed me back, but as soon as I'd purged their minds, they let me go, crying out in surprise.

Moving along the line, I reached for the next person only to realize there was no one left—at least for now. Turning back, I saw Miro awake and on his feet. He was spluttering and protesting, but both of his arms were gripped in firm holds, and from the careful placement of skin on skin, I guessed his captors were both healers. However strong his elements ability, Miro had little chance of breaking free from two determined healers who already had him in their grip.

"Nik," I murmured, running toward the door of the destroyed room.

When I stepped over the threshold, my feet crunched on wooden splinters. The debris littered the entire floor, heaviest around the throne which had somehow been split cleanly down the middle.

No more wood flew through the air, though, and the only upright figures I could see in the room were the captain and his men from the corridor.

"Nik!" I called more loudly, dashing into the room and spinning to try to see in all directions. "Nik!"

The captain looked up from where he knelt over a prone, blood-stained figure, and my heart nearly stopped. But as I raced toward them, I recognized the weak beat of a heart in the patient he was busy healing, and two steps later, I saw his face. It was one of the guards who had been attacking Nik.

I stopped, spinning again, as I peered through the people milling around. There! I caught a flash and then a second one as someone moved again.

Nik.

I raced to the broken throne, falling to my knees in front of Nik. He sat on a raised section of marble floor, his elbows on his knees and his head in his hands. His naked sword lay across his lap, and he was panting, his body streaked in dirt and blood.

"Nik," I said softly, and he looked up at the sound of my voice.

I took his face in my hands, sending my power searching through his body. A cut on his side was easily healed, although another on his arm was more serious. It still took me less than a minute to deal with it, and my heart lightened along with his expression as he responded to the healing.

"Well done." He nodded toward the guards who were busy arresting his opponents. "You got through to them, I see."

"I was so worried," I sobbed.

He carefully placed his sword on the ground before pulling me forward into an engulfing embrace.

"I'm not so easily defeated," he said, eliciting a watery chuckle.

"I see that now." I wiped at my face although I was likely only smearing it with dirt along with the tears.

"What about Grey?" Nik asked, and I stiffened.

"He was gone long before I got out of the room," I said, unable to believe I'd forgotten about him even for a moment.

Nik stood, pulling me up with him.

"We need to find him." He looked dangerous, the fire in his eyes only emphasized by the grime that streaked his face. "I'm not letting him escape this time."

CHAPTER
TWENTY

I tugged him over to the captain who had just completed his healing and risen.

"Do you have any idea where we can find Grey...I mean Slate?" I asked.

The captain frowned. "I know where his office is, but will he still be there?" He looked doubtfully around the wreckage.

"He left before this started," I said. "He might not know what's going on."

Shouts and running feet from outside the room's door made me wince. We'd created enough commotion to rouse the whole hall, so it seemed unlikely Grey wouldn't have realized something had gone awry.

We followed the captain down the hall, anyway. He stopped outside a much plainer door, gesturing silently at it before holding up one finger. One person inside. I could feel their presence too.

I exchanged a look with Nik. He shrugged and flung the door open, striding inside with his drawn sword in hand.

I followed so close on his heels, I nearly tripped over. The first thing I noticed was the size of the room, followed by the opulence of its decor, which seemed a mismatch with the plainness of the door.

But as soon as I caught sight of the man inside, all thoughts of the room itself fled. We had cornered him at last.

He had clearly been on his way from the large desk to the door. Apparently he had noticed the commotion outside, but not quickly enough to escape. Once again, his confidence had betrayed him.

His eyes widened as he took in not only my presence, but also Nik's. However, he recovered quickly and adopted a nonchalant pose.

"Perhaps I didn't give Ignatius enough credit," he said lightly, nodding in my direction.

I narrowed my eyes, and he chuckled, but he couldn't quite regain his earlier confidence. Grey had always known how to exude charm, but now there was an off-putting tension lurking behind his manner.

"I have followed you from one end of this kingdom to another, and even beyond its shores," Nik said. "It ends here."

"I had no idea I'd attracted such illustrious attention," Grey said in an attempt at his normal style, but he looked shaken.

At the beginning, Nik had kept to the shadows in his pursuit of Grey, and I was guessing Grey had been unaware of just how long Nik had been tracking him.

Grey's eyes swept past us to fasten on our companion, his expression growing stern. "I'm surprised to see you here, Captain. You should have put an end to this nonsense by now."

The captain met his gaze calmly, but I could feel the rage simmering underneath. "I'm in the process of putting an end to the nonsense going on in this hall. And it's to my shame I let it go on so long."

Grey's eyes widened, his heartbeat quickening. He was facing two healers, so no amount of acting could hide his underlying fear.

When his calculating gaze shifted to me, his eyes narrowed. I looked back, calm and sure, and he looked again at the captain.

Grey still didn't know about my new skill, so how did he account for the change in the captain? Did he think I had put my own mesmerizations over the top of his?

When he looked at me again, I was sure of it. And I saw something else in his face too. Grey had always surrounded himself with others, finding and exploiting their weaknesses while charming them in the process.

But now his followers had all been stripped away. He was facing us alone, and he no longer loomed larger than life. He looked small and pathetic, an empty shell of a man—all charm and no substance. Even with physical touch, I was now beyond his reach. Grey was weaponless, and he now seemed nothing but weak. Was he the villain we had feared for so long?

The fear I had felt of him drained away, replaced with nothing but contempt and beneath it a swelling sadness. Grey once had a mother who loved him, but he had rejected that love in favor of position and wealth, and now he was left alone with no one who knew his true self, let alone cared about him. It wasn't a life I would live for all the luxury in the world.

My emotions must have shown on my face because Grey's features twisted as he watched me, fury overcoming his polished mask.

In two long strides, he reached me, seizing me around the waist and pulling me tight against him. His other hand cupped one side of my neck, and I pulled up my wall. But he made no attempt to push his power into me, instead leaning over to whisper in my ear.

"You think you've won," he hissed, "but you haven't. You'll see. I've given you a gift you can't give back. You think you have the world right now, but you're the final successor in an illustrious line, and you should ask yourself what's happened to everyone else before you."

"Don't touch her!" Strong hands ripped Grey off me.

"No!" I cried, leaping after him, my hands reaching unthinkingly to pull Grey back. It was one thing for him to threaten me, but he couldn't be allowed to touch Nik.

Grey snarled, twisting nimbly out of the hold Nik had on the back of his jacket. I threw myself forward, convinced he was going for Nik's skin. Latching onto his closest wrist, I took a second to check my wall was in place before pushing my power into Grey. I should have put him to sleep while we had contact earlier, but I'd been distracted and thrown off balance by his words. I would rectify my mistake now.

But Grey pulled back so violently that he ripped his arm from my determined grip. His face had twisted into an expression I had never seen on him before—pure, unalleviated terror. He thought I was going to kill him, and he was ready to fight like a cornered rat.

I leaped after him, expecting him to retreat again, but instead he remained frozen in place. As my fingers circled his wrist again, I looked up at his face in confusion.

He was staring straight ahead, his expression frozen and eyes wide as if taken completely by surprise. I wanted to ask what had happened, but it wasn't a time for calm conversations. It was time to stop the fighting.

I pushed my power into him, but it smashed immediately into an immovable wall. I gasped, trying again and finding the same thing. Now I knew the reason for Grey's shock.

He had finally managed to make a wall of his own. All this time he had tried without success, and it had finally happened now, in the worst possible moment. I growled in frustration, and he grinned. The light that had been missing from his eyes earlier returned. He had thought himself cornered—even his backup plan in ashes around his feet—but now he had fresh motivation and hope.

I let go of his wrist and fell back a step, thrown off by the change. His unexpected discovery had galvanized him, whereas I felt paralyzed and confused at finding us back on equal footing.

As he looked at me, his eyes narrowed, and then he stooped. It took me too long to realize he was reaching for the knife in his boot. By the time I understood what he was doing, he was already lunging at me, his teeth bared and face locked into a grimace.

The blade flashed in my eyes, the steel sharp and the edge jagged. *I've been here before*, I thought numbly, bracing for the ripping pain.

But a body collided with me, pushing me onto the floor. Nik grunted as I heard the sickening sound of a blade plunging into a body.

I screamed, scrambling up. Running to his side, I grabbed one of his hands.

"What were you thinking?" I cried, tears running down my face as I saw his features twisted with pain.

"Had to...be...me," he panted. "You can't...have...more healings."

"And what about you?" I demanded as I sent my power into him. "How many have you had?"

He didn't answer, turning his face away. I tried to twist to see his expression, but my attention was caught by the flash of light on metal. Distracted by his wound, I'd forgotten all about our attacker.

Once again a blade was plunging through the air in my direction, but this time Grey's eyes were on Nik, his target the man next to me.

I lunged forward, my range limited since I was on my knees.

I made it just far enough to grip his arm. Straining, I held it in place, hovering above Nik's torso.

He pushed downward, trying to put more force into the thrust, and I felt my resistance slipping. I was off balance, stretched as far as I could reach and unable to gain better traction.

Movement in my outer vision was the only warning before the captain yanked Grey back, pulling him away from Nik. I was still clamped onto his arm, however, so the sudden movement dragged me with him.

The two of us went down in a tangled heap. Grey had stopped pushing, but the momentum of my counter push remained. It thrust his arm back toward his own chest, my weight twisting it as we both collapsed.

When we landed with a thud, I was on top of him, the hilt of the knife digging into me. I scrambled off, grateful it had been the hilt, not the blade. But as soon as I was free, I realized I had been the only one to be so fortunate.

Grey stared back at me, his eyes wide as his hands clutched the hilt sticking out of his chest. He opened his mouth, but no sound came out. Instead a second groan from behind me made me spin back toward Nik. Grey was a healer. He could deal with the mess he had created.

Nik was in the process of pushing himself up to sitting, groaning all the way.

"Stop!" I cried. "I didn't finish the healing."

I pressed my hands against him again, sending my power toward his injuries. I took my time, making sure everything was fully healed before finally withdrawing.

When I had finished, I turned on Grey in fury. But the emotion faded instantly at the sight waiting for me.

Grey still lay where I had left him. He was utterly motion-less, his hands still wrapped around the hilt of his dagger.

"But...what..." I tentatively touched the back of his hand,

but it only confirmed what my power was already telling me. There was no heartbeat and no breathing rasped in and out. "He's...dead?" I stared blankly up at the captain. "But he's a healer! Why didn't he heal himself?"

"The blade pierced his heart," the captain said. "He was unconscious within seconds."

Nik slowly stood, coming forward to stand beside me. He gazed down at Grey, his face unreadable.

"You didn't help him," he said to the captain. "Aren't you a healer, too?"

A reddish tinge rose up the man's cheeks, but he held his ground, meeting Nik's eyes.

"I have a strong seed, but only non-mage level. Healing a wound like that is beyond me." He rubbed the back of his head. "To tell the truth, I thought he was healing himself at first. I didn't even realize he'd lost consciousness initially."

"So we just left him to die," I said softly, trying to process the thought.

"It wasn't as if we did it intentionally," Nik said firmly, pulling me to his side. "He brought this end on himself."

"On that we agree," the captain said. "And given his crimes, he would have been facing execution in the capital anyway."

"Still..." I rubbed my hand. "As healers, we are sworn to offer healing to all."

"And you did," the captain said. "A royal prince had been stabbed by a murderous traitor, and you were busy healing him. No one could fault you."

Nik squeezed me tighter.

"Is he really dead?" I whispered.

It was hard to fathom. He had been a specter hanging over my apprenticeship from before it even began. With Grey gone, I felt lighter than I could remember in a long time.

But a kernel of heaviness remained within. I had purged Grey's lies from my head, but his final words haunted me. He had left one part of himself in me—the knowledge of how to mesmerize. And there was nothing I could do to purge those memories.

I tried not to think about the other part of what he'd said. It didn't matter what had happened to the Constantines. I wasn't like them. I didn't seek to control anyone, and I would never use the skill again. I was done with mesmerizing forever, and with Grey gone, Tartora was also free of its insidious influence.

"Are you all right?" Nik asked, looking down at me with concern.

I shook myself and managed a wobbly smile.

"We're finally free of him. Right?"

"We are." Nik turned into me, wrapping his second arm around me as well.

I buried my face in his chest and wished I felt more comforted.

TWENTY-ONE

Even with the captain's help, it took time to sort out the chaos at the law keepers' hall. And, like on the island, I once again had to go through every single person connected to the hall to purge any mesmerizations Grey had left behind.

The captain agreed to take temporary charge of the hall until the capital could appoint a new head, and I suspected the king would be sending a whole team to straighten out the messy situation.

"Don't worry," Gia said when she caught me looking concerned. "It sounds like Grey stayed almost exclusively inside the hall. I guess he was worried about being identified if he ventured out into the city. So we only need to track those who came into the hall. And there's no need for you to stay here after you've freed the initial group. We can reassure the Eldridans that you're willing to travel back if they find more people in need of your assistance."

"Are we leaving soon?" I asked, and she nodded eagerly.

"We need to get to the capital as soon as possible to give them a comprehensive report. The unrest in Eldrida is advanced enough that they need to pay serious attention to the city."

"Attention?" I asked tentatively.

"Not like that!" She looked amused. "The last thing Father will want is to sow more unrest. He'll be looking to reassure the easterners that the rest of the kingdom values them. You can expect lots of resources to be sent east in the near future."

While I was relieved at her words, I didn't know how to tell her that my concern hadn't been over the possibility of needing to stay in Eldrida. It was going to the capital that worried me. My old prejudices against both the capital and the Guild were long gone, but the reality was far scarier.

"My parents must be very eager to meet you." Gia's eyes shone as she beamed at me.

Little did she know she had just made my fear worse.

"Do...do you think so?" I asked, trying not to sound as nervous as I felt.

"Of course! You're a valuable asset to the kingdom, you know! As the only person who can free people from Grey's mesmerizations, you've done Tartora a great service. Even though all the mesmerizers are now dead, there's still people left who've been mesmerized."

I stared at her, my mind skimming through our past conversations. It didn't take long to realize that no one had ever told Gia about Grey teaching me to mesmerize. She—and probably the rest of Tartora as well—thought the skill was gone. What would the king and queen think when they learned the truth?

"Plus, of course, they're parents too, not just king and queen." Gia gave me a sly look. "And you're the girl who brought their missing son back to them—the girl he loves. Of course, they'll want to meet you as soon as possible!"

A sick feeling started in my stomach. Gia seemed to have a very rosy view of a situation that was far from simple. Nik might have agreed to accompany us to the capital, but that didn't mean he was back to stay. He was still a reneger.

He clearly didn't feel Gia's optimism about his return given his avoidance of the topic. Even when we tried to discuss plans for the journey itself, he found a reason to excuse himself. I began to grow worried, finally catching him alone when I visited Acorn's stall and discovered him already there.

"You're not planning on backing out, are you?" I asked. "You did promise you'd come."

"And I'll keep my promise, of course," he said.

"Are you worried about seeing your parents again?" I asked softly.

He leaned one shoulder against the edge of the stall, looking down at his feet.

"So much has happened since the last time I saw them." He sighed. "When I left the capital, it was in a fit of anger. Part of me never wanted to see any of them again, and the other part thought I would prove them all wrong and return home in a blaze of glory. I dreamed of having my place reinstated and to hear everyone acknowledge they were wrong about me."

He shook his head. "I thought myself all grown up, but it was a childish fantasy. I can see that now."

I placed a hand on his arm. "You wanted them to change, but you were the one whose attitude changed instead. Of course there's some awkwardness. There's no shame in it, though. You were a child back then—legally speaking at least— and now you're grown up. Surely growth is natural."

He looked up and smiled at me. "You make it sound so normal and straightforward."

"Not quite that, perhaps." I tipped my head to the side, examining his face. "Acknowledging you were in the wrong doesn't mean saying they were entirely in the right, either. It just means maturing enough to recognize there were two sides to the situation. I think your parents will be proud of the man you've become. And even if it isn't the blaze of glory you dreamed of, you have done a great service to the kingdom."

He pulled me against him, resting his chin lightly on the top of my head. "Except you were the one who did it all, Delphine."

I laughed awkwardly, wondering if he'd picked up on my own nerves about going to the capital.

"I couldn't have done any of it without you," I said. "I wouldn't have survived long enough!"

He drew in a long breath. "I'm just glad that's all behind us. I never want to see anyone threatening your life ever again. It's happened far too often already."

"Don't worry." My arms wrapped around his waist and squeezed tightly. "I don't think I'm likely to meet another Grey."

"Thank goodness for that."

I tried to pull away, conscious of everything we still had to do before leaving Eldrida the next morning. He tightened his grip, though, holding me in place.

"Can we stay like this—just for another minute?" he asked.

I settled back against him with a happy sigh. "If it was up to me, we could stay like this forever."

Carriages and teams of horses were provided for our journey to the capital, and we were even given priority for the barge crossing. It was the most physically comfortable journey I'd ever made, but my nerves only strung tighter the closer we got.

Normally Nik would have been the first to notice, but I took extra care to hide it from him since I didn't want to feed into his concerns.

Amara took me aside to check in on me, but there was nothing she could do to ease this particular anxiety.

"There's no denying you've had a tempestuous romance," she said with a sigh. "And I can't promise there will only be smooth sailing ahead." She gazed at me, a thoughtful look on her face. "But I'll do the best I can to ease your way."

I gave her a surprised look, but she only smiled.

"I am your master after all. I should do at least that much for my apprentice."

Although she'd only spoken in generalities, her words comforted me somewhat. I was still only halfway through my apprenticeship, and no matter what else happened, I would still have Amara for a year yet. She had always managed to sort out every situation we'd encountered, so maybe she could somehow sort this one out too.

But when we entered the streets of Tarona, my tension started growing again. As the wheels rolled over the cobblestones, I peered out the window at a city far larger than any I'd visited so far. By the time we arrived at the stone wall surrounding the palace, my churning stomach was making me wish I hadn't eaten lunch.

Large gates opened for us, and we entered an enormous courtyard. I had expected to alight in front of the palace, but to my surprise the horseshoe building in front of us wasn't the largest of the structures within the walls. The towers and turrets of the palace loomed on our left, but the building in front of us was separate although built from the same gray stone.

"Welcome to the Tartoran Mages' Guild." Amara quirked one eyebrow, a slight smile on her face as she watched my reaction. "Does it meet your expectations?"

I gazed in some astonishment at the formal garden beds in the middle of the boxy horseshoe. The effect—which could have been grand—was broken by the occasional section of riotous growth and a sprinkling of odd-looking fountains.

Amara followed my gaze, nodding toward one of the areas where the garden was completely overgrown. "The work of the plants apprentices, of course."

It made sense, but something about it didn't fit the pretentious, image-focused concept I'd always had of the mages and the Guild.

"I don't know what to make of this place," I said at last. "But why are we here instead of the palace?"

The driver of the closest carriage peered down at us. "I thought you were all mages? Aren't you reporting to the Guild?"

I glanced at the other two carriages as everyone climbed out. Obviously he hadn't recognized the prince and princess.

"The Guild is fine," Amara said, and the man smiled in relief.

Whether because of the driver's mistake, or because our exact arrival time was unknown, there was no welcome party to greet us. I suspected it wouldn't be long before one arrived, however.

"What do you think of it?" Nik asked in a low voice from behind me, making me start.

I twisted to see his face, taking in the tight lines of his body and his set expression.

"It's very impressive," I said. "I can't imagine growing up in a home like this."

His eyes grew distant as he gazed across at the castle's towers. I wished I knew what childhood memories were running through his head.

"You can do this," I said in a low voice, gripping his closest arm. "You can do this, Nik."

His eyes dropped to mine, their expression softening as he slowly refocused.

"Of course he can!" Gia bounced over and grabbed him by the other arm. "It doesn't matter how you left. Mother and Father are going to be delighted to see you, Nik."

Looking at the gleam in her eyes, he relaxed further, snorting. "I can see through you, you know. You're planning to take all the credit for bringing me back."

"Of course!" she said with a mischievous grin. "I have to gain points wherever I can since I'm the daughter who turned her back on their legacy, married a foreigner, and spends her days flitting around other kingdoms."

"You know," Nik said thoughtfully, "when you put it like that, I don't seem like such a bad son after all."

"Which is just what I've been telling you!" Gia tugged on his arm, and I quickly dropped my hold on the other one.

As Nik let his sister drag him toward the palace, I watched them go with a slight smile. His sister knew how to ease this particular fear better than me, and she was the appropriate one to be by his side for this reunion. I would have my chance to meet the king and queen soon enough—too soon for my liking. I had no place in the first meeting between parents and son.

The rest of the group followed behind the royal siblings, moving toward the palace at a slower pace. I didn't move, however.

Amara glanced back and frowned when she saw me still motionless beside the carriage. When she gestured for me to catch up, I hurried to do so. But as soon as I reached her, I tugged on her sleeve, pulling her to a stop.

"I know Gia said her parents will want to meet me, but I want to give Nik space to reunite with them first without the complication of my presence."

She examined my face, as if looking to see whether my words were just an excuse to put off meeting the king and queen. After a moment, she nodded slowly.

"That's reasonable enough. Hayes and I need to consult with the Triumvirate immediately, and I'm sure they'll be eager to meet you once they've heard our report. But as an apprentice, we can't include you in the initial meeting."

She glanced uncertainly from the Guild building to the palace. "Luna has already run off to find her Guild friends, I see, but I'm sure there's somewhere you could wait in the palace. Or if you prefer, I could find out which suite will be assigned to us. The Guild keeps suites for the use of visiting masters, so you could—"

"Actually, I'd like to go out and visit the city." I glanced back toward the gates. "It's my first time in Tarona, and I don't know how much opportunity I'll have to explore the actual city."

Amara raised her eyebrows. "I suppose you can do that if you wish. But don't be gone for more than an hour or two."

"You're not worried about me?" I asked, surprised at her easy acquiescence.

She chuckled. "Tarona is a large city, but it's also home to most of the kingdom's mages. Even the criminals know better than to judge someone's strength by their outside appearance." She nodded at Phoenix, who sat on my shoulder as usual. "One glance at that fine fellow, and they'll know you're more than you appear."

I smiled, her words bolstering my confidence. Hayes had noticed her disappearance and stopped for her, so she left quickly. Given their serious expressions, I was glad not to be joining them in their upcoming meeting.

I still felt some trepidation stepping out of the Guild gates, but it wasn't about being alone in the city. Ember had even roused herself from her day's sleep, so I had two companions with me as I set off across the cobblestones.

My sense of anxious expectation came from my true purpose in exploring the city. I had family in Tarona—family I'd never met. It was time to remedy that situation.

I knew Amara, Luna, and Nik would all have gladly helped me if I asked. Even Hayes would have lent his assistance. But just as Nik needed to meet his parents on his own, this was something I needed to do by myself.

My uncle's trip to Tarona, and subsequent desertion of my father, had been one of the major shaping forces of my life. I might not know him personally, but his actions had affected me deeply. And even now, my father was back on our farm hurting because of what his brother had done. I needed to meet my uncle and ask why he never came back.

Since my uncle's strength had been just short of mage level, he wouldn't be found at the Guild or among the courtiers. But with a seed like that, he had to be in one of the nicer areas of the city. Unfortunately, I didn't know where those areas might be.

Since I had nowhere else to start, I asked the guards at the gates for directions to the central market. It turned out there wasn't only one market in such a large city, and they gave me directions to three of them. When I asked which one serviced the nicer areas of the city, they directed me to the closest of the three.

It didn't take long to reach it, and when I walked into the square, I almost forgot my purpose for being there. The rich scent of spices and cooking meat overlaid the bright buzz of the well-dressed crowd. Everywhere I looked, my eyes landed on fine fabrics and sumptuous wares.

I didn't dare touch anything, but wandering among the stalls admiring the goods for sale was entertaining enough. I couldn't let myself get distracted for long, though, not when Amara had given me a time limit.

"Excuse me," I said to a stall keeper whose display of leather goods was momentarily free of customers. "I'm newly arrived in Tarona and looking for my uncle. His name is Olan, and he has a plants affinity. I think he lives in this neighborhood. He might be a customer of yours?"

The woman listened politely before shaking her head with an apologetic expression. "I can't say I know an Olan."

I hesitated, disappointed, although in a city this large it was silly to expect the first person I questioned to know him.

"Have you had a stall at this market for long?" I asked.

She chuckled. "More years than you've been alive, I'm guessing." She eyed Phoenix on my shoulder with interest, her gaze dropping to the tell-tale color difference between his legs. "You're a healer, then? Did you train him yourself? I like what you've done with the shoulder of your dress. It's a convenient way to carry him in a crowd like this. But if you have need of leather gauntlets, you won't find any better quality than mine. All the palace and Guild falconers buy from me," she finished proudly.

"I can see their quality just by looking," I said, eyeing off the two pairs I could see displayed. "But unfortunately I don't have time for shopping today. Hopefully I can have a closer look next time I'm in the market."

The woman accepted my words with enough good humor that I resolved to do my best to come back at the earliest opportunity. Now that I was at the Guild, I was hoping to speak to some of the healing affinity's falconers and get some tips on caring for Phoenix. Quality gloves would no doubt prove helpful.

As I moved down the line of stalls, choosing ones free of customers to approach with my query, I was received with a range of attitudes. But whether gruff, surly, chatty, suspicious, or friendly, every one of them disavowed any knowledge of someone with my uncle's name and a plants affinity. And when I finally found someone who knew an Olan, further questioning established the man in question was barely older than me.

I was about to give up and head back to the palace when a hand pulled softly on my sleeve. I turned to find a small slip of a girl, at least five years younger than me, staring at me with shrewd eyes.

"I heard you asking around the market. You're looking for your uncle?"

"Yes, do you know him?" I couldn't help my voice quickening with eagerness. "His name is Olan."

"And he has a plants seed? Aye, I heard." The girl hoisted a large, wrapped bundle over her shoulder. "If you're wondering about trusting me, ask any of them." She jerked her thumb over her shoulder down the line of stalls and lifted her chin defiantly. "Any of them can tell you. I run errands for anyone who needs it round the market, and I'm known for being the most reliable."

A younger boy ran past in time to hear her remark, slowing enough to call a heckling challenge in her direction. He didn't stop completely, however, and was lost in the crowd as the girl pretended not to have heard him.

"So you actually know an Olan of the right age who has a plants affinity?" I asked, eager for a proper answer. "He would be coming up to five decades by now."

"Aye, I know one. But he don't live in this neighborhood. Likes to talk about his seed, though." She sniffed as if something about that behavior was unpleasant.

"Can you take me to him?" I asked, making a split-second decision. I was supposed to be heading back to the palace soon, but I couldn't let this opportunity slip away. If there was any chance this girl could take me to my uncle, I couldn't walk away now.

"That depends," she said.

"On what?" I asked warily.

"On if you can pay. I'm not trying to cheat you," she added defensively. "Anyone can tell you it's one coin to take goods or a message across town." She looked me up and down. "You're not exactly either, but I'll apply the same rates."

"Very well, then." I smiled at her. "I'll give payment when we reach this Olan."

The girl narrowed her eyes before making up her mind and giving a decisive nod. I was almost glad she'd asked for a coin. It made me less wary that she had some nefarious motive.

"Ember," I called, and the fox appeared out of the crowd.

The girl started, looking uneasily from Ember to Phoenix.

"How many of them creatures do you have following you around?"

I chuckled as I picked Ember up. "Only two. We're all here now and ready to go."

The girl turned without another word and led the way out of the square. I followed a few steps behind, keeping half my attention on her and half on the rest of my surroundings. But nothing suspicious appeared, and no one else appeared to be tailing us.

The girl didn't speak to me other than to give me a disparaging look when I offered to take a turn carrying her bundle. I didn't make the mistake of offering again, and we remained silent across half the city.

At least it felt like half the city. I had no actual way to measure our progress and would have been well past lost without my guide. If this Olan wasn't the right one, then I would have to pay the girl another coin to guide me back to the palace. If he was my uncle, I would have to trust in his goodwill to show me the way back.

But as the houses around us grew more and more shabby, I finally spoke.

"Are you sure this is the right area?" I tried not to let the extent of my unease show in my voice.

"Nearly there," the girl puffed over her shoulder, switching her load to the other side. "And course I'm sure. His youngest attends classes with me in the morning."

I fell silent at this mention of cousins. I had always assumed they likely existed, but I had never expected to meet them.

"Here we are." She stopped in front of a tall, narrow building in a long row of buildings. This particular one appeared to be leaning against the one beside it, and I eyed its upper stories with concern.

"Don't worry," the girl said with a snort. "You're lucky. He's on the bottom."

She rapped loudly on the door, calling through the wood as she did so.

"Patti! Patti! There's someone here to see your Da."

When we heard shuffling from inside, she stepped back, looking satisfied.

The door swung open, revealing a middle-aged man. I gasped, my fingers digging tightly enough into Ember that she protested.

I relaxed my grip, my mind catching up with itself. This wasn't my father, no matter how much he resembled him.

Now that the initial shock had passed, I could see the small differences. There was no doubt about his identity, however. I looked from my uncle to the decrepit house on the rundown street and then back at my uncle.

This might be my Uncle Olan, but nothing else about the situation made sense.

TWENTY-TWO

My uncle was still gaping at me, looking as astonished as I felt.

"She was asking all around the high market, trying to find someone as knew you," my guide said, nodding in my direction.

The man's face flinched at the mention of the market. Was he aware that he wasn't where he was supposed to be?

"Looking for me?" he said slowly, still regarding me with an expression of shock. "You're...you're Osan's daughter, aren't you?"

I nodded. Apparently my uncle wasn't the only one who resembled my father.

"That'll be one coin." My guide held out a hand.

I tore my eyes from my uncle to deliver the promised payment. "Thank you very much," I said with warmth. "I appreciate your help more than I can say."

The girl tucked the coin away. "Always happy to do business with them that can pay."

She nodded once at my uncle before disappearing up the street. I turned slowly back to the open door.

"What are you doing here?" my uncle asked after a painful

silence. "Wait." He rubbed the back of his head. "I should ask your name first."

"I'm Delphine."

"Have you just graduated?" he asked, taking a guess at my age. "And come to the capital looking for work? If you thought I could help you, I'm afraid—"

"No," I said quickly. "I'm still an apprentice."

"An apprentice?" His brows drew together, and he took a step backward, retreating through the doorway. "You've not gone reneger!"

"No, no!" I shook my head emphatically, grimacing at how poorly the conversation was going. "Of course not. I apprenticed to a traveling master, and since our travels brought us here, I wanted to find..."

I trailed off at the expression on his face.

"Did you say a traveling *master*? You just mean that she's your master, I suppose?"

I shifted, realizing my mistake. "Ah, no, she's a master elements mage. Her name is Amara."

He gave a low whistle. "So Osan's daughter has a mage level seed—strong enough to attract the attention of a master, at that. So our family line did have it in us." I detected faint traces of an old resentment.

"I thought you had a strong seed yourself." My eyes narrowed. "At least that's how my father told it."

I ran my eyes up the unstable building, letting all my questions show on my face.

My uncle sighed, his face falling. "I suppose you'd better come in. My youngest is here, but my wife and sons are out at the moment."

I turned my head to murmur to Phoenix. "You wait out here. I'll be back out soon." I shrugged my shoulder slightly, indicating for him to take off.

He did so, his wing sweeping against me as he launched

himself skyward. It looked like a small home, and I didn't want him cooped inside.

"How many sons do you have?" I asked as I followed my uncle into a narrow, dimly lit hallway.

"Three," he said. "My oldest two are twins and would be a little younger than you. They're about ready for activation. In fact, my wife is out talking to a potential master for one of them now."

"What's his affinity?" I asked, trying to wrap my mind around a whole collection of cousins I hadn't known existed.

"Plants, like me."

"You don't want to take him on yourself?" I asked as we reached a living space at the back of the house.

A girl of around twelve looked up curiously. Her eyes jumped from my face to Ember in my arms. She rose to her feet.

"Father doesn't want any of us stuck being builders like him. But who are you?"

"A builder?" I looked at my uncle in surprise. Construction was usually done by those with a plants ability due to their connection with both wood and stone, but I'd always imagined my uncle working with living plants.

He cleared his throat uncomfortably, ignoring my question to answer his daughter's instead.

"This is your cousin, Delphine. Delphine, this is my youngest, Patti."

"Cousin?" Patti's eyes grew even rounder. "Why didn't I know I had a cousin?"

"Because I didn't know myself," Uncle Olan said. "She's from Tarin. My brother's daughter."

"You have a brother still in Tarin?" From Patti's expression, it was clear my uncle hadn't told his children much about his history.

"Yes, my father still lives there on the family farm," I said.

"Family farm?" Patti stared at her father. "There's a family farm?"

"Uncle Olan and Father were supposed to run it together, after Uncle Olan finished his apprenticeship in Tarona. But he never came back." I tried to keep any accusation out of my voice, but it was impossible to do so completely.

"Father, what is she talking about?" Patti asked, a sharp edge to her words.

My uncle cleared his throat again. "I'm sure Osan was glad to see the back of me. He must have a bevy of children to assist him now." He looked at me for confirmation.

"Actually, it's just me." I held his gaze. "And now even I'm gone, as you can see. My father has suffered greatly from your absence."

"He's alone on the farm? Does that mean he needs extra help? Would he still want Father now?" Patti asked eagerly, taking a step closer to me.

"Hush, Patti!" Uncle Olan said sharply. "Don't talk nonsense."

I regarded them both with a creased brow. My uncle clearly felt ashamed of what he'd done, but he wasn't owning to his betrayal. I glanced around the room at the worn and sagging furniture. He certainly wasn't living the life of luxury imagined by my father.

"What happened to you?" I asked softly. "My father always thought...Well, he didn't picture your life like this."

"Reality rarely lives up to our expectations," my uncle said.

"But your seed—"

"Was strong, yes. At least by Tarin's standards. But potential doesn't always equate to success. Osan and I thought we'd saved up a vast sum, but it wasn't as much as we thought. I arrived in Tarona full of hope, but finding a master to take me on and activate me didn't prove as easy as I'd expected." His face assumed an expression so much like my father that I flinched.

"I had neither wealth, connections, charm, or experience to recommend me," he continued. "If I'd been strong enough to become a mage, it might have been a different story."

I shifted uncomfortably, remembering his earlier reaction, but he continued on without commenting on my status.

"In the end, I had no choice but to accept an apprenticeship with a builder, which was not what we'd planned. The experience I gained wouldn't be much use on the farm, but at least I would be activated and could return home once I graduated. Except after I was activated, I discovered my new master had misled me about his strength. The potential of my seed became meaningless once my power was capped at the strength of my influencer."

"Did you report him?" I asked, outraged.

He sighed. "He hadn't made any concrete promises or assurances I could point to—certainly nothing in writing. I was young, naïve, and desperate, without parents or community to guide me, so I was easily fooled. I had already used all my coin by that stage while searching for an apprenticeship, so I had to find a master quickly."

"How awful," I said softly, imagining what it must have been like for him alone in this big city. "But you were only bound to him for two years. Why didn't you go home as soon as you graduated?"

He grimaced. "That had been my plan. But unfortunately my master was a poor businessman as well as weak. He could barely afford to keep an apprentice, and there was certainly no coin left over to share with me. I needed to save enough to cover the journey home, but I couldn't start doing that until I graduated and found proper employment. It took me a while to accomplish that, and by then I'd met my wife."

"After that I suppose it was the twins," I said quietly. "You had more mouths to feed, which would have made it even harder to save. And the journey itself would have become more difficult and expensive as well. I suppose I can see how it happened. But why did you never write to my father, at least? He had no idea what had happened to you—he still doesn't!"

"Yes, I can see I should...ahem...I should have done that."

He wouldn't meet my eyes, and I could read the truth on his face. He had been the strong one—the one with the promise of a great future. But that future had failed to materialize, and he had been too embarrassed to own up to his true situation. Better for his brother to think him dead or absconded with their money than for him to know the truth.

I shook my head at the breathtaking selfishness of that attitude. I wanted to let go of my restraint and understanding and spew out a torrent of recrimination. His useless pride had nearly destroyed my life.

But I kept my mouth closed. This man might be related to me by blood, but we were currently strangers. I wasn't ready to tell him the most painful details of my past—perhaps I never would be. And there was nothing to be gained from recriminations. It might make me feel better in the moment, but the effect would be short. Nothing I could say now would change the past or the effect it had wreaked in my life.

I looked around the room again. My uncle hadn't traded his and my father's youthful dreams for a better life. He was already living the consequences of his choices every day. He didn't need punishment from me.

My uncle's eyes finally settled back on me. "Is your master good to you? You said she's a traveling master—where does that leave you when you graduate?" The concern in his eyes seemed genuine, burning away some of my earlier anger.

"My life is proof that a strong ability doesn't always lead to success," he continued. "You need to make decisions about your future carefully. I know it's too late to change masters, but you should make some connections while you're here in the capital, if you can."

A small smile tugged at my mouth as I thought of Hayes, Clay, Anka, and Luna—and then of Gia and finally Nik. Little did my uncle realize, but Amara's traveling lifestyle had allowed me to make many high-ranking connections already.

But imagining his reaction if I told him about my traveling companions kept my mouth shut. It would only complicate matters to tell him about my connection with the royals.

"Thank you," I said instead. "I'll keep that in mind."

He nodded, relaxing a little.

"And...is he well?" he asked tentatively. "Your father, I mean?"

"He was when I left. I haven't seen him in a year, though."

An unexpected surge of nostalgia caught me off guard. After everything that had happened, I actually wanted to see my father again.

From the wistful look on my uncle's face, I guessed he felt the same.

"I have a little coin of my own," I said slowly. "Not with me, but I could bring some to you later. You could send him a message—even go to see him yourself. I don't know if he would welcome you at first, but I think he would want to see you."

My uncle winced, clearly unsure about his potential reception.

"Go to Tarin? To our family's farm?" Patti gripped her father's arm with both hands. "Oh could we, Da? Could we? Please let us go!"

I watched her with bemusement. She was a number of years away from activation, but on a whim I reached out to test her. She had a plants seed of medium non-mage strength. Had she lived her whole life in this row of buildings? No wonder the idea of a farm was so appealing to her.

"Do all three of your sons have plants seeds like Patti?" I asked.

Both of them turned to me with expressions of mild surprise.

"Oh, I don't think I said, I'm a healer."

"A mage level healer?" My uncle's eyebrows shot up. "That must have been a surprise for my brother."

"It was a great shock for all of us," I said dryly.

"Will you really help us go to the farm, cousin?" Patti asked. "Could we stay there forever?"

"Patti," her father said warningly.

"I don't know," I told her. "That would depend on my parents. But—" I hesitated. "I'm never going back there to live. So they're going to need help from someone."

"Oh, Father, please may we go?" she begged.

The sound of the front door opening presaged a stream of new arrivals. A middle-aged woman was the first to appear, followed by three tall lads. All four of them stopped as soon as they reached the back room, regarding me with astonishment.

My uncle seemed to forget me for a moment, however, his eyes focused on his wife. "Did he agree to...?" His question trailed off at the sad shake of her head.

"Never mind that!" Patti exclaimed. "This is our cousin Delphine. She's a healing mage!"

"Actually I'm still an apprentice," I said uncomfortably as the new arrivals stared at me with even greater astonishment.

"And!" Patti added with increased enthusiasm. "She's been telling us about Da's family farm back in Tarin. She said we can go there!"

"I can help you pay for a visit at least," I said hurriedly. "Whether you can stay would be up to my parents."

The three boys remained silent, but their eyes lit up with the same light showing on Patti's face. Their mother turned to her husband.

"Your parents' farm? Could we really...?"

"Apparently my brother only ever had Delphine, and she's not sure she wants to live there," he said slowly.

"Actually, I'm quite sure I don't," I said firmly.

My uncle had bid me think about my future, and that was one thing I was sure on at least. But neither did I want to follow his advice and make connections in the capital with a view to settling at the Guild. It had only been a few hours, but I already felt the weight of the large city pressing on me. I missed the freedom of life on the road where I could focus on helping people instead of worrying about what impression I would make at court.

When my apprenticeship ended, would Amara be willing to let me continue on as her companion? We worked well as a team since we had different affinities and could cover different needs in the towns and cities we visited.

"Let me properly introduce you all," my uncle said. "This is—"

But before he could say the first name, the latch on the front door popped off, falling to the floor with a thud. The door was thrust forcibly open, bouncing off the opposite wall.

People poured into the cramped building, rushing down the hallway toward us. Patti screamed, two of the boys shouted, and the room became a chaotic muddle of movement and noise.

I remained frozen in place. The stream of arrivals were dressed in the blue and gold uniform of the royal guard, but I couldn't think what they were doing in my uncle's house.

Ember growled, going stiff in my arms. Her muscles tensed, as if she meant to leap down and attack the intruders, but I shushed her. In this chaos, she would only get stepped on. And if she did manage to bite someone, it might get my uncle into further trouble.

But the guards showed no interest in my uncle. They herded all of the house's residents against one wall with stern instructions to remain still. Only I was left in the center of the room, the remaining guards forming a wary circle around me.

Slowly it dawned on me that the guards weren't here for my uncle. They were here for me. Had Nik been worried about my safety and sent them out looking for me?

"You are Delphine, the healing apprentice of Master Amara?" the lieutenant asked formally.

I nodded, mystified.

He stepped forward, his stern expression not quite managing to mask what looked like nerves.

"In that case, you're under arrest. You need to come with us."

TWENTY-THREE

My uncle and his family all gasped, but I was too shocked to pay them any attention.

"Under arrest? Me?"

"You will remain silent!" the lieutenant commanded, a line of sweat breaking out on his brow.

I stared at him, trying to make sense of what was happening. Scanning the rest of his men, I could see no familiar faces. What was going on?

The lieutenant indicated two of his men. They looked even more uncomfortable than him as they stepped forward to grip one of my upper arms each.

When I didn't resist, a third guard tried to remove Ember from my grasp. She snarled and snapped at him, and he whisked his hand away, looking to the lieutenant.

After a brief hesitation, the lieutenant indicated for him to leave Ember with me. I held the fox even tighter as the guards hustled me toward the hall.

Before they had me fully out of the room, however, I dug in my heels and stopped, twisting to look backward. The sudden resistance took them by surprise, and I managed to pull part way free of their hold.

"Go to Amara!" I said, my eyes on my uncle. "At the Guild. Tell her who you are and ask her to give you my coin. You have to go to Tarin and tell my parents—"

"Enough!" The lieutenant's shout cut across my words, silencing me.

The two guards recovered their hold, gripping me more tightly this time, and I was marched awkwardly up the hall. I managed one last look back over my shoulder at my astonished family who were still pressed against their living room wall.

Outside, a covered wooden cart awaited us. I was half thrust, half lifted into the back. The movement dislodged Ember who landed on her feet inside the cart, disappearing unnoticed into the shadows at the back.

Heavy gloves were placed over my hands before they were bound behind my back, and I noticed that the guards all wore gloves of their own. Other than their faces, they didn't have an inch of skin showing anywhere.

When I tried to ask what was going on, they all reacted violently, one of them shoving a heavy gag into my mouth. I made no attempt to resist since it seemed pointless. Even if I could get free from so many guards, where would I go? They were already taking me to the one place I wanted to go—the palace where Amara and Nik were currently located.

But when we arrived in the palace courtyard, there was no sign of either of them. The handful of servants and officials who were moving in and out of the palace and surrounding buildings all stopped to stare at me, but no one offered assistance.

The guards dragged me roughly off the back of the cart and hustled me through a side door and down a set of stairs hewn from stone. I could barely catch my breath with the gag blocking my mouth, and it was hard to see past the tears.

What sort of misunderstanding had sent the guards after me in such an intense manner? If they had just asked me to accompany them back to the palace, I would have come willingly.

Unbidden, Grey's final words came into my mind. I tried to push them away, but they took root, blossoming and growing along with the fear in my belly.

A clanking sounded as yet another guard opened the metal bars of a cell door. When they tried to thrust me inside, I struggled, wriggling from side to side and making garbled, muffled exclamations.

Once again they all reacted out of proportion to my actions, but when I twisted far enough to catch the eye of the lieutenant and thrust out my bound hands, he hesitated. Glancing at the others, he shrugged and removed my bonds.

As soon as the final knot came loose, I was shoved into the cell. Losing my footing, I sprawled across the straw-covered floor. I didn't bother to get back to my feet, merely rolling onto my back and ripping off the gloves. With them gone, I reached up and pulled off the strip of material holding my gag in place. The second I spat it out, I began coughing, sucking in deep lungfuls of air. The gag hadn't actually blocked my airways, but I had been fighting my panicked mind the entire time, trying to reassure it of that fact.

A distant shout made me sit up just in time to see a streak of orange slip through the bars of my cell. Despite everything, I smiled. I wasn't alone.

Climbing slowly to my feet, I picked up Ember and held her close, taking comfort from her warm presence. The cell door had been locked, and no one was in sight. Across from my cell was nothing but a stone wall. I pressed myself against the bars, trying to peer back down the corridor toward the stairs, wanting to see if I was truly alone.

I wasn't.

Sitting in a chair at the bottom of the stairs was a man. He wasn't dressed in the blue and gold livery of a servant or royal guard, and he didn't carry himself like one either. Even from this distance, I could see the quality of his clothes—far finer than a mere servant—and sense the indefinable air of power that hung around him. Even his age seemed too advanced for a guard. And yet he was clearly guarding the row of cells. Why?

He saw me watching and nodded, an unexpected courtesy in the setting. When I opened my mouth to call out to him, though, he shook his head sharply, his eyes conveying a warning. Remembering the gag, I snapped my mouth shut. There was no point talking if he didn't want to hear what I had to say, and I didn't want to end up gagged again. Neither did I want to bring more trouble on myself when I didn't even know what original crime I had committed.

Had the royal family been offended that I had gone into the city instead of coming straight to meet them? It was impossible to imagine they would react in such an exaggerated manner over an issue of etiquette.

Did they blame me for killing Grey, however unintentionally? Perhaps they had intended to question him after his capture and were angry to have missed the opportunity?

I stayed at the bars, waiting to see what would happen, but as the hours ticked by, I couldn't maintain a state of alert. At first I had thought my imprisonment a temporary measure and expected someone to arrive to speak to me at any moment. But no one came.

The old man remained in his seat as the hours wore on, and eventually I stretched out on the single, lumpy mattress that lay on the cell floor. Ember curled beside me, and thanks to her familiar presence, I even managed to doze, exhausted from the travel. But when the sound of an opening door echoed down the cells, I flew back to my feet, rushing to the bars.

But the person who came through the door wasn't an incensed Nik or outraged Amara. A man in the livery of a servant handed the old man on the chair a tray of food and immediately withdrew. The man carefully removed one bowl and plate from the tray before carrying the rest down the corridor in my direction.

"Stand back," he ordered in a deep voice that commanded instant obedience. "I'll only give you one warning."

I scrambled away from the cell door, snatching up a growling Ember as I went. I stared at him as he deposited the tray on the ground just inside the cell.

"What's going on?" I asked. "Why am I—?"

"You will remain silent!" he said in the same commanding tones, cutting across my question. But as he relocked the cell door, he relaxed a little, apparently caught in a moment of compassion.

"We have all been forbidden from speaking to you. But try to have patience. All will be explained in time."

I stayed frozen in place away from the door, hoping for more, but he simply sighed and strode off back down the corridor. I rushed to the bars in time to see him take his seat and pick up the bowl and plate he had left for himself.

Seeing him eat the same food I had been left gave me enough reassurance to consume the surprisingly appetizing meal on the tray. But I still monitored my body closely for hours afterward, watching for any sign I had ingested something unsavory.

Eventually, however, I found myself wishing there might be something secreted in my food. At least driving out the poison would have provided some alleviation from the boredom. Ember alone kept me sane, and I wished Phoenix could have been with us as well. For his sake, I was glad he wasn't, though. The falcon would have hated being restrained for so long without enough space to take flight.

My cell didn't afford any glimpse of outside light, but the regular meal deliveries kept track of the passing hours. Between the food and the two long stretches of slumber from the man in the chair—both punctuated by loud snores—I guessed I had been imprisoned for two days before something new happened.

I spent those days thinking longingly of Nik, Amara, and my other friends and brooding over Grey and his final words, which now felt like a curse over me. Had he known this would happen?

Gia had been convinced her parents would be pleased to meet me, but she hadn't known all the facts. We had never told her that with Grey gone, I was the only one left who could do mesmerizations.

Gia might not have known, but Amara and Hayes had obviously reported the full truth to the Triumvirate, and they would certainly have told the king. Once again, I had been recklessly sure of myself, only to find Grey had been one step ahead, even in death.

My thoughts ran in horrible circles, making it hard to sleep, so I jumped at any opportunity for variety, however small. The opening door had become familiar at mealtimes, but it had been only an hour since the last delivery when it opened again.

I immediately raced to the bars.

When I saw who was standing at the top of the stairs, I almost fainted with relief. Amara had finally arrived.

"I'm here to see my apprentice." She looked wrathful, commanding, and powerful, and my heart lifted just at the sight of her.

The man heaved himself to his feet, and I held my breath. Would he give way before her or attack—even if only with words? He did neither, however, instead sighing sadly.

"No one is permitted to speak to her."

"What sort of ridiculousness is that?" Amara snapped. "She needs physical touch to influence someone's mind. You might not be a healer, but don't pretend you don't know—"

"Their Majesties are not willing to take any chances." The man sighed again. "I know you're biased toward her. She's your apprentice, so of course you are. But you yourself reported that she has exceptional skill at using her power from a distance—more so than many master mages.”

Amara snorted. “Yes, she’s skilled in that area, but that doesn’t mean her power can operate inside someone without physical touch. She’s still a regular healer!”

“I’m sorry,” he said simply.

Amara drew herself up, fury sparking in her eyes. “Delphine is my apprentice and therefore a member of this Guild! Does that really mean nothing, Master Drake?”

I stifled a gasp. Master Drake? The man on constant watch outside my cell was the Master of the Elements?

I shook my head. One of the affinity heads and a member of the Triumvirate had been on full-time guard duty outside my cell. For the first time, I realized just how dangerous they thought I was.

When Master Drake remained silent, Amara continued on. “She’s done nothing wrong! We owe her our protection.”

“Do you think I don’t know it?” Drake spoke in a heavy voice. “It has been weighing on me the whole time I’ve been stationed here. But we cannot deny the very real danger—not just to the throne or the Guild but to the whole kingdom. You know what just two of those Constantines did to us.”

Amara’s shoulders slumped. Seeing her give in made me grip the bars until my knuckles turned white. I pressed myself against them, reaching out with one hand.

“Amara!” I shouted.

She jerked and turned, staring at me with wide eyes. It was obvious from their reactions that neither of them had realized I was hovering there, listening. Her weight shifted, as if she meant to rush toward me despite Master Drake’s earlier prohibition.

But he moved to place himself in her way, his face growing

stern. He no longer looked tired or old but instead full of the same inexorable strength as the tide.

"You cannot," he said.

For a moment Amara met his eyes defiantly, and then she deflated, her shoulders slumping for a second time. Tears pricked at my eyes.

I couldn't blame her, though. Master Drake might be old, but that only meant he had great skill and control. He was the master of her own affinity, and she couldn't possibly fight him.

Was this, then, why he had been placed here? Not to guard against me, but to block those who might try to reach me? My pulse quickened at the idea of who else might try to force entry, but Master Drake continued talking, distracting me.

"Delphine is safe in here for now," he said softly. "If you're concerned for her, expend your efforts where they'll be more useful."

Amara paused for a moment, her eyes measuring his, before she nodded once. She grew tall again, her usual straight bearing returning.

"You are right, of course."

She met my eyes over his shoulder and mouthed a silent apology. I nodded, waiting until she'd turned away to dash the tears from my eyes.

I had just slept, but I felt exhausted in the wake of her brief visit, tossed around on waves of conflicting emotion. Their final words had burrowed into my head, taking up residence there and replaying over and over. The Master of the Elements had issued no overt threat, but I couldn't shake the feeling that there had been danger hinted in his words. The implication that my future safety was in question. What battle had he sent Amara off to fight on my behalf?

And stronger even than my fear about myself was another thought, the one that had come to me earlier. Ever since my arrest, I had been thinking that no one knew where I was. But

Amara had found me. And if Amara found me, then she couldn't be the only one who knew where I was. And if *he* knew…

The longing to see Nik was so intense it took my breath away. Every time I heard new footsteps, my heart leaped, sure it was him. Once he knew where I was, he would come.

But even stronger than the longing was my anxiety about what would happen when he did. Over and over, I silently told him not to come, wishing there was a way for him to receive the message. Wishing he would listen if he did.

Because when Nik came and Master Drake denied him entry, he wouldn't accept it and leave quietly like Amara. Nik would bring down the walls of this prison before he would allow me to remain imprisoned here without charge, trial, or crime.

It was true he had changed, but in some ways he remained the same. Never for a second did I doubt that Nik would throw his full strength into fighting to free me. And he had plenty of strength to fight with. Nik could literally rip out the stones keeping me here.

But he had never finished his training. Master Drake had decades more experience, as well as a host of guards to back him up. If it came to a fight, I feared for Nik. He wouldn't harm his own people, but he wouldn't hesitate to tear apart the prison itself, and they might well hurt him to stop that. And even if they managed to restrain him without causing him physical harm, he would be branded a traitor as well as an outcast. He would lose any chance of reconciling with his family and resuming his interrupted apprenticeship. He had finally agreed to come home, and the last thing I wanted was for him to ruin everything for my sake.

But neither did I want to be stuck in this cell for the foreseeable future. So it was impossible not to indulge daydreams of a dramatic rescue.

But the hours ticked on, and no familiar face or voice

appeared. Eventually night fell, announced by Drake's snores, and then breakfast arrived again, and still no one came for me. I had willed Nik not to come, but sorrow crept over me at his continued absence. I was alone in this cell, with only my fear for company, and I couldn't deny how much I wanted to see his face and feel his arms around me again. He shouldn't come—I didn't want him to come—but my traitorous heart still called for him.

Finally, sometime during the afternoon, my straining ears heard footsteps that didn't belong to a guard. The approaching person was alone and moved briskly, their steps confident.

I rushed to the bars, gripping them eagerly with both hands.

But the figure that came into view was much shorter than I expected, a girl only a handful of years older than me. She threw a curious glance my way, smiling when she saw me watching. But she turned to Master Drake rather than trying to speak to me.

He surged upward, standing with an alert expression. I shook my head at the sight of the two of them facing off. Drake towered over the girl in height, bulk, and years, and yet she wasn't diminished by his presence. She might be young, but she carried herself with an authority that could only come from power in all its forms. Master Drake might be the rolling force of the tide, but she was the sweeping strength of lightning and thunder and gale force winds.

I sucked in a breath, transfixed by the sight of her.

"You've heard?" The girl didn't waste any time on greetings.

Drake sighed and nodded his head once, his stance slackening in the absence of an attack.

"It's utterly ridiculous," the girl continued. "They can't be serious."

"You know they are." The sorrow in Drake's voice made my

stomach turn. What ridiculous decision had been made, exactly?

"Then we'll have to find a way to change their minds." The girl sounded resolute, but Master Drake remained silent.

She threw him a curious look. "I know you don't agree with them."

"Neither do any of them. Not really," he said, making both me and the girl frown.

"No one wants to be responsible for such an atrocity," he said. "No one wants to make the final decision. And yet no one is willing to set her free either. And so we remain stuck in stalemate, no one willing to move either forward or back." He gave her a knowing look. "I've been stuck down here for days, but I'm right, aren't I?"

She frowned. "It would explain why this is dragging on so long. What is everyone hoping for? That someone else will make the decision and absolve them of responsibility?" She sounded disgusted.

Looking my way again, she took in my desperate stance and wide eyes. She tried to muster a second smile but struggled.

"Is it really necessary for you to be down here the whole time?" she asked Drake. "If you could just talk some sense into the others!"

"I'm not sure how well they trust me after all my time down here," he said heavily. "I've carefully refrained from even speaking to her—any healer could see the truth of that if they bothered to ask me—but even so, I think they suspect me of being...influenced..."

This time they both glanced at me, and I rolled my eyes, unable to stop myself.

"That's nonsense!" The words flowed out before I could stop them. "Why hasn't Master Colton been consulted? I'm a healer! I can't influence anyone without touching them, and no one has been close enough for me to touch them since I got here."

For a moment both the Master and the new girl were still, clearly taken by surprise, as if they'd forgotten the barrier between us was erected by their rules rather than any physical impediment. Surely they had realized I could hear their conversation?

Master Drake cleared his throat and addressed himself to the girl again, although I saw his eyes flicking my way as he obliquely answered my query.

"Even if there's been no actual contamination, I believe there is some concern that I might be affected by her unprepossessing outside appearance." A rueful smile crossed his lips. "I've been here many hours after all."

That made me laugh, although I didn't feel much genuine amusement. Was I really such a sympathetic presence that even a captor might grow fond of me and be overcome by pity? I'd seen no sign of it since my arrival in the capital.

"They're afraid," the girl said roughly. "Well, except for Anka. I'm not sure that woman is afraid of anything. But she's playing her cards close—she's too wily to do anything else—so I'm not sure what she's thinking. But the rest of them are letting their fear overpower both their sense and their compassion. Especially Colton. I know he's afraid his entire affinity will be thrown into suspicion, but this is ridiculous."

She ran a hand down her face and groaned. "What a terrible time for Evermund to be away. I know he would do a better job of convincing them than me. But he'd already left for the northern farms before Nik arrived..."

Her voice trailed off, and although I held my breath, my heart beating in my ears, neither of them made any further mention of Nik.

"Airlie," Drake said gently, and I finally knew who the girl was.

Princess Airlie. Sister to the Calistan queen and princess of Tartora. And the greatest living elements mage. No wonder she could stand toe to toe with Master Drake without flinching.

"They know he'll disapprove." Her tone turned hard. "Why else would they be calling for a decision to be made before his return? There's no way Evermund would accept an execution."

Execution? The word rang through my head, everything else fading away as my surroundings grew fuzzy. Execution?

They meant to kill me. And I was stuck here, unable to do anything to defend myself, gagged even from speaking in my own defense.

"As you said, they're afraid." Drake's words pierced the muffled haze around me. "And can you blame them? They have reason to be. The chaos unleashed on this kingdom by the Constantines' insidious lies has already been great. You know how close we got to danger after they burned all those fields. Any further loss of crops, and we would have had people starving over the winter. As it was, it's caused great hardship to many. And all that pain and chaos was caused by only two people who were in the kingdom for mere weeks? Imagine how much worse the situation could get!"

"Of course I know all that. And I know Colton is afraid that lives will be lost if the populace lose trust in healers. But she didn't do any of that. It wasn't *her* who spread those lies!"

"No." He sighed. "And that is why I fear for our kingdom if we take this step. This leads down a road of darkness."

"And we've just got Nik back, too." She sounded close to tears. "You know he won't—" She cut herself off with a glance at me.

My awareness cleared, my thoughts going hard and solid again at the sound of his name. But, as before, they immediately let the topic drop.

Instead, the girl held my gaze. "I'm sorry." She spoke loudly enough that it was clear she meant to address me directly. "I apologize on their behalf, although I realize that must mean very little in the circumstances."

I wanted to reply, to plead my case, but Drake was already stretching the rules by letting her address me. If I pushed too hard—tried to engage in a proper conversation—he might call a halt to the whole thing. I remained silent.

"This really is unacceptable." Airlie's hands balled into fists. "There has to be something we can do. Hayes and Amara are both being treated as if they're already corrupted, but there has to be someone else—some ally we haven't thought of."

Drake sighed again and lowered himself back into his chair. "I wish I had your certainty that she isn't a danger," he murmured. "The certainty of youth."

She gave him an incredulous look. "I know you think this is wrong. You said as much in your message."

He looked my way, his expression weary and heavy, as if he carried the woes of the world on his shoulders.

"I have been helping guide this kingdom for much longer than you've been alive, Your Highness. The burden is starting to grow beyond what these old shoulders can bear."

Airlie snorted. "Don't try to fool me. You're a wily old man with the strength of ten storms followed by a hurricane."

He grinned, his deep chuckle sounding briefly. "I'll take that as a compliment."

"You should." She flashed him a smile, although her eyes were too tense to match the expression.

"I know this is wrong," he said after a moment, "but I couldn't tell you what would be the right decision in its place. And the others are all the same. They aren't bad people. They just feel the same weight I do, the same fear of getting it wrong and watching people suffer as a result. If any of us could figure out an alternative, I'm sure the rest would be easily convinced."

Airlie nodded. "I keep telling myself they won't actually go through with it. They're clearly reluctant to make the final decision. But every day that passes has me more worried."

She looked at me again, and I tried to pour my pleading desperation into my eyes. I must have succeeded to some extent because she flinched, her gaze falling away.

"It's all so pointless." The frustration poured out of her. "Delphine doesn't have a unique ability. She's just a healer, even if she's a strong one. For now, she's the only one in Tartora who knows how to use this skill, but how long will that remain the case? Now that we know something like this is possible, it's inevitable someone will come along with both the strength and the motivation to work it out for themselves. Getting rid of Delphine won't eliminate the threat—it will just ensure we don't know where the threat is coming from."

I slid down the bars to sit, suddenly too exhausted to remain upright any longer. Why had I never thought of that? I had been determined not to teach the skill to anyone—determined it would die with me. But Airlie was right. It had been done once, and that meant it would be done again. There would eventually be someone angry enough or greedy enough to seize at the possibility. I had thought I was the only one who could make a wall, but in the end, Grey had proved me wrong on that. Surely the same thing would happen again.

It didn't matter what the king did to me. He would never be able to eradicate this.

Dimly I heard Airlie leaving, but I didn't look up. My thoughts had turned inward, the futility of it all sparking a desperation that sent my mind flying, exploring avenues I hadn't considered before. Avenues I should have seen already.

This new skill existed now, and we couldn't change that. Others would work out how to do it, as Grey had worked out how to do my skill. But that didn't mean there was no hope. Quite the opposite—that certainty was my best source of hope.

Joy surged through me as I saw the way to save myself.

Despair followed a minute later. Everyone of influence was afraid of getting close to me or even talking to me. The king and Triumvirate weren't going to allow me to stand before them and defend myself. They would decide my sentence behind closed doors, and there was no need for me to ever get close to them at all. In fact, they would almost certainly avoid me as carefully as if I was a known assassin.

Before I could sink too deeply into my fear, however, a face appeared in front of my mind's eye. I didn't know where Nik was right now, but I had no doubt that he would be either searching for me or fighting for me. And if he hadn't given up, I couldn't either.

I leaped to my feet, my hands on the bars as I fixed my eyes on the stationary figure in the chair.

"Master Drake!" I shouted the words.

He startled so hard he nearly fell out of his chair. Leaping to his feet, he whirled to face me, his brows knit. It was the first time I had ever called to him.

I didn't know how many words I would get, so I couldn't waste them.

"Amara. I need to speak to Amara."

The crease between his eyes deepened, and he didn't reply.

I rushed to continue, my words tumbling over each other as I tried to convey my sincerity.

"You said all you needed was a better option in order to convince the others to spare me. Bring Amara here—or if you can't bring her, bring Princess Airlie back—and I'll give you a better option, along with a way to keep Tartora safe."

TWENTY-FOUR

In the end, Drake summoned both of them. And the conversation that followed lasted for a long time. But at the end of it, Ember and I were swathed in a voluminous cloak and smuggled from the prison block.

Airlie went ahead to clear the path while Drake stayed behind to maintain the illusion I was safely in my cell. Only Amara walked beside me as I finally tasted fresh air and saw the sky again.

It was hard not to turn my face up to the sun, but I kept it down, hiding my identity as she hurried me across the short stretch of open ground and through a side door of the palace.

We were heading straight for the king, but Airlie reappeared before we could reach his reported location.

"You can't!" she hissed, making us both stop. "Not now. A delegation from the nomad tribes has arrived a day early and King Marius is in the middle of an audience with them. We'll have to wait until they've finished."

Amara groaned. "What terrible timing! What are we supposed to do now? Should we go back?" She glanced back the way we'd come.

"No," Airlie and I said at the same time, although I said it with considerably more force. I quickly fell silent, however, letting Airlie speak.

"We can't risk that. Drake said the others are suspicious of him already. What if they decide to put someone else on guard duty? She's free now, and there's no point moving backward. We just have to stash her out of sight until the delegation finish their initial business and retreat to their guest rooms."

"I'll take her to my suite," Amara said. "Only the steward knows which one I've been assigned—I don't think most people at the Guild even know I've returned yet—so I won't have any visitors."

Airlie looked uncertain but eventually nodded her agreement. "If someone does discover she's missing and raise an alarm, I'll try to get to you first."

Amara quickly described which suite she was in—a description that meant nothing to me—and then hurried me away. It took painfully long to cross the palace and Guild, but thankfully most of the corridors were empty due to the midday meal.

When we reached the suite, and Amara firmly closed the door behind us, I shrugged out of the cloak with relief. Ember jumped out of my arms and started exploring the room, apparently unbothered by the tension.

"Do you think we'll be waiting long?" I asked uneasily.

She sighed. "I hope not. I'm already nervous enough about this dangerous plan of yours. And I don't want to give Drake or Airlie a chance to overthink it."

"They're good people," I said, although I hadn't known them long. "They won't abandon us."

Amara sighed again but nodded. "If I didn't believe that, I wouldn't have agreed in the first place. I wish Evermund were here."

"Talking of people who aren't here," I said, trying to sound casual and failing.

"Nik's gone," Amara said, without my having to name him.

"Gone?" My heart rate picked up. "What does that mean?"

Had he tried to get to me in prison and been stopped? Had he already been cast out—maybe even from the entire kingdom this time?

"Relax," Amara said gently. "He's fine, or he was when he decided to leave."

"He just...left?" My brows drew together as I tried to make sense of her words. Nik had known I was in trouble, locked away without charge, and he had just left? There was no way that was true.

"He was very angry when he heard what had happened, and he grew even more furious when his father refused to relent," she said slowly, as if picking her words with care.

I relaxed slightly. Nik must have known he didn't have the strength to rescue me alone. Had he left in order to remove the temptation of trying anyway?

That thought didn't sit right, though. Amara and even Airlie had remained to fight for me, but Nik had walked away? I didn't believe it. And Amara clearly knew something more than she was saying.

But she was just as clearly remaining silent on purpose. I wanted to grab her by the shoulders and keep asking until she explained everything, but I couldn't. She was already risking a lot to support me, and I couldn't repay the debt by haranguing her, however desperately I wanted answers.

"What about Phoenix?" I asked. "Is he all right?"

She glanced toward Ember who was sniffing one of the curtains. "I thought he was with you this whole time, although I can see now that doesn't make much sense. A falcon doesn't belong in a cell."

"You haven't seen him?" I bit my lip, trying not to let my concern grow.

"Don't worry," she said, watching the expressions move

across my face. "I believe you can make this plan work. And afterward—"

But before I could hear what was going to happen afterward, a knock sounded on the door. We both froze.

"Amara?" Hayes's familiar voice called through the wood. "Are you in there?"

Amara strode to the closest cupboard—a tall wardrobe—and silently pulled open one door. I remained motionless for a moment, taken too much by surprise to follow her lead. But when she gestured a second time for me to climb inside, I finally responded.

Scooping up both Ember and the discarded cloak, I bundled us into the wardrobe.

"Just a minute!" Amara called as she shut the door on me.

It was dark inside, except for the small bits of light that seeped in around the doors. I could hear perfectly, though, and was able to follow Amara's footsteps as she crossed the room to open the door.

"Hayes," she said in her usual calm way. "You were looking for me? I heard Their Majesties were greeting a new delegation. Are they finished?"

"Not yet, I believe." He stepped into the room, closing the door behind him. "But I couldn't put off talking to you any longer."

"What do you mean?" Amara sounded genuinely bewildered. "Is this about Delphine?"

"Delphine?" He sounded alarmed. "Don't tell me they've finally made a decision?"

She must have shaken her head because he continued in a calmer voice.

"Oh thank goodness. We still have time, then." He paused. "Actually, I came to talk to you about us."

"Us?" My confident master sounded unlike her usual self as she repeated his final word.

I wished I could close my eyes and will myself somewhere else. Clearly this wasn't a conversation I should be witness to. I could hardly start humming, however. Amara wanted me to stay hidden or she wouldn't have stashed me in the closet to start with.

"I know my timing is terrible, and that you're distracted with Delphine's situation, but the whole thing has made me think."

"How could it not?" she said softly. "You dedicated your entire life to serving this court. I remember how passionately you used to argue back in our apprentice days. You said the court was responsible for the good of the whole kingdom. And yet now they're so quick to discredit your judgment and experience."

"Oh, I don't mean that I'm offended," he said. "Not personally, anyway. If they believe I'm compromised, then their actions are reasonable enough. I'm not concerned that anyone is failing to value me as an individual."

He sighed. "I'm concerned at the failure of the entire system. I've believed for so long that I could do the most good by being here. But now I'm questioning that. I'm not sure how much good is possible here after all."

"Hayes." The soft sound of movement suggested Amara had drawn closer to him, perhaps even touched his arm. "You have always done good wherever you were."

He gave a half-laughing groan. "And you've always believed better of me than I deserve. In truth, I was already thinking about leaving court even before we got back to the capital."

"Leaving court?" Amara sounded alarmed. "What do you mean? Where would you go?"

"Wherever you are." The simple statement fell into stunned silence.

I was held frozen inside the wardrobe and could only

imagine Amara was equally so out in the room. Was Hayes saying...

"I love you, Amara," he continued. "I've always loved you. You know that. And spending so much time with you again...I can't lose you a second time. I've lived alone all these years, and I don't want to do it anymore. I was young, and arrogant, and ambitious the last time, and it still hurt terribly. This time I'm afraid..." He drew a shaky breath. "I don't want to feel that pain again. I don't want to lose you. I've experienced firsthand the good we can do together. It doesn't matter if it's at court or elsewhere. I want to stay by your side and work beside you for the rest of my life. I want to marry you, Amara—if you'll have me. Even if that means giving up my life at court."

"You're next in line to be Head of Healing. Everyone says so. Would you really be willing to give that up?"

"I would sacrifice more than that," he said without hesitation.

I could hear the smile in Amara's voice and the tears clogging her throat. "You told me once that it was possible to have ambition without being like my mother. I guess you were right. I should have believed you then instead of running away. But I was so afraid of becoming like her."

"You were never like her." The sound of movement told me they'd come even closer together. "But I always understood why she had such an effect on you."

"Of course you did." Amara was clearly still smiling through tears. "You were always too good to me."

"I dispute that," Hayes said, the smile sounding in his voice too. "Never *too* good. Does this mean you're going to marry me?"

"Yes," Amara whispered, but I was so still inside the closet I caught the word. "I am." Her next words came out stronger. "Because I already came to the same conclusion. Before we arrived in the capital I'd also decided on a major change."

"What do you mean?"

"I mean that you weren't the only one in pain after we went our separate ways all those years ago. And you aren't the only one who has always remembered. I haven't been unaffected by being with you again either. I decided weeks ago that I wasn't saying goodbye a second time."

"Really?" He sounded delighted. "Do you mean it? You've been feeling the same way? I should have said something earlier! I've been so nervous, afraid your feelings had faded into warm friendship after so many years."

Amara laughed. "I thought they had. Until I saw you again."

An unmistakable sound told me Hayes had finally taken firm action and given the appropriate response to her declaration.

But when they finally stopped kissing—much to my relief—their conversation merely resumed again.

"When you said you were planning a major change," Hayes said. "Do you mean you've been thinking about remaining at the Guild? You know I wouldn't ask that of you."

"Actually, since arriving here, I've come to the opposite conclusion as you," she said. "The king and Triumvirate responded badly to the threat from Grey. There's no denying they should have caught what was happening in Eldrida, for one. And now this business with Delphine..." I could almost see her shaking her head. "The king and Triumvirate have been in their positions for too long. They've stagnated. And it's clear that you were right about the impact that has on the rest of the kingdom. We need change, and I think it's time I started working for that change here—at the heart of everything."

"Do you really mean it?" Hayes sounded dazed. "You won't come to feel resentful and constrained?"

"I can't be sure of the future," she said. "But I don't believe so."

"You're telling me I can stay in Tarona and have you too?"

He laughed, an almost giddy sound. "That sounds too good to be true."

The sound of another kiss made me shove my hands over my ears, but it stopped much more quickly this time.

"You'd better come out, Delphine," Amara said loudly.

I startled so badly in response that Ember whined.

"Delphine?" Hayes sounded shocked, and I couldn't blame him.

Reluctantly I pushed open the wardrobe door and blinked in the bright light of the room. I could feel my cheeks growing hotter and hotter as I carefully stepped out of the closet. I couldn't bring myself to look at either of them until Amara chuckled.

"Don't look so mortified, Delphine. I'm sure you had some idea of Hayes and my history. Luna will have told you if no one else."

I gasped as I belatedly remembered my friend. "You have no idea how delighted she's going to be about this," I said, making both of them laugh.

"While I'm delighted to see you walking around freely," Hayes said, "I'm a little confused. What were you doing in Amara's wardrobe?"

I could see the concern slowly leeching away the joy from his face as he realized his new betrothed might be involved in something that bordered on treasonous.

"We're taking her to see the king," Amara said calmly. "But that delegation arrived at the worst possible moment so we ducked in here to wait."

"We?" Hayes asked.

"Airlie, Drake, and me. Gia and Renley by now as well, I'm sure. Airlie was going to speak to them."

He relaxed slightly at the other names, clearly relieved Amara had such powerful allies. "But why was she in the closet? You knew it was me at the door." Slowly understanding spread across his face, his expression falling. "You didn't know if you could trust me."

"Of course we trust you!" I cried quickly, but Amara was less quick to answer.

"I always knew you were on Delphine's side," she said. "You already risked your position and reputation arguing for her release. I never would have expected less. But defying the system is another thing altogether. While I knew you would agree with our intent, I was less sure you would agree with our methods. But then you said you were ready to walk away altogether. Then I knew you were safe to include in this."

Hayes sighed heavily. "I want to be offended that you didn't trust me from the beginning—that you didn't know I would always be on your side. But how can I be offended? I already chose the throne and Guild over you once, so I can't blame you for wondering if I would do it again."

"I'm not wondering anymore," she whispered, and he leaned toward her.

I cleared my throat loudly, and he moved away again, chuckling.

"So what exactly is this plan?" he asked. "Do you need my help?"

"If you're really certain you want to get involved," I said, "then I could definitely use your help."

TWENTY-FIVE

"They've finally left!" Airlie paused mid-step as she took in Hayes's presence. She threw a concerned look at Amara, but I answered for her.

"Don't worry. Hayes is safe. He's on our side."

Airlie looked relieved, but her mouth still turned downward. "I don't like this business of sides. Hopefully this plan will put an end to the matter."

"That's what we're all hoping for," Amara said.

"It's a risky attempt, though," Hayes murmured, making Airlie narrow her eyes.

"If you don't want to be involved..."

"No," he said quickly. "I'm with you. I'm just aware that some are more at risk with this plan than others." He threw me an obvious glance.

Airlie sighed. "It's not an ideal solution, no. But the one most at risk is also the one with the most to gain. If we had another solution, we would have already tried it."

"And that's why I'm with you," Hayes said. "I never would have believed King Marius or Colton could get to this point."

"It's this last winter." Airlie sounded sad. "You weren't here, so you didn't see the situation growing. One of the problems with fear is that it breeds more fear. I'm convinced that if they'd been presented with this situation out of the blue six months ago, they wouldn't have considered such a drastic path. Even now, none of them actually want to be the one to make the call. But we can't leave the situation hanging like this with Delphine at constant risk."

"We appreciate your care for Delphine," Amara said. "I feel terrible that I've been so helpless to rescue my own apprentice."

Airlie smiled at me, the gesture lighting up her face. "Of course we want the best for Delphine—and hope she has a long and prosperous life here in Tartora where her skills as a healer will always be needed. But I would do the same for anyone. We can't start punishing people for what they might one day do!"

"Should we be going?" Hayes asked. "How long do we have?"

Airlie started as if suddenly remembering her original reason for joining us. "Yes, we need to hurry! Drake is keeping Their Majesties and the rest of the Triumvirate in the throne room, but I don't know how long he can stall them."

Amara turned to me. "You're sure about this, Delphine?"

I drew a deep breath and nodded. However it turned out, I had to try something. I couldn't just sit back and let my life be taken away from me without fighting back.

"Where is that fascinating fox of yours?" Airlie looked around the room. "Do you think she would mind being left behind for this meeting?"

"She usually sleeps at this time of day anyway," I said, just before spotting her curled up and fast asleep on one of the padded chairs by the window. I smiled at the sight of her. "Looks like she won't miss us."

She didn't even stir as I wrapped myself in the cloak once again for the trip back into the palace. But with Princess Airlie at my side, no one would have questioned us anyway. From the looks of respect and admiration sent her way, she had obviously won her place in the palace, despite her humble origins.

My thoughts went to Nik again—as they all too often did. Even if the court was willing to accept a princess of humble birth, I had neither Airlie's extraordinary strength nor her temperament. I didn't think I could ever live permanently at court. The current situation might be unusual, but it was enough to put me off a political life forever. Airlie was the perfect wife for Evermund, but if Nik was going to reclaim his rightful position, I couldn't be the wife he needed.

All too soon we arrived at a set of double doors that clearly opened onto a room of importance. I would have preferred my confrontation with the king to happen somewhere less intimidating, but there was nothing I could do about it.

Airlie pushed both doors open without hesitation, making our entrance suitably dramatic. Hayes followed after her, and Amara gestured for me to go next, leaving her to bring up the rear. I appreciated the show of support they were giving me, but I still wished I could have slunk inside without making a fuss.

"Ah, Princess," a deep voice said from the far side of the room, "there you are." But whatever else he'd been about to say was lost when he caught sight of the rest of us.

Surging up from his throne, King Marius eyed me with alarm. His graying hair lent his features gravity, as did the formal circlet he wore, and I wanted to shrink back from his anger.

Beside him, on a smaller throne, sat an elegant woman with a circlet of her own. Standing at her side were Gia and Renley. The princess winked as soon as she saw me, her manner a shocking contrast with her parents. Clearly Airlie had managed to speak to her.

Standing in front of the dais were four more figures, two of whom I recognized. Given the presence of Drake, the Master of the Elements, and Anka, now the Royal Mage, this was clearly the Triumvirate, making the second man Colton, the head of my own affinity. And beside him, the diminutive second woman, whose hair was mostly gray but whose golden face was unlined and full of life, had to be the famous Master of Plants.

The king swung toward them. "What is the meaning of this? Drake?" He sounded furious. "You assured us all was well with your prisoner!"

"She looks quite well to me," Drake said blandly, ignoring the fire shooting from the king's eyes.

I gulped. Apparently Grey wasn't the only one adept at shaping his words around a healer's ability to truth tell.

"This has gone on long enough." Airlie had progressed calmly forward to take her place beside Gia. "You must make a judgment one way or another, and it is only fair that Delphine be allowed to speak in her own defense. You have both Master Colton and Master Anka to tell you if her words are true."

King Marius shot a look at Colton who was carefully avoiding catching my gaze. He might be worried for his affinity and the disaster I might bring on it, but he wasn't completely shameless. As my affinity head, he should have been the one defending me, not Airlie.

He cleared his throat. "I can certainly confirm any lies, Your Majesty." He finally looked in my direction. "You must answer questions directly and without prevarication."

Both Colton and the king glared in Drake's direction, but the Master of the Elements looked unmoved. He might not wear a circlet in his tight curls, but his height and the white of his hair against his dark skin conveyed a powerful combination of strength and age-won wisdom. I was fortunate in my allies.

"To begin with," Amara said, "let's clear up your most immediate concern. Delphine, is physical contact necessary to mesmerize someone?"

"Yes." The word came out shaky and quiet, so I repeated myself in a firmer voice. "Yes. Just like with regular healing, physical touch is necessary to mesmerize. From here I can tell your heart is beating, and your lungs are working, and I could recognize a lie or test a child's seed. But I cannot interfere with another person's body or mind from a distance. Mesmerization is bound by the same constraints as regular healing."

King Marius, Queen Celestine, Drake, and Augusta all turned to Colton. Colton was staring at me, but I couldn't read anything in his expression.

After a prolonged moment, he repeated the question.

"There is no possible way for you to mesmerize someone in any way without touching them?"

"That is correct," I said, holding his gaze steadily.

He looked at the king and nodded slowly. The king looked from him to Anka, who also nodded. Everyone in the room relaxed in response, even me a little.

"Well, then..." King Marius sat back in his throne and regarded me, his face weary and eyes sad. "The princess is right, and you should be allowed a voice in your defense. I apologize for not granting you an audience before now."

Part of me wanted to stammer out that it was fine, awed by my surroundings and company, but another part wanted to rage and scream abuse at his treatment of me thus far. I settled for a stiff nod.

"You were taught this skill by Grey, who is now deceased," the king said, waiting at the end of the sentence for my confirmation.

"That is correct," I said. "I saw him die myself and confirmed it with my ability."

Colton nodded again.

"To your knowledge, the only other ones who knew this skill were Grey's family, and all of them are now deceased as well?"

I hesitated, and the group around the dais tensed.

"As far as I'm aware, the Constantines never taught anyone

outside their family the skill. However, not all the Constantines are dead. One of the grandsons had an elements affinity, and he remains alive. There is also a daughter-in-law who is a healer, but she was never fully accepted into the family and never taught to mesmerize."

Colton nodded a third time, and the king relaxed again. A hint of approval entered King Marius's eyes which I could only attribute to my detailed and specific responses. Apparently I was reassuring him with my openness and careful replies.

But his expression almost immediately grew heavier, his shoulders sinking. My heart sank with them. I had held onto the hope that my words could convince him, but it didn't look promising.

"Have you ever voluntarily planted a lie in another's mind?" he asked, and my heart dropped even further.

"Yes," I said reluctantly. "I mesmerized one of the Constantines at Grey's instruction. I didn't want to, but I felt I needed to allay his suspicions."

The king and queen exchanged a look, and I rushed to keep talking.

"But I regret having done so greatly. It seemed like a relatively harmless lie at the time, but it ended up having devastating consequences. I have sworn that I will never mesmerize again, no matter the circumstances."

"That is an admirable resolution," Augusta said. "But it is one thing to say so when everything is calm and another to hold firm to our intentions through the storm."

Amara shifted closer to me. "Delphine may still be an apprentice, but she has already weathered several storms and faced death more than once."

"Even to save myself, I will not mesmerize again," I said. "I have faced that situation already, and I believe I could face it again if necessary."

The king looked at Colton with a raised eyebrow and again

received a nod. I breathed out, feeling hopeful for the first time, but the king's next words dashed the brief emotion.

"Even so...By your own admission, you have mesmerized before and accept some level of culpability in the deaths which followed."

Hayes stepped forward. "It is a credit to Delphine's sense of responsibility that she claims any guilt at all. The true responsibility for the Constantines' deaths rests at their own feet. They created Grey and set themselves on the path to destruction without any assistance from Delphine."

Colton gave Hayes a hard look, but Hayes continued talking.

"I must also remind you that what happened on the island happened beyond Tartora's borders and is out of our jurisdiction. We are not here today to assign guilt for those murders. If anyone is to seek justice on that account, it must be the islanders themselves. And on the island, Delphine was a protector, not a criminal. If we are discussing the island, we would do better to focus on the benefits of securing an alliance as quickly as possible before one of the other kingdoms beats us to it. And Delphine would be an asset in any such negotiations."

"We have already sent word to Master Clay to begin alliance negotiations," King Marius said. "But as much as we would value such a connection, the safety of our people must be our first priority."

I braced myself, waiting for what I knew would come next. As we had feared, no arguments could prevent the king viewing me as a danger. Seeing his kingdom nearly plunged into famine had clearly had a profound effect.

But before he could speak again, Queen Celestine leaned over and whispered something to him. I couldn't catch the words, but her eyes were on me, and I could have sworn I saw her lips form Nik's name.

The king winced visibly in response to whatever she'd said,

and then slowly nodded. But from Gia's scowl, the queen's intervention hadn't provided any last-minute rescue.

"Delphine, many character witnesses have spoken on your behalf." The king's eyes traveled from Amara to Hayes and then back to his wife, making me wonder what private words had been exchanged between parents and son before Nik's departure. "Bearing this in mind, as well as your testimony today, I cannot in good conscience order your execution. While I would prefer the skill you possess be wiped from existence, that is too high a price to pay."

My whole body slumped with relief. It was good news after all. Except then he continued talking.

"However, regardless of your intentions, I cannot place my kingdom at risk. Therefore, you will be kept in a guarded location and forbidden from any future physical contact."

"Forever?" I asked, not quite grasping what he was suggesting.

He nodded ponderously.

"You will bar her from all physical contact with anyone? Ever?" Amara asked, her tone growing thunderous. "So she is not to be murdered but merely imprisoned for life and barred from using her ability?"

A shudder ran through me. I hadn't even considered that such an imprisonment would mean I could never work as a healer again. Could I spend my life locked in a cage, alone and unable to help no matter how great the need around me? What sort of life would that be?

I had hoped this audience wouldn't require any drastic action after all, but while my life might have been spared, I couldn't accept the future the king demanded. Which meant I couldn't hesitate.

Launching into movement, I leaped onto the dais and reached the king in a single bound. Before he realized what was happening, I had one hand wrapped around his throat. My touch was gentle, but everyone in the room knew what I could do with the lightest of touches.

"Don't move!" I cried. "You know I only need a second!"

King Marius had gone stone still beneath my hand, although his eyes jumped from Drake to Augusta. He had gone without formal guards for such a sensitive meeting, but he had done so knowing the strongest mages in the kingdom were at his side.

But when Drake moved, it wasn't to come to the king's aide. With two steps, he placed himself toe to toe with the Master of Plants. I had fought at Nik's side often enough to know what destruction could be wreaked by a plants master, but she had yet to make any move—no doubt taken by surprise and unsure of the danger I posed to the king.

"Drake," she said in a low, warning tone, but he didn't move.

Amara and Hayes stepped up beside him, the three of them forming a wall with their backs toward the dais. In front of them, blocked from approaching the throne were Augusta, Colton, and Anka. The king's eyes flicked to his daughter, but she shook her head sadly as she, Renley, and Airlie slowly retreated from the dais, leaving the king and queen alone with me.

"Sorry, Father," she said. "But what you're doing is wrong, and you know it. I can't stand with you on this."

"Gia!" the queen hissed. "Your father!"

But Gia just kept shaking her head with a mournful look.

I held my breath, willing my hand not to shake as I kept it in place.

The king met Airlie's eyes next. "We accepted you and made you a princess, and you repay us with treason?"

She remained silent, her face a careful mask.

The king turned his head toward me, speaking through gritted teeth. "I offered you your life."

"If you can call that a life," I replied, trying to sound scornful.

Augusta peered around Drake's crossed arms. "All you're doing is proving us right, girl."

"Perhaps," I said. "But I don't have much to lose at this point."

"And what do you hope to gain if you kill the king?" Colton asked. "If it's a swift death you're after—"

I laughed, the unexpected sound rendering him silent. "If I didn't want to live, I wouldn't be risking this now. But King Marius doesn't have to die. No one does."

"Of course not," Queen Celestine said, a strain in her lilting voice. "If you step away from the king we can talk further, and I'm sure we can—"

"Oh no," I said, shamelessly interrupting her. It had taken every bit of my determination to come this far, but it would all be for nothing if I couldn't brazen it out. "If we're all going to walk away from this alive, it's because Colton will save the king."

I met the eyes of the Master of Healing. "It's up to you to protect your king."

CHAPTER

TWENTY-SIX

Colton's brows contracted, his eyes meeting mine over Amara's shoulder.

"What do you mean?"

"Your Majesty," I said, "please extend your right hand away from the throne."

The king remained frozen for a long minute before reluctantly complying. When the arm opposite to me was fully stretched out, I looked toward Colton.

"That hand is for you," I said.

His eyes flashed as he understood my instruction to make contact with the king. But he clearly still didn't understand my intentions.

Amara stepped to one side, clearing the path to the dais, and Colton slowly approached. He took the king's outstretched wrist in a healer's practiced grip.

As I had expected, he immediately attempted to push his power into the king, no doubt wanting to be prepared to counter any damage I wrought.

I activated the king's wall in response, driving Colton's power out.

He gave a cry of surprise and jerked his hand back, the king's arm dropping limply from his grip.

"What is it?" Queen Celestine asked in alarm. "What has she done to him?"

"I...I don't know." Colton sounded lost. "My power couldn't connect with him."

"What does that mean?" King Marius asked, his voice tense despite the forced stillness of his body.

"That is your wall," I said. "Mesmerization was Grey's weapon, but I had one of my own. This is it."

From the corner of my eye, I saw Anka's face shift. Her narrowed eyes widened slightly. She had always been interested in my wall.

"You asked what I hope to achieve," I continued. "The answer is simple. King Marius intends to destroy my life although I've committed no crime. I need hope for the future. I could end both of us right now—taking my persecutor down with me—unless I have a reason not to do so. You're going to give me hope, Master Colton. And you're going to do it by learning how to activate someone's wall."

"A wall guards not just against a healer's regular power but also against mesmerization?" Anka's face had grown thoughtful as she watched me speak, her brows knitting together.

I nodded. "That's right. It blocks a healer's power from entering the body completely. If you raise someone else's wall, it will drop again when you lose physical contact with them, but, in the meantime, it will protect against another healer."

"That's a powerful tool," Anka said.

I looked from her to the king. "Even if I stay locked up forever, someone else will come along and work out how to mesmerize. Now that people know it's possible, someone will do it eventually. I understand you're worried about what a rogue healer could do, but there's a way to protect yourself against such a person—no matter their intentions. You see me

300

as a threat, but removing all potential threats is an impossible task. The solution is to learn how to defend yourself."

"I thought you'd failed to teach anyone else how to make a wall," Anka said.

I shrugged. "That was true in the past. But I haven't tried to teach the Master of Healing himself." I met Colton's eyes over the king's head. "You're going to learn how to do it right now. And once you can, you'll have another option other than locking me up forever. I'll have a reason to choose hope. So like I said at the beginning: you're our only chance of all walking away from this alive, Master Colton."

One of Anka's eyebrows slowly rose, and I carefully didn't look her way as Colton swallowed. Thankfully his attention was fully focused on me and the king.

Slowly, he took the king's wrist again, and this time I let him connect, giving him time to ascertain that the king was unharmed. Then I activated the king's wall.

As before, Colton's power was immediately driven from Marius's body. But this time he was prepared, and maintained his hold on the king.

"It's remarkable," he said slowly, looking up at me. "But I don't know how you're doing it."

I shrugged. "It's not hard really. You just need to block your own healing power that's connecting with him."

"But how? I've never—"

The double doors creaked open, making him break off as the rest of us turned to look. A young man I didn't recognize strode through the narrow opening. His boots were coated in dust, and his clothes—while fine quality—were rumpled and dirty. On his heels strode a familiar figure in a similar state.

Nik had returned. And on his shoulder rode Phoenix.

The doors clanged shut behind them as the two men took in the scene before them.

"Don't come any closer," Anka called, although her almost

lazy tone didn't match the seriousness of the moment. "As you can see, your father is being held at the point of a healer's sword, so to speak, and Colton is about to try his best to save him. Interference could prove...messy."

"What?" The unfamiliar man's eyes jumped to Airlie, full of questions, and I realized he must be her husband, the missing Prince Evermund. Only the heir to the throne would interrupt a meeting between the king and Triumvirate with such confidence.

Evermund had returned, and Nik had been the one to bring him. I met Nik's eyes, cold washing over me. The tables had been turned. Now he was the one walking in on me doing something apparently heinous. If he assumed I was truly threatening his father's life, I couldn't blame him.

But the confused look on his face faded as he held my gaze. The warmth filling his eyes ignited the same warmth in my chest. Regardless of the situation, he was as glad to see me as I was to see him. He didn't know what was happening, but he trusted me, and his trust filled me with fresh strength.

A sudden whoosh of movement made us all flinch as Phoenix launched himself from Nik's shoulder and flapped his way down the long throne room. The queen sucked in a breath as he swooped toward us, but he merely maneuvered himself onto his usual perch on my shoulder. Once there, he directed one bright eye toward the king. I tried to picture how we looked to others and decided a merlin falcon on my shoulder only helped with the impression I was trying to create.

"That's enough!" I snapped, letting my tension show. Hopefully Colton would think I was on edge at the arrival of fresh backup for the king. "It's time to end this one way or another." I put an edge of desperation in my voice as I added, "Colton, either you block my power right now, or it's all over."

"What?" Colton stared at me. "But I don't know how to make a wall."

I shrugged. "Then work it out. You have ten seconds."

"Wait!" Evermund cried, horrified, and his panic reverberated on Colton's face.

I thrust my power into the king, sending it toward his heart. I knew how Colton would react to my power being anywhere near that part of his body, and sure enough Colton's power was already there, waiting.

The second I reached his chest, my power collided with a solid force. Springing back like released rubber, I was driven instantly out of the king's body.

I pulled my hand away from his neck, joy spreading through me.

"He did it!" I could feel tears on my cheeks, but I didn't try to dash them away. "Master Colton made a wall!"

Cheers erupted from the direction of Gia and Renley, making Phoenix take off and wing around the room in a wide circle. I watched him go, my eyes falling on Amara. She looked deeply relieved. The situation had obviously strained her, but my eyes kept moving, drawn irresistibly to Nik. He still had no idea what was going on, but he ran across the throne room and leaped onto the dais, sweeping me into his arms.

I buried my face in his chest and cried in relief. I might be seconds away from being branded a traitor and dragged away, but at least I had a chance now. And perhaps more importantly, the healing affinity could now make walls. I had proven it could be done, and it was now only a matter of time before walls became commonplace.

Phoenix landed on a nearby urn, still unimpressed with the sudden disruption, but I was enjoying being in Nik's arms too much to care.

"Delphine." Nik murmured my name against my hair, pressing his lips against my head. "I'm sorry." His voice sounded thick.

I pulled back to look at him. "Whatever for?"

I wanted to tell him how much his faith in me meant—especially after I'd failed to show the same trust in him at the beginning of winter—but I was still too emotional for so many words.

"I'm sorry for not coming to you—for leaving you alone in there."

I shook my head. "No, I was glad you didn't come. I didn't want you to throw everything away for me."

He gave me an exasperated look. "Of course I would have come if it could have helped. Surely you don't doubt that?"

I flushed, but before I could respond, a snapped speech from Augusta made me pull away from him.

"Prince Nikolas is as foolish as ever, I see, but I expect better from you, Evermund! Everyone else may have lost their senses, but it is our responsibility to arrest the traitor who tried to kill the king."

Nik growled, his muscles tightening as he tried to pull me back into the circle of his arms. I resisted, and he settled for hovering protectively behind me.

"Of course Delphine wasn't going to kill the king," Anka said in a voice that was quiet but still commanding enough to cut through the tension of the room. "Can't you recognize a piece of theater when you see one?"

She looked with a raised eyebrow from Augusta to Colton, still standing beside the king and queen. "No? None of you?" She sounded disappointed, tsking quietly to herself. "This is why I'm needed as a *law keeper*, not playing dress up in purple robes."

"What are you talking about Anka? Were you in on this as well?" King Marius gripped both arms of the throne, his face white. But despite his obvious fury, he was reining himself in, waiting for answers.

His restraint demonstrated why he had been a successful ruler for decades. I didn't like the decisions he'd been making since learning about mesmerization, but he was capable of putting aside personal insult when it was politically necessary, and he was willing to consider the good and stability of the kingdom over personal revenge. He had proven that when he accepted the Triumvirate putting his son aside in favor of his nephew, and it was that trait I was placing all my hope in.

"Of course I wasn't involved," Anka said. "That should have been apparent. I suppose I wasn't deemed trustworthy enough." She gave Amara an unimpressed look.

"Nonsense, Aunt," Amara said briskly. "It wasn't a matter of trust. I couldn't ask you to get involved in something like this."

"If you didn't know about this ahead of time, then what do you mean?" Colton frowned in Anka's direction. "Are you saying you sensed she was lying when she threatened the king? Because I got no such impression."

Anka shook her head. "This is why I keep telling you that a regular healer is not the same as a law keeper—and why our affinity needs to put greater emphasis on proper truth telling training for all our apprentices."

I could tell from her tone that it was an old argument between them.

"Master Anka, please explain yourself," the king said in a warning tone.

"It's a classic strategy that wouldn't fool any law keeper worth their salt," she said. "The speaker says a series of true statements and allows the listener to assume that those statements are connected to each other."

King Marius frowned. "So in this instance..."

"Delphine said that you intended to destroy her life. True. She said that she needs hope for the future. True. She said that Colton activating a wall would give her hope. Also true. And then she said that without a reason for restraint, she might as well kill the person who was persecuting her. That's true, of course. Freed from all restraints, humanity has shown itself to be perfectly capable of murder. But most of us have restraints already—small matters like self-respect, value for life, and morality for starters. Plus in this case, you're both her king and the father of the man she loves. There was no chance a person like Delphine was going to kill you. She needed restraints to prevent her, yes, but she already had those. She just allowed you to assume that only hope for the future would be enough of a restraint to hold her back. In fact the two truths were never related." Anka looked to me. "Am I right?"

I nodded, impressed.

"But she said I was going to die if Colton didn't succeed in blocking her," King Marius said, looking from Anka to me with narrowed eyes.

"Actually," Anka said, "I think you'll find she said someone would die but never specified who. I believe it was herself she expected to die if she failed in her purpose here. Again, it was all the manipulation of assumptions. It was quite neatly done for a novice." She nodded respectfully in my direction.

"Yes, you're right on that point, too," I said, my whole body shaking with the aftereffects of my earlier bravado.

Nik pulled me against him, and this time I didn't try to stop him.

"I know none of us wanted to punish Delphine in the first place—not when her only crime was being forced to learn a skill she never wanted." Drake met everyone's eyes one by one. "I'm the one who told her that we were looking for another option—a way to mitigate the threat without punishing an innocent person."

"Please don't blame Master Drake or any of the others," I said to the king. "It was my idea. And I went into it knowing that threatening the king might be enough to see me executed, regardless of the outcome. I certainly knew that if I failed— meaning my skills remained an unmitigated threat—then my behavior here would certainly ensure my death. It was always my own death I was referring to, never yours. And while I know it's shameless of me, I beg you to forgive my actions now that you know you were never in any danger from me. Master Colton can make a wall—and hopefully soon other healers as well—so you have a way to protect yourself and others from what I can do. I'm hoping that will give you the reason you've all been looking for to choose a different path."

"Of course it will," Nik said in menacing tones, glaring at his parents. "No one *wants* to hurt you, Delphine."

"I'm not sure I'm following." Evermund had one arm wrapped around Airlie's waist, but his eyes were sharp as they jumped from person to person. "I don't suppose someone could explain what we walked in on?"

"It's quite simple, really," Airlie said. "The king and Triumvirate decided that Delphine should be locked up for the rest of her life without any physical contact for the crime of knowing how to mesmerize."

Evermund looked at Nik. "You were right."

I twisted so I could look up into Nik's face.

He looked grim as he replied. "It's better than I feared, to be honest. But you can understand why we needed to hurry."

"Is that why you disappeared?" Airlie asked. "You must have ridden day and night to fetch Evermund and get him back this quickly."

I frowned at Nik, taking in the lines of exhaustion I hadn't noticed earlier. Airlie had said all along that Evermund might succeed where she had failed. How hard had Nik driven himself in order to bring back the one person he thought could help?

"I talked to Amara," he said, focusing his reply on me. "And we agreed this was the most helpful thing I could do."

I felt a pinch at the memory of what I had once—however briefly—thought him capable of doing compared to the reality of his mature response on this occasion. But the feeling was gone almost as soon as it appeared. Nik had shown me in every way possible that he had forgiven me, and it was time to leave that tragic situation in the past where it belonged.

I looked across at Amara. "Why didn't you tell me?"

"I wasn't sure they would get back in time," she said, "and I knew how hard this was going to be to pull off. I didn't want you to think there was any other hope in case it made you buckle when the moment came."

"So you all hatched a plan to save Delphine?" Evermund asked. "By threatening the king?" He sounded skeptical, and I couldn't blame him.

"Just reckless enough to be believable," Airlie said. "That's what we decided anyway. Drake, Amara, Hayes, Gia, Renley, and I were all in on it, so there were enough of us to restrain the others so that the drama could play out."

"The drama being..." Evermund raised his eyebrows.

"I pretended to threaten the king," I explained. "I claimed I was either going to be saved by Colton learning to make a wall, or else I was going to die on the spot, taking the king with me for revenge. I would never have actually harmed him, though, no matter what happened."

Evermund glanced at Colton who slowly nodded, looking like it pained him to admit I was speaking the truth and he'd been fooled.

"But...why did you need to fake such a thing?" Evermund asked me, sounding bewildered.

"I've tried teaching others how to make their own walls before and always failed," I said. "But then Grey managed to make one during our final confrontation, and while I was sitting in my cell, I came up with a theory about why. Although a wall can be used to block the power of others, it's primarily about blocking a healer's own power. But our power is so central to who we are that it requires true desperation to cut it off. Curiosity, interest—even greed, as Grey previously discovered—aren't enough motivation.

308

"I was raised to hate and fear my power, and my first experience of it after activation was traumatic. So I started with the necessary desperation to separate myself from it. I had that desire before I had any knowledge of what should or shouldn't have been possible. Grey didn't start with that same desperation, but when he had his back against the wall and his life on the line, he was suddenly able to break through and create a wall as well.

"So I took a gamble that the same would be true for making a wall for others. I showed Master Colton a wall so that he understood the concept and truly believed it was possible, and then—"

"You provided him with sufficient desperation," King Marius said. "Am I supposed to be flattered that I was the chosen victim?"

I pulled free of Nik's arms to drop into my deepest curtsy. "It was the most believable and compelling scenario I could come up with. I apologize wholeheartedly for the distress it must have caused you and the lack of respect it showed."

"As to that..." The king paused and looked at his son who met his gaze challengingly. "I can see why it was necessary for me to be in the dark." He looked at Colton, and for the first time, an eager light showed in his eyes. "You can really do it now? As long as we're in physical contact, you could protect me from any attack from a healer?"

"I believe so." Colton also sounded enthusiastic. "Now that I've got the feel of it, I can bring my own wall up and down with ease."

"It's even better than that," I said. "If someone does manage to mesmerize you while you don't have a wall up, just bringing up the wall drives out the mesmerization. I've done it for myself many times, as well as for the people of the island and many in Eldrida."

"This changes everything," the king said before suddenly

subsiding, as if he'd just remembered what had been required to reach this breakthrough.

"The healers among the royal guards will need to be taught it first," Anka said briskly. "And then my law keepers. But we're going to have to put some thought into how to manage the lesson. I don't fancy reenacting a similar scenario to this one a hundred times."

"I'll make it my first priority, of course," Colton said, and I felt a weight lift off my shoulders.

Someone better equipped than me was going to take over the burden I had been carrying. Colton knew how to make a wall, and he could be responsible for teaching others. Maybe—just maybe—I could go back to being no more than a healing apprentice.

"Father. Mother." Nik looked from one to the other. "I brought the woman I love home to meet you, and you considered having her executed. Now that you know Delphine was never going to harm you—no matter what happened with Colton's wall—you can let this matter go. Can't you?" He paused, his eyes hard as steel. "Because if you can't, don't think I'll just stand by. Or that once we're gone, you'll ever see me again."

Marius exchanged a look with his wife before allowing his gaze to roam across the room. Anka and Colton had their heads together, discussing potential strategies, while Augusta was standing back, her eyes narrowed to slits as she took in the scene. But Drake, Amara, Hayes, Airlie, Evermund, Gia, and Renley were all watching the king, waiting to hear how he would respond.

If I had acted alone, I doubted I would have gotten away with threatening the king—whatever my intentions and whatever the outcome. But King Marius was a prudent man. Half his government, and most of his family were arrayed against him, and that would be enough to give more reckless men than him pause. It was certainly far too many people of importance—to both the kingdom and him personally—for him to consider punishing them all for treason. And if he wasn't going to punish them, then perhaps...

When even Anka broke off mid-sentence to look up and wait for his reply, he finally capitulated and nodded to Nik and me.

"Word of what happened here must not leave this group," he said. "This is not a situation that we can risk having repeated." He paused and looked at me. "But I am acutely aware that wrong has also been done to you, and I can understand why you felt driven to extreme measures. I accept the assurance of my healers that you were acting without malice in order to bring about an outcome that would benefit all. In light of that, I think I may issue a pardon for your actions. And Delphine, I hope you will accept my apology for locking you up and threatening permanent incarceration. And Nik—" He hesitated his voice softening more than I had yet heard it. "I'm sorry...for more than just this."

Nik nodded once, the movement rough, but I could feel his relief. It was nothing to how I felt, however. Fresh tears slipped down my cheeks, and Nik pulled me closer.

"Clearly banning all future physical contact wasn't going to work," the queen muttered, and I blinked, unable to process the humor in her voice as her eyes dwelt on her son's arm where it wrapped around me.

Her eyes jumped up to mine, full of concern and sadness. I tried to smile at her—reminding myself she was Nik's mother—but my mouth only twitched.

She stood and came closer, stopping with a hand on her husband's shoulder where he still sat on his throne.

"We have not had the best beginning, Delphine," she said in a quiet voice, "on either side. I'm sure our treatment of you will not be easily forgotten, just as your actions here today will not easily be forgotten by us." Her eyes moved to her son's face before returning to mine. "But we love Nik and have been sorely grieved by his absence. It is clear he has tied his future to yours, and I hope somehow we can find it in us to move past this and start afresh."

Her husband twitched beneath her hand, and she sighed. "Perhaps that is too much to hope for. Let's say instead that I hope we can start now to build a new foundation, and that it will one day prove stronger than this unfortunate beginning."

I thought of my own parents and the way my thinking about my father had changed over the past year.

"Thank you, Your Majesty," I said. "I would like that."

Nik's arm tightened around me, and the warmth of his smile as he looked down at me made the idea of forgiving his parents seem easy. I knew it wouldn't be a simple matter in reality—it had taken me a long time to overcome the image of Nik standing over the Constantines, and I had already been in love with him. But with time, I hoped Nik's parents and I could associate each other with something beyond the events of our first meeting.

TWENTY-SEVEN

The king finally stood from his throne and stepped off the dais, joining the small gathering of men and women who formed both his government and his family. Anka and Colton broke off their conversation to look at him expectantly, and Augusta drifted closer.

"I won't deny a sense of betrayal to find so many of you involved in a scheme against me," he said.

"They wouldn't have been involved if the plan had involved any actual harm to you," Evermund said confidently. He hadn't even been in the city, but he clearly had total trust in his wife and her allies.

King Marius inclined his head in acceptance of Evermund's words. "Betrayal might be my first reaction, but it would be remiss of me if I looked no further than that. The very fact we were brought to this extremity means that collectively we have failed in our task of united government. The immediate crisis seems to be past, and Grey is no longer a threat, but it is clear that serious reflection on these events will be needed."

He looked at Anka. "Not all of those reflections are for right now, but I would like to start by apologizing to you, Anka. You have been a loyal and dedicated servant of Tartora for many decades, and it was wrong of me to force you into a position you didn't want. If you wish to resign as Royal Mage, I will accept your resignation with good will."

She regarded him in silence for a moment, her expression thoughtful.

"I accept your apology, Your Majesty. And at some point I will resign because I have always been a law keeper and always will be. However, I agree that changes are needed, and it seems to me that this isn't a time to be without a Royal Mage."

"Thank you, Anka," Evermund said, sounding relieved. "As always, your judgment is sound. An objective party—one with your wisdom and experience—will be a welcome asset as we repair what has been broken."

She smiled back, and the king nodded. I examined the crown prince. He was young compared to the others in positions of authority, but he was clearly comfortable in their midst.

If I remembered rightly, he had once been Royal Mage himself, and I could see why Airlie had wished for his presence from the beginning. Even with my extremely limited experience of this group, I could feel how the dynamic had changed with his presence. He would be a good king one day, and they all knew it. Already they afforded him some of the respect and authority of his future position.

I wrapped both my arms around Nik and squeezed. He had pushed himself to the edge to bring back the right person. He smiled down at me, but now that the immediate excitement was past, he looked even more exhausted.

"You need some sleep," I whispered, running my hand along the edge of his face.

"Seeing you is better than sleep."

"Today has taken some very unexpected turns," Augusta said acerbically, breaking into the various conversations.

I turned to look at her, my heart sinking as I saw her eyes were fixed on her former apprentice, now turned reneger—Nik.

I had hoped she might be willing to take him back so that he could complete his apprenticeship, but her expression wasn't promising.

"While some rules have always been stretched for those of royal blood, some rules are immutable. I didn't speak previously because I am not totally lacking in compassion and wished to allow a family reunion. But word has been spreading that Prince Nikolas is back, and an example must be set. Renegers cannot be accepted into society, no matter what they might have done in the way of public service."

The queen flinched, her face paling as her eyes jumped to her son. Nik himself remained straight and unmoving, however, his face grave.

A moment of silence passed, and I held my breath, wondering if he would ask her to take him back. But he must have read the answer in her face because he made no such request.

"I do not deny your words, Master Augusta. And I did not come with the expectation that I could remain. Only the gravity of the situation brought me here in the first place. I will be gone by morning. I ask only that I be allowed to sleep before setting off again." He swayed slightly as he spoke, emphasizing the exhaustion behind his words.

"Nik!" For a moment I thought I'd spoken, but the voice had been his mother's. The distress on her face was obvious now, tears springing to her eyes. "You can't just leave again!"

The king put a gentle hand on her arm, looking at her with a set expression that was trying to hide his own distress. "My dear," he murmured, "Augusta is right. However much we want things to be different..."

"Surely there's something we can do." She glanced at Augusta, but the Master of Plants was still watching her old apprentice.

The king glanced at Augusta as well, his mouth tightening.

"Perhaps in the future..." he murmured even more quietly than the queen.

The tempestuous events of the last few days hadn't placed the king in a good bargaining position. Of those around him, Augusta was one of the few who had been unwaveringly loyal, and he must be reluctant to pressure her into something she clearly didn't want to do.

I shook my head, a continuous movement that expressed everything I didn't have the words to say. Nik pressed me against him, whispering into my hair.

"I'm sorry." He sounded broken. "If there was any way I could stay..." His muscles jumped as he held me close. "But you know I will always do everything I can to protect you. Even if that means walking away and never seeing you again. With Grey gone, I've become the greatest threat to your future, and I won't drag you into my outcast status."

My heart broke at his words. The strength of his hold told me the words he would never say aloud. Nik would never abandon me. If he couldn't join society, he would remain in the shadows, watching for anything that might threaten me.

I couldn't bear the idea of that life for him. I wanted to tell him that I would give up everything and become an outcast with him. But I knew I didn't have that choice. Amara had risked everything to stand by me, and I had made a commitment to her. I still had a year of my apprenticeship, and I suspected we would spend at least some of that time with Anka, helping to train others how to make walls.

The king had just shown me great leniency, and I couldn't push the matter by declaring myself an outcast and attempting to leave society all together. They had accepted the risk I posed, but that didn't mean there wouldn't be eyes on me for the rest of my life. I couldn't blame them for that.

"I'm glad you brought up the subject," Amara said with a respectful nod to Augusta. "I had intended to organize a formal meeting to discuss the matter, but all the relevant people are present now so we might as well be done with it."

"I realize your apprentice has strong feelings on the subject," Augusta said, "but we cannot allow emotions to interfere on a matter as important as the status of renegers."

"I agree," Amara said calmly. "I had no intention of attempting to overthrow such rules. The matter I wish to discuss is Nikolas's formal graduation."

Her words sent a ripple through the group, and from Nik's reaction, he was just as surprised as me. Amara sent him a quick warning look, however, and he remained silent, his expression smoothing out.

"My apprentice has not returned to me to complete his apprenticeship," Augusta said coldly. "It doesn't matter what skills he has acquired on his own. He cannot become a proficient."

"No, of course skill alone is not enough." Amara remained unmoved by Augusta's opposition, her expression unruffled. "However, Nikolas has completed his apprenticeship under my guidance which is why I am now putting him forward for graduation."

"You are claiming to be his master?" Drake asked, clearly as surprised as I was. "You know that isn't how it works. Apprentices cannot change masters at will."

"In general they cannot, no," Amara said. "The law is clear that an apprentice must complete their apprenticeship under their influencer, except in the case of death or incapacity of the master. However there has always been a formal exception for royals—an exception that has already been put in place for Prince Nikolas."

"You mean the ruling that allows them to be activated by another royal but complete their apprenticeship under the Guild," Evermund said in an arrested tone. "It's true that ruling was used by Nik. He was adamant he be cross-influenced, so I was given permission to activate him, but the Master of Plants then took on his apprenticeship as had been initially intended."

"Precisely," Amara said. "In Nikolas's case, the law does not require his apprenticeship to be completed under his influencer but rather by the Guild. And I am a member of the Guild."

She slowly gazed across the assembled group, meeting each of their eyes with a challenging look. "Would anyone present like to argue that I lack the necessary strength to take on an apprentice of Nikolas's level?"

She let silence hang in the air as everyone shifted uncomfortably. Even Augusta wouldn't meet her gaze.

"I put forward that I am a member of the Guild and a registered master, and that I am therefore qualified to complete the apprenticeship of a royal student who has been activated by a family member."

"That exception is designed to allow the royal family to pass on their great strength to their children," Drake grumbled, "not to allow royal apprentices to jump from master to master. You know I acknowledge your strength, Amara, but you're one of my people. You don't even have a plants affinity."

"And my other apprentice is a healer," she said. "What of it? The prince is cross-influenced after all. His influencer was an elements mage, so it makes sense for his master to be one too."

"You have all been trapped on that island for the winter," Augusta said, "so you may well have supervised the prince during that time. But he was only halfway through his apprenticeship when he chose to abandon it. A single season is not sufficient to cover his remaining time."

"No, the winter would not be enough," Amara said. "However, I think you will find the prince has been with me far longer than that."

"What do you mean?" the queen asked, her voice eager.

"Prince Nikolas has been tracking Grey for a long time," Amara said. "Last spring, Grey abducted a friend of my other

318

apprentice, and since that time, she and I worked together with Nik to find and free Miranda and then stop Grey. If anyone cares to track our movements, you will see our joint progress. After Tarin, we went to Ostaria, and from there to Caltor. Others can attest that Nik was seen with us in all three places. After Caltor, we traveled east across the northern half of the kingdom all the way to Eldrida. Nik traveled alongside us the whole way. And of course, we were all in Eldrida for the crippling storm before going north into the desert and eventually to the island. If anyone cares to count the months since we first connected in Tarin, I think you will find he has completed the necessary time."

Again, she gazed around the room, silently challenging anyone to deny her words. I was struggling to keep my mouth from dropping open. All her words were true—as a healer I knew no one would hear a lie on them. But she was stretching the truth as far as it could go, and everyone here had to know it. But one glance at the faces of the king and queen showed she was providing a solution they desperately wanted.

"If anyone doubts he has reached a sufficient skill level for a proficient, I invite you to test him," she said with a trace of humor. "I am confident you will not find him lacking in any way."

A dangerous smile spread across Nik's face. "I am more than willing to demonstrate my skill for any doubters."

"I don't think that will be necessary," Drake said dryly. He glanced at Augusta and Colton. "The Triumvirate will need to consult for a moment. If you will excuse us..." He gestured for the other two to step aside with him for a moment.

Hayes started a conversation with those of us who remained, but I wasn't paying enough attention to follow his words. And from the odd gaps in the replies, I wasn't the only one.

When the three affinity heads finally walked back from the

other side of the cavernous room, Drake was smiling and Augusta looked resigned.

"We are happy to accept the graduation of Prince Nikolas to the official rank of proficient," Drake announced. "The Guild will publicly announce the successful completion of his apprenticeship and the lifting of his status as reneger as soon as possible."

Nik met his eyes. "Thank you." The simple words were full of depth.

Letting go of me, he crossed over to stand in front of Augusta. He towered over her small frame, but everything in his manner was respectful as he addressed her.

"Please accept my apology, Master Augusta. I disrespected you and your teaching by leaving in the manner I did."

"Well!" She raised both eyebrows, looking him up and down. "Never did I think to hear such a thing from you. Maybe there really is hope you'll turn into an asset to our kingdom."

Nik's lips twitched upward. "High praise, Master Augusta. I treasure it greatly."

She let out a bark of laughter. "Go back to your young lady, Prince, and don't go trying your charm on me."

Nik glanced at me, his eyes sparkling. Unable to resist, I ran forward and threw myself into his arms. It didn't matter about our audience or the drama of the last few hours. It might not be the right place, but I couldn't wait. After everything we had feared and endured, Nik was accepted back into society. He had a future again.

He swept his arms around me, lifting me completely off the ground and pressing his lips against mine. Lost in my joy and relief, I kissed him back, nothing in my mind but Nik.

Until a moment later when I remembered our audience. When I squeaked, Nik broke off the kiss with a chuckle and put me down.

"If you don't want all these important people to be scandalized," he said, "you'll have to let them know we're going to be married."

"Married?" I asked, the squeak reappearing.

For a second, a shadow marred the joy on his face. "You already know I want you in every part of my future," he said. "I thought you felt the same way?"

"Of course I do," I whispered. "But you just got reinstated as a prince. Aren't there... protocols?"

He grinned, the light blazing back into his eyes and filling me with an answering warmth.

"We can do a formal introduction now, if you like." He put an arm around my shoulders and turned me so we stood side to side, facing the group of bystanders. Phoenix chose that moment to swoop back in to land on my shoulder, as if lending his support to our union.

"This is Delphine," Nik said, "a future master healer and my betrothed. Does anyone object?"

"Would it make a difference if we did?" Augusta muttered.

Nik grinned at her. "Not in the least. I think I've already demonstrated I can walk away from royal life if needed."

"Wait a minute!" I gasped, his words bringing me back to earth. For a few minutes, I'd been thinking of nothing but Nik and the cloud that had been lifted off him, but I wasn't ready for the future he was implying.

"What is it?" The concern on his face was instant.

"I...I don't think I can be a princess and live at court and..." I glanced involuntarily toward the king and queen before quickly looking away.

Nik seemed to pick up on my meaning instantly. "Oh, is that all?" He looked relieved. "Don't worry. If I learned anything in my time away, it's that this isn't the life for me anymore either. I don't intend to settle at court."

"Nik!" Queen Celestine looked at him with disappointment. "Surely you don't intend to disappear again when we only just got you back? I know you were very unhappy with what happened after your arrival, but—"

"I'm not going to disappear, Mother." He gave her an affectionate look. "Gia doesn't live at court, but you still get to see her, don't you?"

"Yes, I suppose." She still didn't look pleased, but her momentary panic had subsided.

"It's not as if I have a role here," he said. "I can do greater good in the rest of the kingdom, especially if I have Delphine by my side. I've done enough travel with Amara to know what it means to the smaller towns and villages to have a master mage come through. And we've all seen how close Tartora came to disaster because the capital wasn't paying enough attention to the remoter parts of the kingdom. We need to increase the connection between the general populace outside the capital and the royal government. And what better way to do it than through a member of the king's own family? Besides," he added, "I am a plants mage after all. I belong in the farmlands, not in a city."

"You're suggesting you become an official royal emissary while fulfilling the same role as a traveling master?" the king clarified.

Nik looked down at me, still tucked against his side. "If Delphine agrees."

"That sounds incredible," I said, hardly able to believe he was suggesting something so perfect.

The king glanced toward the Triumvirate. Whatever he saw on their faces made him nod his head.

"Very well," he said. "Once Delphine graduates, the two of you can take on that role. You'll need to stay in the capital for a while, though. We need to show the court and Guild that you've been welcomed back and give them a chance to see you demonstrate your strength and control."

Nik glanced at Amara who gave him a small smile.

"Delphine and I will also be based here for the time being while we assist Anka," she told him.

Nik looked back at the king. "In that case, I'd be more than happy to stay. I'd like to take some time for study while I'm here. If I'm going to take on the role of a traveling master, I might as well officially pass the mastery exam before I leave."

Augusta's eyebrows shot up. "I see you haven't entirely lost your natural arrogance. You think you'll be able to pass the mastery exam within a year of becoming a proficient? Are you trying to set a new record?"

He gave her a provocative look. "I suppose that depends how well you teach me over the coming year."

She snorted, but I caught the answering gleam in her eyes. You didn't become an affinity head unless you relished a challenge.

"I'm sorry to abandon you the moment I graduate," I said to Amara, feeling a pang at the idea of leaving her.

"Don't be silly," she said. "Since I'll be here in the capital, I'll see you whenever you come back through. I'm actually relieved to know someone will be taking my place."

"You're finally going to settle down and stop all this roaming?" Anka's eyes immediately jumped to Hayes, her expression becoming amused when she saw the way he was beaming at Amara. "I'm glad to see the two of you finally managed to sort things out."

Her gaze shifted slightly to dwell for a moment on Colton. It flashed through my mind that perhaps one of the changes she wanted to see before she left the role of Royal Mage was a change in the Head of Healing. Master Colton had succeeded in activating the king's wall, and for that I would always be grateful, but he hadn't reacted well to the discovery of mesmerization. His desire had been to protect his affinity, but he had abandoned the ethos of a healer in his attempts to do it. Maybe it was time for someone with new vision to take on the role.

"Are you happy?" Nik's quiet murmur made me forget all about the politics of the Triumvirate.

"I've never been happier," I said honestly. "Would you really like to become a traveling master? You won't miss the life of a prince?"

"Once upon a time I thought gaining the throne was all that mattered," he said. "But now I would give up far more than a throne to have you by my side."

"I don't want you to have to sacrifice everything for me."

He shook his head. "Even without you, I wouldn't want to return to court. On Grey's ship, you challenged me to find the role I'm supposed to fill—since it was never that of ruler. I didn't know it then, but I think I'd already found that role while traveling the kingdom with you. Maybe it won't be forever—like it hasn't been for Amara—but it's what I truly want for now. And if the time does come for something different—that's a decision we'll make together."

"In that case," I said, "there's only one possible response."

Grasping the front of his jacket in both hands, I lifted onto my toes and pressed my lips against his, sealing our promises with a kiss.

EPILOGUE

I gazed out the window at the changing leaves. Some trees were still entirely green, but others took my breath away with their fiery hues.

"I'm ready."

I turned to see another breath-taking sight. Amara's long, elegant gown trailed behind her by several feet, and her hair had been arranged on her head in an elaborate arrangement of braids and soft curls.

"You look beautiful," I breathed, making her smile.

"Thank you for helping me prepare," she said. "Both of you."

Luna beamed back at her, her eyes misty with unshed tears. "I would have come from further than Calinara to be at Hayes's wedding. Especially since he's marrying you! I couldn't have dreamed of a more perfect ending."

Amara laughed. "I hope it's not an ending! I like to think it's a beginning."

I chuckled as well. "You're forgetting. Luna is the center of her own story, and she's ready to leave us all behind."

"That's not true!" Luna cried, horrified, before she noticed we were both still grinning. Rolling her eyes, she pulled me into a hug. "I've missed you, Delphine!"

"Are you not enjoying it in Calinara as much as you'd hoped?" Amara asked.

"No, it's not that. I love being back with my family, and it's fascinating seeing the progress already made, as well as the new efforts underway. I just miss all of you at the same time."

"I think that might be the secret to adulthood that everyone was keeping from us," I said with a sigh. "You're always missing someone."

"I can see you've gained much wisdom since turning nineteen and becoming an adult." Luna gave me a cheeky grin. "But who are you missing? I know it isn't that prince of yours since I can't turn around without tripping over him."

"Her parents arrived yesterday," Amara said softly.

Luna's eyebrows rose. "You've reconciled with them, then?"

I nodded, remembering the long-awaited reunion.

In the aftermath of gaining my freedom, I had learned that my uncle had followed my instructions and gone to Amara. He and his family had received funds from her and left for Tarin before I emerged from my cell. I had sent an urgent communication after them to reassure my parents that I had been released and all was well, as well as to inform them of my betrothal. From their reply, I had learned that my uncle, aunt, and cousins had arrived safely on the farm.

My mother didn't go into detail on the meeting between the brothers, but I could read between the lines to know it hadn't gone smoothly. She seemed to be hopeful for the future, however, and with Amara and me stationed in the capital, my mother and I were able to exchange several more letters.

I learned from afar that my cousins had embraced farm life and that my uncle and father had slowly reconciled. By the time Amara sent my parents an invitation to her wedding, Uncle Olan and his family were sufficiently settled to run the farm in their absence. For the first time in my life, both my father and mother would be able to leave the farm at the same time for an extended trip.

I had thrown myself into the wedding preparations with fervor in an effort to distract myself from the wait for their arrival. Amara, in her usual perceptive manner, had understood my mindset and kept me run off my feet from morning to night until their arrival day finally came. Suddenly I had found myself without any tasks at all and no excuses to delay the meeting.

Nik had offered to be with me, but just like his own reunion with his parents, I knew it was something I needed to do on my own.

I had imagined how the interaction might go a hundred times, but I needn't have worried. The moment I saw them, all the pain and worry was overwhelmed by an entire childhood of memories.

I ran into my mother's arms without hesitation, tears streaming down both our cheeks. My father hung back, but when I finally finished hugging my mother, I turned to him with a smile.

"Thank you for coming, Father."

He cleared his throat. "Our daughter's influencer is getting married. How could we stay away? Even if she is a master mage."

I froze, but both he and my mother chuckled. Relaxing, I smiled back. If they felt calm enough to joke about it, that had to be a good sign.

"I'm sorry, lass," my father said softly, catching me off guard. "Your mother and I have had some long talks in your absence, and I know I was in the wrong with how I handled things."

"Obviously." My mother put her hands on her hips. "What am I going to do with the two of you? Of all the ridiculous things, keeping something like your squeamishness from me…" She shook her head.

"You've forgiven Father?" I asked, wanting to hear the reassurance, even though her manner made it clear she had.

She smiled. "He had to clean the henhouse on his own for a good month, but we got there in the end." She linked her arm through mine and squeezed. "You'll find out yourself soon enough, but you can't maintain a partnership through an entire lifetime unless you're willing to forgive each other along the way."

I nodded. Nik and I weren't even married yet, but we had already learned that lesson.

"Where is this man of yours?" Father asked. "He's not here to greet us?"

"He wanted to be," I said quickly. "But I wanted to meet you on my own first."

My mother nodded her approval, squeezing my arm again, but my father went quiet.

"I'm sorry, Delphine," he said. "I'm sorry for the way I treated you. I'm sorry for teaching you my anger and fear."

My mother nodded approvingly. "And he was sorry even before that brother of his showed up and made it even more clear how wrongheaded his ideas were."

"I forgive you, Father." I tried to surreptitiously wipe the moisture from my eyes. "I forgave you a long time ago."

My mother beamed at us both. "You were always a better daughter than I could have hoped for, Delphine. I've missed you, even if the house is full of people now."

"Are things going well with Uncle Olan?" I asked eagerly.

My mother smiled. "Better than I feared in the first week. Those cousins of yours have proved a mighty boon on the days my back aches."

"I'm so glad you finally have proper help," I said. "It makes me feel much better about not returning to the farm." I watched my mother's face, trying to gauge her reaction to my words, but she just chuckled.

"Don't look so worried. We already knew you weren't coming back. You outgrew the farm a long time ago."

"But not you!" I wrapped my arms around her, reveling in the familiar embrace. "I'll never outgrow my mother."

She chuckled. "I'm glad to hear you say it because I have every intention of spending a good portion of my old age bouncing my grandbabies on my knee."

"Mother!" I drew back and whacked her lightly, my cheeks heating.

She just laughed again. "So when do we get to meet Nik?"

"Right now, if you want," I said.

"And his parents?" my father asked gruffly, clearly uncertain about the prospect.

"They've invited us all to join them for the evening meal." I tried not to look as nervous as I felt at the idea.

"A meal with the king and queen?" My mother's eyes widened, and she glanced nervously at my father.

But despite all our fears, the meeting went better than expected. Nik's parents treated mine with more warmth than I anticipated, and my parents managed to overcome their awe at my future family's rank—at least enough to converse with sense.

"Delphine?" Luna bumped my hip with hers, startling my thoughts back to the present.

"Sorry." I shook myself and looked at Amara. "We shouldn't be talking about me. Today is your day."

"You're the envy of both the Guild and the capital, you know," Luna said cheerily. "Hayes was already the most eligible unmarried mage and that was before he became Head of Healing."

"Don't remind me about his new appointment." Amara sighed. "It's the reason we had to have a formal state wedding."

"Can you really begrudge us all the excitement?" Luna asked. "It's been a very long time since one of the Triumvirate got married."

"I heard Hayes is the youngest Triumvirate member in three generations," I said.

"Not that you're one to talk about youthful accomplishments." Luna snorted. "I overheard Augusta boasting about how that betrothed of yours is going to be ready to take the mastery exam by the start of winter."

I groaned. "Don't remind me. Nik's not only graduated, he's going to be a master before I'm even a proficient."

"He doesn't appear to mind," Luna said with a chuckle.

"It's not the difference in rank that's the issue." Amara was clearly trying not to smile. "Delphine has to graduate before they can be married."

Luna exploded into laughter. "Now that would definitely chafe Nik, if I know anything about him. I'm surprised he hasn't smuggled you off in the middle of the night."

"He would have both me and my betrothed to answer to if he tried anything of the sort," Amara said with a militant light in her eyes.

"Talking of your betrothed," I said, ignoring their teasing. "It's time for you to go and make him your husband."

Amara's face softened at the word, a glow radiating from inside her and making her even more beautiful. And the glow only grew brighter when the doors of the throne room opened, and she saw Hayes waiting for her at the end of a long stretch of red carpet.

I followed behind, but my eyes were on the man standing to one side of Hayes. Asking Nik and Evermund to be his two attendants had been a typical Hayes move—combining kindness with political acumen. His wedding had generated intense interest among both the Guild mages and the general populace, and Nik's inclusion had clearly demonstrated the former prince's return to favor and power.

Nik looked down the room and caught my eye. His smile grew as he watched me, and I sighed wistfully. It was right that Amara was getting married first, and I couldn't be happier for her. But spring seemed like a long time away.

The ceremony passed quickly, and all too soon, Hayes and Amara were swept up into a whirl of good wishes as everyone of wealth and power in the kingdom vied to congratulate them. I hung back, taking a moment to admire the white flowers that decorated the rows of chairs and the bright velvet of the carpet that had been used to form the aisle.

Arms came around me from behind. "That carpet will be purple the next time we're here for a wedding," Nik's deep voice said.

I smiled at the vision his words created. Hayes might be a member of the Triumvirate now, but only members of the royal family were permitted to walk down the aisle on a purple carpet.

A flash of the same purple caught my eye, drawing my attention to Anka. She was congratulating Amara, a delighted expression on her face.

She had been working hard for months but was finally starting to talk of retiring from the Royal Mage position. And I had an inkling who might be asked to fill it in her place.

"Do you think Amara will be happy in the capital in the long term?" I asked.

"Hmmm..." I felt the rumble of Nik's response in his chest. "I think she will be. But not as happy as we will be when we finally get back on the road."

A brush of movement near my feet made me flinch, but when I looked down, the sight of orange fur told me who had joined us.

I chuckled. "I'm not sure you're supposed to be in here, Ember."

"If the steward informed her of that fact, I don't think she was listening," Nik said. "No one ever manages to keep her away from you for long."

"I'm fortunate in my friends." I stealthily picked her up before leaning back into Nik's arms.

"She's not alone either." Nik pointed to an urn against the closest wall. Apparently Phoenix had taken a liking to the perch he'd found on his previous visit.

"Oh no," I groaned. Falcons were harder to keep hidden than foxes.

"Don't worry, today is about Hayes and Amara, and neither of them will kick him out. Isn't it fitting that he and Ember are here? They've spent almost as much time with Amara as you have."

"When you put it like that, I defy anyone to kick them out."

I leaned my head back against him and closed my eyes. For once, everyone I loved was together, and I intended to enjoy it while I could. Before long, I would be on the road, far from all but three of my loved ones.

When I thought about it like that, I knew the remaining months would fly by, especially given how much study Nik and I both had to get through. Before we knew it, our new life would be upon us. Tartora would wait for us, and we would be ready to explore every part of it when the time came.

NOTE FROM THE AUTHOR

I hope you enjoyed the conclusion of Delphine, Nik, and Amara's story. If you missed the beginning of Nik's journey, you can read about how he ended up as a reneger in the A Mage's Influence series, starting with Seeds of Glory and Ruin.

Or for more adventure, intrigue, and romance in an academy setting, try the Spoken Mage series, starting with Voice of Power. Set in a world of written power, it tells the story of a girl who discovers she can wield power through spoken words.

To be informed of future releases, as well as A Mage's Apprentice bonus shorts, please sign up to my mailing list at www.melaniecellier.com.

And if you enjoyed A Mage's Apprentice, please spread the word and help other readers find it! You could start by leaving a review on Amazon or Goodreads or Facebook or any other social media site. Your review would be very much appreciated and would make a big difference!

Acknowledgments

I'm glad to finally reach a happy ending for Nik, and I want to thank all the readers who have stayed with me for the journey. I apologize for leaving you all hanging at the end of book two, but I hope you enjoyed how everything was wrapped up in this book.

And many thanks to my faithful team who have stayed with me through the series. Rachel, Greg, Priya, Ber, Katie, Mary, Dad, James, Karri, Rebecca, Marina, Cheri, Shari, Brittany, Kitty, Aya, Lyra, and Marc, I thank you every time, but it never seems like enough.

And, of course, a final thank you to God who is always ready to forgive our mistakes and help us find peace from our past.

ABOUT THE AUTHOR

Melanie Cellier grew up on a staple diet of books, books and more books. And although she got older, she never stopped loving children's and young adult novels.

She always wanted to write one herself, but it took three careers and three different continents before she actually managed it.

She now feels incredibly fortunate to spend her time writing from her home in Adelaide, Australia where she keeps an eye out for koalas in her backyard. Her staple diet hasn't changed much, although she's added choc mint Rooibos tea and Chicken Crimpies to the list.

She writes young adult fantasy including books in her *Spoken Mage* world, her *Mage's Influence* world, and her various *Four Kingdoms* and *Kingdoms of Legacy* series that are made up of linked stand-alone stories that retell classic fairy tales.

www.ingramcontent.com/pod-product-compliance
Lightning Source LLC
Chambersburg PA
CBHW061624210726
48287CB00001B/278